I0730590

*Discover the land of Baljehni,
where magic hums through rock and bone.*

Beyond the Humming Downs

Tales of Ellir

Ellen Starsmore

First published 2025 by Starsmore Forge

Copyright © 2025 by Ellen Starsmore

All rights reserved.

ISBN: 978-1-7641592-0-3 (ebook)

ISBN: 978-1-7641592-1-0 (paperback)

No part of this book may be reproduced in any form or by any electronic or mechanical means, including information storage and retrieval systems, without written permission from the author, except as permitted by Australian copyright law and fair use.

Any use of this publication to "train" generative artificial intelligence (AI) technologies to generate text is expressly prohibited.

For permission requests, contact the author at ellen@ellenstarsmore.com.

This is a work of fiction. Names, characters, places and incidents are either the products of the author's imagination or are used fictitiously. Any resemblance to actual persons (living or deceased), places, buildings, products, businesses, companies or events is entirely coincidental.

Edited by Tracey Rolfe.

Book Cover by 100 Covers.

Created with love by a human.

For my mum, dad and siblings, who know exactly how long it's taken to get here…

and my nieces and nephews, who are blissfully unaware and just think it's really cool I wrote a book.

Author's Note

This novel uses Australian English (including spelling).

Except for words that are entirely made up. Of which there are many. Pronounce these as you will.

See ellenstarsmore.com for a glossary and other bonus content.

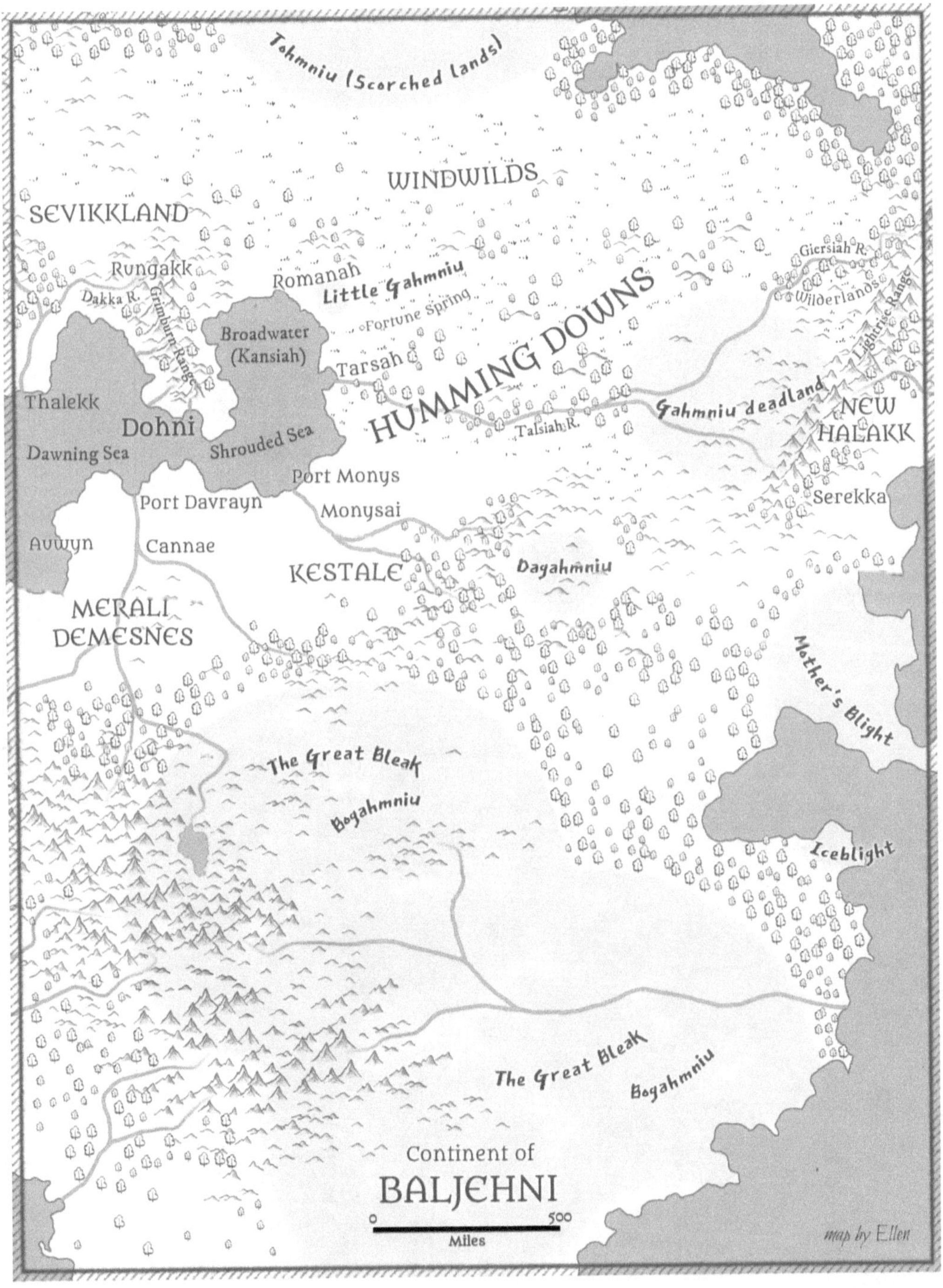

Tohmniu (Scorched lands)
WINDWILDS
SEVIKKLAND
Rungakk
Dakka R.
Romanah
Little Gahmniu
Fortune Spring
Giersiah R.
Wilderlands
Grimburn Range
Broadwater
(Kansiah)
Tarsah
HUMMING DOWNS
Lightrise Range
Thalekk
Dohni
Gahmniu deadland
NEW
HALAKK
Dawning Sea
Shrouded Sea
Talsiah R.
Port Monys
Serekka
Port Davrayn
Monysai
Avwyn
Cannae
KESTALE
Dagahmniu
MERALI
DEMESNES
Mother's Blight
The Great Bleak
Bogahmniu
Iceblight
The Great Bleak
Bogahmniu
Continent of
BALJEHNI
0
500
Miles
map by Ellen

Part One
Heartstorm

1. Rattled her bones

A pair of riders surged towards Adehl across the wild grasses of the Humming Downs. She'd spotted the horses a few minutes ago, tiny specks at first, growing larger. They flowed up and over a swell, angling down a slope where loophorns feasted on the bounty of recent summer rains. The animals scattered like disrupted ants.

Adehl slowed Cloud and the extra horses to a walk. The downs rolled in all directions — rocky outcrops, clumps of woodland and sprawling grassland, vibrant with new growth. Amid the spears of green, brilliant white daisies, yellow sunfaces and purple flax-lily blooms swayed. Bees hummed, and a flock of black-and-white birds fossicked for insects — until the oncoming riders thundered into their midst, sending the birds into the air.

The horses' gaits slowed as the pair approached Adehl. At last, they pulled up before her, a chestnut and a blood bay. The riders were men she didn't recognise, but they were doubtless from the Vuusah company camped at Fortune Spring. Like her, they wore undyed summer mahgans over leather leggings and long boots. They sized her up, one large and expressionless, the other keen-eyed and graceful, leaning forward in his saddle as he scrutinised her. Adehl held the slighter man's gaze. The fine braids keeping his dark, waist-length hair in check were threaded with gold, copper and blue velinkah beads that matched the vibrant samah bound around his middle.

"Soul bright and balanced," Adehl said. Her voice came out husky after nine days of riding. She'd passed only two Vuusah camps since leaving her own, the most recent at Wandering Well three days ago. She gestured at the string of four geldings she was leading. "You're from Fortune Spring? I've brought you some horses."

The larger of the men was already examining the animals and nudged his chestnut mount closer. He wore his braids at a more conventional length, their ends brushing his shoulderblades. The patterns woven into his samah proclaimed him a noumenor, a zehli able to manipulate a person's llirah. She suppressed the urge to tell him these were the pick of the horses her company had bred in recent seasons.

The man with the stupidly long braids smiled. "Soul bright and welcome," he said. "It is good to finally meet you."

Not sure of his meaning, Adehl felt her cheeks heat under the intensity of his regard. She studied the patterns on his samah, unable to make them out. "Thank you. I look forward to reaching your camp."

The light in his eyes faded, and Adehl wondered what she'd said. His clean-shaven face was expressive, exuding curiosity, intelligence and something else she couldn't define. He swung his pale-amber gaze to his companion, then back to her. "I've been marking your progress. You camped at Upper Well last night." It wasn't a question.

"You're a farsenser?"

He smirked and tilted his head, beads clinking together. "The old man wanted us to come out and meet you."

The large noumenor shot him a look. "We're here to collect the horses," he said. "Our doyen thought it would save you time."

"I appreciate it." While Adehl could have found Fortune Spring without assistance, she welcomed anything to speed up the journey to a hot meal and some company. "Do we have long to ride?"

"You misunderstand." Some of his severity slid into awkwardness. "Gentah doesn't want —"

"That can wait. We've been rude." The farsenser's gaze fixed on Adehl's. "I'm Roh. That's Frahto. Will you tell us your name?"

Adehl blinked at the unexpected information, delivered so casually. She knew the name *Roh*. Everyone did. "You're Little Atali?" It explained the complicated markings on his samah. She'd known the zehli destined to be Atalah rode with Gentah's company, but this man was not much older than her. His smile broadened, and she regretted using the nickname. He was doubtless arrogant enough already.

The noumenor, Frahto, grunted with something like resignation. "The one and only."

Roh chuckled, stood in his stirrups and swatted Frahto on the back of the head. She watched their byplay for a few moments. This was the zehli rumoured to have the greatest affinity for ellir in several generations? She raised her hand and spoke her own name. The beads and charms on her srih clinked as the leather wrapping slid down her arm.

It was Frahto who first nudged his massive chestnut alongside Cloud, his upright palm offered to Adehl's in the traditional greeting between zehla. "Soul bright," he muttered as their palms touched for a few heartbeats, long enough for their inner rhythms, their llirah, to thread briefly together. She sensed his discomfort and wondered at it, but neither she nor Frahto revealed much of themselves.

With an unreadable glance at his companion, Roh came forward on the blood bay. The surrounding air seemed charged, and Adehl was burningly aware of Frahto watching on as Roh joined his palm to hers.

She gasped, couldn't *help* it, as his llirah slammed through hers. Unfettered, Roh's energy surged and soared. How could a mortal body contain a rhythm of such amplitude? It rattled her bones until she thought she'd shake apart. Then her llirah blended with his in a natural resonance as cool and smooth as silk. She stopped shaking, shivered at the shocking intimacy. Uneasy, she tried to pull away, break this connection that was *too much*; but, with a sound deep in his throat, Roh threaded his fingers through hers in a firm clasp.

Roh was laid bare before her, his soul a shimmer of ellir. Adehl sensed his shock mirrored her own. Their rhythms had combined so instinctively she hadn't been able to resist. It felt inevitable, as though her llirah's natural state was to be melded with his.

Sanity returned with a jolt, and she wrenched her hand from his. The motion jerked Roh half out of his saddle and, by the time he'd righted himself, Adehl had moved Cloud to a safe distance. They stared at each other. Adehl scrambled to regain control of both her llirah and facial expression. If she could see into Roh's soul, then he could see into hers. Sun's fury. Had he *seen*? Her heart hammered.

"Roh, what in the burning bright sun did you do?" Frahto's voice held an edge.

Roh twitched, fingers curling as if unsure what to do with his hand. "Nothing. Don't drop your rein. Everything's fine." His gaze bored into her, alight with recognition and astonishment.

With effort, she dragged her attention away, looked

anywhere but at him. High up and to the south, a hawk hovered over the downs.

Frahto cleared his throat. "Well, as I was saying before, Gentah asked us to meet you so we could take the horses back to camp." His words were loud and jarring. "That way, you can start your return journey now. We brought provisions."

"What?" Adehl shook herself. She groped for her water flask and took a swig. "Did you say *provisions*? That would be appreciated, but I'm heading to Tarsah." The reminder of her destination made her heart ache. She needed to see her father, hoped desperately he was all right after his accident. "I was intending to stay overnight in your camp."

Frahto slapped a fly off his arm. "There might, uh, be a problem."

"Plans change," Roh said, as though continuing an argument. "If Adehl is riding to Tarsah, of course she should stay with us."

Frahto said nothing, but his frown made his sentiments clear. Doubtless sensing Adehl's escalating unease, Cloud tossed his head, and she laid a hand on his neck, calmed his llirah with a thread of rhythm. "How far is Fortune Spring from here?" she asked, to fill the silence.

"About four hours ride." Roh smiled and his confidence almost reassured her — until she remembered what had just happened. She couldn't let him get too close. Maybe she *should* take the provisions they offered and avoid the camp. Her spirits fell at the diminishing prospect of a convivial evening around a fire, with fresh-cooked food and a sleeping pallet.

Frahto said, "Roh, I don't think —"

"Enough." Roh sat still in the saddle. "Gentah wouldn't want a Vuusah zehli to skirt our camp when it's on the way."

"You're taking full responsibility."

"Look," Adehl said, trying to make sense of their exchange. "What's going on? You said there was a problem — is someone ill?"

Frahto shrugged and glanced pointedly at Roh.

"There's no problem." Roh's jaw jutted stubbornly, and Adehl didn't believe him. "Our doyen thought you could cut off a day from your journey if we met you out here. But that's obviously not the case, so now we'll escort you to our camp. All right?"

Adehl allowed Roh's conviction to override her doubts. Surely one night couldn't hurt. They could feed her, give her somewhere to sleep, and she'd leave first thing in the morning. As long as she kept to herself, everything would be fine. She wouldn't let her guard down again.

She adjusted her grip on the lead rein. Despite being strung closely together, the horses all had their heads down, grazing furiously on clumps of weeping grass. She'd been letting out the rope gradually as they moved away and now hauled them in. "Let's go then," she said.

Muttering something that was lost to the breeze, Frahto wheeled his horse around and set off the way he and Roh had come, following their trail of trampled grass and flowers. Adehl let out the cry that would spur all her horses into action. The wind riffled her hair as Cloud launched into a canter after Frahto's chestnut, Roh's horse right alongside hers.

ROH IGNORED Frahto's attempts to catch his attention as they approached their camp, revealed by a smudge of smoke in the clear afternoon sky. He didn't need to see the jut of his friend's chin, or the fingers clenched around his rein. He didn't need to see the glint in Frahto's eye.

Hookbeaks swirled noisily through the skies, and flies zoomed around the sweaty horses. Adehl rode beside Roh, keeping a few paces between them. She moved as one with the animal, effortlessly controlling the four horses on lead rein. The ornaments of her srih clinked, tiny glints of copper, green and amber. Similar beads adorned her many long, dark braids. A movement in her cheek, as though she gnawed the inside, made her look apprehensive — although she met his smile with one of her own readily enough. His llirah surged and reached for hers again, straining for that unexpected resonance. At her quizzical glance, he averted his gaze and reasserted control.

The situation was confusing. Never had his llirah responded as it had to Adehl's. He always kept it tamped down to avoid overwhelming people. But when he'd touched Adehl, her rhythm all honey and wind and speed, his restraints had dissolved. It had been instinctive, that need to blend with her rhythm as though it were a missing fragment of his own. He didn't know what it meant.

He did know he hadn't been able to let her leave.

They were close to Fortune Spring now. Despite the cook-fire smoke, the hollow wasn't easy to spot amid the undulating sea of grass and scattered silverbark woodland. Frahto kicked Melon into a canter and headed down a slope past a rocky rise. Behind the hill lay a wide, natural depression, where tents, horses and trees clustered around a waterhole. Fortune Spring was his favourite of all their annual camp sites, and Roh found he wanted to show it off to this intriguing young woman.

"What's going on over there?" Adehl asked.

Roh looked to the staked-out area where the old former Bladekor warrior drilled groups of zehla in swordplay. The Kestali man's black uniform contrasted against the green of the grass, unlike the neutral garb the zehla wore. Roh met

Frahto's gaze, annoyed by his friend's grim amusement. This was why Gentah hadn't wanted a zehli from Doneyah's company visiting their camp. "They're being trained for a mission," he said.

"What mission?" Her gaze remained fixed on the weapons field, where all had gone still while old Mentus demonstrated a few moves.

"Uh… Gentah will explain."

They were almost among the tents now, and Adehl murmured to her horses as they passed the picket line and a pen of laying hens. Her presence attracted attention. Hands stilled amid weaving flankah or sewing leather. Conversations faltered. Children ran, bare feet thudding on the worn turf between canvas walls, squeals cut off by cuffed ears and sharp words.

A girl scrambled between a pair of tents, batting away garments suspended from a drying line. She pulled up when she broke free of the laundry and came face to face with the horses. Roh recognised Sorah, Lenatoh's half-Kestali daughter. Her gaze, keen and intelligent above her scarred cheeks, took in Adehl with interest. Then she caught Roh's eye and flushed, before ducking out of sight.

"Lenatoh ought to deal with her," Frahto muttered, staring after Sorah. "It's getting dangerous."

It had shocked everyone two years ago when their senior nedoyen had brought his eleven-year-old daughter out of a Kestali sailor into Gentah's company. Before Sorah, Roh had never encountered a pidakah child with such a strong affinity for ellir. Many Vuusah would consider it unthinkable, but Sorah's llirah was big and vibrant, impossible to ignore. Were she full-blood Fiugreh, she would have begun training as a zehli this summer gone. Instead, she would have to be quelled or she wouldn't survive her llirah going wild. "I'm sure he's keeping an eye on her," he said.

"He knows what he has to do. He should have done it already."

Roh didn't bother responding. The Vuusah precepts were clear, and no one doubted Lenatoh would adhere to them. Roh couldn't help feeling sorry for the girl, though. To quell her considerable affinity would be devastating for her, no matter her lineage. He became aware of Adehl watching them, but she made no comment.

Gentah himself came forward to greet them, his mouth tightening as he noted Adehl's presence. Roh dismounted and thrust Sprig's rein at the nearest acoleh, went to Adehl's side as she swung off her horse. On foot, she stood at average height, her knee-length mahgan flowing below her samah, its markings declaring her Urgreh lineage and empathiser skills.

The big moonskin whuffed and nosed her hair as she looped up the rein. "There's no need to hold him," she said as an acoleh arrived at her side. She stroked the pale gold mane of the sunskin she'd been leading and turned to Gentah. "Soul bright and balanced, Doyi. I bring greetings from Doyi Doneyah."

"You have our thanks," Gentah said stiffly. "Soul bright and welcome to Fortune Spring." He grazed his palm against Adehl's.

"Thank you for sending your zehla to meet me," she said. "I understand you hoped to save me some riding, but I'm on my way to Tarsah, so…"

Gentah inclined his head. "Of course."

Roh frowned. "Doyi —"

"Frahto will help you get the horses settled," the old man said, not looking at Roh.

"Yes, Doyi," Frahto said.

"But —"

"Not now, Roh."

Frahto gestured for Adehl to follow with the horses, then

set off towards one of the pickets. She raised her brows as she passed Roh. He couldn't help grinning in response and watched the easy sway of her body as she walked away, her influence on ellir a bright new song. Her mount followed without being led, and Roh kind of understood why.

"Black sun burn you, boy." Gentah's voice jabbed at him. "Why is she here?"

"You heard what she said. She's heading to Tarsah. It would have caused more comment if we forbade her to come."

The old man's hands clawed in search of something to throttle. "She saw the exhorters in training?"

"She's Vuusah. I don't see —"

"Enough. I see rather more than you."

Roh resented being the target of Gentah's sharp tongue, especially when the doyen was keeping secrets. "What aren't you telling me?"

"When you are Atalah, you will have the right to ask that question."

"If I am ever Atalah," he said, "I had better not need to ask." He wondered how the current Atalah would feel if she knew how often Gentah said things like that. As though she were in her dotage, soon to be replaced, rather than a hale woman barely in her fifth decade.

Inexplicably, Gentah chuckled. "True." He watched Roh in silence for a moment. "What's wrong?"

"Nothing, Doyi."

"She's attractive."

"I suppose she is."

"Hmm." The doyen considered him. "Keep away from her, do you hear me?"

Having no intention of following this directive, Roh thought it best to say nothing at all.

2. Spiced flah

Frahto stroked the flank of the new buckskin gelding while Adehl fastened the lead rope to the overhead picket line. Among the new horses were also a sunskin, a dun and a black. They were all beautiful animals.

"He's up to your weight," Adehl said.

Frahto looked up to find her watching him, mouth quirked in a hesitant smile. It was the first time he'd felt the full force of her attention. Her amber eyes glinted with humour above bronzed cheeks framed by her braids. Slender and lightly muscled, she moved with compact grace, not giving much away. He stepped back from the horse. "Probably. He's not for me, though."

"That's a shame. For you, I mean." She rocked on her heels, brushed her hands on the fabric of her mahgan. "Um, do you think I might have some warm water to wash?"

He supposed she had discerned Gentah's reluctance to have her here. Should he apologise? Roh would. "I'll see to it. Do you need anything for your mount?" He gestured at her horse, still saddled, grazing untethered nearby.

"He's fine for now." When she patted his neck, the moon-skin lifted his head as though paying attention to words she wasn't speaking. Then he resumed his enthusiastic foraging.

Adehl said little as they returned to the camp area, where Frahto asked Sorah to organise washing water and anything else Adehl might need. Lenatoh's daughter nodded and peeped at the visiting zehli through her lashes.

"Thank you." Adehl smiled at the half-Kestali girl, whose scarred cheeks flushed. "Could you find some tohroot for my horse? I'd like to give him a treat."

"I think so." Sorah glanced at Frahto; then her dark braid slapped her shoulders as she spun towards the cook-fires. Sorah seemed to have grown taller. It was difficult to recall the sailor brat she'd been two years ago, hair ragged and short, face shockingly mutilated from some barbaric Kestali ritual.

"Who is that girl?" Adehl asked.

"Sorah?" Frahto considered what to say. The girl's presence in the company remained a touchy subject. "She's the daughter of one of our nedoyens. Her mother is from Kestale." He waited for Adehl to express surprise or even disapproval that Gentah's company harboured a pidakah child. There was no point trying to conceal her Kestali blood: Sorah's skin was too pale and her eyes too dark to be of pure Fiugreh lineage. And then there were those scars.

"How old is she?"

"Thirteen or thereabouts." Old enough that her llirah needed to be quelled before it shook her apart.

"She's not wearing any srih."

"Srih?" He eyed the strips of woven leather, beads and metal twisted around each of her forearms. "Why would she?"

Adehl looked incredulous. "All Fiugreh girls weave them when they are twelve."

"But Sorah is pidakah… It would not be appropriate."

"Why not? Since when does a girl's lineage matter for weaving srih? She's still approaching womanhood. Is it not enough —" She bit off her next words, her face flushing. "Where is her mother?"

"On a Kestali merchant ship somewhere, I assume. That's where the girl came from. Believe me, she is better off riding with us than losing her innocence among that bawdy lot." And here at least were zehla aplenty to ensure her talent didn't kill her.

"Maybe not if you treat her as though she's less than human."

"I hardly think —"

"She's half Fiugreh," Adehl said. "By denying her srih, you are denying half her identity. Her father can't want her to be an outsider among the Vuusah all her life."

Had the woman not heard him? "She's *pidakah*," he said. "How can she not be an outsider?"

Adehl pressed her lips together. After a time, she said, "My apologies. I didn't mean to preach at you. I'm weary and forgot my manners. I am grateful for your hospitality."

It sounded like an honest apology, but Frahto felt disquieted. He made some acknowledgement, and they exchanged meaningless conversation until Sorah returned with a few pieces of tohroot and word that Adehl's washing water was heated.

Frahto watched Adehl's interactions with Sorah, wanting to make sure she would let the matter rest. Sorah didn't deserve for some stranger to upset her with suggestions of things she couldn't have. He already regretted giving way to Roh's insistence that Adehl come here. Not that Roh ever listened to him.

GARBED in clean leggings and mahgan, Adehl towelled water out of her washed hair, then grabbed her comb. She'd scrubbed every inch of her skin with warm, soapy water and felt ready to face whatever awaited her in this camp. It should have been unremarkable for her to bring horses they'd *requested* and stay a night before heading on to Tarsah. The tepid welcome and reluctant hospitality made her wonder what was going on.

She told herself to ignore it. Best to keep her head down and leave first thing in the morning. She'd betrayed too much of herself already.

The shadows were growing long amid the silverbarks where Adehl had secreted herself to bathe. The trees grew in numbers around the water, filling one end of the hollow. Grassy hills ringed the natural depression, except for a section behind Adehl where time had exposed craggy walls of heartrock. Bushland birds chittered, and a mob of ravakah clustered on the opposite bank of the spring. Some of the grey animals watched her; others drank before loping up the hillside to graze. It was easy to see why Fortune Spring was a popular camp among the Vuusah.

When Sorah returned, the girl smiled shyly. "The evening meal is being served. The doyen invites you to join his fire."

"Thank you," Adehl said, sitting on a log and pulling on her boots. Overhead, leaves rustled as tiny barkwrens flitted among the branches. "Did you give Cloud the tohroot?"

"Yes." Sorah giggled. "He licked my hand and then tried to stick his nose in my ear!"

"Means he likes you."

The girl's radiant expression made the half-truth worth it. Adehl's blood still burned at the fact Sorah was being denied srih. She also wanted to know who was to blame for those terrible scars. "Do you tend the horses often?"

Sorah's face sobered. "Sometimes, when everyone else is busy."

"Help me now, before dark falls," Adehl said. No doubt Sorah got lumped with all the worst chores around camp. "I'll eat afterwards."

They walked together to where Cloud was grazing partway up the slope of a hill. Adehl removed his saddle and laid it on the grass; then Sorah helped her rub him down.

"Why don't you tether him?" Sorah asked after a while. "Won't he run off? My father says horses all want to be free."

"He's right. But Cloud won't run off because he and I share a bond." Adehl removed Cloud's halter and smiled at Sorah's furrowed brow. "Do you understand what it means to be soulmelded?"

Sorah's small jaw hardened. "My father is soulmelded to Rahda."

Presumably not her mother. "My bond with Cloud is similar, although not as strong. Our rhythms fit together." She interlocked her fingers, held them up.

"You're lucky." Sorah gazed after the horse as he dropped his head and moved off. She looked like she needed a hug.

"Now, where's this meal you promised me?" Adehl said instead, gathering all her gear. "I think I've kept the doyen waiting long enough."

"He'll blame me, don't worry."

"I won't let him blame you."

By now, the day had almost faded. Pink and orange stained the underbellies of high, wispy clouds, but the hollow lay in full shadow. Gentah's company gathered around two fires set about fifty paces away from the tents and the trees. Voices drowned out the flock of hookbeaks wheeling across the glowing sky, and the aromas of roasting loophorn and spiced flah made Adehl's mouth water. Beside her, Sorah's steps faltered as a score or more faces turned towards them.

A hush fell, and *now* the hookbeaks' screeching resounded loud in the dusk. Adehl attempted a smile and wished she'd found the time to braid her hair, rather than leave it loose down her back. It made her feel partially undressed.

She faced the shrewd visage of the doyen. "I'm sorry to keep you waiting." It was hard not to look at Roh, seated at Gentah's side, his gaze pricking her skin.

"It was right for you to tend your horse first. I hope the girl was not a nuisance?"

A delicate anger threatened Adehl's calm. "On the contrary. Sorah looked after me very well." Turning to Sorah, she almost joined their palms, as she would thank an acoleh for the same service. Her hand landed on the girl's forearm instead, where her srih ought to have been. The girl's unrestrained llirah threatened to erupt with anxiety; Adehl instinctively calmed her rhythm as she would a frightened horse.

Gentah's eyes narrowed. "You may go."

Adehl momentarily thought he spoke to her, but Sorah mumbled something and slipped away.

The doyen indicated a vacant mat in the circle around the fire. "Please join us."

"Thank you," Adehl said, as mildly as she could manage. She was not, fortunately, seated near Roh, although being placed beside his dour friend was not ideal either.

"Sorah seems to like you," Frahto said, almost accusingly, as a boy of about seven handed her a carved plate piled with food. Frahto's own plate, smeared with grease and shards of loophorn bone, lay discarded on the ground.

"Is there any reason she should not?"

He huffed. "I just hope you said nothing to —"

"I'm not that cruel." Adehl held his gaze a moment. She saw too much of herself in Sorah. Safer to focus on her meal. Roasted loophorn, dampah bread, boiled tohroot seasoned with cinnamon and wilted butterflowers. "This looks fantastic."

"Better than trail rations, I imagine."

"Just a little." She ventured a smile. "Do you always eat this well?"

"We like to make visitors feel welcome," he said with a straight face.

Adehl raised an eyebrow and turned back to her meal. It tasted as good as it looked, the flavours rich and complex. She'd love to see what they fed visitors they'd invited.

"Why are you heading to Tarsah?" Frahto asked.

She chewed, swallowed, refrained from saying her reasons didn't concern him. "I have family there." Her voice came out rough.

The man looked unimpressed. "Just about everyone has family in Tarsah."

She shrugged as a girl brought her a bowl of spiced flah. Adehl inhaled the sweet scent before taking a sip. Perhaps if she focused on the flah, Frahto would leave her alone. Why hadn't she prepared a believable lie?

"It's the height of summer," Frahto said. "I imagine the foals are weaning — doesn't your doyen need you?"

She eyed him over the rim of her bowl. "There are others to handle the foals. But, if you must know, I received word my foster-father's had an accident. My doyen gave me leave to visit him." It hurt to think of the letter. The letter from Mikka, some woman she'd never heard of, calling her home.

Frahto crossed his arms. Then his attention shifted to something behind her, and a hand landed on her shoulder. Ellir fizzed through her — already she recognised Roh's energy. She leant forward to break contact, and he dropped onto the ground beside them.

"I'm sorry you keep getting lumped with this oaf. He's

not much company." Grinning, Roh gave a ceramic flask to Frahto.

"And now you're here, things are much better." Frahto unstoppered the flask and took a swig.

"I did bring wine." He held out a hand for it, but Frahto lifted it high above his head. "Oi, bloodhead, we're sharing that. Give it here."

"You called me an oaf."

"And a bloodhead. Give it here." He pounced on Frahto, and a moment later they were wrestling in the dust.

Adehl drained her bowl of spiced flah and returned to her meal. She ate, too hungry and grateful for proper food to leave anything on her plate. Beside her, Frahto pinned Roh on his front with a knee, Roh's arm twisted up his back. The flask of contention stood, mercifully unspilt, on the ground near Adehl's foot. "You ought to know better," Frahto said. "Do you yield?"

"Umph." Roh tried to buck Frahto off, but the man was half again his size.

Adehl picked up the flask and sniffed the contents. "You might as well yield," she said. "I have the wine now."

Both men laughed, and Frahto released Roh, who dusted himself off. "Please forget that happened," he said.

"I could try." Adehl sipped the wine and smiled at the smooth, deep flavour. "How is it you have wine, anyway? In my company, we only have tohba."

Roh grinned. "Gentah is partial to Haiffin red. We always have crates on hand."

"I suppose you raided the supply cart without permission," Frahto said.

"The occasion warranted wine." Roh met Adehl's glance with an intense expression, and she hoped the fading light hid the heightened colour in her cheeks. She'd blame it on the drink. After another sip from the shared flask, she moved her empty plate to one side and stretched out her legs, enjoying the slight buzz the wine was already having on her senses.

On the other side of the fire, an older man in a black uniform talked to a couple of women, his sword hilt prominent behind his shoulder. It reminded her of the weapons training she'd seen riding into the camp. Gesturing with her head, she said, "Tell me more about him."

Frahto glanced behind and frowned, but Roh said, "That's Mentus. He's a retired Bladekor warrior."

She had suspected as much, but finding one of the Kestali swordwielders here surprised her. "Why is he training your zehla?"

Roh glanced at Frahto, who gave a small shake of his head. Across the fire, someone guffawed.

Adehl scrutinised Roh, who shifted on the grass. "For how long?" she asked.

"Over a year," he said. "At the Summersdawn Conclave before last, the Atalah —"

"Roh." Frahto's voice held a warning.

"She might as well know." Wine sloshed over his arm as he gestured.

Frahto plucked the flask from Roh's hands. "I think that's for the doyen to decide."

"You've been training zehla in weapons for a year?" Adehl tried to imagine zehla fighting with swords, but the picture wouldn't come. "Why?" she asked again.

"They're being sent out to make sure kalkah zehla are not breaking our precepts," Roh said.

That gave Adehl pause. Although trained by the Vuusah, kalkah zehla typically took on contracts with businesses, administrative bodies and wealthy citizens. "Surely most kalkah zehla follow the rules," she said.

Frahto gave a rough laugh. "I doubt it. If they intended to

follow our precepts, they would remain with the Vuusah, not sell their services for coin."

It was an opinion she'd heard many times. Many kalkah zehla didn't have a choice after the Vuusah deemed them unworthy. The whole discussion was a timely reminder of why she needed to keep her distance.

"You should hear all the stories," Roh said. "The kalkah in Tarsah or Romanah are bad enough, but at least we have more control over them."

"But why do these zehla need swords?"

"So they can protect themselves."

"From what?"

"Anything. Who knows what threats may lie in gravohl places like Dohni or the Merali Demesnes."

Adehl's eyes widened. The city–state of Dohni lay hundreds of miles away across the Broadwater, and the Merali Demesnes were even farther. She'd never considered the Vuusah might send zehla that far abroad. Most Vuusah rarely left the Humming Downs; many avoided setting foot in the Fiugreh cities of Tarsah and Romanah.

Roh shuffled closer. "Adehl…"

She clambered to her feet, head reeling from the wine. They gaped up at her. "Sorry. I just need…" She waved out into the darkness beyond the ring of firelight.

Roh's face cleared. "Of course. You'll come back?"

"Perhaps," she said, trying to sound mysterious, rather than anxious. Fury, she'd known not to get too comfortable with Roh. The wine had been a bad idea.

3. Under the Stars

Adehl stumbled over someone's discarded plate as she headed out of the firelight towards the trees. It was cooler away from the fire, a light breeze rustling the silverbark leaves. Her footsteps made little sound on patches of worn grass, leaving the night free for the music of crickets and frogs and darkbirds. Back at the fire, drums came out. Ankle bells soon followed.

Her gear lay in a heap where she'd left it near the edge of the trees. She braided her hair first, moving by touch in the darkness. She kept the adornments simple and functional, opting instead for speed. As the strands of hair flowed between her fingers, she embraced ellir through the ground, casting out her senses to locate Cloud.

Maybe she *should* mount up and ride away tonight.

Cloud grazed over the hill, coat gleaming silver in the starlight. Tail twitching, he lifted his head as Adehl approached. "How are you going, beautiful?" she murmured, energy ebbing between them via the land. The horse whuffed and nosed her hair. "You think I've brought you more treats, huh? Always wanting more." She palmed a few pieces of tohroot between his questing lips.

Besides the distant fireside music, the night was quiet. Adehl buried her face in the horse's warm neck, relishing the exchange of energy between them. It was enough. She wouldn't flee in the darkness; it would only give rise to more questions. She would be strong and calm, an ideal Vuusah zehli. Early tomorrow morning, she would leave.

A whisper of movement behind her. "I thought you were returning to the fire." Roh's voice came from the darkness.

She turned, her eyes straining to locate him. "How did you sneak up on me?" She didn't feel equipped to deal with him just now.

He chuckled, and she could just make out a dark shape moving towards her. When he reached out to Cloud's neck, she imagined the dark mane trailing through his long fingers. "Your company breeds beautiful horses."

"We do." She couldn't keep a hitch of hesitation from her tone.

A pause. "Someone else bred him?"

Forget the wine, coming to this camp had been a bad idea. "My foster-father bred Cloud." She usually avoided talking about her family, her father in particular, because it meant she had to lie. Lying to any zehli was always inadvisable; lying to someone as strong as Roh was sheer folly. For ten years, she had barricaded thoughts of her family in the back of her mind. She'd kept her promise to cut off all ties with them. But ever since Mikka's letter had reached her a couple of weeks ago, the walls had been crumbling. *Your father had an accident...*

"Is he Vuusah?"

"No. He breeds and trains horses in Tarsah." That at least was true. *One of the stallions kicked him in the head...*

"He's kalkah then?" He sounded disapproving.

"No. He's not a zehli. He's just good with horses." *He's still unconscious. It's been a week…*

"I see."

She frowned. "People don't exist for you unless they're Vuusah, do they?"

"That's not true. It's just…" A tense pause. "Oh."

Roh behaved as Adehl would have expected of a zehli groomed to be Atalah, yet he continued to surprise her, too. Standing close, he brushed her hand where it lay on Cloud's neck. The touch was fleeting, perhaps accidental — but the surge of energy made Adehl's llirah thrum like randomly plucked lute strings.

"You said he is your foster-father," Roh said.

She didn't dare respond.

"He means a lot to you."

"Of course. He raised me and instilled in me my love of horses." Emotion clogged her voice, and tears wet her cheeks. She hoped he was all right.

Roh was silent for a moment. "What aren't you telling me?"

She didn't answer at first, not wanting to lie further. "Many things, no doubt." She tried for a light tone. Thank the stars it was too dark for him to see her face.

He laughed. "You're right. I'm sorry. I just…" He moved closer to Adehl, but he didn't touch her this time. "Will you be at the Wintersmorn festival?"

"Um…"

"We're gathering at Singing Canyon this year. Will you be there?"

Adehl's fingers clenched the folds of her mahgan. "No."

"Why not?"

"I'm sorry, but…" She cast about for something true. "I don't know where I'll be, come Wintersmorn." The equinox fell in about a month and a half.

"How long are you visiting your family?"

"I'm not sure. Perhaps a few weeks." Perhaps indefinitely.

"We'll be here for a while yet." A pause. "You could visit on your return."

Adehl sucked in a breath and clamped down on her llirah, which had flared at his suggestion. He was standing so close his breath warmed her cheek, his voice hopeful, almost vulnerable, all arrogance fled. She didn't understand the connection between them, but it was undeniably present. Something about Roh made her want to confide in him, trust him. She reminded herself not to be a fool. "I don't think so," she said, surprised at her genuine regret.

"Why not?"

"You must have noticed your doyen would banish me to the Gahmniu deadland if he could."

There was a pause, but he didn't contradict her. She wished she could see his expression, but the moon had not yet risen. "The old man will come around. Say you'll return."

"I can't."

"Your doyen can do without you. You said so yourself."

She tried to think of an excuse that wouldn't involve lying.

"You know you can't lie to me, Adehl."

She couldn't help an involuntary chuckle. "I know! I don't suppose anyone could."

"Well?"

"If I can't lie to you, I had better say nothing."

"You can tell me anything. Please?" Finally, he touched her, took her hand in his and held it between them so their elbows brushed. Her llirah blended with his like honey in watermint tea, sending tingles down her spine. But this time he kept his llirah restrained.

"You won't like the truth," she said.

He pulled away without breaking their clasp. "You have someone else?"

"No." She didn't count Deneh, although they'd enjoyed their time together.

"Good." His shadowy form drew nearer once more. His hand traced over the srih wound around each of her wrists, then moved up to her hair.

Adehl had lost track of the conversation, no longer sure what he was asking. She leant towards him, certain he was about to kiss her. Then, remembering her predicament, she pulled away. Time and again, she kept on forgetting how dangerous he was. "I think you should go now." Her heart battered at her rib cage.

It took him several moments to gather himself. "Why are you so afraid of me?"

His hurt was unmistakable. In the darkness, Adehl rubbed at her face. Too many secrets. Too many lies. "It's just..." He was going to be *Atalah*. And she... "This feels like... something. And I don't think it's a good idea."

"Why?"

"Because I'm not..." Fury, what could she tell him? "I'll be away for a while."

A surge of distant laughter came from the fire.

"What are you saying?"

"Can't you leave it at that?"

"No." The beads in his hair clacked together. "Are you going somewhere?"

"I'm staying in Tarsah."

"With your family."

"That's my intention."

She could almost feel his mind turning it over. "For a few weeks, you said."

Adehl made no reply, willed him to understand.

"You don't mean…" His voice became sharp. "No, you *can't* mean…"

She refused to deny it. Maybe it was time for bald truth. "I'm leaving the Vuusah. When I return to Tarsah, I'm applying for a kalkah licence."

A stunned silence met her words as Roh backed away, leaving cold air around her. "*Why?*"

"Does it matter?"

"Yes!"

"My f-foster-father needs me. This is something I have to do." And it was true. Her father had risked everything for her to be trained as a zehli… But she'd stayed away for ten *years*. Surely that was long enough. She was a horse empathiser, and her family bred horses. It was time to go home.

The night air hung thick, almost too thick to breathe. Roh's dark shape had gone still. Only Cloud, a silver figure grazing across the hillside, proved time hadn't stopped.

"You're serious," Roh said after a moment. "You'd choose… *that* over the Vuusah?"

Adehl sighed and shook her head, braids sweeping her shoulderblades. She couldn't explain any of this to him.

He closed the gap between them, his hands to her waist. "How can I change your mind?"

Adehl tried to pull away. "You can't." She couldn't think properly as he held her, his face inches from hers in the darkness. "Roh…" Their rhythms threaded together, fizzing through every corner of her being, at once breathtaking and terrifying. She battled to stop her core self from unfolding, baring her soul along with her secrets. "No. *Stop.*"

His hands dropped, and the storm of ellir drained away. "I'm sorry."

Adehl staggered back, her whole body shaking. "You can't just — You're too strong."

"I'm *sorry.*"

They stared blindly at each other while Cloud tore at the grass. In the distance, a pipe joined the lively drumbeat and dancing bells.

"Make me understand," Roh said in a low voice. "Explain to me why you're throwing everything away to become kalkah."

"I'm not throwing anything away! I'll still be a zehli. A zehli can *exist* without the Vuusah. They are not the same thing."

"But the Vuusah train all zehla," he said. "And we need talented zehla to keep the world bright and balanced."

"Why confine zehla to Vuusah enclaves on the downs, far away from everyone? Why not use our abilities to serve others — and, yes, earn some coin? The Vuusah have already ensured all zehla must have pure Fiugreh blood…"

She hooked back the next words unuttered, mouth suddenly dry. Her stomach gave an awkward lurch. Not a wise topic to bring up.

Roh took a step back. The fireside drums echoed Adehl's rampaging heartbeat. She told herself he couldn't possibly guess she had more than a passing interest in whether pidakah Fiugreh could be trained as zehla.

"Blighted sun," he said, his voice rough. "Do you truly believe all that?"

"You asked me to explain."

"But you speak of ellir as though it's something to be *used*."

"What about every time you farsense? Or read someone's llirah?"

He made a noise of protest.

"How can you distinguish between my working with Vuusah horses and those of my family?"

"But it is different. Don't you see? Out here, ellir is wild and free, untamed. Zehla belong on the Humming Downs,

Adehl. Not working like gravohl in cities for coin." He sounded revolted.

She ought to have known the future Atalah of all people wouldn't understand.

Ellir burst into her as he took her hand again. She wasn't ready — would never be ready — for the way her llirah responded, surged to meet his. She shook him off, stumbled in her haste to gain distance. But distance didn't seem to matter anymore. Even with several paces between them, she was intensely aware of Roh's immense rhythm, cascading in resonance with hers. "You feel it." His voice came low.

"Stop." She couldn't move. The magnitude of Roh's talent overwhelmed her. "What are you doing?" She was pleased with how composed she sounded.

"I'm not *doing* anything," he said. "This is... something else."

She wished she could make out his expression in the darkness.

With difficulty, she extracted her llirah from his, clamped down on her rhythm, confined it within her core. When she spoke, her voice shook. "You need to forget about... what happened. I doubt we'll see each other again."

"I don't accept that." The words, the way he said them, made Adehl shiver.

She looked over at Cloud. "I'll go now."

"Wait." He sounded resigned. "Don't flee in the dark. I'll leave you alone, I promise. Let me get someone to find you a pallet."

Adehl closed her eyes, tried to think. Weariness seeped into her limbs, and she acknowledged how little she wanted to ride onwards tonight. If she grabbed a few hours sleep now, she could sneak away early in the morning. Whatever happened, she couldn't risk encountering Roh again.

4. Distant cry of darkbirds

Frahto paced as he waited for Roh to finish dallying with Adehl out near her horse. He quashed his guilt at spying on his friend — not that the darkness allowed him to see. He didn't trust this woman. Some of her views were… unusual.

He halted at the sound of voices approaching. Arguing. Peering into the blackness, he made out a pair of dark shapes. Their voices broke off as they neared him and the smaller shape veered away, leaving Roh to arrive alone in front of him.

"What are you doing here?" Roh asked.

"Waiting for you."

"Nosy."

"Worried."

"I can take care of myself." Roh gazed after Adehl's silhouette against the camp glow, lifted his chin as something caught his attention. With a muttered oath, he strode towards the fire and music.

"Don't ignore me." Frahto hurried to grab Roh's arm. "Tell me what happened."

"Nothing happened." Roh shook him off and kept moving.

"I don't believe you."

"Leave it, Frahto." His voice held an edge.

"Roh!" This time Frahto used his greater strength to restrain his friend. "Be careful. There's something about her that's... suspicious." At Roh's snort of bitter laughter, the unbridled confusion and distress in his rhythm, Frahto relaxed his hold. This was more than a woman rejecting his advances. "You know you can talk to me."

Twisting free, Roh resumed his progress towards the fireside. Frahto only just kept up. He'd never known Roh to act like this. There'd been women, of course; girls really. They'd been throwing themselves at Roh for as long as Frahto had known him. One daring young zehli had offered Roh her srih; Frahto still didn't know how his friend had refused without offending the girl. But none of them had affected Roh like this. Not one of them had led Roh to shut Frahto out.

Most tents glowed from within as their occupants settled for the night, but a group still clustered or danced beside the fire. A good number were acoleh, Roh's younger brother, Johre, among them. The youth cavorted with Lenatoh's younger daughter, Kalihra, the pair grinning at each other. Roh, meanwhile, skirted the dancers to where Lenatoh himself stood with one arm around Rahda, his injaleh and Kalihra's mother.

"Listen," Roh said. "Has anyone arranged for Adehl to sleep somewhere? She has crawled underneath the tack wagon."

Lenatoh and Rahda blinked at him. As well they might. How could Roh know that?

"Who looks after such things?" Roh demanded. "Or do we like guests sleeping rough?" He flung a look at Frahto as though expecting assistance.

Frahto stilled. Fury, was he supposed to have organised something? "Uh, we could ask —"

"Don't bother." Roh gave a short laugh. "Perhaps I shall offer her the hospitality of *my* tent. I should have thought of that first."

He wasn't serious. At least, Frahto *thought* he wasn't serious, but Lenatoh's eyes widened. "I don't think that's ideal. We'll lay an extra pallet in our tent."

"I suppose she could sleep in with the girls," Rahda said. "I'll go see to it."

As she left, Roh regarded Lenatoh with hooded eyes. "Thank you." He paused, then pivoted and disappeared into the night.

Frahto stared after him, contemplated following. What in the burning bright sun had that woman said?

"What happened?" asked Lenatoh.

Frahto turned to find the nedoyen's attention also fixed in the direction Roh had gone. "I'm not sure."

"Hmm. I'll keep an eye on him." He sounded pensive. "And her."

"You don't mind putting out an extra pallet?"

"No. Roh was right. We should have organised that."

He beckoned his younger daughter to him, chuckled as Kalihra dragged her hands out of young Johre's. She wore an embroidered mahgan over her leggings, the vibrant scarlet and emerald threads similar to those woven through the srih adorning each narrow wrist. She wore the latter self-consciously and, since he could not recall having seen them before, Frahto supposed them to be a recent addition. Strange to think the girl could have reached twelve already.

Lenatoh bade Kalihra go help her mother. "Yes, *now*. It is growing late. Your sister is already abed."

The piper's lively tune trilled to an end, its absence heavy on the air. As the dancers broke apart, perhaps catalysed by

Kalihra's departure, the tinkle of ankle bells punctuated the dull murmur of conversation.

Lenatoh looked at Frahto. "Best leave Roh alone."

"I suppose." Frahto wished Roh would talk to him. He wanted to shake some sense into his friend. He knew exactly which corner of Fortune Spring Roh would seek for solace.

"Gentah will speak to him," Lenatoh said. "Leave him to us and go get some sleep."

It was a direct instruction and Frahto had no option but to obey. If Roh would listen to anyone, it would be Lenatoh, their calm and rational nedoyen. "I've never seen him like this."

"He's not the first man to be upended by a woman."

These words didn't reassure Frahto, but he nodded and bade Lenatoh goodnight. Tomorrow, he would stick beside Roh and make sure that woman didn't get near him alone.

THE MOMENT she crawled into her bedding beneath the wagon, exhaustion ached through Adehl. She curled into a ball, took deep breaths and tried to let the pipe music and the sound of bells wash over her. If only she'd heeded Frahto's suggestion earlier in the day, taken the offered provisions and kept riding. Hindsight was no use at all.

Grass tickling her cheek, Adehl opened to the heartstorm, the wild tempest of ellir in the depths of the world. The energy flowed through her, strummed her llirah. It was chaotic and free, untethered. Every part of her vibrated until she felt cleansed. But she pulled out before the heartstorm tugged too hard and swept her away. It was always a danger, even among zehla if they opened up and lost concentration. Instead, she tuned in to the many surface rhythms of Fortune Spring and the surrounding downs. Farsensing wasn't her primary skill, but she easily found Cloud among dozens of unfamiliar horses. The company lay quiet, except for a group lingering around the fire. One rhythm came to her clearer than all the others.

As she wondered, chest uncomfortably tight, at Roh's prodigious talent, she felt him approaching. Her lungs stilled as she lay motionless. He paused beside her wagon. "I know you're awake."

She released the breath she'd been holding. "Go away. I'm trying to sleep."

"Come out of there. I've found you somewhere more comfortable." He shifted, clothes rustling against the grass, boot scuffing against some part of the wagon, which creaked as though he had braced himself against it. His voice next came close to her head. "Adehl?"

If she didn't oblige him, he would probably drag her into the open. "Where?" she asked to stall for time. Burn him, she didn't want to move now she was settled. "How did you know where I was?"

He gave a bitter half laugh. "You knew I was approaching."

A frisson of understanding came, and she clutched her bedding close. He kept slipping beneath her defences, and she'd already said far too much. Why would he not leave her alone?

In the end, she crawled out, dragging her gear and bumping her head on the undercarriage. Roh reached for her, but she thrust her bag forward to avoid touching him. Cursing, rubbing at the self-inflicted ache, she staggered to her feet. The music had faded, the quiet broken only by low voices and the distant cry of darkbirds.

"Are you all right?" Roh asked.

She huffed and swayed out of his reach. "I'm fine."

"This way," he said, the words clipped.

Adehl followed him back through the camp.

They reached a large tent that glowed from within, one of few not shrouded in darkness, and Adehl realised it had grown late. Voices, hushed yet animated, then not so quiet, as a woman allowed her biting reproach to breach a whisper. "No, not there, you stupid girl... There! Next to Kalihra's pallet. Sorah, bring yours over here."

Roh moved under the awning and put his hand to the tent flap. "May we enter?"

The tent flap tore open to reveal a slender woman whose frown made Adehl's own tentative smile falter. Her braids were long and mostly dark, although lamplight picked out a few threads of silver. She was so fine boned and small that Adehl wondered how she'd manage a horse. "We're almost ready," the woman said.

"Look, if this isn't convenient... I was fine beneath the wagon."

"No, you were not." Roh's jaw jutted. "Rahda, thank you. This is Adehl."

The woman made a soft noise of assent and stood aside. Adehl reluctantly entered. Inside, the main chamber of the tent featured woven flankah floor mats that looked regularly shaken and a low, central table surrounded by bright cushions. Two girls stood beyond Rahda, and Adehl recognised Sorah. The girl had exchanged her clothes for rough sleeping garb and, from her puffy eyes and tousled, unbraided hair, looked dragged out of her bedding. Adehl was about to greet her when Sorah's eyes widened, and she shook her head. Adehl hurriedly returned her attention to the woman. "Hello and thank you. I'm so sorry to disrupt your evening."

"It's no trouble." Rahda strode into another chamber within the tent. "Your pallet is here. Sorah" — her voice grew even sharper — "I told you to put it *here*." The sound of dragging.

Sorah expelled a breath but said nothing. She fidgeted with her hands, rubbed her light-brown eyes.

"I'm sorry they woke you," Adehl said in a low voice. The girl darted her a nervous smile, shrugged.

A surge of ellir claimed Adehl's attention. Roh had touched her arm, but she couldn't make herself shake him off. "I'll leave you here," he said. He hooked a finger and drew a strand of hair away from her face. She tensed, not knowing what he might do next. But his mouth twisted, and he did none of the things that flitted through Adehl's mind, before releasing her. "Thanks, Rahda," he said on his way out.

Adehl hefted her gear into the sleeping chamber and deposited it onto the threadbare pallet that had been prepared for her. Given its lack of stuffing, she doubted it would be much softer than the grass beneath the wagon.

"Do you need anything?" Rahda asked her. Her attitude was hard to figure out — not hostile exactly, but not welcoming either. She kept glancing nervously at Sorah, and it struck Adehl Rahda was ashamed of the girl's presence. How ironic. "I've put your pallet next to my daughter's."

"Thank you," Adehl said, wary of betraying herself further. "I am sorry. I tried to tell him —"

"It's really no trouble." This time, Rahda offered a smile. "I hope you sleep well."

Adehl toppled wearily onto her pallet. Really, that wagon had been just fine.

The two girls clambered into their own bedding, Sorah's shoved against a billowing wall to make room. The other girl turned down the lantern and hung it on a support pole, then sat among her blankets. Snuggling into her own bedding, Adehl closed her eyes and tried not to notice the now-familiar rhythm beating from somewhere over near the spring.

Rustling garments and the jingle of srih caught her attention. When it didn't subside, Adehl opened her eyes to find the chamber still lit by the dull glow of the lamp, and Sorah's sister fingering the srih she wore on each slender wrist. Sorah lay still in her bedding, although Adehl could tell from her breathing she wasn't asleep.

"How long have you worn your srih?" Adehl asked.

The girl flushed. "Only a week. I am still getting used to them." She held out her wrists. "Aren't they pretty?"

"Yes." Adehl fingered one of the woven bands, twisted several times around the girl's delicate arm. Scarlet threads and a vibrant blue. Tiny charms wrought in gold and copper threaded through the knotted strands of spun flankah and leather. "Do you have someone in mind already?" she said, teasing.

The girl flushed again. "Not really."

Adehl turned to Sorah, lying wrapped in her covers, watching the exchange. "I'm sorry, Sorah," she whispered. "It's not fair." She could be this girl, denied everything. So easily.

Sorah shrugged, her scarred features expressionless — too expressionless for a girl her age. "My mother raised me. Her people do not covet such things."

Hearing her pain, Adehl laid a hand on her arm and tried to soothe her llirah. This poor child deserved so much more.

Her sister regarded Adehl with fascination. "You do not mind?"

"Mind?"

"That she's..." The girl looked at her sister and chewed her lip.

"That she's pidakah? Of course not." Adehl caught Sorah's sister in an urgent gaze. "Sorah is no lesser a person for being pidakah. Do you understand?" She paused, clamped down on everything else she wanted to say, aware of the flimsy tent walls. "Go to sleep," she whispered.

With a shrug and a rattle of her wristbands, the girl finally lay down and drew up her covers. Adehl turned down the lamp and groped her way back into her bedding, thankful she could no longer see their expressions.

The tent chamber grew quiet. Beyond, tent poles creaked and fabric billowed, creatures rustled the grasses. In the distance, somewhere beyond the fire, the distinctive cadence of muffled voices.

Adehl lay on her back, eyes wide open, staring at the faintly glowing tent ceiling. She couldn't bear to think of them quelling the bright young girl lying near her.

She thought about her father — who wasn't her foster-father at all — and wondered what the Vuusah would do if they discovered her deception.

5. Cleaved

Under the risen moon, Roh crossed the grass to Gentah and Lenatoh. Cross-legged on woven mats, the two leaders held private conference some distance from the main camp.

The doyen looked up, moonlight shining full on his furrowed brow. "Where have you been?"

Roh lowered himself onto the grass. Lenatoh's mild expression was unreadable, his hands busy with knife and whetstone. "That's none of your concern," Roh said.

"I told you to keep your distance from her."

"I took it as a suggestion." He withdrew a smooth disc of heartrock, one of his favourites, from the front pocket of his mahgan.

Ought he have listened to the doyen? For the past hour, seated on top of the craggy rise overlooking the camp, he'd turned Adehl's words over and over in his head. They gouged at him like a stone embedded in a wheel. He'd spent all his life roaming the Humming Downs. They were at the heart of Baljehni, the wild humming land, part of the ancient homelands of the Fiugreh clans. His heart hurt at the thought of zehla living like gravohl in the city. The thought of Adehl doing so… He recalled those melded moments in the darkness, the starlight glinting in her eyes. Fury, he wished —

"Frahto is worried about you," Lenatoh said.

"I'm fine."

"You're not." Gentah's voice lashed like a whip. "You're so on-edge I daresay the entire camp can sense it. And don't tell me Frahto was exaggerating. What's going on?"

"Nothing." And that was true. Had to be true.

"Roh —"

"What did she say to upset you?" Lenatoh asked.

Roh squeezed the piece of rock, and the words tumbled out. "She told me she's leaving the Vuusah. She's going to Tarsah to apply for a kalkah licence."

The scrape of knife on stone ceased as Gentah and Lenatoh exchanged a glance.

"I know she's within her rights to do that," Roh said. His heart stabbed out a mix of emotions he couldn't identify. Even now he couldn't drag his attention from Adehl, who lay in Lenatoh's tent, her rhythm imprinting itself on ellir. He shoved the disc back into his mahgan. "I couldn't persuade her to change her mind."

"Sun's blood," Gentah muttered. "This is just what we need."

"Did she say anything else about her plans?" Lenatoh asked.

"She intends to work for her foster-father, who breeds horses in Tarsah." He was trying to forget the other things she'd said.

"That's interesting, at least," Gentah said. "He'll bear watching too, I daresay."

"Watching?" Roh said.

"Yes, watching." Gentah glared. "Things are at a delicate

stage, Roh. I told you I didn't want this woman in our camp, yet you brought her here anyway. And now this!"

Roh had temporarily forgotten about the secrecy surrounding the exhorters. Adehl had not approved of them either.

The doyen held his gaze. "I must ask you to listen now, Roh. I need you to be open with me." He shuffled closer so their knees were almost touching. Roh allowed his hands to be appropriated and felt Gentah's familiar rhythm thread through his. "I sense this woman means more to you than you're admitting."

Roh shifted on the hard ground. He ought to have known the doyen would detect something of his reaction to Adehl. "Perhaps," he said, energy fizzing between them. "If she weren't determined to leave…"

"I feel the turbulence within you." Gentah's tone was soothing. "But she is not for you."

"What do you mean?"

"You are to be Atalah, Roh. Your injaleh will be carefully chosen."

Roh felt a wave of heat spread through him. The doyen had put a name to the connection between him and Adehl. He ought to have realised. *Injaleh* meant *soulmeld* in the old tongue. It was a sacred, permanent bond between lovers. But becoming injaleh involved a formal ceremony, and a noumenor zehli to align the llirah of those being melded. It couldn't happen spontaneously. Not completely or on such short acquaintance.

Blighted sun. Even now, he felt her at the edge of his senses. He did need to keep his distance.

Then the rest of Gentah's statement sank in. "What do you mean by *chosen*?"

Gentah regarded him, infuriatingly unapologetic. "With

your agreement, of course." The old man's llirah nudged more insistently.

With a jolt, Roh realised the doyen was attempting to impel him.

His breath hitched with incredulity, and Gentah's bony grip tightened. Roh yanked his hands away and rolled to his feet, toppling the old man onto the grass. "What in the blighted sun was that?"

Roh had somehow kept his voice low, but the night air rang loud with shock. Gentah lay flat on his back, moonlit silver braids haphazard around his head. It took obvious effort for the old man to edge his elbows underneath his body; then he levered himself upright with Lenatoh's help. Shaking hands smoothed out the folds of his mahgan across his knees. "You must not see this woman again."

Roh's shock at Gentah's betrayal surged into anger. The old man had broken a sacred Vuusah tenet without justification or apology — simply to ensure Roh stayed away from Adehl? "You wasted your effort, old man," he said. "She wants none of me. But if you ever try that again, I will break your fingers."

"Roh!" Lenatoh's head snapped around.

"Don't manipulate me like I'm a junior acoleh."

"That's not —"

"Peace, Lenatoh," Gentah said, holding up a hand. "That was wrong of me, Roh. But it's vital you —"

"I don't want to hear it," Roh said. He couldn't look at either of them. "Was there anything else?"

A pause. "We're going to decamp in a few days. Head to Romanah."

"I thought we were staying here, then heading to Singing Canyon," Roh said.

"I've changed my mind."

Burn you black, old man. With nothing polite to say, Roh

stepped around Gentah and left. Inside, he raged and shattered all at once. That sort of behaviour was the whole reason for sending out the exhorters. Was this the first time his doyen had attempted to impel him?

Partway to his tent, he changed direction. Between Adehl's proximity and Gentah's perfidy, Roh was in for a sleepless night. He made instead for the picket line and his horse, Sprig. The moon was blessedly bright, the perfect night awash with stars. In the distance, a hunting dog howled.

IN THE HOUR BEFORE DAWN, Adehl crept up a hill and summoned Cloud. Her heart hammered, and her head snapped around at every tiny noise. But soon she had him saddled and her gear attached. She guided him into the trees to drink at the spring, hoping none of the camp's early risers would see her. It was stupid. She was free to leave. Yet she wouldn't relax until the tents lay far behind.

The rustle of something moving towards her made her spin. A figure approached. Not a tall figure, though, only a child, her hair unbound. Adehl released a shaky breath.

Sorah clasped a wrapped bundle against the front of her mahgan. At first, Adehl thought Sorah was running away, but she held out the package. "I've brought you some supplies."

"Food?" Adehl made room in the bag strapped to her saddle. "Thanks. Did I wake you?" Beyond her own whisper, all remained still and quiet.

The girl shrugged, shook her head. Adehl took Sorah's hands in hers. She wanted to tell Sorah not to lose hope, that Adehl had become a zehli despite being pidakah. But that would be cruel and dangerous.

The sadness in Sorah's expression made her seem older than her thirteen years. She tried to pull her hands out of

Adehl's. "I should not be talking to you. She will make me polish all the pots again."

Adehl squeezed Sorah's fingers and cast a glance towards the camp. "One day, things will be different," she breathed. "One day it won't be the end of everything to be pidakah."

Sorah nodded, her eyes wide.

"Go now, little sparrow."

Sorah hesitated. Her thin, unadorned wrist extended, shaking.

Ignoring the voice in her head that screamed at her not to be stupid, Adehl swiftly placed her palm against Sorah's. The girl's energy soared within her, raw and wild. Denying her — or any child with affinity — the chance to meld with ellir was cruel. Adehl forced a smile.

Sorah smiled in return. "Thank you. I hope we meet again," she said.

"Me too. Be strong, Sorah."

As the girl nodded and slipped away, Adehl reached for Cloud, his muzzle dripping with water. She needed to leave before she did anything else foolish. Without further delay, she tightened the girth and made sure the rest of her gear was secured.

They broke out of the shadows surrounding the spring, and tension cut into Adehl's neck. There was nowhere to hide now, and Cloud glowed like the moon itself; but the pre-dawn air stayed quiet and still as his smooth gait carried her out of the hollow. The camp diminishing behind her, Adehl began to breathe.

Then a horse and rider appeared ahead. A dark, hybrid shape atop a rise, silhouetted against the lightening sky. Even as she swore under her breath, Adehl's pulse leapt. She didn't bother attempting to evade the rider. Instead, she nudged her horse into a canter and met the challenge head on, almost certain it was Roh, only half hoping it wouldn't be.

He waited for her, as still as a tree.

The thud of Cloud's hooves echoed in her heart as the animal surged up the slope. From the top of the rise, the Humming Downs fell away in gentle folds to the horizon, wide and mysterious and beckoning in the rising light.

Roh's expression was unreadable as Adehl pulled up alongside him. He sat his horse without a saddle, a cooler, more distant version of the man who'd sought her out in the starlight. His mouth, yesterday so quick to smile, was immobile. Only his eyes betrayed a glimmer of the warmth he'd displayed last evening, until that too became over-shadowed by darker emotions. He looked like he hadn't slept.

"Have you been out here all night?" Adehl asked, noting his dishevelled braids.

He gave a short laugh. "How could you tell?" With a shrug, he leant forward and stroked his horse's neck, fingers pale against the red-brown coat. He had strong, graceful hands.

Adehl looked past him to the south, where mobs of ravakah and loophorn herds dotted the grass. "Are you all right?"

"What do you think?"

She had no answer. She ought to keep riding, but tearing herself away was hard. His rhythm bounded, chaotic and complex, scraping against Adehl's despite the air between them.

"Burn you, Adehl. I don't understand *why*."

"I'm sorry," she said, not sure what she was apologising for. She had been unwise last night, indiscreet. But she'd done nothing wrong. Well, mostly.

Another bitter laugh. "I told myself it would be better if I didn't see you again. Yet here I am, waiting. Why are you sneaking away before the camp wakes?"

"It seemed best. I presume you told your doyen about my plans?"

His brow furrowed. "I did."

That left little to discuss. Adehl shook her braids off her shoulders and straightened in the saddle. "Are you going to let me leave? You can forget all this ever happened."

"You don't get it, do you?" His voice grated the words into shards. "There will be no *forgetting*. Don't you understand what's happening?"

"Whatever it is —"

"We're injaleh."

Something shifted inside Adehl, as though the word, spoken aloud, cleaved them together.

No. They couldn't be. People didn't become soulmelded without a great deal of ritual effort. It wasn't something that simply happened one day while exchanging a greeting out on the downs. But even now, with them both on horseback, not touching, she was aware of Roh's llirah thrumming, *synchronised* with hers. She pressed the lower part of her breastbone, as though that could make it stop.

"How?" Her mouth was dry. "It doesn't work like that."

"Not usually, no."

"Are you sure?"

"Near enough." He nudged his horse closer to hers. "Will you change your mind?"

Adehl tried to think. Under different circumstances, she might have changed her mind. A part of her yearned to stay with Roh and figure out what everything meant. Her soul wept at the prospect of their parting, but Roh didn't know the truth. "I can't."

"*Why?*" It started as a wail and ended in a roar.

"There's no point in — Sun's fury, I'm leaving the Vuusah. You're supposed to be the next Atalah. Where does that leave us? Better we part now, before —"

"Go then!" His eyes flashed. Anger pulsed out of him, vibrant and unfettered. "Go live like a gravohl in the city with all its chaos and corruption. Discover the mundane life of a kalkah zehli."

"I'm not meant to be Vuusah. If you knew, you'd understand."

He stared at her, bewilderment and confusion pushing the fury off his face as quickly as it had arrived. Whatever he read in her expression made him sigh deeply. "Burn you, Adehl." His hands gripped the rope of his rein, knuckles white. "You'd better just go."

Adehl's chest felt clamped in a vice. She gathered her rein into one hand, straightened Cloud's charcoal mane so it sat flat against his neck. Met Roh's rigid expression a final time and nodded.

At the bottom of the slope, Adehl slowed Cloud and permitted herself to twist in the saddle. A thin seam of sun had breached the horizon, spinning a thread of gold onto the grassy expanse she and Cloud had descended. A flock of hookbeaks wheeled, squawking noisily, but whatever had startled them had already disappeared from Adehl's view. The ridge line was empty.

6. Waiting for an Invitation

THE GATE to her father's property had not been there ten years ago. The solid timber construction swung inwards, supported on both sides by tall posts carved with images of horses. She brought Cloud alongside and managed the latch from saddleback. It caught again behind them with a clunk as she guided Cloud down the well-tended gravel road.

Home. Finally.

Adehl had pushed Cloud for four days, needing to put distance between herself and the events at Fortune Spring.

Distance from Roh.

But, when she had curled in her bedding — in the lee of a hill, amid a copse of trees or on the open, grassy plain — the heartstorm had called and Roh had found her.

He was a skilled farsenser, so perhaps it ought not to have surprised her. But even as the miles between them accumulated, his rhythm came to her across the wild cadence of the downs. His llirah conveyed a mix of yearning, frustration and awe. Adehl could only stare up at the glittering sky and wonder what he sensed from her. It was disconcerting, but comforting, too.

He'd have more difficulty reaching her now she'd entered Tarsah. Too many people, too many influences. Perhaps she could banish him from her mind and focus on what lay before her.

After ten long years, she was home.

She tried to look at everything. Horses grazed in the fields to either side of the road, and clumps of purple starflowers danced in the late summer breeze. She'd forgotten about her favourite climbing tree, a stately old shaggybark in the middle of the field, the platform still high in its branches. Then she spotted her old pony, Bimble. Her call came out strangled, but he whinnied and streaked across the green with the verve of a yearling. Adehl vaulted off Cloud and met her beloved boy at the fence, feeding him a nub of tohroot and scratching his neck under the long, silver-streaked mane. When she remounted Cloud, Bimble followed along the fence line, whickering.

It was farther to the house than she remembered, but at last it stood before her. Her childhood home, where her brother and father still lived. Its propped-open windows and stone facade conveyed a quiet prosperity that made her heart swell with so many emotions her throat choked up. Beside the house, the first of several fenced yards lay empty of all but dust and dung.

No one appeared at the sound of Cloud's approach, and Adehl took a slow, deep breath. It probably meant everyone was out in one of the back paddocks, checking on foals perhaps, or working with a yearling. It had been seven weeks since her father's accident. At this time of day, he wouldn't be lazing about the house.

Then somewhere a bell rang, and feet pounded along the corridor inside.

Pulse thudding, Adehl dismounted. Gravel crunched under her boots, ellir thrumming through the soles. As she waited for the door to open, she wiped her hands on her mahgan, smoothed down the fabric. Cloud stood calmly at her shoulder, and she took a firm grip on her llirah and her nerves.

The door stayed shut. Inside the house, a man spoke and laughed, a voice she didn't recognise. An unfamiliar woman replied, her words soaring out the window to reach Adehl in the front courtyard. "Mind you don't forget it, or I might forget I'm going to wed you!"

Adehl froze, then backed away, dragging Cloud's head around. The horse snorted and clattered on the gravel. Within the house, the banter ceased and footsteps again thumped along the floorboards. The front door opened to reveal a young woman garbed as though she'd just come in from the stables: sturdy trousers and short tunic, muddy boots, straw sticking out of her night-black hair, which she wore tousled and short like a child's. Not Fiugreh. Sevikk, perhaps, from the hair and pale skin, the blue eyes. Hands on hips, the girl examined Adehl, mouth puckered as she sucked on her cheeks.

"Oh," Adehl said. "I thought… I'm sorry." She laid a hand on Cloud's neck and ran her fingers through the charcoal silk of his mane. Tried to keep the worry out of her voice. "I'm looking for my father. Paluh. Is he here?"

The woman's blue eyes widened, and she clapped a hand over her mouth. "You're Adehl?"

Adehl could only nod.

"Your father will be so pleased to see you."

"He's recovered?"

"He's been up and about for a couple of weeks." She sucked on her cheeks again. "I'm sorry if I worried you. Tohanuh wouldn't write, but I know if it were my father…"

"You're Mikka?" Adehl smiled as the fear she'd barely acknowledged faded away. *Up and about.* "Thank you for letting me know."

"I'm very glad to meet you," Mikka said. Her gaze moved to Cloud, and she stepped forward with a wide grin. "This fellow looks almost familiar. Hello there, beautiful."

Inside the ajar front door, a familiar hall table stood against the wall, but the blue-green swirls of the rug looked new.

Mikka ran expert hands all over Cloud. "You look like you're out of Bella," she crooned. "Sired by… Winterblue? I'm so pleased to meet you." Bending, she lifted his legs to inspect each hoof, massaged his wither, then looked at Adehl. "Your da says all Winter's get are headstrong, but he seems a lamb to me."

Adehl strived to remain patient. "Is my father here?"

"Of course. And your brother." She stepped a few paces back from Cloud and turned towards the house. "Come here, Toha! It's your sister!" Then she strode to the nearest yard rail and hollered for a stablehand.

A man arrived at the front door. He was taller, broader, than she would have predicted, his hair in a single, thick braid that hadn't been there before. Except for those telltale blue eyes, he would pass for pure-blood Fiugreh, as she did.

"Hello, Tohanuh," Adehl said, her throat clogged. "I'm not sure I would have recognised you."

Framed by the doorway, Tohanuh crossed his arms over the grimy leather of his work vest. "What are you doing here?" He'd be nineteen now, and his voice was deep. Behind him, something glinted on the wall above the table. A timber-framed mirror Adehl didn't remember.

Before she could reply, a freckled boy arrived in answer to Mikka's summons. Adehl handed over Cloud's reins, confident in her father's people, but gave the boy a few instructions. When she returned her attention to Tohanuh, he had moved out onto the gravel. Glancing askance at Adehl, he issued his own instructions to the stablehand. As Cloud's dark tail swished and disappeared around the corner towards the field behind the house, Adehl steeled herself.

"I hope you have a good reason for coming," Tohanuh said.

"I heard Da was hurt."

Tohanuh's eyes narrowed; then he turned to Mikka, who leant on the fence rail. "I told you not to write to her!"

Chin raised, Mikka met his fiery gaze. "I know, my dear one. But —"

"She stayed away for a reason."

"It's been *ten years*," Adehl said. "If Da had died —"

"It's too risky." Her brother scowled. "Especially now, while he's still recovering."

Mikka pushed off the fence and went to Tohanuh. She nudged his hands away, bringing her own up to cup his face. "Your father needs to see her." She kissed him as his arms went around her shoulders. "It'll be all right."

Tohanuh's face softened with Mikka in his arms, reminding Adehl of the boy she'd left behind. She wanted to hug her brother. Once, she wouldn't have hesitated. Instead, she stood in the middle of the forecourt, separated from her brother and his intended by cool air, and realised she was waiting for an invitation to enter the house.

In the end, it was Mikka who herded Adehl inside, towing Tohanuh by a hand. Mikka glanced at the formal reception room but strode past to the large kitchen. Here, Mikka's influence was obvious. Every shining pot occupied a different place, every utensil hung on new hooks. Adehl yanked out one of the wooden chairs and sank onto it — her first chair in many months. Mikka flitted about the room, clearly at home. She filled the kettle with water from the bucket outside the back door and hung it over the hearth, then collected bread, meat and apples for the table. Adehl felt too churned up to eat but yearned for her father's watermint tea.

Tohanuh leant against the doorjamb, arms once more folded across his man-sized chest. "You shouldn't have come," he said. "I thought we all agreed —"

"You and Da are my family. When I heard what had happened —"

"We stopped being your family the day you passed yourself off as full-blood Fiugreh and apprenticed yourself to the Vuusah."

Adehl flinched. "You know why I did it." She wasn't used to this new, adult, hostile version of her brother. It didn't help that he was right. She *had* agreed to stay away. It had seemed the surest means of concealing her true lineage, and the Vuusah would quell her affinity for ellir if they knew she was pidakah. Unable to meet her brother's gaze, she realised uneasily that there might also be repercussions for her family.

"Yeah, I know." He bit off his next words and strode out through the back door. His footsteps crunched across the gravel of the kitchen courtyard.

Adehl glanced at Mikka, busy with the contents of a canister. "Are you making tea?" she asked.

"Not tea," Mikka said, her singsong tone at odds with the tension. "Something that will lift your spirits. I daresay you've been riding for days and need a better welcome." The girl then embarked upon a stream of light chatter about her life with Adehl's family as they waited for the water to boil. Eventually, she produced a mug filled with a hot beverage that frothed at the rim. "This is what we drink at home."

The mug warmed Adehl's hands. It contained some dark-brown concoction smelling of soil and spices. "You're Sevikk?"

Mikka nodded. "That's one reason your father took me

on." She raised her brows. "Go on. Taste it. It's made from ground karvva nuts."

The froth tickled her lip as she sipped. "Urghumm." The mug clunked onto the table. "It's rather, er, bitter."

Mikka clapped her hands and laughed. "Let me add some honey," she said, reaching into the cupboard. "Trust me."

It wasn't much of an improvement, but Adehl sipped at the muddy brew. Mikka poured herself a mug, eschewed the honey, and joined Adehl at the table. She started asking about how Vuusah breeding and training methods differed from Adehl's father's. Adehl responded, but her attention drifted. This room, the family kitchen, had once been the centre of her world. Ellir had always been present, of course; even as a child, she had caught tugs of its rhythm. But now… Now those rhythms and influences were unveiled. It was as though a thread of conversation had emerged, clear and intelligible, from a fireside gathering. She read the history of the table beneath her fingertips, its grains etched into relief by years of wear — decades of service as a food preparation and eating surface, a stint in the laundry, and occasionally put to more innovative uses. She pulled away, cheeks heating, as recent, vivid images of her brother and Mikka — and this table — flowed out. Tohanuh's llirah, even quelled to a safe amplitude, was strong and left a substantial imprint.

The table bore impressions of her father's energy, too, and she suspected she was sitting in his favourite seat. She drained her drink and rose, her chair scraping the floor.

Mikka placed down her mug. "Shall I get you something? Would you like to rest?" She grabbed at the cutting board, laden with a loaf of crusty bread. "You haven't eaten. It's today's. Fresh."

"No, thank you. I need to see my father."

"Of course. He's still on light duties, but we could check the near yards," Mikka said, also rising.

"It's all right. I know my way around."

Mikka's pale cheeks reddened. "Of course. Sorry." She resumed her seat, looking suddenly small in the large kitchen. A hand snaked out and, ignoring the knife, broke off a chunk of bread. Adehl left her to it.

She crossed the kitchen courtyard, smaller and neater than she remembered it, with new iron hooks driven into the two walls for hanging buckets and ropes and old leather harnesses. The other two open sides led to the sheds and training yards and, beyond them, the fields. The old familiar hills rose in the distance, rocky outcrops visible near their crown.

Reaching with ellir for her father's rhythm, she sensed he was close by. Adehl made her way past deserted yards to the barn, where her father's old bay mare, Flighty, was tethered outside. She whickered at Adehl's approach, making Adehl wish she had some tohroot left for the grand dame of her father's enterprise. Stroking Flighty's neck, she probed for the mare's llirah, spoke into her ear.

Boots scuffed behind her. "Well, girl?" her father said, his voice not quite steady.

Eyes misting, Adehl smiled and released the horse's llirah gently so as not to startle. "Are you angry with me as well?" she asked, turning.

Upon sighting her father, she stilled. He looked robust enough, she noted with relief, although his face bore new lines and his skin sagged around his bones. But his once long, dark hair had been shorn, the iron-grey regrowth revealing an ugly, raw scar behind his left ear. Between that and his deep blue eyes… For the first time in Adehl's memory, her father looked more Sevikk than Fiugreh. The familiar srih around his left wrist, given to him by her mother so long ago, looked distressingly out of place.

"Not angry, never that," he said, his expression soft.

She swallowed. "I've brought Cloud. Did you see?"

He smiled, and at least that was familiar. "He's in the hexagon field."

From behind, the sound of water on gravel as Flighty relieved herself, then the stench of urine. Adehl gathered her resolve. "How are you? Mikka wrote to me." Her voice trembled. "I needed to see you."

"I'm holding together." Her father led her into the barn and the scent of fresh hay. "You didn't need to risk this."

"You were unconscious for a week! I thought you were going to die." A knot formed in her stomach. "I've missed you so much."

He plucked a leather strap off a nail driven into a post, then produced a needle and thread. "I've missed you too, Dehl-Dehl. Wasn't sure I'd ever see you again."

The implication hurt. After receiving Mikka's letter, Adehl had convinced herself her family would welcome her arrival.

She spied a low stool in the corner and fetched it for her father. He sank onto the stool and gestured. As she had many times as a girl, Adehl dropped onto the straw at his feet, tucking her legs under her. She watched his expert fingers draw thread through the leather.

His llirah pulsed its familiar rhythm, much clearer to her now she was a trained zehli. Threading her llirah with his, she applied a gentle healing rhythm designed to bolster the body's natural healing processes. Although she usually worked with horses, the principles were the same.

"What's that you're doing, then?" he asked after a time.

"Helping your body heal. You can feel it?"

He smiled. "My head no longer aches."

"Good." She laid her head on his knee.

That evening, they ate together in the kitchen, as had always been the custom. Mikka presided, passing round mugs of her noxious brew, which she named karv. Adehl watched to see whether her brother and father drank the stuff, or whether they humoured her and secretly tipped it into the garden. But Tohanuh seemed to enjoy it. Much of his outward hostility had dissipated, although he shied away from meeting her eyes. Adehl didn't need zehla skills to know they still had much to discuss.

Despite her family's evident assumption that Adehl would never return, her old bedchamber remained untouched. Mikka supposedly slept in a room above the stables. Adehl took the familiar route down the corridor and paused at the solid timber doorway that still bore the scratched figures of horses near its base. Crouching to regard them more closely, she grimaced. She'd never been an artist.

She dumped her gear onto the narrow bed. First a chair and now a bed. Sitting down, she almost sighed at the cushioning of the mattress. Her brother appeared in the doorway. In the soft light cast by the oil lamps, he looked younger, and she almost recognised the boy who had wept on her departure ten years ago. She hauled herself off the bed and hugged him, his return embrace so hard it hurt. His llirah fizzed into her, and she threaded it with her own, hoping he would sense her love.

He tensed, shoved her away. "Don't."

"Toha, what is it?"

He shook his head. "Are you really that oblivious?" He stepped away from her, poised on the threshold of her room. His arms hugged his chest. "How long are you staying?"

"I thought I could help here. Da could never afford a zehli."

He stared at her. "You can't mean — Are you insane?"

Adehl returned his gaze, her vision blurry.

"Adehl, you can't *stay* here. I might have been a child, but when you joined the Vuusah, I knew I was losing my sister."

She retreated to the end of the bed farthest from the door.

She wanted to reassure Tohanuh the Vuusah wouldn't discover the truth, but her mind was in turmoil.

Tohanuh held up a cloth, embroidered with a horse in one corner. Their mother's work. "I came to bring you this. Mikka says she filled the water pitcher but forgot a towel." From the doorway, he dropped it on the bed. "You always knew the price, Adehl. Don't make it higher than it already is."

After he left, Adehl drew up her knees and huddled on the bed until the lamp flame flickered and died.

7. Miles of grass

A shout came from up ahead, and Roh dragged his gaze from the southern horizon. The distraction was a relief: he was getting a cricked neck. There was nothing to look at anyway — the rolling downs extended to the sky.

He was riding near the back of the column, which had bunched up before him, voices rising in urgent chatter. He soon spotted what had caused the commotion. On top of a higher swell, standing in relief against the bright northern sky, twin warning cairns perched side by side. He'd been so preoccupied he hadn't noticed they were drawing close to the cold, dead expanse of Little Gahmniu.

Riding nearby, Gentah twitched his reins. "Don't worry," he said to one of the acoleh. "We'll give it a wide berth."

It was two years since Roh had skirted one of the dead-lands. On the rare occasions they went to Romanah, they usually approached from the east, not the south. No one knew why ellir shunned some parts of the land, but there was no question of crossing the lifeless expanse.

Their northwestern trajectory had brought them to the

southern rim, and the column of horses and wagons adjusted course to go around. Still, Roh's attention remained fixed on the cairns. "I'm going to ride up to the markers," he said.

Gentah thumbed his rein. "Why?"

"Sprig could do with a run." In truth, Roh could do with some distance from the doyen. But that wasn't his only reason.

"If you must," Gentah said. The old man had trodden carefully since the incident four nights ago at Fortune Spring.

"I'll stop at the markers." Probably. Little Gahmniu itself would start a mile beyond the cairns, the deadland extending over ninety miles across. He wondered what it would feel like to step upon its surface, to be temporarily severed from ellir.

"Can I come, too?" asked someone behind.

Roh twisted to see his brother, Johre, grinning at him from the back of a sunskin with a pale mane. "Is that one of the new horses?"

"Yeah. He's fast," he said hopefully.

"All right. Let's see how he goes." Roh nudged Sprig into a canter and then a gallop. Streaming air blew away the flies and dried the damp hair at the back of his neck, and their thudding progress scared marmots into their burrows. Johre brought the sunskin up alongside Sprig, and they sped up the slope towards the twin cairns. It would normally be Frahto riding with Roh. He'd never ridden out with Johre before. The boy rode well, although he'd not grown into his young man's body yet.

The cairns grew larger, but more gradually than Roh expected. By the time he and Johre crested the hill, the cairns dwarfed them: each was thrice as tall as a man, blocks of weathered stone fitted together. They were designed to be visible for miles. Below, the horses and wagons of Gentah's company looked like a long, dark snake slithering through the grass, as they pushed on west towards the next set of markers.

"Not what I expected," Johre said.

Roh turned to find his brother surveying the terrain beyond the marker cairns. The downs continued unchanging for a distance — swaying grass, some scattered trees. A flock of hookbeaks dived and danced in a swirl of vibrant red and blue. Then the green abruptly became a vast and rocky expanse of brown that seemed without end.

"Nothing grows on the deadlands," Roh said. "Nothing lives. It's said even the birds fly around." At its westernmost point, Little Gahmniu came within just twenty miles of the coast, permitting passage to Romanah around the edge. The cairns marking out its massive rim looked like a brace of thorns.

"Have you ever…?"

"I've never been closer than this." Roh swung his leg over Sprig's rump. "Luckily, we have more than eyes at our disposal."

Grass yielded beneath his boots as ellir vaulted up into him, strumming his bones. The wild rhythms of the downs came to him, but Adehl's llirah was missing. He'd farsensed her progress across many miles of grass and scrub as she headed to Tarsah, far to the south. But the chaotic energy of the city had swallowed her distinctive melody of honey and wind and speed.

"What do you sense?" Johre asked him.

Roh wrenched his attention back to his brother, who had also dismounted, reins held in a slack grip. "Nothing."

Johre lifted a dark eyebrow. "It's her, isn't it? That zehli who visited our camp the other day."

Bright sun burn you, little brother.

"Before he left, I overheard Frahto say you were obsessed with her."

Roh frowned at the smirk on his brother's face. "I'm not obsessed."

"Who are you trying to convince? You've been mooning about for days."

Roh glared. At fifteen, Johre was more intuitive than Roh had expected. And impertinent. "Don't presume too much, little brother."

Johre shrugged. He didn't seem overawed by Roh, unlike all the other acoleh. Good for him. "Are you going to show me Little Gahmniu, then?"

"You sure?"

"Yeah. Might as well get some benefit from being your brother."

"It's not pleasant."

Another shrug of bravado.

"All right," Roh said. "Take my hand."

Despite knowing what to expect, Roh would never be ready for the utter *lack* of energy. The region was dead. Not a judder of ellir emanated from it. Roh guided Johre into resonance with the heartstorm. He gathered in the strands of rhythm from the land before them, described to his brother the source of each influence, explained how to identify the void of Little Gahmniu a mile distant.

"Blighted balls," Johre said, face leached of colour. "That's... I can't..."

"Sorry." Before releasing Johre's hand, Roh extracted them from ellir and threaded energy to soothe his brother's youthful llirah. "That better?"

Johre flashed a grin, but sobered as he swung his gaze back towards the deadland. "It feels so wrong. It made my bones go cold."

"Yeah."

"Why did you come up here?"

Roh stared into the blue above the waste. "Sometimes it's

hard for me to separate myself from ellir. I suppose I wanted to remind myself of how bad the alternative is." He dredged up a smile and brought his horse into position for mounting. "Why did you come with me?"

Johre reddened. "You're my brother," he said, as if that explained everything.

Roh realised he'd spent little time with his brother since Johre had joined Gentah's company as an acoleh a year ago. Before that, Roh hadn't seen him in a decade, not since Johre was five and Roh a boy of thirteen, leaving his family to begin his own zehla training. "I've been meaning to ask how you're, uh, enjoying your training."

Johre let out a laugh. "I don't think you've given me much thought at all." He fiddled with his rein. "I'd like to know my brother."

"I'd like that too, Joh-Joh." His heart swelled at his brother's blinding grin.

They talked of inconsequential matters as they headed back to the column, which by then was past the next pair of marker cairns; Roh was relieved when Johre peeled off to ride with his friends among the acoleh. Roh's thoughts drifted back to Adehl. No matter what he said aloud or what he told himself, he didn't accept he'd never see her again. He missed her. Which was ridiculous. He tried to think more objectively about kalkah zehla. How many were registered, and who employed them? For what? He should know if he were to become Atalah.

He missed Frahto, too. Gentah had sent Frahto to Tarsah with the newest circah of exhorters bound for Dohni. The old man had given Frahto some separate mission — but his friend wouldn't tell him what it was. It was unlike Frahto to keep secrets from Roh, even Gentah's secrets. Come to that, Roh usually confided in Frahto. But he hadn't discussed Adehl and the doubts consuming him with Frahto or anyone.

The fact Frahto was on her trail, would be in the same city as her in a few days, only made it worse.

Despite his previous resolution, Roh wished he had gone with that new circah of exhorters in Frahto's place.

Late in the afternoon, they reached Sage Well, and Gentah called an end to the day's riding. They'd arrived in a wide, shallow valley, where an ageing wooden hut stood in a meadow of wild herbs and grass. Gentah dispatched someone into the hut to oil the windlass and identify any need for repairs. The wagons carrying the water troughs drew up alongside the hut, while the rest of the company dispersed to make camp.

When Roh dismounted, the void of Little Gahmniu prodded him like dead fingers on his spine. Far to the south, Tarsah's chaotic influence was a seething mass of energy and noise. He concentrated harder — searching, yearning. But he still couldn't resolve any individual rhythms within Tarsah from this distance.

Sprig nudged him and snorted into his ear. He reached up and stroked the horse's cheek. "Sorry, hotfoot." He noted where the horses were being picketed. "Let's remove this gear."

After attending to his horse, Roh helped his brethren draw water for the animals. As was customary on travel days, they set no fires, instead gathering in loose groups to share a cold meal of dried meats wrapped in fresh legah leaves gathered during the day.

The evening dragged on, mild and sweet-aired, crickets chirping as the stars came out. Roh stared into the night and wished Frahto were here to distract him. Then a delicate probe of ellir made his shoulders tense. Lenatoh sat cross-legged a few paces away, back straight, a daughter on either side. Kalihra had inherited the fine bones and delicate beauty of her mother, her dark hair in two neat braids as befitted a girl her age. Talking with Johre, she sat with her arms looped around drawn-up knees, the charms on her newly woven srih clinking. Lenatoh's other daughter, Sorah, looked more like her father. Not that Roh had ever seen her mother to compare. Sorah could almost pass for Fiugreh, her Kestali–Senn lineage barely changing the cast of her scarred features. She stared off into the distance, her thin body angled away. Despite the Vuusah company surrounding her, she somehow looked alone.

The probe of ellir continued to tease at him, and Roh glared at the nedoyen. *"Don't,"* he said with more force than he'd usually use.

Lenatoh rubbed his forehead. "I'm worried about you."

"I'm fine."

"You keep saying that, but I don't believe you." The nedoyen's gaze bored into him. Perhaps he wanted to say more without his daughters in earshot.

Roh discovered a perverse desire to make the man uncomfortable. "I've been thinking about some things Adehl said."

Lenatoh held his gaze and waited.

"I've been trying to figure out why some zehla choose to be kalkah."

"Did she not tell you?"

"I know why *she* wants to be kalkah. I already told you that."

"What exactly did she say?"

"Some rubbish about zehla enclaves of little use to anyone. She implied zehla should be available for hire indiscriminately."

"And what do you think?"

"It goes against everything the Vuusah stand for. But I

want to understand her perspective. How could any zehli reject the Vuusah as easily as they would a broken saddle?"

"Why does any zehli become kalkah?"

"I thought most kalkah zehla are those not claimed by the Vuusah." Roh withdrew his favourite piece of heartrock, needing something in his fingers. "They are inferior. In affinity, I mean."

"Mostly. Yes."

"She's not, though. She's…" Honey and wind and speed.

Straightening, Lenatoh slanted a look at his daughters. Kalihra faced Johre, immersed in the harmless flirtation of the young. Sorah stared up at the darkening sky, her expression dreamy. Lenatoh adjusted his sleeve. "Some zehla are not meant to be Vuusah," he said eventually.

Adehl had said something similar. "I don't believe that. She *belongs*."

"You may wish it so, but —"

"I think Adehl is amazing and brave and the kindest person I've ever met," Sorah said suddenly. She shifted her weight on the woven mat beside her father.

Roh stared at her, throat clogging. "What did she say to you?"

"Not much." Sorah shrank back into herself, her llirah flaring with an odd mix of guilt and excitement. "But she was nice to me. And I think you should leave her alone."

Roh gave a dry laugh. "What do you think I'm doing?"

"What about Frahto?" she demanded. "He's gone to Tarsah after her, hasn't he?"

"Sorah, that's enough," Lenatoh said. "Time for you and your sister to go to our tent." He tapped Kalihra on the shoulder.

As Lenatoh wrangled his daughters, their limbs angling and twisting in argument, Roh thought about Sorah's words. Frahto had regarded Adehl with suspicion. Not for the first time, he wondered uneasily what instructions Gentah had given his friend.

As Sorah stepped past him, Roh gently caught her wrist. Her llirah flared at his touch, vibrant as driving rain and fragrant green herbs. "I think she's amazing and brave and kind too," he said, chest tight.

When the girls had gone, Lenatoh came to sit beside him. He fished out a flask from the front fold of his mahgan and offered it to Roh. "Try not to think about her."

Not so easy. Even now Roh's llirah searched in vain for Adehl's. A few days ago, he wouldn't have hesitated to confide in Lenatoh about the connection between them, but tonight he kept silent. He pulled out the flask stopper and took a swig. The tohba burned as it went down. "You should quell Sorah soon," Roh said.

"I'm sorry for what she said. I'll reprimand her."

"Not because of that. She only said what she felt."

Lenatoh made a soft, sad sound. "That poor child. She has all the affinity. Kalihra will never be a zehli." He grabbed the flask and took a swig of the distilled tohroot spirit.

"You could get someone else to do it."

"No." Lenatoh exhaled. "I'm a noumenor and her father. It's my responsibility. But not yet… I can't quite bear to quell her yet."

Roh picked up his stone. Sorah was talented enough to be a zehli, her tainted lineage the only obstacle — albeit a huge one — to her being trained. It made him realise how important it was for zehla to procreate only with full-blood Fiugreh. Otherwise, a great number of children would confront a similar predicament — affinity for ellir, but unable to be trained. At least Lenatoh was here to ensure Sorah's llirah didn't go wild.

He tried to block out the memory of Adehl's bitten off

words. *The Vuusah have already ensured all zehla must have pure Fiugreh blood…*

He looked up when Lenatoh touched his knee. "Forgive me, Roh, but there is something else we must discuss."

Roh flicked the hand away. "None of that," he said in a sharp whisper. "Not that you would succeed where Gentah failed."

"I wasn't…" Lenatoh sucked in a breath. "You must forgive him for his actions the other evening."

"Must I?"

"He was only…"

"Overstepping? Betraying my trust?"

"Worried."

"That's no excuse." Roh struggled to keep his voice down.

"I know." Lenatoh paused. "Understand that Gentah — all the doyens — have invested much in you, Roh. You're the future of the Vuusah."

"And that gives him the right to *control* me? Break precepts?" Every bone trembled as fury surged through him with renewed intensity. "What was he so worried about, anyway?"

"I think you can guess." When Roh remained silent, Lenatoh shifted on his mat. "Did you think we would not sense what was between you and Adehl?"

"He implied she's my injaleh."

"I wasn't sure you heard him."

"I heard."

"It happens sometimes, this instinctive melding of llirah. And, yes, it can presage becoming injaleh." Lenatoh leant forward, a dark and earnest shadow. "But not if you ignore it, keep your distance."

Although he'd spoken quietly, Lenatoh's words hung heavy in the night air between them. Roh didn't know what to think. *Instinctive melding of llirah* implied he had no control over what had happened. As though it were chance. Adehl's rhythm had drawn him from the moment he'd begun tracking her across the downs. He pressed a hand to his midriff, where his llirah hummed silently, no longer quite whole. "So none of it's real?" His throat was tight, the words strained with the remnants of anger and burgeoning pain. "It's just some colossal coincidence?"

Lenatoh touched Roh's leg again, comforting, and this time Roh allowed it to remain. "Not entirely. The meld is but a facet of your attraction for her — albeit a powerful one."

Relief eased some of the tension in Roh's neck and shoulders. He hated the idea that everything he felt for Adehl could be a sham. But if it were real, *instinct*, he didn't want to fight it anymore. Those minutes with her alone in the darkness had changed him deep within. He should have tried harder to persuade her to stay. "What if she returns? To the Vuusah, I mean."

Lenatoh took a moment to respond. "You're going to be Atalah, Roh. With that comes certain obligations. It will be important to surround yourself with —"

"I won't allow Gentah to control my entire life." Some of the anger came rushing back. Roh had been so irate at Gentah's attempt to impel him the other night, he'd almost forgotten the rest of the doyen's words: *Your injaleh will be carefully chosen.* What the blight did that mean?

Lenatoh nudged him with the tohba flask. "He's only trying to protect you. We all are."

"Is that supposed to be comforting?"

"Is it not?"

The spirit burned Roh's throat and made his head swim. It sounded like Gentah had plans he hadn't seen fit to share. "What's the old man up to, Lenatoh?"

"You know better than to ask."

Roh scowled. "Then tell me why he's sent Frahto to Tarsah after Adehl. She's done nothing wrong."

"Frahto is merely going to ask some discreet questions. We would have preferred a kalkah zehli not to visit our camp."

"She's not kalkah."

"Not yet."

Roh thumbed the stone in his hand. Adehl had seen the exhorters. He'd become so accustomed to the Bladekor warrior's presence over the past year that he'd ceased to wonder at it. "Why are the exhorters being kept secret, even from other Vuusah companies?" he asked.

"The Atalah wishes it so." It sounded like an excuse.

"So, that's it?" Roh said. "Frahto's just going to make sure she doesn't reveal any of our precious secrets?"

A hesitation. "Of course." And there was the lie.

Roh's body ached from two long days in the saddle after months at Fortune Spring. Or maybe it was his heart that ached. He tilted back to lie on the grass, inhaling its comforting scent. Overhead, the constellation of the twin scribes glittered, one of the wandering stars bright near the tip of the quill. The moon had not yet risen.

Out here, ellir was pure. The energy thrummed through him, and he felt connected to every creature of the downs — his brethren settling down to sleep, their many horses tearing up the meadow grass, a pack of distant hunting dogs, and the colony of marmots below. Human influences were transient and everything else was bound into the natural ecology of the Humming Downs. Even the terrible void of Little Gahmniu. Out here, the Vuusah existed in harmony with ellir. Roh had never thought to want otherwise.

Lenatoh leant over Roh, little more than a dark shape blotting out a section of starlit sky. "I understand this is difficult," he said.

"I'm fine." When Lenatoh didn't move, kept hovering, Roh said, "I need to be alone now."

"All right." The man pushed to his feet. "I'm for my tent, then."

"I think I'll just sleep here." Roh shifted to find a more comfortable position. "It's mild enough." It would also save time in the morning. He would need to leave early, before anyone noticed. Perhaps even late tonight.

"I'm sorry, Roh," Lenatoh said. "We'll speak more tomorrow."

Roh exhaled as Lenatoh's footsteps retreated through the grass, but nothing could dispel the weight on his chest or the tight coil of tension within.

He tried to focus on things he knew. Things he could control. He could reach Tarsah in four days. Sprig was in excellent condition, and Roh wouldn't need to carry much. Just a bedroll, some provisions, and a couple of water skins.

8. Answer Enough

Adehl woke to the sound of rain.

It was one of those light, steady summer rains that made the downs bloom. The kind of weather that made her want to turn over and sleep for another hour — especially since, in a bed in her father's house, she had no fear of flooding.

For the fourth night in a row, she had slept badly. The soft, cushioning mattress and snug blankets ought to have lulled her into immediate slumber, but she couldn't reach the comforting energy of the heartstorm. Although imbued with traces of ellir, wood was a poor conduit for the world's energy — the Vuusah had built the Tarsah compound of stone for a reason. Adehl missed the heartstorm flowing through her at night. And she missed Roh's intangible presence, burn him.

When she stumbled into the kitchen, her father and brother were eyeing the rain outside and discussing whether some merchants would keep their appointment. Apparently, Mikka was out bringing in a string of horses for viewing.

"There's tea in the pot," her father said, as Adehl drifted

over to the hearth. Tohanuh grunted good morning before resuming their discussion. The watermint had steeped into bitterness, but she sipped it anyway, letting the conversation fold over her as she planned how to make herself useful with the horses. She had the chance to show them what she could do. After three days of being treated like an awkward, barely tolerated houseguest — by Tohanuh, at least — she'd make them see.

From outside came the familiar sounds of hooves, voices and snorting horses. Adehl trailed after her father and brother towards the second yard, which now contained eleven three-year-old geldings churning the dust into mud. Mikka, mounted on a dainty brown mare, issued instructions to a fleet of handlers.

One horse, a broad-shouldered sunskin, whinnied and bounded away from the girl trying to untangle his mane. "Whoa, whoa," the girl said. She looked up as the sunskin's tail lashed. "He doesn't like the rain."

Adehl moved closer. "Let me help." Caressing the sunskin's wet neck, she sought his llirah, set about coaxing the tension out of his rhythm. He rubbed his head against Adehl's chest, his presence warm and solid.

Her father came to the horse's head, placed his large hand over Adehl's. "There you go, sunny boy." His expression was unfathomable.

"Any others who hate the rain?" Adehl asked, wiping water out of her eyes. For ten long years, she'd been working towards the moment when she could apply her zehla training for the good of her father's horses as her mother had once done.

"You should get inside," Tohanuh said, adjusting the halter on a bay.

"I'll need to settle them all down if you keep grumping around them. Don't you remember anything Ma taught us?"

He went rigid. "Don't you *dare* presume —" His fingers fumbled with the rope, and it took him three attempts to tie the knot. Mikka moved alongside him, laid a hand on his arm until he stilled. Spearing a glance at Adehl, he said, "The buyers will be here soon. Make yourself scarce."

Adehl wanted to argue. Wanted to be useful. Wanted to show them. But that dream was swiftly dying. It was impossible not to feel the worry emanating from both her father and brother. Worry caused by her presence here. She went inside.

By the time voices reached the kitchen courtyard, sunlight streamed through the window. On entering, her family pulled up short. Her father's smile faltered only slightly, but Tohanuh's faded into a scowl. Mikka slipped out from under his arm and rummaged in the pantry.

Heart hurting, Adehl rubbed at a gouge on the kitchen table. Her father came close and gripped her shoulders. "You always wanted to be a zehli of the Vuusah, my sweet girl. Don't throw it all away. You can see we're doing fine here."

She stared at the rough timber. "I do see that," she said with difficulty, unable to ignore the underlying meaning in her father's words. He didn't need her. He'd never expected her to return.

But it was the fear he tried to hide that seared Adehl. She'd always known the Vuusah must never learn her true lineage. Their retaliation against her would be swift and brutal. To her shame, she hadn't considered what they might do to her family. After all, it had been her father who had arranged for her lineage documents to be falsified, his own name replaced with another's as her blood father. Coldness swept through her at the realisation that she'd used her father's injury, Mikka's earnest letter, to rationalise a terrible decision. Ten years wasn't long enough. No amount of time could hide their true relationship if anyone started asking questions.

Her father squeezed her arms and released her. "You would be wasted here, Dehl-Dehl. You shine like your mother." He accepted a mug of tea from Mikka. "My one regret is they forced her to give up the Vuusah for me. I don't want that for you."

"She didn't regret it." It was like talking through gravel. "She told me often how lucky she was to have found you. She loved working with the horses."

Her father smiled. "Yes, Solanah and I were happy." He glanced at Tohanuh, who was laying out food on the table. "I hope both of you will be as happy as we were."

Tohanuh and Mikka exchanged a warm glance. Adehl stupidly thought about Roh. And it *was* stupid. She would probably never see him again. Ought not, anyway. She wasn't taking up with the zehli who might become Atalah. Even if they were injaleh. But they *weren't*. They had shared… something back at Fortune Spring, but it couldn't be that.

She'd been foolish that night. Under the glittering stars, she'd confided things to Roh she now regretted. Her family thought she could return to Doneyah's company with no one knowing she'd intended to leave.

"I'm sorry," she said thickly. "I guess I should go." The resounding silence was answer enough.

Eventually, Mikka said, "Surely she can stay one last night? After all this time…"

"Of course," her father said. "Those Vuusah exhorters in town don't ride out this way often. They know we don't employ any zehla here. There's no reason anyone should suspect anything."

"Da…" Tohanuh said.

"Hush. I'll hear no more of it today." He picked up a slice of bread and smeared it with butter and jam.

Adehl found it difficult to breathe. "Exhorters?"

Tohanuh squinted at her. "There's a bunch of them roaming the city, making trouble." He grimaced at whatever he saw on her face. "Zehla with swords, Adehl. We're lucky they haven't already paid you a visit."

She wet her mouth. "Why didn't you say anything, before?" *They're being sent out to make sure kalkah zehla are not breaking our precepts,* Roh had said. If his doyen had sent word about her intentions, they were bound to show up here.

She ought not wait. She ought to leave immediately.

No wonder her brother was so angry with her for coming home.

FRAHTO'S FINGERS itched to draw back the leather cover of the folio lying on the table. Instead, he took a draught of ale. Dinah and the rest of her circah sat with him at the long table, still eating their meal. They'd been enthusiastic company on the ride to Tarsah, eager to take up their responsibilities as exhorters, but Frahto wanted privacy when he looked over Adehl's records.

Several groups lounged at tables in the main gatherhall of the Vuusah compound in Tarsah. It was barely a quarter full, with a dozen tables providing seating for two hundred. Banks of windows along two sides of the hall looked out over wild, coastal herbs and grasses — and, beyond them, Broadwater and the Shrouded Sea.

Frahto glanced again at the folio, ignoring the banter going on around him. The records clerk had made him wait to see Adehl's documents. Frahto had visited the administration building yesterday afternoon as soon as he'd stabled his horse and dumped his gear in the lodge assigned to them. He'd been burning with purpose, his ears ringing with

Gentah's instructions to find out everything he could about Adehl, something they could use to break her hold over Roh — but the clerk had refused to give him access until this morning. He contemplated what might lie within. It felt like snooping, but it was the logical place to start. Gentah wanted to know who Adehl was. So did Frahto. He didn't know everything that had happened between Roh and Adehl that night at Fortune Spring, but Gentah was obviously worried about it.

At last, Dinah pushed to her feet, casting a curious glance at the folio lying unopened on the table. She made no comment, however, and towed her zehla out for some sword practice.

The leather was smooth beneath Frahto's fingers; it hissed as he dragged the folio across the timber surface towards him. Inside were loose papers with writing on them. Different inks and varied scripts. Documents written at different times by different people. The coarse leaves scratched against each other as Frahto sorted through them.

On top were two documents signed by a Vuusah doyen called Doneyah. The first was Adehl's certificate of graduation after five years of training; the second confirmed she would ride with Doneyah's company for at least three years. Adehl had signed the second document, her handwriting so haphazard Frahto struggled to read it.

He sat back in his seat and drained the rest of his ale. Having served her three years, and more, Adehl was within her rights to leave the Vuusah. But the general understanding — expectation, really — was that any decent zehli would ride with the Vuusah until physically incapable. Even old or infirm zehla rarely left the Vuusah. Some lodged here at the Tarsah compound; others lodged in Vuusah settlements along the river.

Most kalkah were zehla the Vuusah didn't want. Those

who didn't serve their three years repaid their debt in annual tithes.

Behind the zehla documentation was Adehl's lineage chart. Another standard document for all zehla. As custodians of ellir, the Vuusah kept the zehla bloodlines pure. Adehl's lineage chart listed her mother as Solanah, daughter of Kotaruh and Nonihra of the Urgreh clans. All three names were marked with the zehla symbol — as he would have expected. Much as his distrust of her was growing, he had to admit Adehl's affinity was strong. She was bound to be descended from a long line of zehla.

He moved to her father, listed as Jontah, son of Bintoh and Lehl. All zehla of the Nargreh clans. Nothing untoward there, either. Frahto summoned the server and ordered another ale.

The only other document in the folio was Adehl's application to the Vuusah. Ten years ago, a Vuusah zehli called Dalanah had sponsored her. Frahto wondered why her parents weren't mentioned — then he discovered the explanation, and something else as well.

Dalanah had sponsored the girl because both Adehl's parents were dead. Dalanah, he read, had once known Adehl's mother. Frahto remembered Roh saying Adehl was returning to Tarsah to work for her foster-father, which fitted with her blood father being dead.

He frowned at the various documents, nibbled at some sharp cheese left on one of the meal platters. Outside, several toolkah geese wandered into view, their sturdy grey bodies twitching as green beaks shredded clumps of tussock grass.

The papers rustled as Frahto gathered them with care and replaced them inside the folio, brushed some crumbs off its leather. Everything seemed legitimate, but he had the nagging feeling he was missing something.

ADEHL HAD NEVER SEEN the firehead trees in bloom. There were several in the grounds of the Vuusah compound, upthrust boughs decorated with scarlet blossoms, long leaves the colour of flame. It was a dramatic display, made somewhat macabre by the blood-red shadows cast over Cloud's pale coat as they passed beneath.

She stroked the horse's neck beneath the play of colour and took a few slow breaths. She could do this. Earlier, as she shoved gear into her bag, the tears had flowed.

The Vuusah compound sprawled on a sea cliff outside Tarsah. It comprised multiple buildings of different shapes and sizes, joined by courtyards and pathways, surrounded by fields and untamed coastal vegetation. Adehl had lodged here a few times in the last ten years, but Doneyah's company more often wintered at one of the inland river settlements. It had suited Adehl to escape the temptation of visiting the city where her family lived. Now, as she headed towards the stables, she wondered if she'd ever return.

In the stable courtyard, a lively girl took charge of Cloud, promising to give him tohroot treats and a good brush before setting him out to graze. Adehl was about to head towards the Mainlore building to organise lodging, when the rumble of voices and clash of steel caught her attention. In a courtyard usually employed for staging horses, a dozen men and women sparred with swords. A dozen more gathered around, laughing and shouting out comments and suggestions. None of them paid Adehl more than a passing glance.

There were more armed zehla than she'd expected. Thank the sun she hadn't yet applied for a kalkah licence. For the thousandth time, she wished she'd kept her mouth shut at Fortune Spring.

As she waited in the Mainlore building for the clerk to assign her a room, Adehl's memories had extra-sharp edges. It was behind one of those faceless doors that her grandmother had handed over Adehl's fake papers. Papers with Jontah as her fake father. It had all gone as planned, there being no reason for anyone to question, but she wondered uneasily how much probing her cover story could withstand.

Room key in hand, Adehl didn't immediately make the trek to Citrine Lodge. Instead, she wandered out to the resonator at the cliff edge. It was tucked into a natural contour of the precipice, a paved, circular area some fifteen paces in diameter. Its fitted blocks of pale-silver heartrock surrounded a waist-high pillar at the centre. About fifty paces below, waves broke onto the rocky shoreline.

She lifted her face to the wind, feeling its bite on her cheeks, tasting salt on her tongue. Silver gulls circled above the waters of Kansiah, the Broadwater, harrying the fishing boats below. Farther out, ships approached the port of Tarsah, the city sprawling on the banks of the Talsiah River. She missed this — the bitter salt wind, the squawking gulls, the sound of waves breaking. She loved riding the Humming Downs, where ellir strummed her soul, but Tarsah would always hold a place in her heart.

As always, the heartrock radiated a warmth unrelated to the sun shining upon it. Standing at the centre of the resonator, she opened her llirah and welcomed the world's energy, her body a vessel for ellir. It bounded through the heartrock, channelling and amplifying the heartstorm. At first it was wild, buffeting her soul; then, with a final tweak, her rhythm slid into resonance as perfect as the single note of a singing bowl. Every limb tingled, but most of the energy concentrated in her core, humming silently.

She was one with the entire world. Her body sighed.

Impulsively, she cast out, seeking the influences from the lands beyond. She wasn't much of a farsenser, but a resonator made everything easier. She found Cloud's rhythm where he grazed in a nearby field and brushed against the unfamiliar rhythms of some of the zehla inhabiting the compound. The cacophony of interweaving and overlapping rhythms in Tarsah was almost impossible to untangle, but beyond the city, everything calmed again. On a whim, she reached for living influences out on the downs — a herd of loophorns, perhaps, or some goats.

Then a single, powerful rhythm, closer than expected. Freakishly distinct. And familiar.

Adehl's heart clattered. She knew whose rhythm that was, whose llirah she touched. She tried to tell herself she hadn't been searching for it.

When Roh noticed her presence, she gasped as his llirah threaded through hers. Maybe she ought to have expected it. Their llirah fitted together across the distance, their two rhythms blending to create a music both simple and beautiful.

For a minute, she revelled in it. It was like air after days of holding her breath.

Then her mind reasserted itself. What the fury was she doing?

Adehl wrenched herself away, ripped her rhythm out of the meld.

There came jagged, tearing pain as her flesh and bones threatened to shake apart. Stone pressed harshly against her body, scraped at her cheek. Coloured lights flared behind her eyelids, and her stomach threatened to eject its contents.

An exclamation. Boots rustled through the grass. She lifted her head, setting off a fresh wave of pain and nausea. Through swimming vision, she identified a hulking figure barrelling towards her; then her head dropped again to the stone, and darkness descended.

9. About to Unravel

Adehi. wrenched open the window to let air into the tiny room. The cloying stench of her own sweat and the part-filled waste bucket sickened her. Leaning on the sill with her eyes closed, she inhaled the summer breeze, scented with grass and a hint of the ocean.

She took deep breaths as her insides churned. How could she have been so stupid? Her memory was hazy, but she had the impression of someone carrying her here — presumably her assigned room in Citrine Lodge. She'd roused herself enough to heave into the bucket, but the room hadn't stopped spinning, and the floor kept tilting beneath her feet.

Groaning, she forced her eyes open — squinting at first because, fury, the day was bright. Several floors below her window, a swathe of wild coastal grass stretched toward a grove of silverbarks and firehead trees, the sea glinting beyond. Her narrow bed with rucked sheets stood against the wall of the tiny room, but she headed for the washstand opposite and peeled off her clothes. The wash water was fresh and the soap fragrant. In clean leggings and mahgan, she combed and rebraided her hair, gritting her teeth against the dizziness.

The door opened onto a corridor, where a young woman about her own age leant against the wall, with one knee bent and her boot braced behind her. She wore typical Vuusah summer riding garb of leather breeches and lightweight mahgan, with a striped red-and-blue samah, and a short sword hanging from her hip. Her many braids were gathered and tied at the back of her neck with a strip of leather, her srih bound around her muscled upper arms to keep them out of the way.

"Hello," Adehl said, bracing herself against the doorframe.

The woman pushed off the wall and swiped stray hair from her face. "How do you feel? They thought you'd slumber awhile yet."

Adehl closed her eyes. "I know. I was an idiot. Who brought me here?"

"Frahto found you at the resonator just after midday."

Adehl recalled the figure bounding towards her as she passed out. Hoping she'd misheard the name, she asked, "Frahto?"

"From Gentah's company, remember? We arrived in Tarsah yesterday." The woman introduced herself as Ketahl. "You were pretty out of it. We found out which room you were assigned."

Adehl struggled to get her aching head around that. The fact Frahto had ridden to Tarsah unsettled her, especially since Roh was out on the downs somewhere. "Why are you waiting outside my room?"

"Just making sure you wake up." Ketahl stepped forward and stopped Adehl from swaying in the doorway by grabbing her shoulders. "Maybe you should stay in bed."

"I'll be fine." Adehl's cheeks heated as she realised Frahto had witnessed her ineptitude. Burn him black for being the one to rescue her. "How many of you came with Frahto?"

"Just the six in our circah. We're trained to mesh."

Adehl glanced at Ketahl's sheathed sword. "And in arms too, I understand."

A nod. Ketahl's llirah betrayed her excitement.

Adehl allowed Ketahl to support her as they moved down the corridor. The zehli guided Adehl to the top of a timber staircase and started helping her down.

"Are you still dizzy?" Ketahl asked.

"A bit, but it's getting better." Adehl clutched the banister with her free hand and focused on staying upright. "I think I'll swear off resonators," she joked feebly. Ketahl huffed a laugh but said no more until they reached the ground-floor foyer, her grip steady at Adehl's elbow.

By the time they reached the gatherhall, Adehl had recovered enough to walk unassisted, but Ketahl followed her inside. The room was full of zehla waiting for the evening meal. They were loud. Just how many of these armed zehla were stationed in Tarsah, anyway? Adehl headed towards a vacant table.

Frahto rose from a raucous group at a table full of tankards. Back at Fortune Spring, he'd been stand-offish around Adehl, but of course Roh had occupied most of her attention. At Frahto's gesture, Ketahl joined the group of zehla Frahto had abandoned. Adehl smiled her thanks, then braced herself for whatever ridicule Frahto might dish up.

He sat opposite her, placing his mug of ale on the table. A muscle twitched in his jaw, but his deadpan expression gave nothing away. Somewhere, a bell rang. As though it were a signal, Adehl's head started pounding, and she rubbed her temple.

The corners of his mouth quirked. "How is your head?"

Adehl dropped her hand. "It's been better."

"What were you doing at the resonator to invite such carnage?"

"Obviously something stupid," she said. He was about to speak again, but Adehl lifted her hand. "Look, thank you for stepping in. I appreciate you not leaving me there for the birds to crap on, but I don't owe you an explanation."

"Fair enough." Leaning back, he scrutinised her.

Adehl wondered what he'd come over to say. Once a server had taken her order, she said, "You didn't mention you were riding to Tarsah."

"Should I have?"

"Considering you knew I was coming here — why wouldn't you?"

He smirked. "You thought we could have ridden here together? That's sweet, but you left our camp precipitously, if you recall."

"True." They were sparring with words, but Adehl wasn't sure of the topic.

"I suppose you wish Roh came instead," he said.

"Not at all." But she felt heat suffuse her cheeks.

His eyes kindled, and he leant forward, his voice a low growl. "What the blight did you say to Roh that night? Did you think to seduce the future Atalah? Is that it?"

"What? No!"

"Because if that's your plan, you're going to be disappointed. Roh told Gentah everything."

"So? None of it's a secret." Except perhaps for one or two things.

"You think the doyens will let him get distracted by you?"

"Nothing happened between Roh and me. Other than talking. You should know: you were watching."

"I was *waiting*." He took a draught of ale, thunked the mug onto the table with a glare. "Tell me what happened."

Adehl stared, taken aback by the magnitude of his hostility. Emotion bubbled out of him like a cook pot on high flame, and it belatedly occurred to her that he'd been looking out for her arrival. "Why are you here?" she asked.

"That's none of your concern." Then he shrugged. "This is Little Atali we're talking about."

She closed her mouth. It was starting to make disturbing sense. "Did Gentah send you to… buy me off or something?" She shoved her braids out of her face. "Your doyen must know I'm no threat to his precious baby Atalah. We talked. I left. Surely Roh told him —"

"That you're applying to be kalkah?"

Sun's fury. "Well, about that —"

"Gentah will never let Roh soulmeld himself to a kalkah zehli like you. Why have you come to the compound?"

"What?" Adehl's heart clattered. "What are you talking about? We're not —"

"And now I find your mother left the Vuusah under interesting circumstances."

Breathing was suddenly difficult. Frahto met her horrified stare with a smug smile and raised his mug to his lips. A surge of anger swept Adehl's panic aside. "My mother is none of your concern. Nothing about my life is your concern! I don't know where you learnt —"

"The records clerk was very helpful."

Adehl's jaw dropped. "You've been reading my records?"

"And both your parents' records." He looked shamefaced. "I had permission."

"But why? What are you hoping to find out?" Adehl hated the fact her voice shook. "I don't know where you got the idea that Roh… Burn you, I'm nobody."

"Come on, Adehl!" Frahto's voice was rising again. "I was there, remember?"

"I did nothing!"

"You certainly did something." His gaze bored into hers. "Tell me why your mother was expelled from the Vuusah."

"I thought you read her file?" Her mouth was dry. This was bad. Very, very bad.

Frahto grimaced. "That information is restricted."

Thank all the stars and the sun. She eyed the door leading to the kitchens, wishing her ale would arrive. She needed to calm down and think. He couldn't suspect the truth yet, or they wouldn't be having this conversation. But her cover story was almost certainly about to unravel. *Think.*

All this because Roh and she... Fury, they couldn't be injaleh.

"Well?"

She shook her head. But Frahto raised his brows and attacked from another direction. "Roh mentioned you have a foster-father here in Tarsah."

"Burn you, Frahto. That's not a secret."

"I presume that's where you've been? What's his name?"

No no no. "I will not have you harassing him."

"You won't tell me his name?"

"Whatever you're after, it has nothing to do with him." It had everything to do with him.

Frahto watched her, his arms crossed on his broad chest. She forced herself not to look away from his bland facade until a serving girl arrived with a tray holding a plate of food and drinks. Adehl took a long draught of her ale.

"Who is Dalanah to you?" Frahto asked next.

Adehl wanted to tear her hair out — whether from fear, frustration or fury, she wasn't sure. "This feels like an interrogation."

"Would you prefer we conduct a forced candour ritual?"

"On what possible grounds?"

"On the grounds Doyi Gentah wants to know certain

things, and I think you're hiding something." When Adehl shook her head, he said, "Why else are you refusing to answer my questions?"

"Because you're being a stonehead!" Ale spilt when she slammed the mug down. "And you don't have authority —"

"What does it matter if you have nothing to hide?"

If only Adehl's glare had the power to slit his throat. "Dalanah was my mother's doyen." That was the truth, at least. "My mother rode with her company many years ago." Before she fell in love with the doyen's pidakah son, and the wrong people found out.

"But your mother was expelled from her company. Why did Dalanah sponsor you to the Vuusah?"

"Perhaps they valued my affinity." Adehl laced her tone with honey.

Frahto's eyes were like small stones. "It doesn't make sense. I think someone was a smooth talker."

Adehl shrugged and pretended to misunderstand him. "She's a well-respected doyen. Her word counted for a lot."

He took a slice of bread from Adehl's plate, chewing as he watched her. He might as well eat his fill; if Adehl tried to eat, she would gag. As though sensing her turmoil, he gave that smirk she was fast coming to detest, then rose from his seat, drink in hand, the timber bench scraping across the floor. "I thought Gentah was overreacting, but now I can only applaud his instincts. Whatever it is you're hiding, I'm going to find out."

Adehl waved him off, striving for nonchalance. "Go do whatever you need to do."

"We'll talk later," Frahto said ominously, then stalked away to rejoin his brethren.

Adehl could only stare after him, gut churning. This was worse than she'd imagined. Roh was the sun-cursed Atalah-in-waiting. Little Atali. She supposed his doyen *would* want to know details about anyone he… favoured. No matter that they'd already parted. The damage was done.

THE RECORDS CLERK turned and banged her elbow when Frahto entered the records room. "What now?" Rubbing the bone, she clambered down from the stool she'd been standing on, a box partially withdrawn from the shelf above her head.

"Have you thought about my request?" Frahto tried to produce the smile Roh always used to get what he wanted. It was, after all, his third visit since this morning. He drifted across to the window, which overlooked a patch of wild greens being eaten by another gaggle of toolkah geese.

"No," the woman said. She was older, with greying hair and the thicker waist typical of zehli retired to administrative roles in the compound. "I told you already. Those records are restricted. You'll have to make do with Solanah's standard files."

Frahto made a face. He'd already established that Solanah's files didn't hold the information he sought. He'd uncovered nothing about Adehl's mother or the reasons the Vuusah had expelled her. It was infuriating.

He'd pored over Adehl's father's records, but they held nothing useful, aside from confirming Jontah had died a young man. Dalanah's involvement remained a mystery, though. Her records had shed no light on her relationship with Solanah or Adehl; in fact, they hadn't mentioned them at all. According to her papers, Dalanah was a respected Vuusah doyen riding in one of the Kiagreh companies.

The clerk crossed her arms and glanced at the door. "If that is all?"

"Not quite. Could I please see Adehl's records again? In case I missed something."

"They would be the records you removed from this room against explicit instruction?"

"I've already apologised for that." When the woman's jaw jutted, Frahto scowled. It felt more natural than reaching for a smile. "You already let me see them once. Will you just give me the fire-cursed records?"

"They are still on my desk."

"I'll wait."

The clerk eyed him balefully, then left the room. Not stopping to consider possible repercussions, Frahto grabbed the key from outside and locked the door behind her.

The packed shelves were badly labelled. Frahto edged down the first aisle, trying to avoid knocking anything over with an errant shoulder or knee. Each timber shelf held stacks of small, flat boxes. Tiny writing he could barely read. Names and places he didn't recognise. Burning bright sun, it would take him hours to find what he sought.

He didn't have hours.

After a muffled exclamation, someone began pounding on the door. Furious yelling. Frahto kept searching, squeezed his frame into a crouch to peer at the bottom levels. The records clerk kept pounding on the door and shouting for him to open it.

Frahto wiped sweat off his brow, felt it trickle down his spine. Tried to go faster. Eyes scanning meaningless words. Hunting for… something.

Expelled. The word was scratched on a box about halfway to the floor. He got down onto his knees to make sure. *Expelled.* Scratched on not one box, but several. All boxes on this shelf, in fact. And the shelf below it. His blood thudded, and his fingers left clammy prints in the dust on the shelf.

The furore outside the room continued, and the clerk

announced she was informing Doyi Barenah. Well and so. Whatever punishment the doyen doled out would be worth discovering the truth.

There were numbers scratched on the boxes. Dates. Frahto couldn't help grinning as he calculated an approximate date from what he'd gleaned already and found the relevant box. It was sandwiched between two others, but the sanded-and-oiled timber helped it slide out. Inside lay a pile of loose parchments, all different thicknesses and sizes, some pinned together. The inked writing on all was thin and faded.

Still on his knees, Frahto shuffled to the end of the aisle. He held the box before him, laid it down on the floor in the light near the window. The writing resolved into words, and he restrained a crow of triumph as he found Solanah's records in the middle of the pile. He drew them out, scanned the contents… And there it was.

His breath caught with shock. Sitting back on his heels, he stared through the window above him. A minuscule cloud was the only blemish in the blue sky.

The muffled shout came through the door. "Frahto! This is your last warning before I go to the doyen. Open the door. Now."

He read through the document again more slowly. Momentarily, he considered stuffing it into his mahgan — but, when all was said and done, the information wasn't complicated. And it would be easily proven under candour, now he knew the right questions to ask. He shoved the records into the box and replaced it on the shelf.

Mind spinning, he staggered to his feet, shook out a leg gone numb, then limped to the door and turned the key. The red-faced clerk pushed past him, spluttering with fury and mortification.

"Get out," she said.

Frahto stared into space for several heartbeats, his mind

churning over what he'd learnt. And what it meant if the dates added up...

"Just get *out*." The woman was about to explode.

"I'm going," Frahto said. He rapped his knuckles against the doorframe.

He'd found what he was looking for.

10. As shadows filled the kitchen

ADEHL WAITED on the front porch of her father's house, her arms wrapped around her middle in an attempt to calm herself down. After her conversation with Frahto, she'd drained her ale, eschewed her uneaten meal and gone straight to the field where Cloud was grazing. She needed to warn her family.

When her brother opened the door, she pushed past him. "Where's Da?"

Tohanuh grabbed her shoulders. "Not so fast." His fingers bit into her flesh. "What are you doing back here?"

"I need to talk to you and Da."

She twisted out of his grasp. Her baby brother, once no taller than her shoulder, crowded the tiny entrance hall. On cue, he knocked the delicate, carved table against the wall with his knee, and Adehl reached out to steady the lamp her mother had treasured.

"Da's in the barn," Tohanuh said.

Adehl released the lamp. Her mother's influence had long

since dissipated from the brass, but Adehl felt loss on realising she would never touch its cool surface again. "Would you…" She swallowed. "Would you get him?"

"I'll call Mikka too."

"But —"

"She's part of this family," Tohanuh said fiercely.

Adehl expelled a breath. "I'll wait in the kitchen."

Mikka arrived first, entering via the back door. After a glance at Adehl, she bypassed hearth and pantry, instead taking a chair at the heavy timber table. A bright headscarf, damp with sweat, bound dark unruly hair off the girl's face, and she drew her feet up onto the chair, arms circling knees. In that position, she looked about twelve. Adehl found it hard to look at her, knowing she would stay here, would get to be part of Adehl's family.

Her father appeared at the door, his shorn head smeared with grime, clothes crumpled. Rising, Adehl almost knocked her chair over. Her father enfolded her in his arms and squeezed until Adehl thought her ribs would crack. "What's happened?" he asked.

She pulled away, guided him to the table and resumed her own seat. Tohanuh had followed her father inside and now glowered at her from beside Mikka. The worn ridges of the timber pressed beneath Adehl's probing fingertips, as she cast about her jumbled mind for what she needed to say.

"Will you just spit it out?" Tohanuh said. "Some of us have animals to tend."

In one of the back fields, a horse whinnied and another replied. Outside, someone was chopping wood. Adehl wished she had thought to boil the kettle.

"What is it, Dehl-Dehl?"

She moistened her lips. "I think they're going to find out the truth about my lineage. They're looking into my background… reading my records. Asking questions." Her voice faded to a whisper.

The woodchopping continued; then a log clunked onto a heap.

"What did you do?" Tohanuh gripped the table, knuckles white. "What did you *do*, Adehl?"

"Nothing!" Her head pounded, and she rubbed at her temple, going over Frahto's words. He'd implied it related to Roh.

"Obviously it wasn't nothing." Tohanuh's gaze scoured her face. "Did they find out your insane decision to leave the Vuusah? Is that it?"

"Not exactly —"

"What were you *thinking*?"

"I have every right to leave! It's hardly a crime to —"

"Your very existence in the Vuusah is a crime!" Tohanuh stood, his chair scraping across the floor. "First, you begged for Da to help apprentice you to the Vuusah. And now, as if the deception we're all living to fulfil *that* dream wasn't risky enough, you decide to toss it aside." Voice shaking, he stood over Adehl; his words lashed at her. "What happens when the Vuusah discover what those amber eyes of yours are hiding? If they see you alongside Da — alongside me — do you think they won't guess the truth?"

"That's enough." Their father had not raised his voice, but, at the unmistakable command, Tohanuh's head swivelled.

"It's necessary!" Tohanuh growled the words, presenting no trace of the boy she'd climbed trees with. Adehl mourned the years she'd lost, even as her heart cracked in the face of her brother's onslaught. "She needs to understand what's at stake here! They could shut us down, maybe even lock you up, Da. Or worse!" He returned his fierce gaze to Adehl. "You don't get to choose, Adehl. You cheated your way into the

Vuusah, and now you owe it to all of us to protect that secret."

Their father thumped the table. "Tohanuh!"

Her brother shrugged. "I'm done."

Adehl set her shoulders and blinked back tears. "It's not that simple! Do you think I *want* that secret to come out? I've been careful for ten years, and no one has ever suspected anything."

"And now?" Tohanuh demanded. Mikka slipped away from the table, took one of his hands and smoothed it between her own.

"I didn't expect these zehla exhorters getting in everyone's business, and…" It was hard to explain the situation with Roh when she didn't understand it herself. "At another company during my ride, I met the man —"

"This is because of a man?" Tohanuh said, his voice rising further.

"No!" Well, yes, probably. "It's not what you think. Don't look at me like that." The kettle sat empty beside the hearth. Shaking inside, she rose to fill it with water and set it over the coals. Keeping her back turned, with trembling hands, Adehl gathered the things she needed to make tea. "It's just… I met the zehli they are grooming to be Atalah, and…" Nothing penetrated the silence in the room behind her. Even the woodchopping had stopped.

A chair creaked. "Dehl-Dehl… you had better tell us the whole."

Adehl took a deep breath and faced them. Her father sat with his hands folded on the table; Tohanuh propped himself against the sideboard, and Mikka resumed her seat. Adehl's voice cracked as she described her encounter with Gentah's company — most of it, anyway. "And now the doyen has sent zehla to ask questions."

"Yet you came here?" Tohanuh asked, pushing forward.

"They didn't follow me." Besides, Frahto would find his way here soon enough.

With a sharp glance, her brother stormed down the hall, floorboards shuddering. Adehl imagined him peering out the front window into the fading light, head thrust behind the curtain.

Her father looked as though wolves had caught his prized stallion. "This is all my fault."

"No!" Adehl went to him, knelt beside his chair. He took her hands, and she threaded their llirah together. "It's *my* fault and I'm so sorry. You gave me everything I thought I wanted."

"We didn't think far enough ahead, Dehl-Dehl, my mother and I."

"It would have been all right if I hadn't…" She paused, Frahto's interrogation ringing in her ears. How long before he learnt Dalanah had a pidakah son who ran off with Adehl's mother? "I'll never forgive myself if anything happens to you because of this."

Face sorrowful, Mikka laid a hand on Adehl's shoulder as she headed to make the tea. At least, Adehl hoped she was making tea and not that awful Sevikk stuff.

"We knew the risk," her father said, the pressure on her hands tightening. "You were just a child, and I take full responsibility for my own actions. Besides, despite your brother's carrying on, there's not much the Vuusah can do, other than stop buying our horses. I'm far more concerned with what they'll do to you."

"But —"

"Hush now." He regarded her with sad eyes. "You shouldn't go back, Dehl-Dehl."

Her father's words lodged in her chest. He was right. She could no longer return to Doneyah's company. She probably ought not even return to the compound where she'd left all her belongings.

But she couldn't stay here, either. Once the Vuusah knew what she'd done, they would quell her affinity for ellir. She knew they couldn't — wouldn't — completely quash her llirah: that would kill her. But they would suppress it. Make her rhythm small and insignificant. The thought of being unable to sense ellir made her feel ill.

"I don't know what to do," she said into her father's leg. "I should probably go far away from here… far away from Tarsah and the Humming Downs." Her voice faltered as she tried to think where she could go.

Mikka brought four steaming mugs to the table. "You could go to Dohni or Port Davrayn," she said.

Dohni and Port Davrayn were across the Shrouded Sea, hundreds of miles from Tarsah, the Humming Downs and everyone she knew. Miles, too, from the Vuusah. By all the stars and the sun. Adehl had only wanted to rejoin her family.

Tohanuh returned from the front of the house, his restless energy filling the room. "Will they be able to track you here?" he asked.

Adehl lifted her head from her father's knee, then hauled herself up from the floor. "I'll go."

"Wait." Her father took hold of her wrist. "You said they haven't uncovered the truth yet."

"Da, this isn't wise," Tohanuh said.

Their father cut him off with a sharp gesture. "Enough!" He gestured for Adehl to take a seat at the table and nudged a mug towards her.

"Da!" Tohanuh crossed his arms. When their father ignored him and rose to gather food for the table, Tohanuh shot a look at Adehl. "You didn't answer my question."

"What?" Adehl perched on the edge of her chair.

"Could they track you here?"

"I don't know. I don't think so. But it won't matter. They'll know Da's name by tomorrow." Her temples throbbed. She should go. She knew it. She couldn't.

Tohanuh made a disgusted noise deep in his throat and went outside, dragging Mikka with him. Adehl remained alone with her father in the large kitchen, watching him methodically gather and lay a meal on the boards of the table. A plate of grapes and figs joined a wedge of hard yellow cheese. A roasted fowl. Goblets carved of silverbark intended for wine. Adehl fingered one, ellir thrumming between it and her fingertips, but not even that could make her smile.

She clutched at her father's hand as he moved past. "I'm sorry, Da. I never meant…"

"Hush." He sat down and drew her close, holding her against his chest as the day faded and shadows filled the kitchen.

It was full dark outside by the time Mikka and Tohanuh returned. Her brother grunted and lit the lamps; then they all sat down to the meal.

A sharp knock at the back door broke the uneasy peace. Tohanuh was on his feet in an instant, a club in hand; he hefted it meaningfully.

Again, the rap on the door.

Adehl, whose heart had raced to double time, reached out with ellir. It could be Frahto. Or the exhorters. She knew it wasn't.

Tohanuh directed Mikka to open the door, while he stood beside it with the club raised.

Adehl surged to her feet, swayed as ellir thundered through her. "No, Toha," she said, the words strangled.

The door opened and her brother tensed. Adehl made it to his elbow, caught his arm, hung onto it as she searched for balance. Her lungs weren't working properly.

Roh stood on the threshold. "Here you are," he said, his smile like the morning sun. Adehl could only gape as Tohanuh wrested his arm free from her grasp. Roh ignored him, his llirah radiating joy and relief and need as he gazed at Adehl. She felt it, even with two paces between them. "It seems I could not, in fact, let you go."

He wore riding leathers, his mahgan stained, his long braids frayed. Behind him in the dark courtyard, his horse drank from one of the water troughs, sweaty flanks gleaming in the kitchen light.

"What are you doing here?" Adehl asked through the constriction in her throat.

"May I come inside?"

She nudged Tohanuh aside and stood back in wordless invitation. Roh crossed the threshold. Dishevelled and travel-worn, he looked out of place in her family kitchen. Her llirah flared at his proximity, but she pushed the energy deep within her.

"Adehl?" Tohanuh's grip on the club had not eased. He was taller than Roh by about half a head, broader too. He eyed Roh with dark suspicion.

She laid a hand on Tohanuh's arm. "It's all right… I think. This is Roh. He's a friend." At least, she hoped so. From Tohanuh's narrowed eyes and the way he hefted the club, she gathered he drew his own conclusions. She turned back to Roh, who was looking around, taking in everything, everyone — her father, her brother, her. His smile faded, but Adehl held his gaze. "I don't think he's here to make trouble," she said.

Confusion met her. Denial. His body had gone still, arms hanging like dead weights at his side. He was quick on the uptake, Roh was. "Blighted sun," he said roughly.

Adehl waited. Her whole life was now laid bare before him, just like her soul. She wished he hadn't come.

"You said they couldn't track you here," Tohanuh muttered. He peered into the courtyard, perhaps checking for companions. When he swung back inside, he addressed Mikka. "See to his horse, would you, Mikkasha?" He touched her shoulder as she passed him, then closed the door and leant against it, arms crossed on his chest, the club close to hand.

Their father drew out a chair for Roh, who gave him a wild look of disbelief as he sank onto it. Da poured wine into a goblet, then urged Roh to eat. "You look as though you've been riding all day, young man," he said.

Roh stared at the remains of the meal in the centre of the table. Then he appeared to recollect himself and turned to Adehl. "Are you all right? I was worried."

Adehl's cheeks burned, and she took a seat opposite him. "That was your fault, you know."

"My fault?" His eyes kindled. "It was not me who sought you."

"I did not *seek* you," she said, growing even hotter. "I was at the resonator and…" She pulled herself up, aware she was babbling in a desperate attempt to stave off the inevitable accusations and recriminations. Sun's fury, what would he do? Dizziness suffused her at the enormity of the situation. "Why are you here?"

Roh's fingers clenched his goblet. "I could tell it knocked you out cold." He took a sip of wine and clunked the goblet on the table as though he wished its contents were something else. "I had to come," he said. "I hope I didn't ruin my horse."

"Adehl, what happened?" Her father's voice sharpened with concern.

She kept her focus on Roh. "How did you find me?"

Roh's hand jerked towards hers across the surface, not quite all the way. He managed a faint, wry smile. "You know how. But…" His gaze returned to her father, sitting forward in his chair, offering Roh a plate of food. The mild blue eyes regarded Roh without flinching. "Blighted sun, Adehl." His voice tore apart on the words. "Tell me this man is your *foster-father* and not…"

Adehl's heart wrenched. But whatever happened, she would not lie to Roh anymore. "I'm so sorry," she said.

11. Cheekbones

Roh's thoughts were bouncing like stones. Maybe covering sixty miles in a day had made him delirious. Or perhaps Sprig, protesting, had thrown him onto his head. For four days, his one thought had been to reach Adehl. He'd travelled fast, and today had been especially brutal. Exhaustion. It was making him stupid.

She closed the gap between their hands on the table, but he pulled away. "You said you wanted to work for your foster-father," he said. The man sat beside her, watching, while the younger man leant against the door, fingers white around the handle of a club. Roh tried not to see the similar slant of their cheekbones, the common ridge of their brows.

"This is Paluh. He breeds and trains horses," Adehl said.

"Then he is…?" Perhaps she would refute it. Perhaps Roh had it completely wrong.

"I think you know who he is," she said, voice rough.

Roh's head started shaking in denial and wouldn't stop. This man, with his lightly tanned skin and shorn grey hair, not to mention his blue, blue eyes, looked to have a potent dose of Sevikk blood. "Tell me he's your uncle."

She smiled wryly. "Now, you know everything."

"Everything?" Roh winced at his own sharp tone. Someone else's voice was coming out of his mouth. "If I knew everything, I would know what I'm supposed to do. What I'm supposed to say." Sun's blood, he could barely breathe. He shoved himself to his feet.

"Don't go. Let me explain."

"What's there to explain? You're pidakah." The word tasted bitter, final. All pretence gone. Until this moment, he'd actually believed he could persuade her to stay with the Vuusah. "How did you think to get away with it?"

"I *already* got away with it." She lifted her chin. "For ten years. My lineage has made not a whit of difference."

"But —"

"Even you could not tell."

It was true. But he'd been distracted. Sun's blood, her llirah called to his even now. Regardless of her lineage, they were injaleh. "Does anyone else know?"

"No." Then she sighed. "But Frahto will soon figure it out."

Roh's throat clenched. His heart felt trampled by a herd of horses, but one thing he knew. He didn't want Frahto to find out.

He didn't want anyone to find out.

Roh yanked out the chair and sat down again. He rubbed his hands over his face, took deep breaths. Someone moved behind him; then came the sounds of the fire being stoked. "You've seen Frahto?" he asked, pleased with how calm he sounded.

"Unfortunately."

"What's he been doing?"

"Asking questions."

The ferocious young man at the door slammed his club into the timber. "This is just great." A thread of worry tempered his harsh tone. "Are we sitting around drinking now?" He glowered at Paluh, who was bringing a pitcher to the table.

"Hush," Adehl said.

"Is this the zehli you mentioned? The one they're grooming to be the next Atalah?" Almost as large as Frahto, the young man had Paluh's blue eyes. "Do you think he's going to do nothing?"

"Your brother?" Roh asked.

She nodded. "Tohanuh." She poured more wine into Roh's goblet, then her own, sloshing the red liquid onto the table.

"What sort of questions has Frahto been asking?"

"He's been looking at my records and asking about…" She grimaced. "My lineage says my father was someone else."

"You falsified your lineage chart?"

"I falsified it." Paluh calmly brought an extra portion of meat and some apples, moving with the casual grace typical of most Fiugreh.

"Hush, Da!" Adehl and her brother said together.

Roh eyed the partially consumed meal on the table. He'd not eaten anything since that morning, but his stomach wasn't about to let him eat now. "What about your mother?"

"She was a zehli, cast out when she fell in love with Da."

He nodded. She must have borne remarkable affinity to produce Adehl. He wondered what had happened to her.

"My father could have been a zehli too, if —"

"Enough!" Roh glared at her. "He is pidakah. You are pidakah. Neither of you can be zehla. It's not permitted!"

Her chin came up again. "I *am* a zehli."

Roh pressed fingers into the knotted muscles at the back

of his neck, his thoughts skittering all over the place. They kept landing on the fact Adehl's mother had given up her entire world for this pidakah man.

"What are you going to do?" Adehl sounded angry and scared. He wanted to shake her. Sun help him, he wanted to wrap his arms around her too. "You're different from them," she said. "You know you are."

"Yes, I'm different. Your brother said it. I'm going to be Atalah."

Adehl's expression almost broke him. Trepidation, hurt… something deeper and stronger. Her amber eyes beckoned him into their depths. He didn't know what she saw, but eventually she sat back. "I'm in your hands."

"Is that it?" Her brother sounded incredulous.

"What choice do I have?"

Roh dug his fingernails into the tabletop. It was not for this he'd abandoned Gentah's company and followed Adehl to Tarsah. Not for this he'd risked his horse. How could she be pidakah? Her llirah blazed as brightly as any he'd known. He closed his eyes, but the memory of hers, clear and earnest and deeply determined, stayed imprinted in his mind. He longed to be anywhere but here.

"What will he do?" Tohanuh demanded in a low, urgent voice.

"I don't know."

"What will happen to Da?"

"I don't *know*. Nothing, I hope," Adehl said.

"But what about those exhorters?" Her brother's voice rose, but she didn't answer.

Roh tried to think. He had known from the start there was more to Lenatoh's assertion Frahto would monitor Adehl. He didn't know why Gentah had instructed Frahto to investigate Adehl's lineage, but he didn't like it. "You can't stay here," he said. "If Frahto comes —"

"I know." She slumped in her chair, fingers toying with the stem of her goblet.

He hardened his heart. She was pidakah. She had deceived everyone, tainted the integrity of the Vuusah. The other circumstances didn't matter.

He felt a touch on his shoulder and an accompanying llirah like apples and hay. "There's no fighting it," Adehl's father said. "Pidakah or no, the heart doesn't discriminate."

Roh stared at the man, at the srih on his wrist. "It's impossible."

"Solanah said the same at first. But in the end..." Paluh shrugged.

"Adehl's mother?"

Paluh nodded. "She paid a high price for choosing me. But she could sooner have stopped the sun from rising than chosen otherwise."

"Hush, Da!" Adehl's cheeks flushed.

Roh's chest tightened. Adehl's mother had been cast out of the Vuusah. Expelled. "I can't."

"I know you'll look after my girl," Paluh said.

"Oh, hush!" Adehl sprang at her father and dragged him aside. She kept her back to Roh as she gripped her father's shoulders and shook him gently. Roh wished he could see her expression. "He can't," she said. "Don't you see it's not like that? It can't be like that."

Roh wanted to refute the older man's words. Wanted to pretend he didn't know what Paluh was talking about. But Adehl's denial was like a hammer striking glass. Despite the impossibility, he had the nagging feeling it very much *was* like that.

When Adehl had begged her father and grandmother to break laws to get her into the Vuusah, she'd had no notion of what she'd be giving up. How could a girl of thirteen have understood what it meant to sever ties with her family? To pretend to be someone else?

Now, as her gaze swept across the once-cherished belongings in her bedchamber — not hers anymore, she reminded herself — she saw the full extent of her youthful naivety. Among her possessions were a box holding jewellery that had been her mother's and a hairbrush inlaid with pearl shell. And her old leather-bound book of zehla tales, featuring beautiful hand-coloured illustrations. She would never have abandoned these things had she accepted she'd never return. Even when she'd departed this morning, she hadn't truly believed it.

She found an old blanket, spread it out on her bed, and began piling things into the centre. None of these items would aid her journey into the unknown, but if she were being cast adrift, she would cursed well take some memories. She swiped at her eyes and sniffed.

Measured footsteps approached down the hall; then her father stood in the doorway. Clutching the carved stone horse he had given her for her sixth birthday, Adehl said, "If you thought I was never coming back, why did you leave my room like this?"

"Hope. Stubbornness." He moved into the chamber, nodded at the carving, about the size of his fist. "That'll weigh you down, Dehl-Dehl."

"I don't care." She placed it on the pile and put her arms around her father's shoulders. Beneath the roughened leather of his vest, his hard-packed muscle and bone hummed with his unique rhythm. She'd been dreading this moment all evening. Her whole body ached. "I'm sorry," she said, clinging to him.

"For what?" Her father chuckled. "If you could have seen yourself at thirteen, the fire in your eyes… You'd understand why we couldn't deny you."

"You should have denied me." Adehl wiped her nose. "Had I known then what I know now, perhaps I would have chosen differently."

He tightened his arms. "Or perhaps not." Outside, hooves scuffed on stone, and low muffled voices drifted through the window.

"It hasn't turned out as I planned."

"Life rarely does." Her father kissed her forehead and held her away from him. He traced her cheek with a knuckle, his eyes filled with emotion. "I'm proud of you, Dehl-Dehl. I'm glad I got to see the woman my little girl became."

Throat thick with suppressed sobs, Adehl forced herself to let him go. Hands shaking, heart breaking, she gathered the four corners of the blanket and used a spare samah to tie her possessions into a bundle. She heaved it in her arms, refusing to acknowledge its weight. Dear world, she couldn't do this. She didn't even have a destination. Her grief threatened to erupt, but she forced it down. "I'm ready," she said.

When she re-entered the kitchen, Tohanuh was alone. He rose from the table and gathered her into a hug, the first genuine warmth he'd shown her. His llirah betrayed worry and fraying anger, revealed his affection and, yes, pride. It was just as well he didn't speak. Better to remember this fragile peace.

Her father and brother followed her out into the lamplit kitchen courtyard. Roh fussed with straps on his saddled horse, who bore it with a flick of his tail. Mikka stood near Cloud, also saddled and ready.

"This is for you." Her father gave her a pouch of coins. "I daresay you could use more, but it's all I have on hand."

"I can't —"

"Take it, Adehl." Roh looked up. "You might need it."

Adehl's hands shook as she stowed the pouch, allowing Tohanuh to fix her bundle of belongings to Cloud's back. She felt like a horse driven out of the herd, banished to roam alone. Inhaling deeply, she ran her eyes one last time over the dark house and stables, the training yards and kitchen garden beyond. Mikka. Tohanuh. Her father. "Will you be all right?" she asked.

"I'll make sure your family is unharmed," Roh said, swinging onto his horse.

A clamp around Adehl's heart eased. With a long, last look at her family, she mounted Cloud, then followed Roh around the house towards the road.

In one of the back fields, unprompted, her old pony, Bimble, whinnied farewell.

12. Hours before midnight

Leaving behind the glow of her father's house, Adehl stared ahead into darkness. There was no moon, only starlight, and she judged it a few hours before midnight. Although she could barely make out the gravel lane before them, the horses walked sure-footedly enough. Roh rode a few paces ahead, an almost invisible shadow, radiating tension. She couldn't think what to say, wished she knew what he was thinking.

As soon as they reached the road, Roh kicked his horse into a canter. It wasn't a safe pace in the darkness, but Adehl urged Cloud to follow. At least it gave her time to get her head together. For about three miles, she trailed in Roh's dust as the road descended out of low, rural hills towards the mass of twinkling lights beside the river. Ought she seek accommodation in Tarsah? She didn't know how much coin was in her father's pouch, nor how much anything cost. She didn't know how much time she had until Frahto uncovered the truth. Maybe it didn't matter, since Roh already knew.

When they drew near the city, Roh slowed his horse to a walk, and Adehl brought Cloud alongside. She left space enough for another horse between them — not too close, not yet. In the darkness, the air between them thickened with all the words unsaid.

"Will you let me explain?" Her voice cracked in the middle.

"How will that change anything?"

"It won't change who I am." She peered through the blackness, tried to see his expression. "I'm still the same person."

"But you're not the person I thought you."

"Because I'm pidakah? I thought more of you than —"

"Because you *lied*, Adehl. For ten years, you've lied to everyone!"

Deep inside Adehl, a flame kindled. "Yes," she said. "I lied. I wanted to be trained as a zehli."

"You had no right to be trained."

"Because *only the pure blood of Buljehni can meld with ellir*? I suppose you memorised that at age one."

"It's the first precept."

She attempted a level tone. "I understand you're outraged and shocked. But if you think about it... keep an open mind... what's so terrible about me being a zehli? Doneyah said I'm the best horse empathiser she's ever worked with."

"The Vuusah are the custodians of ellir to keep it bright and balanced." He recited the familiar doctrine in a monotone. "If we allow just anyone to interfere, they could compromise the heartstorm."

Adehl felt like jabbing him in his well-muscled arm. "But what about everything else that influences ellir? Every living thing leaves its imprint. Our horses treading the road, the smallest ant trail. Even a tree influences the rhythm as it grows. You can't control those."

"That's different. Those influences are part of the natural cycle." His tone implied she ought to know better. "A zehli's influence is much greater, and we must take care. Can you imagine what would happen if everyone could exert their influence on the heartstorm? This is basic zehla training."

Adehl didn't respond for a moment. A herd of emotions stampeded through her, led surprisingly by hurt. She waited until she could speak calmly. "We're not talking about everyone."

By now they had reached the outskirts of Tarsah, the road lined by a clutter of buildings, lights shining in windows. There was just enough residual light for Adehl to make out Roh staring at the road ahead, his lips pressed together.

"So, you don't trust me to be careful?" Adehl said. "Because I'm pidakah? How can you be that narrow-minded?"

Roh still didn't look at her.

"What if *you* had been born pidakah, Roh? What then?"

His head swung round. "What?"

She gave a twisted smile. "Do you think it impossible? You cannot be unaware of all the pidakah children with affinity who are quelled when their llirah becomes unstable. Take Sorah, for example. Your nedoyen's daughter. She could be trained as a zehli; fury, she should be trained, and —"

"She's pidakah!" His mouth snapped shut.

"Yes." Adehl remembered the way Sorah's llirah had soared. "Just imagine if that were you."

He turned away from her again, riding with his attention fixed forward, back straight, his braids tangled across his back. Adehl tried not to despair at his stubbornness. Roh was Vuusah to his bones. They had shaped him and commanded his loyalty. They would never let him go.

Adehl forced herself to ask, "What are you going to do?"

He cast her an angry glance. "I don't know. Sun's blood, Adehl, this is serious. If they find out, there will be repercussions. Aside from anything else, they'll quell you."

"I know."

Roh's horse shifted beneath his rigid frame. "I know what I *should* do…" He cursed under his breath.

Adehl tried to ignore the gnawing hollow in her gut. She badly wanted Roh to forgive her, but if he protected her secret, he would be turning his back on everything he knew and believed in. She didn't think she could ask it of him.

They reached the centre of Tarsah in silence. It was the largest of the Fiugreh cities, established when the Merali, recently arrived on the continent, came in their sailing ships, looking to trade. History told of a small Urgreh farming settlement in the fertile river valley. A thousand years later, Tarsah sprawled for a few miles along both sides of the river. Coming in from the northeast, the road from her father's property brought them to a vast square bordered on three sides by multistoreyed buildings, lights shining at the windows. The fourth side opened to the river, where fishing boats were moored at a quay. The market stalls were long packed up, but people milled outside several taverns edging the square.

Adehl reined in Cloud. "I'm not going to the Vuusah compound," she said. Despite her gear being in Citrine Lodge, she searched for a likely inn. Or maybe she needed to leave town immediately.

"That's an awful idea," Roh said. "Frahto will ask even more questions."

"I think it's gone past that." When Roh didn't answer, she added, "You won't tell him?"

He muttered something under his breath. Adehl thought she caught the word *insane.* "Not yet. I told you I don't know."

"Roh, I need to disappear." Her heart hammered, but she forced herself to go on. "Perhaps there's time for me to retrieve my gear, but —"

"*No.*" His harsh tone caused an inebriated sailor to crane his neck and look. Roh's expression could have torn strips off a hunting dog.

"What's the alternative?" Adehl said. "You said it yourself. They'll quell me for this. You can't ask me to let them."

"Blighted sun." His hand covered his eyes. Dishevelled, dusty, and no doubt exhausted from his long ride, he looked wild. A true child of the Humming Downs. Ellir bounded in him so brilliantly, Adehl fancied she could almost see it.

"I'm sorry." Adehl fought to stay composed. "I know there's... something between us. But I *am* pidakah and I cannot change it. And I will die before I let the Vuusah quell me."

FLEETINGLY, Roh considered riding with Adehl out of the city into the wilderness. Blighted bloody sun and stars and moon combined. He wished it were a few hours ago, when his worst fear was that Adehl had knocked herself out using a resonator.

"I will not let them quell you," he said, meaning it. And that ought to tell him something, but he was too exhausted and distraught to think coherently. Fury, they were having this conversation in the middle of the square, where anyone could hear. "I'm going to talk to Frahto."

"About what? I'm still pidakah, Roh."

"Not so loud!"

She eyed him sideways. Eventually, she said, "You think you can talk him around?"

"We don't even know what he's uncovered yet."

After a long pause, in which Roh held his breath, Adehl slowly nodded.

They resumed their journey, the horses plodding side by

side across the Konnor Bridge, then up the hill. Roh's mind churned. There was little about Adehl that revealed her Sevikk blood — perhaps a slight roundness to her jaw, perhaps a darker shade to her hair. Nor did her llirah betray her. It called to his, and he'd never been more certain they were injaleh. What if he *had* been born pidakah?

He shivered. He desperately needed sleep.

As they neared the Vuusah compound, a maze of stone and iron and lamplight rising before them, Adehl broke the silence. "Roh, whatever happens… I'm glad you know the truth."

He stared at her. She was a pidakah impostor zehli, who had lied and deceived, but he could not despise her. "I need to talk to Frahto," he said. "Find out what he knows."

"Promise you'll warn me if —"

"I won't let them quell you." It was all he knew. "Promise you won't run."

A pause, then a reluctant nod.

They crossed the grounds of the compound without speaking, offloaded the horses to a sleepy stable lass. Adehl's pale face and jittery energy sliced through his soul. It wouldn't get any easier.

After Adehl headed to her room, Roh entered the gather-hall alone. Frahto stood so violently that ale spilt from the mug in his hand. He'd had a few already, Roh judged, recognising the signs in Frahto's flushed cheeks and slack jaw.

"What the blight are you doing here?" Frahto said.

Roh weaved through tables towards Frahto's group of zehla in the corner. Dinah was there, along with others he'd seen training at arms in the camp at Fortune Spring. The circah leader slumped with both elbows on the table, head propped in her hands, examining him through narrowed eyes. Roh turned to Frahto. "I hope you've left some ale in the place for me."

"Bring ale for my friend!" Frahto called to the room, lifting his mug. His next words came from beside Roh's ear. "I need to speak to you."

Roh schooled his llirah; he'd decided on a direct approach. "I hear you've been making a nuisance of yourself."

"Meaning?"

"Adehl says you've been reading her records."

"You've seen her already?" Frahto's breath smelt of dark ale. "Where is she?"

"She's going to her room."

His friend expelled another ale-soaked breath. "Good. Come with me."

Frahto led him to a small chamber holding a circular table with eight chairs. Frahto shut the door and drew heavy curtains closed against the night outside, releasing a cloud of dust. Roh, having swiped one of the hall lamps on their way, laid the light source in the centre of the table and collapsed into a chair. He put his feet up on one of the other chairs and wished he'd waited for the ale. Frahto, the bloodhead, had brought his half-full mug. "What is it?" Roh said, bracing himself.

Frahto fiddled with the curtains, inspected a worn patch in the woollen folds. "I know she means something to you," he said eventually. "But I've felt from the start she was hiding something."

Roh rubbed the back of his neck and closed his eyes. He wished he didn't have to deal with this now. "Sit down, will you?" Frahto took a chair opposite, his shadow large on the wall behind him. He fiddled with the handle of his ale mug. "Frahto, out with it!"

"I found out her mother was cast out of the Vuusah."

Roh tried to pretend shock and curb his very real apprehension. "Do you know why?"

"You won't like it."

"You're a good friend, Frahto." Roh smiled faintly, despite his hammering heart. "But there's no need for coddling."

"This is bad. Shocking, really." Frahto rose from the chair, his shadow bounding around the room. "Look, Adehl might not be who she seems."

Mouth dry, Roh eyed Frahto's abandoned mug of ale. He forced himself to meet Frahto's gaze and saw he'd paused for too long.

"You already know," Frahto said.

Roh mustered his most guileless expression. "What do I know?"

"You're a rotten liar. This is me, remember?" Frahto's gaze speared him. "You already know Adehl's mother took up with a pidakah man."

Burn it. Roh reached for Frahto's mug. He took a long pull, then replaced it on the table, ignoring Frahto's raised eyebrow. "All right, yes, she told me. He's her foster-father."

"Why would she tell you that?"

"I don't know. We talked. Does it matter?"

"But don't you see what it means? Her lineage…" Frahto paced the room. "Her lineage must be in question."

"What? No! You can't go around making that sort of accusation."

"But what if —"

"No." Roh kept his voice low and even and firm. Fury, he couldn't believe he was doing this. But the words kept on coming, each like grass seeds in his mouth. "Think about what you're implying — and the trouble that could cause. Her lineage is fine, and her llirah is strong. If anyone ought to know, it's me."

"But it fits. What if she was lying when she said she was heading to her *foster*-father in Tarsah? What if he's —"

"I said *no*. Do you think me stupid?"

"I think you don't think straight around her."

He had that right. "Look. She told me. Her blood father died before she was born. She was raised by her foster-father."

"Her mother's pidakah lover. The horse breeder. Named Paluh, I believe."

"Yes." Bright sun, forgive him.

Frahto came to rest against the wall. He retrieved his ale and took a mouthful. "Why pretend you didn't know?"

Roh huffed. "Isn't it obvious?"

"I think…" Frahto stared into the space above Roh's head. "I think we should verify her story. There's something going on. Did she tell you how she gained entry into the Vuusah?"

"Her mother's former doyen presented her. It was all quite unremarkable."

"You don't find that strange?"

Committed now, sun help him, Roh stood and gripped Frahto's forearms, not caring when ale spilt on his own dusty sleeve. His friend's llirah bounded with suspicion and doubt. "Look, you need to leave this alone. It's a serious accusation, and there's nothing to warrant it."

Frahto chewed his cheek. For a terrible moment, Roh considered impelling his friend to force him to back down. He banished the treacherous thought, although he wasn't beyond schooling his own llirah to false sincerity. He felt Frahto's resistance break and released him roughly.

"All right. I believe you." Frahto frowned. "What —"

"No more tonight. Please. I'm about to keel over." He took a few more mouthfuls of Frahto's ale. It tasted sour, and he grimaced.

"Stay and have a drink with me. I'll get us a pitcher." Frahto pulled out a chair. "I promise not to mention Adehl again tonight."

"Tomorrow. I need sleep. I rode sixty miles today."

Frahto shot him a knowing look. "You knew she knocked herself out at the resonator?"

"Leave it. You promised," Roh said. "I'm going to bed."

"Are you going to her?"

"I said I need sleep." Fury, he wished he could, though. The thought had his blood stirring.

"We're in Yellowbrush Lodge," Frahto said, sounding mollified. "There are plenty of beds free."

Roh found the room easily, a dorm with eight sets of bunks built into the walls. Frahto and the circah had spread their gear around. He recognised Frahto's brightly woven blanket on one of the bottom beds.

As was his custom, Roh climbed onto the top of the bunk farthest from the door and unrolled his bedding. If denied the starlit sky, he would rather not stare at the underside of someone else's bed. He laid his hand on the stone wall beside him, connecting him with ellir. Skimming atop the heartstorm came all the local rhythms and influences from nearby.

Adehl's rhythm was easy to pick out. She was asleep. He allowed her energy to pulse through him, serene in her repose, all the turmoil smoothed away. It warmed his heart. Folding his other arm across his eyes, Roh wondered what in the bright sun he should do.

13. The ocean sighed

The early morning sunlight was sharp and fragile as Adehl trod the path along the cliff top. She'd woken alone in Citrine Lodge, thrust out of some fitful dream, every instinct urging her to flee. It didn't matter where, just away. Somewhere the Vuusah couldn't reach her. Maybe one of the outer clans would shelter her — she'd heard there were a few Malgreh groups in the Wilderlands, a secluded pocket of high downs beyond the vast deadland known as Gahmniu. The Vuusah avoided all the lands around Gahmniu.

A note from Roh, slipped under her door during the night, stopped her. *Don't run. You promised. I've spoken to Frahto.*

What did that last part even mean? Uncertainty prodded her like rocks under a bedroll.

She ought to have grabbed her horse and belongings and ridden deep into the downs. Instead, she headed on foot towards the sandy cove on the other side of the headland. The cliff path wound through clusters of twisted moonah trees festooned with bower spinach, interspersed with pigface succulents and clumps of fragrant coastal rosemary. It then descended to the cove, where jagged reefs of rock clawed at an expanse of pale sand. The waters of Kansiah, the Broadwater, surged and sucked, foam streaming in runnels over the rocks. Overhead, silver gulls surfed on air currents.

Adehl followed the beach, feet struggling for purchase, until she found the firmer sand close to the tideline. Beyond the next headland lay another small bay, enclosed by dunes and tufts of seagrass and scrub. Along the broad beach, pairs of red-beaked plovers patrolled their territories.

Sand and rocks, seaweed and seclusion.

There was an old wreck too, fragments of disintegrating hull rearing at odd angles. She settled onto the sand, soaked up the morning sun as birds explored decaying timbers and the ocean sighed. Bounding from the roots of the world, ellir thudded through her like a pledge.

The heartstorm didn't care who her father was.

SOMETIME LATER, a familiar prickle of ellir touched Adehl's senses. A mere brush of presence, as though Roh had reached out on waking. Her apprehension escalated.

When at last she felt him approaching, she sat rigidly, her gaze fastened on the headland, even though she knew it would take him at least half an hour to reach her. He seemed contained, his llirah held in check, not allowing her to read him. By the time he appeared, silhouetted against the restless sea as he rounded the point, Adehl thought she was going to lose her breakfast.

He drew nearer, graceful across the sand, anxious plovers wheeling around him as he crossed their patch of beach. And then he stood before her. Upturned mouth. Eyes that glittered. His washed hair flowed loose down the back of his knee-length mahgan. He'd shaved as well, his jaw smooth and strong. Yesterday he'd been exhausted, she realised. This morning, he looked full of vital energy.

"Well?" Adehl tried to keep her voice steady.

"What are you doing out here?"

"Making myself scarce." Under his scrutiny, she found her cheeks warming. "What happened with Frahto?"

His jaw tightened. "He's a stubborn, interfering bloodhead."

"I already know that."

Roh dropped to his knees beside her, sand flicking onto her lap. "He knows your mother took up with Paluh, and it made him suspicious. I told him he was wrong."

His words rolled over her. She was braced for Frahto to discover the truth about her mother. Although not common knowledge, it had never been a secret. It did, however, invite speculation — which was why Adehl had been a fool to draw attention to herself. On hearing about Solanah and Paluh, anyone could do sums and arrive at the truth of Adehl's parentage. Bad, bad, bad.

But… Roh had refuted it. Roh had lied to his friend, lied to the Vuusah. To protect her. Her heart squeezed so tightly she could barely breathe. "Do you think he believed you?"

"Why wouldn't he?" He shrugged. "I hope so."

Adehl struggled to control the haphazard kilter of energy inside her. Slowly, Roh reached out, trailed a knuckle down her arm to her hand. Strong fingers threaded through hers; then he tugged her closer, until they knelt thigh to thigh in the sand. He hadn't touched her like this, as though they were starting something precious, since that night at Fortune Spring. She'd held back then, holding her llirah bound, clinging to her secrets as the tide threatened to sweep them away. This time, she let go. Ellir glided between them, blending in sweet harmony like a ship flying before the wind.

"I don't…" He smiled ruefully. "I don't know what to think, but I can't help what I feel."

"I'm still pidakah."

"I know." His face was close to hers. "I wish many things were different, but… you've toppled my world, Adehl." She couldn't move, couldn't speak, could only hope she wasn't misunderstanding his expression. "Come here," he said, and his arms went around her.

Finally able to breathe, Adehl buried her face in his neck. His arms tightened in response. He felt good against her, as though it wasn't just their llirah that fitted together. Her body trembled. Then she felt his lips against her skin and turned her face to meet his. He kissed her softly at first, but with growing intensity, his heart thumping against her breast. Ellir whirled through them until Adehl's bones sang.

She rested her brow against his, their blended llirah spiralling around them. "Back at Fortune Spring, you said we were…"

"Injaleh."

She could no longer doubt it. It was how he'd known where to find her. It was why, despite meeting him only a week ago, Adehl couldn't seem to leave, even knowing Frahto was about to unmask her. "But *how*?"

"Lenatoh said it happens sometimes. An instinctive meld."

She pulled back to look at him. "That first time we met?" She remembered their llirah cascading and cleaving together. She'd put it down to his considerable affinity.

He nodded. "I couldn't hold myself back with you. My llirah just… surged."

"But…"

"Lenatoh said it would unravel if we went our separate ways, but I don't know." He frowned as though at a memory. "I came after you because I didn't want it to."

Sand slipping under her, Adehl dropped onto her heels, tried to sort out her thoughts. She remembered the way her llirah had responded to his when they'd touched palms under the sky. Losing control hadn't been one-sided. *Why* had it happened, though? How would she have reacted to meeting Roh otherwise?

"Does it matter?" Roh asked, his gaze fixed on her face and apparently reading her expression. He offered a smile. "I prefer to view it as the world knowing our hearts before we did."

She smiled too, but it was brief. "This is why your doyen sent Frahto after me, isn't it? Because he knows we're *injaleh*." From the little she'd seen of Gentah, he wanted Roh under his thumb. That would extend to anyone Roh became close to.

"I fear so." He looked at once furious and sorrowful. "They knew about us from the start. I'm sorry."

"And now Frahto knows…"

"I told you: I spoke to him."

"But if he does find out" — which Adehl thought likely — "I can't rely upon him doing nothing." She willed Roh to understand what she wasn't saying. She would be unmasked as *pidakah*. They couldn't take this any further. She needed to run.

Roh subsided onto the sand with his knees raised, gazed towards the wrecked ship, where a couple of silver gulls perched atop an upthrust board. Adehl moved beside him. When Roh's arm came around her, she leant into him, laid her head on his shoulder. She could get used to the *ellir* rippling between them, the warmth of his body.

She mustn't get used to it.

"It feels like they've been grooming me my whole life to become Atalah," he said after a while.

"I know."

"I never thought it would mean… Gentah seems to think he can control my whole life." His arm tightened around her shoulders.

"I guessed as much."

Surprisingly, he chuckled. "Adehl, I have no intention of letting the old man choose my injaleh."

Adehl said nothing. He couldn't choose her if she were revealed as pidakah. And not even Little Atali could preserve her secret through force of will alone.

Perhaps his own thoughts echoed hers, because he didn't speak again for several minutes. Then he said, "If we can keep Frahto quiet, you can join Gentah's company. The old man will come around."

"Roh…"

"Wait. Hear me out. We could do with a horse empathiser."

It was so absurd, Adehl laughed. "Has anyone ever refused you anything?"

"You're pretty good at it."

Shaking her head, Adehl rose onto her knees and swung across to straddle his lap, wound her arms around his neck. "That's because you're dangerous."

"I'm just fighting for what I want." His arms encircled her.

"And it means everything to me." She brushed her lips against his. "I wish it could all be as you want."

He drew her close and held her. Adehl ought to disengage — her body, her llirah, her heart. But she couldn't make herself move; the bonds between them seemed almost physical, beyond her power to sever. They sat so still that a fearless gull hopped towards them across the sand. It flapped away when Adehl lifted her head. The movement roused Roh from wherever his mind had gone, and he shifted underneath her.

"My leg has gone numb," he said. "No, wait."

Adehl crawled away. "I don't want to squash you." She

put a yard of distance between them, and they stared at each other. She suspected Roh was truly seeing her for the first time. He knew everything now. She had nothing more to hide.

He exhaled and shook out his leg. "Tell me how it happened, Adehl. I want to understand."

Seated cross-legged on the beach, she lifted sand in her palm, watched it rain through her fingers. Beneath the sunbaked surface, the grains were cool and damp. "One of my earliest memories is of my mother rocking me in her arms, singing to me after I'd fallen off one of Da's stallions. I was about three years old. I had climbed over the gate to the stall and clambered onto Berry's back, thinking myself so clever." She smiled. "You can imagine what happened. My mother came running. She went first to Berry's head and, within moments, he was calm, snuffling her hand. Then she gathered me up, wrapped me in ellir, and everything was all right. Next, she put me back on top of Berry and explained how I'd frightened him. She showed me what to do next time."

Roh chuckled. "It's tried and true."

"Yes, but it showed me what a zehli can do. And as I grew older, I understood what my mother had given up for my father. And what had been denied him because of his Sevikk blood. It used to make me so angry. Especially when his Sevikk blood was going to affect me, too. I hated the Vuusah for that."

Roh sat with his arms looped around his knees, the ends of his long hair trailing in the sand. "Who were your father's parents?"

She regarded him carefully but told him the truth. "His mother is Dalanah, a doyen of one of the Kiagreh companies. It was she who sponsored my application and… arranged things. His father was a Sevikk trader she met somewhere."

"What happened to your mother?"

Adehl sighed and clambered to her feet, dusted sand from her leggings and mahgan. She pulled Roh upright, fingers threaded through hers, then drew him along the expanse of silver sand. On their right, the waves eased themselves endlessly in and out. "My mother and I were close," she said, her throat thick. "She was kind, wonderful with the horses. I wanted to be just like her."

"She was an empathiser, too?"

Adehl nodded. "She was killed in a stupid accident on my father's property when I was eleven."

He squeezed her hand. "I'm sorry."

"It was a long time ago."

They walked in silence for a while, the breeze catching their hair, hands clinging together, awkwardly navigating rock pools as they rounded a point. At one of the pools, Roh stooped to sift through shells and rock fragments and clumps of bobbly seaweed. He crouched, precariously balanced, something held between his cupped hands. After about a minute, he rose and placed the object in Adehl's palm. It was a piece of dark rock, irregular but worn smooth by the waves and sand. He closed Adehl's fingers around it, and she instinctively sought ellir in the stone. Hope, encouragement and love imbued with Roh's rhythm bubbled out at her.

When they reached the next curve of sand, she said, "I was twelve when I decided to find a means of joining the Vuusah." She glanced across to find him shaking his head. "It was the only way! I wanted to be a zehli."

He pressed his lips together, but his eyes were dancing.

"Fortunately for me," Adehl said, "I look a lot like my mother."

"You said you despised the Vuusah."

Adehl sobered. "It's not that simple. I've been with the Vuusah for ten years, breeding beautiful horses. And we need the Vuusah precepts to guide behaviour, or people could get hurt. But…" She caught his gaze in hers, challenging him to disagree with her. "But I don't think it's fair or valid to exclude me — or *anyone* — because of lineage."

He grimaced. "I've never thought about it before. But what you said yesterday… I imagined myself in your place. In Sorah's, too."

"That girl is talented."

"I know." He looked troubled. "But the Vuusah precepts have stood for centuries. I can and will make an exception for you, because I couldn't bear the alternative. But you cannot expect —"

"Oh, Roh," she said, shaking her head. "I expect nothing. Not even you can stop what will happen."

"I won't let them hurt you."

Dear world, it was hard to be afraid when Roh looked at her like that, spoke in that low, desperate, determined tone. "I need you to make sure they don't hurt my family," she said.

"Adehl —"

"Please promise me. Officially, the Vuusah can't hurt them, but they're terrified."

He drew her close and wrapped his arms around her shoulders. His warmth and energy bolstered Adehl's fraying calm, and she burrowed beneath his hair to hug his waist. "None of them know anything yet."

"Promise!"

"Hush, I promise. I promise I'll protect all of you." He kissed her hair as the breeze gusted, sent dried-out seaweed and leaves cartwheeling along the sand. "But Frahto will listen to me. It'll be all right."

When Frahto staggered out of bed, head thumping to remind him of the ale consumed last night, Roh was already gone from his bunk.

Upon further investigation, Adehl also proved to be missing from the compound. Since both had stowed their gear on their respective beds, Frahto refused to panic. They would be back. It was good neither would be around this morning to interfere with his actions.

Gentah had commanded him to gather all the facts, and the final piece was Adehl's foster-father, Paluh. Solanah's pidakah lover. Not even Gentah could have predicted just how colourful Adehl's background was. Roh was so twisted into knots he couldn't see what Frahto now considered obvious. He worried about his friend. Roh would take it badly, but the idiot needed to know the truth.

Paluh, it turned out, was well known in Tarsah for his horses, and directions to his holdings were easy to obtain. When Frahto rode out, he took Dinah's circah of exhorters with him.

14. Towards the cliff edge

Roh didn't want to leave the beach.

Hand in hand, he and Adehl returned barefoot along the hard expanse between wet and dry, ellir humming between them. The beach stretched fine and white, crossed with reefs of rock and belts of seaweed. Silver gulls squabbled over the water. Beneath Roh's feet, the heartstorm sang a chorus just for him and his injaleh. Or so it seemed.

Adehl's lineage didn't matter. How could it, when her llirah flamed as brightly as any he'd known? Ellir had claimed Adehl as surely as it claimed any zehli. But the Vuusah would see it differently. If Roh couldn't convince Frahto of the lie, perhaps he could persuade him to say nothing. Or maybe he and Adehl could hide in a remote corner of the downs — at least until this faded.

He was unaccustomed to feeling this powerless.

They reached the small cove closest to the grounds of the compound. Before taking the narrow path leading through coastal scrub back to reality, Roh stopped and turned towards the roiling blue sea. Adehl paused beside him for a few heart-beats, then tugged on his hand.

"Wait," Roh said, counting the seabirds.

She slid under his arm, and he pulled her closer until she faced him, her srih tangling in his hair. Her mouth brushed his, the lightest of kisses, and her thumbs wiped sand from his cheeks. "Come on," she said.

"My knees are shaking — look." And it was true. Only it wasn't just his knees: it was all of him, trembling like a child facing the owner of a horse he'd just lost.

She smiled sadly. "Mine too."

They put on their boots; then Adehl towed him up the narrow track. His grip on her hand threatened to pull her off balance, but he couldn't let go. Scrub gave way to the city pastures of the Vuusah, where grazed a few fat horses. Then the outer buildings of the Vuusah compound emerged, a grey and imposing labyrinth of stone.

The sound of raised voices — not shouting but pitched to carry — snagged Roh's attention as they approached the gatherhall. Adehl's hold tightened, her mouth a tense line. In unspoken agreement, they followed the voices past the gath-erhall, across the grounds.

A brief silence. A man groaned.

Then the chanting began.

The sound of zehla raising their voices in unison always sent a thrill down Roh's spine. Chanting helped them tune in to each other, helped blend their rhythms when they needed to work together. Usually, a goreyah chant meant they intended to create a resonant mesh of ellir to amplify the strength of a doyen. Usually, it meant the doyen was attempting something out of the ordinary.

"Dear world," Adehl breathed. She dropped Roh's hand and ran.

The chanting grew louder as Roh followed. Adehl cut

across the untamed grass towards the cliff edge, her figure lithe against the sky and the sea.

Then the resonator came into view, a jut of rock farther along the cliff. High above the sea, it almost looked like it was floating. A crowd of people gathered around its landward edges, leaving the heartrock platform free for the goreyah chanters. There were five of them standing in a circle, the sea breeze pressing their mahgans to thighs, teasing the ends of their braids. Barenah, the elderly doyen who presided over the Tarsah compound, lifted her face to the sky, one hand on the central pillar.

At her feet, cuffed to a metal ring, was Adehl's father. Paluh sagged against the stone, his face bruised, one of his eyes swollen shut.

Adehl made a strangled sound that was part yelp, part gasp. Her rage swept through Roh like a herd of spooked horses. She pushed through the crowd of onlookers — witnesses, Roh realised with a sickening jolt — until she stood between her father and the doyen. "Stop this. You have no right!"

The goreyah chant faltered and ceased. In the sudden silence, the entire world could have heard Roh's thunderous heart.

Barenah stepped back. She considered Adehl without speaking, then swung her gaze to where Frahto stood among the crowd. Roh hadn't noticed him.

"This is Adehl," Frahto said, coming forward. His gaze found Roh. "I tried to warn you."

Roh felt like a horse had kicked him in the chest, but he rammed a shield over his emotions. "Doyi Barenah." He tried to sound unconcerned as he approached the doyen. "Soul bright and balanced."

The doyen squinted at him. "Soul bright, Roh. I understand you're aware of the accusation brought against this woman?"

Roh glanced at Adehl, whose fingertips trailed along her father's jaw as she inspected him. Her mouth moved in soft words only Paluh could hear. Unsure of what Frahto had revealed, he scrambled to determine a path through this. "Last I heard, it was mere speculation."

"It's a serious accusation that we cannot ignore." Barenah pierced him with a look that reminded him of his obligations.

"Have you tried asking him if it's true?" Even as he said the words, Roh knew they were futile.

"Of course. He failed candour."

"She's been lying to you from the start, Roh," Frahto said. "She has deceived the Vuusah for years."

"We'll know soon enough," said the doyen.

Roh felt Adehl's gaze on him, desperate and pleading. He wanted to tell her everything would be all right. He wanted to return to the beach. Instead, he moved to Adehl's side, where she bent over her father. "How is he?"

"Don't let them do this."

"Stand aside, both of you," Barenah said.

"No!" Adehl cried out. She plastered herself to her father's front. "I will not let you do this."

The doyen regarded her balefully. "Do you wish to confess instead?"

No no no. Roh searched for options. Maybe he could somehow help Paluh withstand forced candour. He edged closer. If he could bolster Paluh's llirah, stop Barenah from manipulating him…

"Roh, what are you doing?" Frahto asked.

Roh took Adehl's hand in one of his and her father's in the other. Her eyes widened as he guided their combined rhythms to weave with Paluh's.

"Roh!" Frahto's glare lashed at him, demanding, incredulous and, finally, bewildered. Taking advantage of his greater strength, Frahto broke Roh away from Adehl and Paluh, then hauled him through the onlookers, out of earshot of the doyen. Pain skittered through Frahto's rhythm, but he kept his voice low. "You *knew*. You knew last night!"

"I thought we had an understanding," Roh said in a biting whisper, aware the doyen watched them.

Frahto's jaw dropped. "You lied to me! I thought she had you fooled!"

"Why couldn't you have kept this to yourself? I thought you trusted me."

"Just as you clearly trust me," Frahto threw back at him.

Ellir roiled within Roh, threads of anger and frustration and despair. "I would never go behind your back."

"Don't hide your head in a hillock!" Frahto said. "She's pidakah. There's nothing you can do about it!"

Before Roh could respond, the doyen's raised voice cracked their heated bubble. "What's going on?" She shoved some of her white braids behind her shoulders. "Is this pertinent to the situation? Or can I get some answers now?"

"Apologies, Doyi," Frahto said, casting a warning glance at Roh.

"Doyi…" But what could Roh say? As soon as Frahto summoned the doyen, the situation had leapt out of his control. He couldn't prevent what would happen next, despite his plan to protect Paluh. He found Adehl being held by two zehla at the edge of the circle.

Amid the gathered crowd, the silence was heavy. No one so much as scuffed boots on stone. Barenah transferred her scrutiny to Adehl. "Well?" she said.

Adehl lifted her chin and nodded.

Adehl breathed.

Pain bloomed under the hands gripping her arms. They dragged her away from her father. Chained to the resonator, he watched her; his head moved in small jerks of denial, the movement obviously painful from the pounding someone — Frahto? — had inflicted. The anguish in her father's rhythm reached her through the heartrock, and she did her best to soothe him. While she still could.

Dear world. She breathed. From below came the crash of waves.

She'd always known this day might come. But, over the years, the danger had receded like the horizon on the Humming Downs. Then she'd delivered horses to Fortune Spring… and now she was about to fall off the edge of the world.

No one spoke. Doyi Barenah waited in the centre of the resonator. The goreyah zehla held their silent circle, velinkah hair beads and metallic loops glinting in the bright noonday sun. The rest of the zehla edged back, leaving space around Adehl and the two restraining her. Roh looked agonised. She thought he might do something stupid, but he paused a few paces away, Frahto behind him.

The doyen beckoned her forward. Adehl tried to breathe, but the salt wind whipped the air out of reach.

The exhorters flung away Adehl's bruised arms as though they were diseased; then one of them pushed her in the back. Adehl stumbled to her knees halfway to the doyen. Face hot, kneecaps stinging, she clambered upright and held her head high. "I will answer your questions," she said with as much composure as she could muster. "But first, release this man."

After a moment's hesitation, the doyen nodded. Although her father shook his head, mumbled refusal, it was Roh who came forward to remove the cuffs. He assisted her father to his feet, supporting him with an arm as they moved to the grass. Fury threatened Adehl's composure when she saw again his swollen face and ginger movements — then she noticed his bare forearm.

"Where is my mother's srih?" she asked hoarsely.

Her words scraped at the silence. Someone behind her snorted. The doyen raised her eyebrows. "Did this man wear a srih?" she asked Frahto.

"He did," Adehl said, before the odious man could answer. "My mother gave hers to him, and he is entitled to wear it."

Barenah's brow furrowed, but there was no prohibition on Fiugreh women giving their srih to whomever they pleased. Adehl's father had checked years ago. "Return the srih to him," Barenah said, her expression unreadable.

Adehl glared at Frahto as he withdrew the familiar strip of leather and beads from his pouch. Mouth set in a line, he dropped it into her father's trembling fingers. Murmurs among the zehla onlookers made Adehl thrust her own wrists behind her back.

Barenah returned her attention to Adehl. "You will submit to candour?"

"Yes." She ignored the muffled protests from behind her. By confessing, she could save her father the discomfort of forced candour. Either way, the truth would come out. Her body started shaking.

"Stand at the post," the doyen said.

Adehl complied, unable to stop the shudders racking her body. She faced the onlookers, at least two score of them, eerily quiet as they watched. Her heart expanded on finding Roh with his arm around her father's shoulders. She held her father's gaze for a few heartbeats, trying to send reassurance. It was harder to look at Roh. His face was pale, the sunlight gone from his eyes.

At a signal from the doyen, the goreyah zehla resumed their chant.

Ellir tumbled in the heartrock beneath Adehl's feet. In the depths of the world, the heartstorm churned, feeding its energy up towards the surface. The zehla tuned in — first to the heartrock they stood upon, then to each other, exerting their combined wills on the rhythm. As the goreyah chant lifted to the sky, Adehl felt the mesh forming, all strands of ellir forced into synchronisation. A single rhythm for the doyen, standing at the central pillar, to wield.

Adehl was a zehli, and she felt it.

She felt Roh, too. He wouldn't let her face this alone. Emotion clogged her throat, her nose, her eyes. The thought of being quelled, unable to feel the wild rhythms, unable to meld with Roh, almost released the dam of tears.

Almost.

She clung to the fact she wasn't being quelled today and embraced the vortex of rhythm spiralling into the centre. It was excessive for a candour ritual in which she was cooperating. Adehl had no intention of lying, and verifying truth would take the doyen far less effort than extracting it. But she supposed Barenah might as well make use of the assembled goreyah circle.

After interminable minutes, the doyen shoved her white braids off her shoulders, straightened the folds of her mahgan, and began asking questions.

It didn't take long.

Yes, Paluh was Adehl's blood father.

Her lineage documents had been faked.

Adehl was undeniably pidakah.

There were other questions, scores of them, and Adehl answered them all. The result was the same. Her deception was revealed, and she had ruined everything.

Afterwards, Adehl was numb. She couldn't look at her

father, or Roh, or anyone, as they led her away from the resonator, ripped the srih off her wrists, and locked her in the basement of the Mainlore building with only her guilt and despair for company.

ONCE ADEHL WAS CONFINED to await judgement, Frahto went looking for Roh.

He'd expected to find his friend lurking outside the Mainlore building like a besotted puppy. Or petitioning the doyen for Adehl's release. Or, failing that, seeking comfort in a pitcher of Haiffin wine. The longer Frahto searched, the more incensed he became. He was already furious — with Roh for concealing the truth and with Adehl for seducing him away from it. Thwarted in his plan to rip into his friend, Frahto felt like pushing someone off the cliff.

It finally occurred to him Roh might have left the compound. Upon confirming that Sprig was indeed missing from the near field, Frahto cursed and headed to the gatherhall.

Several hours and more mugs of ale later, one of the stablehands signalled Frahto from the doorway. He went outside, where the sun hunkered near the horizon, and found Roh leaving the stables. His friend checked his step on sight of Frahto but didn't stop.

"Where have you been?" Frahto demanded, falling in beside him.

Roh slanted a glance at him without slowing. "I escorted Paluh home."

"The doyen released him?" Once Adehl had confessed, Frahto hadn't paid her father another thought.

"Yes."

"But he's almost as guilty as Adehl. He helped conceal…"

Now Roh stopped. The look he gave Frahto could have seared stone. "Are you not satisfied?" he roared. It was so unlike Roh to raise his voice that Frahto stepped back. "It is proven. She will be judged! Must you destroy her father, too?"

"I —"

"The man is harmless. He can't hurt the Vuusah. I've convinced the doyen of this."

"You interceded for him?" At Roh's expression, Frahto swallowed the rest of his words. He supposed Roh had a point. Adehl's crime was ten times greater than her father's. If the Vuusah dealt with her, perhaps no one would notice or care what became of the horse breeder.

Frahto trailed Roh across the compound. His friend headed without hesitation for the lodge where Adehl had slept last night, then swept around her room, gathering up personal items and shoving them into her bag. He lingered over some stone velinkah beads in a wooden bowl on the dresser. After holding the red, blue and green ornaments in his palm for a long moment, he poured them into a small pouch that also went into her bag.

"Someone else could deal with that," Frahto said from the doorway. Her possessions would be returned to Adehl, he supposed, once she was released. Assuming she was released.

Ignoring him, Roh scanned the room. None of Adehl's gear remained as far as Frahto could see. These rooms were plain, and she clearly hadn't unpacked. Roh shouldered the bulging bag, and Frahto flinched at his expression.

"Roh —"

"You're blocking the door."

Frahto searched for the right words. He didn't recognise this version of Roh. "I'm sorry things turned out like this."

"You went behind my back."

"I was protecting you."

"I told you I vouched for her."

"You *lied* about her relationship with Paluh. To my face!" Resurgent anger got the better of Frahto. How dared Roh take the moral high ground in this? "If you want to debate betrayal, then look at your own actions. It was not *me* who tried to deceive the Vuusah!" He shook his head in disbelief. "You almost made me unwittingly complicit in something that goes against everything I believe." He'd thought Roh believed in it too.

Roh drew a sharp breath. For several heartbeats, he didn't move; then he retreated and slumped onto the bed. "I'm sorry." His eyes now held naked desperation. "I don't know what to do."

Frahto pushed off the doorjamb. Roh's bristling hostility had dissolved into fear for a woman he should never have met.

Roh fiddled with the strap of Adehl's bag on the bed beside him. "Was she all right when you left her?"

"Of course." Frahto edged to the window and perched on the sill, watching Roh's face. "She went without resistance. No one harmed her."

"Did she say anything?"

"No."

Roh rubbed his neck, some of the steel returning as he gathered himself together. "If they quell her… that's permanent. There's no coming back from that."

"Of course they'll quell her, you idiot. And expel her for good measure."

"I can't let that happen."

Burning bright sun, they were back here again. "You need to *forget* about her. Once and for all. Roh, this obsession will ruin you."

Roh glared at him, and Frahto shivered. He did not like

being on the receiving end of Roh's ire. Then Roh straightened his expression and suppressed his llirah until it betrayed no trace of his emotion. "You're right," he said flatly as he stood, leaving Adehl's bag on the bed. "I hate feeling this helpless."

"I guess it's rare for you."

Roh's chuckle held little mirth. "Not so much lately."

"More reason to forget about her."

This time, Roh grimaced. "I'm trying." He shook out his shoulders and moved towards the door. Frahto had the impression he was trying not to look at Adehl's belongings. "Come on. I'm starving."

Frahto's stomach wouldn't let him eat, of that he was sure. "And then?"

Roh's shrug didn't fool Frahto for a moment. "I'm still trying to figure that out."

15. Run like the wind

Sometime after midnight, Roh gave up pretending to sleep and slipped outside. He needed to feel the night air on his skin, smell the grass, hear the darkbirds wailing.

The grounds outside were black. Yellowbrush Lodge was one of the outermost buildings in the Vuusah compound, surrounded by grass and wild greens where toolkah geese liked to forage. Roh's restless feet took him, perhaps inevitably, towards the cliff edge where the resonator stones gleamed pale under starlight. The wind whipped his hair into knots, and the sea crashed onto the rocks below.

Seated on the warm heartrock, his back resting against the pillar, Roh listened to the waves and the mournful darkbirds. Ellir brushed his senses, but he kept himself separate. He needed to approach this with a clear head.

Roh understood why his recent actions wouldn't — couldn't — make sense to Frahto. They barely made sense to him. Only ten days ago, his primary concern had been how to make sure he beat Frahto in the flag race come Wintersmorn. Now the autumn festival loomed as an obligation, because

Adehl wouldn't be there. In a span measuring mere days, his entire world had changed.

Still, Frahto might consider him knocked off course, but in reality Roh felt more centred than he'd ever been.

Adehl was pidakah, but she was also his injaleh. In the eyes of the Vuusah, the two couldn't be reconciled. How could the future Atalah be soulmelded to a pidakah zehli? But ellir had brought him and Adehl together, matched his immense llirah with hers. They couldn't be more connected, even if she *were* pure blood of Baljehni. Who was he to argue with the heartstorm?

His heart hurt and his head ached. He tried to imagine what Gentah would do if Roh carried out his plan to free Adehl. The testy doyen was undoubtedly on his way here. It was surprising he hadn't arrived already. Roh would have to break precepts. Would he be able to look the old man in the eye?

Blighted sun. He knew he would do it — even if it jeopardised his future as Atalah. He could no sooner allow Adehl's bright llirah to be quelled than leap off this cliff into the sea.

He'd promised her everything would be all right.

Well and so. He would deal with the consequences. Maybe he didn't deserve to be Atalah after all.

He couldn't hold off any longer. Opening to ellir, Roh found Adehl where she lay unsleeping in a basement cell. At his touch, her llirah surged with a mix of emotions — misery, fear and a flare of relief before she quashed it. Her llirah was so vibrant, so *real*, that he marvelled they couldn't converse. He tried to reassure her through emotion instead. Love, courage, hope.

To save Adehl, he would do anything.

TWO HOURS BEFORE DAWN, Roh stopped in the shadows outside the Mainlore building, where steps led to a sunken door and a row of basement holding cells. Adehl's guard, one of the zehla exhorters, was already half asleep, so it took only a light weave of ellir to nudge him wholly into slumber.

Creeping inside, heart pounding at the base of his throat, Roh smoothed out the rhythm of his passage as he'd brush out footprints in sand.

All the cells were empty, except for the one that confined Adehl. Even without her energy pulling him, he would have identified her door by the sleeping guard beside it. Lantern light bathed the inert form and illuminated Adehl's slender fingers gripping the bars of the grille.

"Where's the key?" he asked.

"Front fold."

Weaving ellir to ensure the guard didn't wake, Roh found the key inside the zehli's mahgan and unlocked the door. Adehl fell into his arms, pressed her face to his neck, arms tight around him. Their llirah entwined and meshed, and he breathed her in. "Are you all right?"

"Yes." She shifted in his hold. "How is my Da? He already had a head injury, and those pit scums —"

"Ssh." He kissed her hair. "I took him home. I'll tell you everything later, but now we need to move." He disentangled her arms from behind him, but the sight of her bare wrists brought him up short. "Where are your srih?"

"Frahto took them."

"Frahto did?" The devious bloodhead. Roh clamped down on a spike of fury.

"They don't matter," Adehl said, shivering. She glanced at the slumbering guard. "What did you do to him?"

He pretended not to hear. "I wish I'd known earlier that Frahto had your srih. I could've —"

"Forget the srih." She nudged his arm. "The guard. You

drowsed him? How many precepts have you broken to get me out?"

"You're a fine one to talk about breaking precepts," Roh muttered as he smoothed out the influences they were creating and made sure the guard would stay asleep for a while longer yet.

"I'm not the Atalah-in-waiting. I shouldn't be letting you do this." But she clung to his hand and allowed him to lead her towards the door.

It was still dark when they emerged from the basement, but Roh sensed the serving staff stirring and knew they needed to hurry. He selected the darkest route to the main gate, his senses on high alert. All the while, he erased their influence along the path. They passed the gatherhall, still in darkness, then one of the administration buildings and rounded a corner into the final courtyard.

A hulking figure stepped out from the shadow of the wall. Roh halted, his jaw clenching, and Adehl drew a sharp breath. In the building above, a light came on in a third-floor window.

"I truly hoped I was wrong," Frahto said, his arms crossed.

"How did you know?" Roh asked. Somehow, Frahto had concealed his energy, despite grumbling frequently he couldn't fathom how Roh did it.

"I know you and your belief in your own invincibility."

Adehl bristled with tension, but she said nothing. Roh found it hard to remember this was his closest friend, standing in their way. "Stay out of it, Frahto."

"Someone needs to save you from yourself."

"Now that's just insulting." Roh struggled to keep a grip on his temper. "You could have stayed in bed. You didn't need to get involved."

"I'm not getting involved. I'm trying to stop you from making a huge mistake!"

"It's not —"

"Don't you see this will give Gentah even more control over you?" Frahto's voice was low and urgent. "Oh, I daresay he'll let you get away unscathed as usual — although you've never gone this far before. Meanwhile, he'll send exhorters to deal with Adehl, who could end up dead instead of simply quelled. And all the while, he's manoeuvring you right where he wants you, under his bony thumbs."

Coldness slid down Roh's spine. He hadn't forgotten the night Gentah tried to impel him. Bile rose in his throat. "We need to go. Where are Adehl's srih?"

"Roh, listen to me —"

"Don't!" Roh held up his hand, horrified when it appeared to be shaking. He clenched it into a fist. "Her srih. Do you have them?" Roh asked through gritted teeth. He wondered whether his friend knew how close Roh was to doing something he'd regret.

"Roh…" Frahto looked like he wanted to keep protesting, but maybe the light had grown sufficient to reveal Roh's expression. Muttering under his breath, Frahto pulled out a pouch from the front fold of his mahgan and dug around inside. After withdrawing a tangle of leather and beads, he thrust the mess at Adehl as though he couldn't bear to touch her.

She caught them with both hands, the beads and links tinkling as they draped through her fingers. Roh sensed her emotions roiling like a bitter sea as she tried to untangle the bands; then she cursed and shoved them into her mahgan.

Frahto shook his head at Roh. "I feel like I don't know you right now."

Roh wondered if he'd ever known himself. He felt about

to fly apart. With a glance at Adehl, he made to move past Frahto.

He might have held himself together had Frahto let them go. Instead, Frahto's huge hands came down on his shoulders. Rage surged from deep within Roh, wild and unfettered. He tried to haul it in, but it fed on all his turmoil from the past few minutes, days, weeks. Everything he'd been holding in check unravelled. His mind roared as he thrust Frahto away with his arms and lashed out with his llirah. *Away!*

Frahto fell a few steps back, reeling from the forbidden strike of ellir. Roh grabbed Adehl's hand and fled.

ADEHL HAD little choice but to run.

Roh's grip threatened to crush her hand, and it was all she could do to stay on her feet as he dragged her through the compound grounds. After that brief, shocking strike at Frahto, he'd withdrawn his llirah deep inside, and she couldn't read him.

Her lungs and muscles burned by the time Roh stopped at the main gate, where Cloud and Roh's horse stood saddled and waiting. Adehl found her packed bag strapped behind Cloud's saddle, and there was gear behind Roh's saddle, too. She stared up at him. "You organised this?"

"Get on!" he said.

In the distance, unmistakable shouts. More lanterns had been lit, and it wouldn't be long before hoof beats followed. With a surge of fear, she swung onto Cloud and gathered the reins as Roh mounted his own horse in a fluid movement. Within moments, they were galloping down the road.

In the pre-dawn dimness, it wasn't a safe pace. The road descended steeply, following the contours of the headland as it dipped towards the river and the town. Adehl concentrated on riding: best not cut this escape short by tumbling headfirst off the cliff. She couldn't stop herself from fretting, though. The Vuusah were on her trail; even if she evaded them, any zehli with limnor skills could track her. There was nowhere to hide. Her heart hammered at the prospect of being shoved back in that cell and quelled by her brethren.

Afterwards, maybe she could still work with her father's horses. She didn't need ellir to muck out the stables.

Enough! She gritted her teeth and reminded herself she wasn't quelled yet.

They reached the town as the sun breached the horizon. Their horses made an awful racket as they veered around farmers' carts and narrowly missed market goers forced to leap out of their way. Angry shouts followed them through the market, where stalls were being set up; Adehl winced as someone dropped a crate, spilling peaches all over the square.

Without slowing, Roh headed over the Konnor Bridge, then swung onto the road leading to her father's property.

"No!" Adehl urged Cloud alongside Roh's blood bay, and the two horses matched each other stride for stride. "I can't go there." She'd rather the Vuusah quell her right now than bring more trouble to her family.

Roh shook his head. "Not your family. We can hide in the deep downs, maybe with one of the outer clans." When she didn't respond, he added, "I can hide our influence. They won't be able to find us."

Adehl struggled to make sense of his words. It seemed the rumours vastly underestimated Roh's ability. She thought of the slumbering guard and the lash of compulsion against Frahto and couldn't help feeling she was leading him some- where he ought not go. She had to stop this. No matter how tempting it was to keep galloping down the road, to hide with Roh out on the downs, she couldn't let him keep breaking Vuusah precepts to help her. If he didn't end up despising her, he'd despise himself.

Before she could talk herself out of it, she brought Cloud to a halt in the middle of the road. They'd reached the first fields outside the town, a mile or so before the road climbed into the hills where her father's property sprawled. The morning light was clear and sharp.

Roh pulled up and circled back towards her, his expression tight. "What is it?" He scanned her and Cloud as though looking for injuries.

"You can't come with me." She recalled Mikka's words from the other day. *You could go to Dohni or Port Davrayn.* "I need to go alone."

"I'm not leaving you." He peered down the road towards Tarsah. "We need to keep moving."

"Roh —"

"You won't stand a chance without me. They have limnors." He dismounted as he spoke. Crouching, he placed his hand on the roadside grass.

Adehl bit her lip. "I think —"

"Can we argue about this later?" He rose to his feet. "We only have a few minutes until they're upon us."

Burn everything bloody and black. Without waiting for Roh to remount, she nudged Cloud into motion. But she didn't take the east road into the downs, the road that went past her father's property. Instead, she galloped back the way they had come.

Roh hollered after her, and she flinched at the fear in his tone. But he was right. The Vuusah limnors would find her in the downs. It might take them longer if Roh were with her, but it would happen. She had to go farther away. Beyond their reach.

The road followed the river into town. Half a mile downstream soared the distinctive arch of the Konnor Bridge. Cloud's strides ate up the distance, the bridge growing larger, its traffic primarily market carts and merchants. If Roh were correct, the Vuusah exhorters would soon arrive at the bridge and... Seven horses emerged from behind buildings and began ascending the span at speed.

"Sun's blood, Adehl! What are you doing?" Roh's panicked shout came from her left.

"Stay here and distract them!" About ten more strides to the intersection. She flung out her hand, and Roh clasped it, their llirah blending. *Goodbye.*

"What are you...?" His grip tightened when she tried to let go. A tactical error on her part.

She slowed Cloud, forcing Roh to drop her hand, or risk one of them falling. It was enough. As Roh started swearing, Adehl crossed onto Catwhistle Street. It was one of the oldest streets in Tarsah, where the early merchants from the Urgreh clans had built their houses. It led, she knew, straight to the mouth of the river and the merchant wharf.

Run like the wind, she thought at Cloud. Her heart broke as she realised she'd need to leave him, too.

Impossible to know whether Roh had stayed — until shouts came from the main road behind her, along with the clatter of hooves. She risked a look over her shoulder. Horses circled at the intersection about fifty paces back. Roh and Frahto faced off in their midst until one rider shouted and broke out of the circle. As the woman started galloping after her, Adehl turned and gave Cloud his head.

16. Gone too far

Within heartbeats, all the Vuusah riders were on her tail.

Adehl's world narrowed to a blur of stone and shutters, the thunder of hooves and a breeze scented with salt and fish and tar. Cloud's rhythmic gait thudded through her. It was like flying.

The merchant wharf lay tucked into the mouth of the river. Catwhistle Street brought them to the downriver end, nearest the Broadwater. A row of ships lined the wharf, their decks full of activity beneath tall masts flying coloured flags. Two ships had recently departed, cutting west under full sail through a flotilla of fishing boats.

Adehl guided Cloud in the direction of a ship bearing the distinctive blue-and-yellow markings of Merali House Davrayn. Through the teeming activity of dock workers, livestock and cargo, she could just make out the name *Seabird*. At the base of a ramp near the bow, a blond Merali woman stood with a wharf official, shuffling papers between them.

Enraged shouting rose behind Adehl as she passed a stack of crates filled with tohroot bulbs and carts holding bundles shrouded in hessian. The official looked up and, frowning at the commotion, raised a whistle to his lips. Adehl drove Cloud towards him. Even if it ended badly, she was committed now.

She dismounted within ten paces of the ramp. Dock workers bustled around her, lugging goods onto the ship. Others had come to a gawking halt, but a sharp word from the Merali woman got them going again. Then a new commotion farther down the wharf revealed a band of guards.

Adehl flung out her hands in supplication and addressed her desperate words to the Merali woman, who she took for the captain. "I seek asylum and passage!"

The woman's eyebrows shot up. She was slight of stature, with long, fair hair plaited in a thick braid. The wharf official, a tall, spare man of middle years, glared. "Halt right there," he said, his command including Adehl's pursuers. "No horses or weapons on the wharf!"

"*Please.*" Cloud's warm body buffeted Adehl as her Vuusah pursuers arrived and dismounted. "I seek asylum and passage!"

"We claim —" The rest of Frahto's words were lost as the wharf guards surged to confront the Vuusah, steel flashing in the morning sunlight. On foot, the exhorters looked like children with toy swords next to the hardened guards. Adehl scanned the group for Roh and found him shouting at Frahto. Roh wrenched his arm out of Frahto's grasp and tried to reach her, but the wharf guards blocked him.

The official snarled. "Enough! Get them off the wharf." Gesturing at Adehl, he added, "This woman as well."

"No, please!" Adehl twisted away from grabbing hands. "I have coin. I seek asylum and passage!"

"Look, I don't care what you've done. But I don't need Vuusah trouble on my wharf," he said. "Come back when you don't have vermin on your tail."

"You can have my horse!" she said, although her heart broke at the thought of Cloud in this clod's hands.

He appeared to consider this. Then Frahto said, "That horse belongs to the Vuusah."

"He does not!" Adehl spun to face Frahto; he and Roh alone had somehow avoided being evicted from the wharf. "My father bred Cloud. You shall *not* have him."

"You and your horse will return with me for judgement like the pidakah liar you are!"

Adehl spun back to the Merali captain. "Please? I have coin for passage. Any corner in the hold will do. I don't care where you're bound."

The official gestured irritably at two of his guards. "I've had enough of this."

"Wait." The *Seabird*'s captain examined Adehl. "What are you accused of? Be frank."

Adehl winced as the guards grabbed her already bruised arms but met the woman's steady gaze. "I'm a zehli. Having discovered I have a Sevikk ancestor, the Vuusah wish to quell me."

"It's not *permitted* —"

"Burn you black, Frahto!" Roh reached Adehl's side. "Let her leave, I beg you!"

"I'll be more than happy to see her leave — as soon as she is judged and quelled," Frahto said. He drew himself to his full, impressive height and addressed the guards restraining Adehl. "Thank you for your assistance. Please bring her this way."

"Just a moment," the captain said. "I have a spare passenger berth as far as Dohni."

"Thank you." Relief made Adehl momentarily dizzy.

"No!" Frahto said.

"I'll take the horse," said the official with a satisfied leer.

It hurt, but Adehl nodded. Ignoring Frahto's protestations, a guard took Cloud's rein and detached Adehl's bag, which she slung over her shoulder. Before she could farewell her beloved companion, Cloud was led away. She gazed after him, heart cracking, reaching for him with a final, soothing thread of ellir.

"He'll be all right," Roh murmured, his arm coming around her.

"I've had him since he was a foal." She knuckled tears out of her eyes and struggled to breathe past the pain in her chest. "Tell my father. Maybe he can buy him back."

One of the *Seabird*'s crew appeared at her shoulder, waiting to escort her aboard. Sun's fury, not yet. Cloud had disappeared from sight, and she couldn't breathe.

"Adehl? You don't need to leave. I'll talk to… someone." Roh's voice sounded strained.

"This is for the best," she said. Behind Roh, Frahto was arguing with the Merali captain. "It's gone too far."

"I'm sorry. I misjudged him."

"He's your friend."

"So I thought." He wrapped his arms around her in a fierce hug. "I don't think I can let you go."

Tears slid down Adehl's cheeks as their llirah melded. It would be like rending herself in two to leave him, but she had no choice. She drew away, aware of the sailor waiting. So many things she wanted to say, but her voice had deserted her.

"Are you ready?" the Merali captain said, striding over. "If you're boarding, it needs to be now."

Adehl nodded, adjusting the weight of her bag. All her worldly goods were slung over her shoulder. She couldn't look at Roh again, or she might not leave. Almost blinded by tears, she stumbled towards the boarding ramp.

Roh stared after Adehl, stricken. He clung to the shared rhythm strumming through him; in a few moments, she'd be aboard ship, cut off. Water barely conveyed ellir. She'd be aboard ship for days, perhaps a week, and then extremely far away.

Frahto hustled past him towards the *Seabird*. Roh lunged and grabbed his arm and, although Frahto shook him off, it gave Adehl time to step onto the ramp.

At once, Roh's sense of her receded. It was like the tide sucked out, leaving him stranded alone on the sand.

He couldn't do this.

"You're being a woodbrain," Frahto said furiously, keeping his distance.

"I'm sorry."

"You *impelled* me." Frahto's tone was unforgiving. "There'll be consequences, even for you. I hope she's worth it."

"I shouldn't have done it." But he'd do it again.

Frahto grunted. Roh hated leaving things between them like this.

Adehl gained the deck of the ship and took a position at the rail facing them. Dock workers stood by each bollard on the wharf, ready to unfasten the heavy ropes restraining the vessel. The deck crew bustled, and the Merali captain moved towards the boarding ramp. Soon, the ramp would be unhooked and hauled back onto the wharf.

Blighted bloody sun.

Roh had always been able to picture his future. From a young age, he'd known he would ride the Humming Downs with the Vuusah. He lived for the heartstorm and the song of the land under the sky. When others had decided he could one day be Atalah, he'd felt honoured by the thought of serving ellir and his brethren in that role. Now that future seemed… bleak. It no longer made sense. He couldn't rejoin

Gentah's company, soak up the sun at whichever camp they visited next. It felt like someone else's life.

Adehl's gaze bored into him, her mouth a straight line. The *Seabird*'s captain stepped off the ramp, and the crew on the wharf surged forward.

"Wait," Roh said, moving.

"Roh, don't you dare!"

But he dodged around Frahto before the man could restrain him. In another three strides, Roh reached the ramp. Protests came from the crew who were halfway through unhooking it, and it twisted precariously as he scrambled to the top. Then he clambered onto the *Seabird* into Adehl's arms.

"Roh!" Frahto sounded winded.

"You can't," Adehl said, her voice choked up.

"What's going on?" barked the captain. "We're about to sail."

"Do you have enough coin for two?" Roh asked. Eyes wide, Adehl nodded. He favoured the captain with his best smile. "Apologies, captain. I beg passage as well. We can share the cabin."

"Presumptuous," murmured Adehl, clinging to him.

The captain glared. "The *Seabird* is not a hire cart, you know. Will you share rations as well?" But a moment later, she bit off a curse and ordered the ramp removed.

Roh breathed into Adehl's hair as the dock workers unwound the ropes from the bollards, and the ship's crew hauled them in. "Sorry, jaleh, was that too presumptuous? I just..."

"Stars and sun, *no*," she said, holding him tighter.

With a shudder, the *Seabird* moved. Keeping Adehl under his arm, Roh turned to face the wharf. Frahto stood there, face pale with shock. He stared at Roh, slowly shook his head. Behind him, Roh's horse Sprig stood with his head resting on the back of Frahto's mount, as they had rested many times before. Bound to Sprig's saddle was Roh's bag containing all his gear.

"Look after Sprig for me," Roh called. Then, as the ship pulled away from the wharf — "Tell them I'm sorry!"

Frahto's jaw dropped, but the breeze whisked away whatever he said, filling the sails as the *Seabird*'s prow began to swing. The bustling wharf panned out of view to reveal the wide river mouth. The Vuusah compound stood high on a headland, and to the south stretched the golden beach where he and Adehl had walked yesterday. Behind Tarsah and the strip of coast, the terrain rolled up into the vast, high plateau of the Humming Downs.

All too soon, the ship completed its arc, and the coastline receded as the *Seabird* headed west into the Broadwater.

FRAHTO STARED in disbelief at the departing ship, his feet rooted to the thick planks of the wharf. His mind stumbled through options, needing to *fix* this, but kept coming up blank. There was no fix. He couldn't change what had just happened.

Yet he couldn't seem to drag himself away. If he turned from the *Seabird*, he'd have to acknowledge the fact Roh had abandoned everything they both believed in. Once Frahto had forced himself to accept that awful truth, he'd have to tell someone.

He closed his eyes against the swelling nausea in his gut. It was bad enough that Adehl had escaped without judgement, without being quelled. But Roh's defection... Maybe Frahto ought to take the next ship in pursuit. Anything to avoid facing Gentah when he arrived.

Frahto's rage at Adehl, temporarily banked, flared again

with a ferocity that made him shake. It was all her fault. She'd come between him and Roh from the start, made them stop trusting each other. She'd seduced and twisted Roh with her lies and outrageous beliefs and made Roh impel him. And now she'd lured him away.

She wouldn't get away with it. The doyens would never permit a rogue pidakah zehli to exist. They would retrieve Roh and make Adehl pay. Frahto hoped he'd be around to witness it. Maybe they'd even let him help.

He startled when a furry head nosed his shoulder, then lifted a hand to caress Melon's soft cheek. Sprig came up on his other side, the two horses enfolding him in warmth. Frahto calmed his llirah to prevent distressing them.

"Roh will be back, you'll see," he murmured to Sprig. "He's just confused right now." The blood bay rubbed his nose on Frahto's head.

Frahto knew he ought to return to the compound. Dinah's circah was doubtless waiting for him at the edge of the wharf — had the exhorters seen what had happened?

He still couldn't make his feet move.

So he stayed, watched the *Seabird* get smaller and smaller, until she was a speck on the blue-green horizon.

Interlude

17. Door number five

THE SHIP'S timbers creaked and heaved as it ploughed through the rolling swell, sails angled to catch the wind. Gripping the rail of the high aft deck, Adehl watched the coastline recede from view. Roh stood beside her, close but not touching. They didn't speak, the moment too big for words.

A bubble of numbness insulated Adehl from reality, but it could pop at any moment. She was leaving behind everything she knew.

Ahead lay boundless water and unknown territories. Exile.

Distance ultimately squeezed the thin green line of the Humming Downs over the horizon. Adehl stared at all the blue, struggled to believe this was happening.

Roh put his arm around her shoulders. She couldn't fathom how he was here.

Someone cleared their throat behind them. "Welcome to the *Seabird*, er…" The woman looked bemused. "Your cabin is ready."

Roh released her, and Adehl pulled herself together. The lower deck, stained with guano and tar, showed no sign of her gear.

"We took your bag to your cabin," said the sailor, as though she retrieved passengers' abandoned belongings from the deck all the time. "A meal will be served at midday."

They followed the woman's swinging club of blond hair across the rocking deck, dodging the crew as best they could with their balance compromised. The air smelt of salt and damp. Inside a low, narrow corridor, the woman stopped before a door marked number five and produced a large key, which she fitted to the lock.

The door opened onto a small cabin with two narrow bunks and few furnishings. Adehl's bag had been dumped onto one of the sleeping pallets. Roh, she realised, had nothing. "Thank you," Adehl said, as the woman handed her the key and departed. Then to Roh, loitering in the corridor — "Get in here."

He brushed past her, and Adehl closed, latched and locked the door. She turned, leant against it and regarded him. He wasn't a large man, not much taller than her, but he seemed to fill the cabin. His wind-scourged hair tumbled over his shoulders. He met her gaze with a look that made her blood burn.

They thudded together hard. Hands held her tight against him, his warmth and energy pressing into her. Their mouths tore breaths from each other, more urgent than yesterday on the beach. She couldn't get enough of him. His light. His strength. She started clawing at his clothes.

He groaned. "You're so — I can't —" He shuddered as her fingers fumbled at the shoulder ties of his mahgan. "Are you sure?"

Did he even need to ask? She wanted nothing more in the world than him just now. All the emotion she had been holding contained was erupting out of her. All her fear and sorrow and anger were transformed and overwhelmed by the desire she'd been keeping in check. In reply, she unfastened her own mahgan and shucked it to the floor.

His eyes gleamed, and he wrapped her in his arms again, his mouth devouring hers. He pressed kisses to her jaw, trailing towards her ear and the tender skin below it. As he started moving lower, the deck rocked beneath their feet, making them stumble. With a grin, Adehl nudged him towards the unencumbered bunk. It was barely wide enough for one person, but it would be enough.

The heat in his gaze made her breath catch. He released her for as long as it took them to tear off the rest of their clothes, then lifted her onto the bunk. His fingers trailed along her skin, mouth following in a trail of warm breath and lips and tongue.

Burning beneath his touch, Adehl reached for him. "Come here."

He squeezed himself onto the bunk with her, and they again pressed together from thigh to hip to chest, this time with nothing separating skin from skin.

"That's better," she murmured and wound her arms around him, her fingers catching in his hair.

Roh's heart thudded almost painfully — and not entirely because of his recent exertions, or the fact Adehl lay warm and soft and naked on top of him. She stared down through glazed amber eyes, her tumultuous emotions flowing through him as though they were his own. Sorrow and fear and guilt were all layered beneath her love, binding him with velvet thorns.

He thumbed a tear from her cheek, lifted his head to kiss

the place he'd just touched. Nothing should have tarnished this moment, but it would be fixed forever between fear and flight and whatever adversity came next. He wanted to delay the inevitable for as long as possible.

"I'm sorry," Adehl said thickly. "I shouldn't be so glad you're here."

He kissed the corner of her mouth. "I'm glad I'm here."

"No, you're not. At least not entirely." She framed his face with her hands. "You can't hide what you're feeling from me anymore."

"Then I hope you felt how much I enjoyed the past half hour."

She flushed, even more beautiful, all satiated and undone, hair a silken stream on his chest. Then she placed a hand across his mouth, her eyes like pools of honey. "I never wanted you to break precepts for me."

"I know."

"I never wanted you to hurt your friend."

Roh's heart clenched at the memory of his dealings with Frahto over the past two days. First lies, then accusations, culminating in the ultimate betrayal. Frahto had been doing his duty, and Roh had broken the most important precept of all. He bitterly regretted the necessity and wished he'd seen an alternative. If only Frahto had not interfered.

"You belong with the Vuusah, Roh."

"Hush." He'd always thought so, but he'd broken so many precepts of late, they might expel him too. "Let's not think about that." He couldn't do anything about it, either. Back on the wharf, he'd acted according to his heart. There hadn't been time to weigh potential outcomes and repercussions. For the time being, at least, the Vuusah couldn't reach them.

Her gaze raked his face, trying to penetrate and decipher emotions Roh couldn't identify in himself. He wrapped his arms tighter around her and brought their mouths together. Time suspended as they explored each other again, ellir humming between them.

Much later, she lay with her head on his chest. "They're going to come after us, aren't they?"

"Probably."

"Now they've got those exhorters..." She shuddered. "Frahto hates me."

Roh's first instinct was to brush off her concerns, but he sighed and stroked the smooth skin of her back. "He's not too fond of me right now, either."

"Thank you for getting me out of there," she whispered.

"I will *never* let them quell you."

"I've wrecked your life."

He stopped her with another kiss. Right now, he'd take being jammed into this tiny cabin, this cramped wooden bunk. The rest could wait.

She lifted her head. "So, we just shut out the world?" she said, proving how well she read him.

"For the time being."

"Spend the whole voyage naked in our cabin?"

He shivered. "What are you trying to do to me?"

She laughed, then inexplicably pulled away.

"Where are you going?" he asked as she began pulling on clothes.

"Hungry." She smirked. "They said a meal would be served, and I've worked up an appetite." When he just stared, she chuckled. "You'd better come too. You'll need to keep your strength up."

Part Two
Soulspark

18. At the feet of mountains

On a sunny afternoon, the *Seabird* swung around a grassy headland to reveal the ancient trade city of Dohni. Adehl's whole being skittered with apprehension — and a skerrick of excitement.

She stood with Roh in the ship's prow, trying to take everything in. The first sign of the city had been the massive lighthouse on the headland just passed. The *Seabird* now sailed below a robust guard tower high on the starboard side. Along with another guard tower and lighthouse across the water, the tower above marked the entrance to Dohni's famous harbour. The high sun sparkled on the waves, brightening the sails of other merchant vessels and fishing boats.

Directly ahead, impossibly large, the city itself clustered at the feet of mountains. The harbour waters curved around immense walls that barricaded a jumble of stone, coloured roofs and pockets of greenery. The terrain climbed away from the shore, peaking in a craggy rise with grand buildings on top. The mountains swept up behind the city, their forested flanks shimmering green.

Beside Adehl, Roh bounced on the balls of his feet. They'd been at sea for a week and were both desperate to step ashore. It was no wonder zehla avoided sea voyages, with uncountable fathoms of water blocking them from the heartstorm. The muted cadence coming from the ship's timbers was no substitute.

"This ought to be interesting," Roh said, his attention riveted on something in the distance.

Adehl followed his gaze to the crag thrusting up in the midst of the city. Its lower flanks were wooded, but the top comprised cliffs of pale, grey rock. The faint purple sheen could have been a trick of the light. "Do you think that's truly heartrock?"

He grinned. "So I've heard. It might make this visit worthwhile, eh?"

Adehl squeezed the rail. *Visit.* She couldn't blame Roh for viewing this as temporary. They hadn't discussed anything of importance during the week-long voyage. Every time she had broached the future, Roh had diverted her with tales of an impromptu rig-running competition or dragged her aft to throw quoits. More than once, he'd pulled her into their cabin and locked the door. In the end, she'd followed his lead and tried not to think about what lay ahead.

Now, though, with Dohni laid out before them under the sun, Adehl tried to imagine living in this enormous, unfamiliar city. As an independent city–state steeped in history and Baljehni's most important hub of trade and commerce, Dohni made Tarsah look like a fishing village.

Several slow, deep breaths entirely failed to calm Adehl's thudding heart.

Timbers vibrated and creaked as the *Seabird* swung farther starboard around the headland into Dohni's deepwater port. A third lighthouse marked the narrow entrance to the small cove, which was almost entirely ringed by land, the city curling around the water like a mother protecting a child. The busy wharf stretched along a broad expanse of the shoreline, prickled with wooden piers and moored ships.

Amid shouts and thuds and clangs, the *Seabird* nudged into a vacant berth. Land and sea crews scrambled to make the vessel secure, throwing down thick ropes for winding around bollards. A land team rolled out ramps that hooked against the ship's sides.

One of the *Seabird*'s crew hailed Adehl and Roh with a brisk wave. "All clear to disembark!"

"Our thanks!" Roh called to the man's departing back. He turned to Adehl. "Let's do this, jaleh."

She released the rail. They had their arrival papers from the *Seabird*'s captain, who had told them what to do. Now it was all before them. Roh grabbed their bag from the deck and bounced down the passenger ramp ahead of Adehl. When she reached the timber wharf, its rigidity jarred her knees.

They pushed through the chaos of cargo movement towards the large customs building, located in the middle of the wharf. Inside, at one of several booths, a careworn official looked over the documents Captain Terrell had supplied. He rubbed a hand over his stubbly chin and scrutinised them from boots to braids.

"You don't have any further documentation?"

"Captain Terrell of the *Seabird* said these would suffice," Adehl said.

"It's only the two of you?" Frowning, he peered behind them, as though expecting a horde. "I gotta say, we're getting jack of you hooters showing up here." His fingers twitched and Adehl had the impression he wanted to crush their papers into a tiny ball.

"I don't think..."

The official glared. "Barging in, thinking you own the streets..."

"We're here on *personal* business," Adehl said.

"You look like hooters. You sure you don't have any weapons?"

"Definitely no weapons," Adehl said. "Please, we're not here to make any trouble."

After a long moment, the official grunted and scrawled something on their papers, made a note in a ledger, then handed them back, saying they must be kept on hand at all times. He named a fee that made Adehl flinch, but she handed over the coin, and he waved them through into the city.

She was about to comment on the official's attitude, when they stepped off the timber wharf onto the cobblestoned road.

Ellir swept in like a wildfire.

She ought to have braced herself. Dohni was said to be built on a foundation of heartrock, and this was wilder, stronger than anything she'd known. The heartstorm felt closer to the surface here; it stoked the cobblestones' energy into a blaze.

Roh closed his eyes and tilted his face to the sky. "I guess the rumours were true," he said.

Adehl wasn't sure she could speak with the barrage of ellir rattling her rib cage. She took Roh's hand, bringing their threaded fingers up between them. They grinned stupidly at each other as their llirah melded and danced in the tempest. She was vaguely aware of traffic swirling past, someone shouting. Then she blinked back to full awareness to find three black-uniformed guards glaring at them.

"Oi, hooters! Out of the way."

Roh expertly disentangled their llirah and drew her to the edge of the street. "Apologies, friend. We meant no harm," he said.

The guards stalked after them, and one thrust out a hand. "Papers!"

Flustered, Adehl handed them over. The guard, a stocky man with short dark hair and heavy jowls, scrutinised the documents. "Is there a problem?" Adehl asked.

"Aye. We've got a hooter problem in this city."

"That has nothing to do with us," Roh said. "We've just arrived."

"Hmmm." The guard handed back the papers.

Adehl said, "Look, we're not, er, hooters —"

"Good morning, Captain," a new voice said breezily from somewhere behind. "May we be of assistance?"

"Just what we need," muttered one of the other guards.

The approaching group of Fiugreh men and women were dressed similarly to Adehl and Roh — undyed flankah mahgans over leather breeches, brown boots and clusters of beaded braids. Each bore a short sword at their hip, and their samahs were striped red and blue — exactly like the exhorters Adehl had seen back in Tarsah. Their hair beads were red and blue, too. Standing in a distinctive formation, the six of them looked like militia on patrol.

The leader of the circah, a tall, lean woman with sun creases at the corners of her eyes, flashed a grin. "Well met, zehla," she said. "You have the wide-eyed look of brethren just arrived." She turned her attention to the guards. "Thank you for welcoming our new arrivals. We'll escort them to the lodge."

"Not hooters, huh," the guard said, scowling at Adehl.

"They don't answer to you, Captain," the Vuusah woman said easily. "Run along now."

The man loudly thumped his sword hilt in its sheath. "Things are changing in this city, hooter. You mark my words."

"Indeed they are." The woman's smile was ferocious. "I'll take it from here."

The captain thumped his sword hilt again in evident

disgust. Turning to Adehl and Roh, he said, "If I catch you lying to me or making a nuisance of yourselves again, I'll clap you in irons. That's a promise." Then he pivoted and led his companions along the wharf road without a backward glance.

The Vuusah woman laughed. "That was enjoyable." Holding up her hand, she said, "Soul bright and balanced, zehla. I'm Tallah, and we are the Blue Fox circah."

"Soul bright, Tallah of the Blue Fox," Roh said. He stepped forward and met Tallah's hand for no more than a few heartbeats. There seemed to be no recognition between them, and Adehl was relieved he didn't give his name. "Thank you for rescuing us. What did we do wrong?"

"Oh, the Bladekor Guard are the council's dogs. They despise us as a matter of principle," Tallah said. She next touched her palm to Adehl's, a polite brush of ellir the only exchange. "As to what you did wrong... I can guess." She looked amused. "You wouldn't be the first zehla to step off the wharf and hold up traffic while the city welcomed you."

Roh chuckled. Adehl could only marvel at him. Her own nerves were stretched so taut her head was starting to ache. "It will take some getting used to, that's for sure," Roh said. "How long have you been in Dohni?"

"Almost a year. We were the first circah deployed here." She glanced at the glowering passersby. In a lowered voice, she said, "Our presence is long overdue. Dare I hope you've accompanied another circah? We're in sore need of reinforcements."

"Actually, no. We're here on other business," Roh said.

"Oh well. We'll escort you to the lodge. It's miles from here, and our doyen would have our hides if we left you to get lost in the city."

"That's really not necessary," Adehl said, hoping she managed to conceal her alarm.

"We're glad for the excuse. It's not every day we get new blood from home."

Adehl was trying to work out how to get out of this, when one of the other zehla said something she didn't catch. Tallah spun round to watch someone or something in the crowd. The street teemed with people from all over Baljehni — it was impossible to distinguish residents from visitors. Adehl couldn't be certain who had caught the exhorters' attention.

"My apologies," Tallah said. "It looks like we shan't have the honour of escorting you, after all. Take this road past the Great Market and ask for directions to Four Nations Plaza on the other side of the harbour. Our lodge is about a mile beyond. I look forward to hearing all your news over a meal tonight." With that, the circah of exhorters surged into motion, carving a route through the throng.

Roh stared after them. Wordlessly, Adehl started walking in the direction Captain Terrell had told them would lead to the Old Kestali Quarter, where they would find affordable lodgings. It was the same direction Tallah had indicated, but that couldn't be helped.

Her mind churned. She'd expected to find Vuusah exhorters in Dohni, but not within half an hour of setting foot in the city — and not roaming the streets emulating Bladekor Guards.

A few minutes later, she showed their papers at Traders Gate, a massive stone construction leading through the thick city wall into the oldest parts of Dohni.

"Let's do this, jaleh," Roh said, once they were through. The heartrock crag ascended inland to their right, but the wide, heavily trafficked road led along flatter terrain at the base of the hill. He took her hand. "The city awaits."

"I look forward to learning her secrets." Adehl strived for a light tone. Despite Roh's discretion, she hadn't missed his easy camaraderie with the exhorters. He hadn't seemed too surprised to meet them.

For the entire sea journey, they'd resolutely shut out responsibility and consequences. They'd loved each other and pretended it would be enough. But setting foot on land had brought reality crashing down.

Roh was Vuusah to his bones, the Atalah-in-waiting. He'd abandoned the life laid out for him in the impulse of a moment. How long before he regretted it?

19. SPENDING COIN

ROH ALMOST FELL out the window when the bells started ringing. Three distinct notes chimed an unfamiliar strain from somewhere close by. Loudly.

Gripping the window sill, he leant out over the shadowy plaza. The space below, cobbled with a green square in the centre, measured about fifty paces across and was hemmed in by buildings. To the west, a narrow belltower soared above the roof line of the Old Kestali Quarter, its blue-and-green cladding illuminated by the newly risen sun. As the bells chimed, people crossed the plaza three floors below, most garbed in fine, brightly coloured garments under dark cloaks. Small groups exchanged hushed greetings before heading down a narrow street towards the belltower.

"Ugh, what's that?" Adehl croaked from behind him. She plunged her head beneath her pillow, holding the edges down around her ears.

Roh smothered a chuckle. Since leaving Tarsah, he'd discovered Adehl was not a morning person. They'd arrived in Dohni yesterday, and he hoped for both their sakes that early morning bells were not an everyday occurrence. The chimes stilled after several minutes, the air ringing with a final, piercing note, and the procession of people slowed. A pair of tibbies landed on the lawn in the centre of the square. At least, they *looked* like tibbies: the black-and-white birds below were smaller than the ones back home, and their warbling song differed slightly.

"What are you doing?"

He turned to find Adehl squinting at him from the bed, her hair in all directions. "I didn't want to wake you." Meeting her look, he laughed. "I didn't reckon on the bells."

"Are those tibbies I can hear?"

"Yep."

She scrambled out of bed and pulled on her mahgan from the day before. He put his arms around her as they stood at the window, sunlight painting the upper floors of the opposite buildings yellow and orange. A man thrust open the doors of a tavern across the square and began setting up tables outside, spooking the tibbies to flight.

Roh and Adehl had taken lodgings in the Old Kestali Quarter at an establishment called the Wild Colt — mainly because they liked the name. The Wild Colt wasn't the lodge where his brethren could be found, but it was clean, functional, with meals included. So far, it seemed adequate, except possibly for the morning bells — even if the price for a week, which Adehl had paid upfront, made Roh's brain bleed.

The morning meal was served in the gatherhall on the ground floor. A few groups of patrons were present when Roh and Adehl entered, including a pair of women, their brown hair cut short in the Kestali style. They were eating hurriedly in silence, long ornaments swinging from their ears. As soon as Roh and Adehl sat down, a server brought over plates laden with moist breakfast cakes made of some type of red grain, smeared in a paste of pulverised nuts. There was also a bowl containing segments of a pink-fleshed fruit and hot, herbal tea to wash it all down.

Just as Roh finished his first mug of tea, the bells rang again. This tune was different — more sedate and somehow sombre but joyous at the same time. All the Kestali in the room, including several newly arrived, surged to their feet and hurried to the door, abandoning partially eaten meals. One man drained his mug and slapped nut paste on a piece of breakfast cake to take with him.

Roh snagged the attention of the server. "Forgive our ignorance, but what do the bells mean?" he asked.

"Birthing ceremony," the server said, balancing plates on a strong forearm. Perhaps seeing their confusion, he added, "The herald bells this morning marked the start of the labour. Then the covenant bells will ring twice an hour for the songs of exchange." He made a face. "Sometimes they go all night. Later today, the bestowal bells will mark the rei-tarn's gift and, an hour or so after that, the proclamation bells will announce the birth." With that, he swept away to continue clearing the tables.

Roh laughed at Adehl's expression. "Some obscure Kestali ritual?" he said.

Over more than a thousand years, Dohni had been occupied and governed by four different nations. No doubt there would be many unfamiliar traditions. How would they celebrate Wintersmorn here? It was only a few weeks until the long days tipped into long nights and, after that, the coldness of winter. He was supposed to be spending the festival at Singing Canyon… Shutting that thought down, he plucked up one of the pink fruit segments, its bitter juices coating his tongue.

"You need clothes," Adehl said, her gaze travelling over

the crumpled attire he'd been wearing for over a week. She smiled ruefully. "We both probably look like vagabonds."

Roh massaged his unshaven jaw. "How much coin do we have?"

"Enough."

He nodded. He had no idea how long their bag of coin would last or how they would replenish it. Normally, he would apply to the Vuusah for anything he needed. Fingering his putrid undershirt, he said, "This can be burned, as far as I'm concerned."

They ventured into the city midmorning as the covenant bells pealed for the fourth time. Walking along a cobbled street, Roh was once again struck by the storm of ellir coursing through the bedrock of Dohni. His llirah thrummed in response.

The Great Market, which they'd passed through yesterday, was easy enough to find again, being less than a mile away. A steady stream of foot traffic and donkey-drawn carts bore them down the hill to the market's entrance. Inside was organised chaos, a massive built-up maze of tiny shops and laneways so narrow the sun barely penetrated. They eventually found a row crammed with vendors selling bolts of wool, flankah, mulberry silk, agave silk and other fabrics. This led to a section of the market devoted to seamsters and tailors, where racks of pre-made garments in many colours and styles cluttered the aisles.

Roh picked at a loose thread on the sapphire-blue tunic Adehl had persuaded him to put on over dark trousers. Clean clothes would be welcome, but this would take some getting used to. It was knee-length, similar to his usual mahgan, but the new tunic was cut to a looser fit. He'd always been more comfortable in the natural tans of undyed flankah and in the leather leggings worn out on the downs.

Then Adehl, who had looked beautiful in everything she

tried on, emerged wearing a long garment in muted tones of purple, deep green and gold. It flowed from her shoulders down to her calves, with a matching sash at her waist, and made her look like a forest queen.

Roh cleared his throat. "That looks nice." She certainly wore it better than any of the other women he'd seen in similar garments.

"It's called a gobeila." Flushing, she bundled her Vuusah garb into a tight ball and shoved it in a sack she'd procured earlier. "You look pretty fine yourself."

He frowned down at himself. "I don't look like me."

"We need to blend in." She trailed one of his long, beaded braids through her fingers, then brought her hand to his jaw. "Is it too much?"

Roh didn't answer for a moment. He'd always taken pride in his Vuusah identity, and the thought of intentionally concealing it made him feel strange. But this was for Adehl's safety.

"I'm sorry," she said. "We've already attracted attention, and I thought —"

"Hush." He gently pushed one of her braids over her shoulder. "I'll adjust."

"You're sure?"

He nodded and took her hand. "I think we still have some shopping to do."

They eventually settled on three outfits each, along with undergarments, comfortable boots made for city walking and some other things Roh needed. They were in the heart of the market, having just purchased a shaving kit, when a raised voice nearby made Roh jerk to a halt.

"Soul bright, zehli. Please present your kalkah licence." It was a light, mocking tenor Roh knew well. Heart slamming against his ribs, he pulled Adehl behind a display of finely crafted leather aprons as the voice continued. "I assume you have it on your person?"

"Do you mind?" A male voice, indignant. "Of course I don't have it. We're in the market."

"In that case, we are authorised by the Atalah to prove your registration using other means."

"Wait, you can't just —" Sounds of a scuffle and a muffled protest. Adehl's grim gaze met Roh's as they listened to exhorters force candour in the middle of the marketplace.

Roh felt ill as the interrogation progressed. These zehla were from Gentah's company. He'd ridden with Chah, the circah's leader, for years and helped train the newest members of his circah. The line of questioning was innocuous enough. Nothing more than confirming the zehli's kalkah registration and his employment details. It was over quickly, but the man's legitimacy only made the incident all the more horrifying. There were protocols around forcing candour, not least that it had to be performed in the presence of a doyen.

Eventually, Chah thanked the man, and Roh sensed the circah moving along the aisle towards the stall where he and Adehl were sheltering. He couldn't meet Adehl's gaze as he pulled in his llirah to leave no recognisable impression.

"I take it you know them," Adehl muttered, lifting one of the aprons from the stand as though intending to buy it. A few stalls away, the harassed zehli uttered a string of curses.

He nodded, drawing back as the exhorters passed. Ninah barked her distinctive laugh in response to something Chah said.

"Did you know they'd be doing that?" Adehl's tone was taut.

"No."

"Forcing candour is not permitted! It's a *violation*."

Roh didn't respond. He'd impelled Frahto while freeing Adehl.

"We been here barely a day," Adehl said. "How many exhorters are here? Is this what you meant by regulating kalkah zehla?"

"No!"

"What then?"

"I don't know." Roh's head pounded, and he pressed fingers to his temple. He hadn't thought about what regulating kalkah zehla would involve in practical terms.

"They said the Atalah authorised it."

"Well, I'm not the Atalah!" He took a few deep breaths. Frahto had accused Roh of letting Gentah control and manoeuvre him, and Roh hadn't even noticed. Their company had been training zehla to wield swords and work in circahs for nearly two years. He should have asked more questions.

"How many here will recognise you?" Adehl asked.

"I don't know."

"Because that could prove a problem."

When they arrived back at the Wild Colt with their parcels, Roh muttered something about going to find a wine merchant. Approving wholeheartedly of this idea, Adehl handed him her dwindling purse. She took all their purchases up to their room, where she flopped down on the bed, her booted feet dangling over the side. A breeze drifted through the window, bringing the tangy scent of citrus.

The potential number of Vuusah in Dohni disconcerted her, especially when some of them knew Roh. The city was supposed to have been a safe haven where she could catch her breath and figure out what she was going to do. She ought to have had time before the Vuusah tracked them down. Yet the exhorters seemed already entrenched in Dohni;

not to mention they were acting beyond the limits of their own precepts. The Bladekor patrol she and Roh had met upon arrival had tolerated the Vuusah presence, albeit grudgingly. Did the guards know the extent to which the exhorters were overstepping?

Adehl had hoped to register as a kalkah zehli immediately, then take on some work. The sea voyage and city entry fee had consumed more than half their coin, leaving funds for little more than a few weeks lodging and ancillary extras.

Now, the prospect of intense scrutiny by the Vuusah gave her pause. She couldn't afford for them to force candour on her as part of the application process. Besides, if any of them recognised Roh…

She hoped he returned quickly with wine.

From somewhere outside came the high-pitched whinny of a horse. Adehl rose and went to the window, but there were no horses in the square below. The horse whinnied again, and she could faintly hear a handler trying to calm the animal.

She made her way down to the Wild Colt's rear courtyard, where a man was trying to gain control of a stunning pewter gelding. The horse strained against a lead rope, head tossing, hooves clattering, clearly favouring his left hind leg. A tall, blond woman frowned nearby, her hand gripping the collar of a stable lad.

"Stay back please!" the woman said as Adehl approached.

Adehl ignored her, keeping her movements fluid and gentle. She allowed the horse to get used to her while she embraced ellir, channelling a soothing thread of energy through the ground to the animal. The gelding tossed his head and snorted. Adehl walked slowly up to him, murmuring soothing words as she threaded ellir between them. Before long, the gelding allowed her to lay a hand, and then a cheek, on his soft, warm neck. The horse trembled and stilled, his llirah subsiding under Adehl's influence. Adehl crooned to him for another minute, then beckoned to the man holding the lead rein.

"You should be able to tend the leg now," Adehl said softly, stroking the beautiful blue-grey neck. "I'll make sure he stays calm."

The man handed the lead rope to the wide-eyed stable lad and came forward with a medical kit. "My thanks, mistress."

The blond woman leant against the wall of the stable building, arms crossed on an expansive chest. She wore her hair in a single horse's tail that reached down her back. "Impressive," she said, keeping her voice even.

"Oooh, that be something special, mistress," whispered the boy clinging to the rope. He looked about twelve, with a shock of brown hair and brown eyes. Round face, dimples. "How you do that?"

"I've worked with horses all my life," Adehl said with a smile.

"As have I," the woman said dryly. "You're a zehli, I assume?"

Adehl nodded. "Are you the stable mistress? I'm very happy to help with your horses while I'm lodging here. I'm Adehl."

"Yes! You teach me what you just did?" The boy's whole body quivered with hope.

"Ai, Chanti. You know what a zehli is," said the stable mistress. To Adehl she introduced herself as Maesenna. "We usually get by just fine with Chanti and Orkoh here, but this horse's injury was neglected by his darkspawn owner. We're grateful for your assistance."

"Do you need a healing?"

"I doubt his owner would pay for it," Maesenna said. "Never fear, Orkoh is good with a poultice, and the leg will be fine. Chanti will look after him." The gaze resting on the boy was fond.

Chanti's chest puffed out. "I look after all the horses."

"I can see they're very lucky," Adehl said. "How many horses do you have here?"

"Seven permanent residents. A few of the local business owners stable their horses with us, and we keep a couple of mounts for hire. Obviously, we also stable guests' mounts." Maesenna ruffled the boy's hair. "Keeps this one out of mischief."

Beneath Adehl's hand, the gelding stood peacefully while Orkoh tended the nasty gash on his leg. Orkoh finished by affixing a poultice and rose. "I don't know how you got him to stand so still, zehli, but I thank you."

"I channelled his pain away," Adehl said.

"Indeed?" Maesenna said. "I did not know such a thing could be done."

"Are there not zehla in the city for hire?"

"It depends on what you wish done and how much you wish to pay. The guild sets its prices high."

That gave Adehl pause. "The guild?"

"The Zehla Guild." Maesenna regarded Adehl curiously. "All zehla in Dohni who hire out their services must register with them."

There was a Zehla Guild in Dohni. Of course there was. *Someone* in this city must have been regulating kalkah zehla all these centuries. Absurdly, Adehl felt like laughing. "Where might I find this guild?"

"It's in Donellon Plaza — less than a mile from here."

"I know the way!" Chanti jiggled with excitement only suppressed, Adehl suspected, by the injured horse.

"Thank you," Adehl said. "I'm curious about these Vuusah exhorters we've seen. How do they fit in?"

Orkoh snorted and Maesenna chuckled drily. "The

hooters have been making a nuisance of themselves for nigh on a year, and it seems all the guild's efforts to be rid of them have failed. Make of that what you will."

"It sounds like an interesting situation," Adehl said. She carefully disengaged her llirah from the gelding's, then stepped aside so he could be led away. "Please let me know if he starts fretting, and I'll come."

Maesenna hesitated. "The owner won't pay you, and we can't..."

"There'll be no charge," Adehl said. "I'm a guest here. I'd like to make sure he's all right."

Roh was waiting for Adehl inside, his eyes bright. "There you are!" He took her hand and drew her towards the front door of the lodging house.

"You promised me wine," Adehl said.

"And I will deliver. It's this way."

He led Adehl through the plazas and narrow streets of the Old Kestali Quarter for about ten minutes, until they arrived at a leafy, cobbled square bounded by shopfronts with coloured awnings. Chalkboards listed the year, grape varieties and vineyard of wine barrels tapped for that day. Patrons clustered at tables in the square, filling the air with a merry hum of conversation.

"They call these Kestali wine taverns *sildai*," Roh said, looking smug. "Will it suffice?"

Adehl grinned.

They spent the rest of the afternoon at a table spending coin they could ill afford. They sampled the wares from three different sildai, the smooth, red wine coming in colourfully glazed pitchers. Other establishments served spiced-meat pastries, exotic fruits, and soft, white cheeses. All the wine came from the Senn nation of Kestale, which occupied the low hills between the Humming Downs and the Merali Demesnes, squeezed between the Shrouded Sea and the Blood Range. According to Roh, the best wine came from the tiny town of Haiffin near Port Monys.

When dusk fell, and staff began lighting strings of lanterns above the square, Adehl finally brought their conversation around to more serious matters.

"We need to decide what we're going to do," she said. "Now that we're here, and the place turns out to be full of Vuusah."

"We can avoid them."

"For how long? Some of them know you." When Roh didn't reply immediately, she said, "I knew they would come after us, but I didn't count on Vuusah exhorters running rampant through the city."

Roh grimaced. "We've seen two circahs."

"In little more than a day. It's not a good sign."

"Are you saying you want to leave?"

Considering the question, Adehl lounged against the chair's backrest and watched a young woman step down from a stool after lighting a lantern. The *Seabird* had brought them to Dohni. It had seemed opportune. If they couldn't hide in the largest, most diverse city in Baljehni…

Could Roh avoid his Vuusah brethren?

Would he?

Adehl sighed. "Either way, we don't have enough coin to leave."

"Oh." Roh scratched his still unshaven jaw.

Adehl almost smiled at his evident consternation. Neither of them was accustomed to worrying about money. "Avoiding them might be our only option. But, whatever we do, we need coin. We're on our own now." At least, Adehl was. Roh could go back. She didn't say it.

"Right."

"I know you're not ready…" Might never be ready. "But I'm going to apply for a kalkah licence tomorrow."

"You just said we need to avoid the Vuusah."

"I learnt this afternoon that I can register without consulting them."

"What do you mean?"

"The stable mistress told me there's a Zehla Guild that oversees such things."

Roh stilled. Then, carefully, he centred his mug on a sunflower in the tablecloth's bright, floral print. "Go on."

Adehl flicked a pastry flake from the surface with a fingernail and repeated Maesenna's words from earlier. Roh dropped his forehead to the table.

"This is a good thing," Adehl said. "We can avoid the Vuusah."

"I'm glad you think so." The words came out muffled.

Eventually, Roh sat up and refilled his goblet. He plucked a pastry off the plate and ate it with ferocious concentration. Adehl sipped her own wine, cool on her tongue with hints of aniseed, and watched Roh trying to come up with, she supposed, an alternative means of earning coin. At least he looked less disgusted with the notion of her becoming kalkah than he had back at Fortune Spring.

"Roh, I need to earn a living. Would you rather I muck out stables?"

"Of course not."

"This is the best way. If we don't earn coin soon, we'll be sleeping in alleys."

"I *know*." He grabbed at his goblet so hard he knocked it over. "Sun's blood," he muttered.

Adehl leapt back as dark-red liquid spread across the tablecloth, besmirching the printed flowers. Roh gathered up the cloth and squeezed out the wine onto a planter box. With careful deliberation, he blotted every drop of red liquid from the wooden table.

"That was a sad waste of Haiffin red," he said, picking up the empty pitcher from the bare, and now slightly damp, wooden table. "I'll get this refilled."

Roh weaved through the tables towards a sildai, disappearing into the gloom. Adehl slowly resumed her seat and hoped none of that wine had spilt onto her new gobeila.

That conversation had gone… about as well as she'd expected.

When Roh returned a few minutes later, carrying the pitcher brimming with wine, he looked stricken. "Fury, I've just gone and spent more coin."

Adehl suppressed a smile. "I believe you just made my point for me."

He muttered something about wine being a necessity. "I just don't see how we let this happen. Allow the Zehla Guild to exist, I mean. Why haven't we done anything about it before now?"

We. Meaning the Vuusah. The word scraped at her. "Maybe that's why the Vuusah are here."

"Maybe."

He swirled wine around his mouth, closed his eyes and swallowed. Had he been a cat, he might have purred. Fascinated, she watched him savour the entire goblet.

When he was done, he poured another. Adehl held out her own to be filled.

Cradling his goblet on the table, Roh said, "I can avoid any zehla who might know me. I promise."

Adehl studied his face. "All right."

"But I'm going to find out what's going on."

20. Circle of Wind

Morning sunshine glittered on the harbour as Roh stepped onto the Lokk Janikk Bridge.

He'd woken early, his mind unsettled as the sea. An afternoon spent dulling his senses with wine had given him nothing but a sore head with which to contemplate his situation: stranded in a foreign city, cut-off from his misbehaving brethren. Irrevocably bound to a woman who was about to become kalkah — and was probably already expelled.

There was nothing to be done about the latter: Adehl was his injaleh. The Vuusah, though… Without stopping to analyse what he was doing, he'd left Adehl sleeping and crept out of their room.

It wasn't difficult to navigate the city's awakening streets. Remembering Tallah's instructions, he asked for directions to Four Nations Plaza and discovered the route marked with signs, made from coloured tiles, affixed to the walls of buildings. The motif for Four Nations Plaza was a white square surrounded by myriad small tiles in shades of blue and green, like the shifting colours of the sea. This sign could be found every fifty paces or so, along with other signs leading to other places.

Roh followed the white squares beneath the shadow of the silent belltower rising high above the Kestali Prayer Hall and across gardens resplendent with pink crepe myrtle blooms. Gardens aside, most of the streets were narrow, the buildings pressing in on the early morning traffic.

Beyond Bridge Gate, the sky opened up again.

The Lokk Janikk Bridge spanned the narrowest point of Dohni's harbour. Built centuries ago, during the Sevikk occupation, the bridge was a wonder of Sevikk engineering — wide enough for carts to pass in opposite directions, long enough that it took minutes to cross.

Roh paused at the crown of the bridge. Behind him, water lapped the wall surrounding the cramped Old Merali and Kestali Quarters. Ahead, on a small promontory at the foot of the bridge, stood Four Nations Plaza, the gleaming, white seat of Dohni's governing council and a symbol of peace after centuries of conflict.

Four Nations Plaza, beyond which — according to Tallah of the Blue Fox — lay the Vuusah lodge.

Roh had no difficulty in locating influences left by his brethren in the stones of the bridge. With dozens of zehla using this route daily, their passage stood out like a loophorn trail up a hill. He followed the trail across the plaza, past buildings he took for administration halls, then through a newer section of the city, all wide streets and unweathered stone.

He arrived at a busy junction. Traffic from five incoming streets flowed around a small plaza, on which stood a monolith, taller than two men and carved in the crude shape of a horse. Long grass grew around the base of the sculpture, lush and green with feathery seed heads, reminiscent of the downs back home. Most of the faces swirling around the plaza bore the dark cast and amber eyes of the Fiugreh clans.

Roh was about to cross the stream of pedestrians and living horses, when he became aware of people scattering on the opposite side of the junction. At first, the reason for the disruption was obscured by the sculpture — but then a circah of exhorters moved into view, and Roh swore under his breath. He casually entered a nearby shop and pretended to inspect its wares. Through a scrupulously clean window, he marked the progress of his former brethren. They sauntered past his hiding place, fortunately not glancing in his direction.

He knew every last one of them.

"See anything you like?" The shopkeeper hovered at Roh's elbow.

Roh prepared to politely extricate himself, then noticed the objects in front of him. They were tiny animals exquisitely carved from coloured stone — swirls of blue, green, dark red. Stupidly expensive. Frivolous. But several were horses in various attitudes — docile grazing, stretched out in full gallop, rolling joyously in a meadow. He traced a finger along the smooth back of a rearing horse carved out of an iridescent, white stone, traces of ellir fizzing beneath his touch. He wanted to buy it for Adehl. Not that they could afford to spend their coin on tiny stone horses. Their lack of funds was something he was trying not to think about.

Outside the stone carver's shop, Roh proceeded carefully through the junction. A signpost indicated the Saddlers Guild to the west; another pointed south to Settlement Quay. The zehla trail led him down a small, residential street between the two.

He came upon the Vuusah lodge sooner than expected. It was broad, white and three storeys tall, with a pair of zehla stationed at the top of a short flight of steps.

Roh sucked in a breath and mentally chastised himself for being a fool, especially after the near miss a short while ago. He didn't recognise the current sentries — thank the bright sun. But if they knew him… It was too late to back out, so he strolled past, trying to look as though he were headed somewhere.

The zehla paid him little attention. It seemed, while he wore the local clothing Adehl had forced him to purchase, no one would take him for a zehli, let alone the supposed Atalah-in-waiting.

It was no excuse. He'd promised Adehl last night he could avoid his brethren. He would do better.

But he still needed answers.

Using back alleys, Roh found his way to a narrow lane diagonally opposite the building. Aside from the two sentries, little marked the building as Vuusah headquarters. Its architecture was unremarkable for this district, which appeared less ancient than the districts on the opposite shore. Like its neighbours, the Vuusah lodge featured a portico in the centre of the building and banks of large windows on the three levels of each wing.

Roh carefully read the impressions coming from the lodge. Overlaying the embedded rhythms of the building were the vibrant llirah of perhaps a dozen zehla present inside. He dared not probe deeper, lest they detect him. There was something unusual in the basement. The rhythms of the heartstorm seemed to swerve around it, like a stream parting around a rock.

He couldn't help thinking it would be so easy to stroll up to the green front door, give his name and be welcomed inside. They might not be expecting him, but they wouldn't turn him away. Under normal circumstances, he'd be staying there.

He could have a drink with Chah and Ninah, whom he

hadn't seen in almost a year, and find out how they'd been faring in Dohni. They could tell him what the Vuusah were doing about this upstart Zehla Guild and explain why Chah had forced candour on that innocent zehli yesterday.

Roh rolled deeper into the shadows of the lane, cold stone pressing into his back. Even if he hadn't promised Adehl, it would have been a terrible idea.

Once the Vuusah knew he was in Dohni, what then?

Voices across the street drew his attention back to the lodge. A Fiugreh woman in a rumpled green mahgan and wild, dark hair staggered down the front steps. The sentries made no move to help her, despite the fact she could barely walk. Roh winced as she stumbled and fell heavily to her knees on the street. She stayed on all fours, gasping, hands clutching at the cobbles. Was she retching?

With horror, Roh realised she was weeping.

He reached out via ellir with some vague notion of soothing her, wishing he dared go out on the street to help her. As soon as his llirah found hers, her head jerked up, her angry amber eyes scanning for threats as she thrust him off. Roh hauled in his energy and withdrew down the lane.

The woman was clearly a zehli — but probably not Vuusah. Kalkah, then. But that didn't explain her presence in the Vuusah lodge. Or why she looked like she'd been incarcerated for a week. In the moments Roh's energy had touched hers, he'd sensed her desperate meld with ellir. She'd plunged into the heartstorm like a deprived drunk seeking oblivion.

By the time Roh returned to the corner, the woman was gone. The same two sentries were chatting casually, one of them giving a shout of laughter.

Roh waited, unsure what he was waiting for. Flies buzzed annoyingly in his face as the morning grew warmer. Light traffic — some carts and horses, but mainly pedestrians —

flowed along the street, and a mounted courier clattered to a halt outside the Vuusah lodge. So far, no one appeared to have taken any notice of Roh loitering. He kept out of sight, using his ears and ellir to mark any changes. It seemed zehla made poor sentries.

About half an hour after the courier's visit, several new voices enticed Roh to sneak another peek at the lodge. A different circah of zehla gathered out the front, making ready to leave on patrol. Roh didn't recognise any of them.

Here was his chance to learn more.

Soon enough, the circah set off in the direction Roh had come. He waited about thirty heartbeats before slipping out of the lane to follow.

Two hours later, Roh found himself returned to the semi-familiar streets of the Old Kestali Quarter.

It had not been a fun two hours. The exhorters had dragged him around the oldest parts of the city while demonstrating that yesterday's incident in the market was far from an isolated event. They had forced candour on three indignant kalkah zehla — one of whom had fainted on the steps of the Auwyn Trade Hall — and demanded to see the kalkah licence of at least five others.

Each time they sighted another zehli, Roh's heart cracked a little more.

The Bold Lynx circah — for that was how they introduced themselves to their victims — now led him to a bustling plaza not too far from the Wild Colt. Plaza Korim was large and round, streets radiating out like the spokes of a wheel. These included a wide road ascending towards the craggy hill dominating the eastern skyline. Buildings topped the distant rise, one bearing a green dome of tarnished copper.

Closer to hand, most of the official buildings surrounding the plaza were tiled in vibrant colours: shades of just about every colour Roh could name — and some he couldn't. The grandest was Kori Lodge, traditionally inhabited by the Kestali delegate to the Four Nations Council. Opposite, on the uphill side of the plaza, stood the Bladekor garrison, off-duty guards lounging in a forecourt. The garrison was blocky and utilitarian, built of dark stone, the only unadorned building.

Roh allowed the exhorters to go on without him. As the circah passed the garrison, the guards out front jeered and hollered.

A statue stood in the centre of the plaza. Carved from red marble, it depicted a woman, three times larger than life-sized, holding a pitcher and a cup. Laying a hand upon the sun-warmed surface, Roh idly allowed the marble's rhythms to flow through him, telling the story of many bird visitors and the devoted attendants who cleaned the statue daily.

Deeper, the heartstorm enticed him. Ellir flowed through the heartrock underlying the city, sweeping his attention towards the hill in the east. The steeper, seaward flanks of the outcrop were wooded below the cluster of buildings at the summit. Inland, the hill flowed into the northern, walled reaches of the city.

With a glance in the direction of the Wild Colt, just a few twists and turns south of the garrison, Roh took Moi Boulevard, the wide, uphill road towards the crag. A flame-haired woman pushing a barrow of small plants told him the hill was called Goldayn Rise and the buildings were Dohni's renowned Heights University.

The gradient increased. Roh missed his horse.

He was not long past a high-walled cemetery in the shadow of Goldayn Rise, which was starting to feel like a small mountain, when he came to the foot of a stairway carved into the face of the escarpment. The path zigzagged back and forth past clumps of greenery clinging to the rock and appeared to provide a direct route to the summit. Men and women wearing red sashes across their chests bustled in both directions.

Roh climbed, lungs and legs burning, the heartstorm bearing him upwards.

At the top, the green-domed building and another bordered a balustraded terrace and viewing platform. Roh sank onto a stone bench to catch his breath. His gaze swept past the city towards Haventown Bay in the south, farmlands and fields to the west, untamed mountains to the north. This land felt far away from the Humming Downs. A persistent onshore breeze swept across the pinnacle, licking the sweat from Roh's skin.

Once he'd recovered from his exertions, Roh became aware of a nagging rhythm tempting him. He unfurled his llirah and opened to the energy spiralling through the embedded core of heartrock. There was an unexpected order to the rhythm, a constraint, as though halfway between chaos and coherency. It was like the mass of heartrock stood ready to mould ellir into a familiar resonant pattern…

Roh surged to his feet.

He weaved through the university, a haphazard arrangement of buildings, paths and quadrangles. Ornate stonework. Pockets of lawn. A growing number of scholars and students bore satchels or piles of books. The place reverberated with a quiet hum of productivity and the silent thrum of ellir.

He came to a path along a stone wall. Although the wall was too high for him to see over, he sensed what was on the other side and followed the path to a wrought-iron gate. Beyond was a lush garden containing many plants he didn't recognise. Weathered pillars of heartrock peeked through the foliage.

His pulse quickened. As he'd suspected, a resonator. A direct conduit to the vast reservoir of ellir surging within the hill. But, unlike the single-pillar resonators he was accustomed to, this was more. This was a resonant circle.

The gate squeaked as Roh pushed it open. Blood fizzing, he strode towards the nearest heartrock pillar, which stood about shoulder height — then abruptly checked his step.

The garden was not empty. It held a man who had been concealed by greenery where he stood near the focus stone. His colouring and the broad plains of his face proclaimed him Fiugreh, but his braids were short, reaching no farther than his shoulders. He wore a red sash over a plain mahgan of burnt orange, and his blue samah bore markings indicative of a limnor zehli from the Selgreh clans. Around a decade older than Roh, he judged.

Having clearly interrupted the man in the middle of a meld, Roh brought forth his best smile. "My apologies for intruding, zehli. I sensed the resonator and couldn't keep away." Most of the pillars in the outer circle were concealed, but he sensed there were seven.

The man scrutinised Roh, eyes narrowing. "May I ask how you learnt of it?"

"The resonator? I felt the coherency in the hill."

"You felt it?"

Roh paused at the scepticism in the man's tone. It had been a long time since anyone doubted something Roh did. Of course, this man didn't know who Roh was. He grinned. "Yep. It's magnificent. I would love to wield it. Once you've finished, of course. I am sorry for disturbing you."

"The Circle of Wind is the property of the university. We do not permit outsiders to *wield* it, as you say."

"No?" Roh's grin faded. "Why not?"

"It's a finely tuned instrument… In fact, few outside the Ellirisi know of its existence."

Roh took in the high wall, the overgrown foliage. It wasn't much of a disguise. The resonator was so vibrant he could almost hear it humming. He decided not to take offence at the implication Roh would mess up its tuning. "What does the university need a resonator for?"

"Research."

Roh battled against a frown. "I'd be interested to know how you use it for research."

The scholar smiled without warmth. "You are visiting Dohni, I think."

"I arrived recently, it's true." Roh glanced down at himself, realised he wore nothing to identify him as a zehli. Even the kalkah zehla he'd seen wore mahgans and samah with markings to denote clan and affinity.

The scholar moved out of the circle. "Perhaps introductions are in order." He held up his palm. Roh met it with his own and allowed their llirah to touch. The man's rhythm conveyed wariness, also considerable affinity and excellent control. "Soul bright and balanced. My name is Gordoh. I am First Scholar of the Ellirisi."

"Soul bright." At the man's pointed glance, Roh grimaced. "My name is Roh."

Gordoh twitched, and Roh watched him make connections. "Roh. Not… Little Atali? *That* Roh?"

"I can't believe that stupid name reached this far."

Gordoh's tone cooled almost to hostility. "You're Vuusah."

For several heartbeats, as the breeze whipped foliage around the stones, Roh couldn't think how to respond. He wanted to declare that of course he was Vuusah. But he had deliberately confined his hair to a single braid and wore a local-style tunic instead of a mahgan. Then, there was Adehl. "I'm not here on Vuusah business," he said. "They don't know I'm here."

"That's painfully obvious. Otherwise, the news would be all over the city."

Roh rubbed the back of his neck. "I would prefer it stay that way."

A bird chittered. Roh shifted under Gordoh's scrutiny. "And I would prefer the Vuusah not learn about the Circle of Wind," the scholar said.

"They'll not hear of it from me." It seemed impossible the Vuusah could be ignorant of the resonator, but Roh was thankful the scholar hadn't asked for an explanation. Perhaps he didn't want to answer questions, either. "You mentioned something called *Ellirisi*."

"We Ellirisi are scholars of ellir."

Scholars of ellir… Sun's blood. "What exactly…"

"Our research is fully sanctioned by the Zehla Guild and the Four Nations Council."

"And the Vuusah?"

A dry laugh. "What do you think?"

Roh didn't know what to think. The idea of a bunch of kalkah zehla researching ellir — whatever that entailed — was just another thing to shatter his brain. "How many kalkah zehla live in Dohni?"

"A few hundred, I suppose."

"As many as that?"

Gordoh regarded him steadily. "About a dozen arrive each year seeking new opportunities."

It seemed a large number to Roh. "They're all members of the, uh, Zehla Guild?"

"It's a requirement of their residence in Dohni. Even the hooters." With a hint of amusement, Gordoh added, "If you stay beyond a month, you will be obliged to join, too." Roh didn't know what expression he'd made, but Gordoh chuckled. "Are you intending to stay beyond a month?"

From his tone, the scholar assumed not. But, in truth, Roh

had no idea. "How many Vuusah are here?" It came out more abruptly than he intended.

"About fifty, at last count. They keep coming." Gordoh speared Roh with a gaze. "Why are *you* here, Little Atali?"

"Personal reasons." Roh straightened. He eyed the resonator. Sun's blood, he itched to get his hands on it, but the scholar stood before it like a guard dog. "Since we're friends now, will you allow me to…"

"Friends?" Gordoh said dryly.

"Not yet perhaps." Roh dredged up another of his most charming smiles. "She'll be in good hands. I promise."

The other man continued to examine Roh. "Friends," he muttered, almost to himself and appeared to reach a decision. "Very well. I grant you leave. Don't make me regret it."

"I'll take good care of her. My thanks, zehli."

Roh waited until Gordoh had gone before moving to the focus stone in the centre of the circle. The stone radiated warmth beneath his hand. At first, he drew the natural heartrock rhythms into him; they were less coherent than before, Gordoh having allowed the earlier pattern to dissipate. But the echo of that pattern was there, the result of repeated use.

Mindful of the resonator's status as a *finely tuned instrument*, Roh didn't mess with it. He wove the same pattern of ellir through the stones above and the rock below. It felt different from a mesh created from a circle of zehla: steadier and completely under Roh's control.

The city opened up to him. He'd never known anything like it. He could probably have discovered a kitten up a distant tree.

But Roh cared little for kittens at that moment. Instead, he set about tracking down all the exhorters in the city.

21. Take your hand

The morning was well advanced by the time Adehl awoke. She lay in the tumbled sheets for a few minutes, listening to the sounds of the square outside. The sweep of a broom against stone, a conversation between two women who were clearly friends, a sign squeaking in the breeze. She threw off the covers, wondering why Roh had let her sleep so long.

The morning meal had long been cleared away when she got downstairs, but she scavenged some watermint tea and bread smeared with nut paste from the kitchen. Roh was nowhere to be seen.

Back in their room, she found a polished nugget of blue agate on the windowsill.

It looked to be from a small bag of mixed stones Roh had deemed essential to purchase at the market yesterday. She picked it up and attuned to the tiny rhythm nudging at her fingertips. Roh's instilled impressions reached her clearly: love, reassurance, apology, absence. Reluctantly impressed, she stared at the stone until the impressions dissipated. It looked like she was braving the Zehla Guild alone.

A glimpse of the stable mistress reminded her she ought to check first on the injured gelding.

In the stable, the straw smelt clean and fresh, with recently oiled leather tack hanging on a wall above sacks of horse feed. The sound of a shovel scraping stone accompanied the ragged whistle of someone hard at work mucking out the last stall in the row.

Chanti straightened as she approached. "Bright day, mistress." He seemed pale and subdued this morning. She hoped he hadn't spent a long night tending to the horse.

"Bright day," she said. "How is our patient this morning?"

"Nightdancer be happy to see you, mistress. His leg be healing good."

Adehl slipped into the stall Chanti indicated and gently greeted the horse. He nuzzled her hand, and she wished she'd brought some slices of apple from the kitchen. "He's doing very well," she said. "Orkoh must indeed be good with a poultice."

The boy grinned.

Adehl wandered down the row of stalls, greeting each inhabitant. She missed being around horses. It had been weeks since her life had been this uncomplicated. Her heart ached for Cloud, left with that clod of a wharf official. She couldn't bear to think of her horse stabled permanently, brought out only when the man felt like prancing about the town. She hoped her father found out and bought him back.

Clinging to that thought, Adehl came to a stall holding a nightmoon horse, black with silver-grey points. Joy jolted through her. "Who'd have thought we'd meet again here, eh, Blackseed?" He nosed her hand, just as he'd used to do, and whuffed at her.

"Why you call him Blackseed?" asked Chanti. "That not be his name. It be Shadow."

Adehl turned to see the boy hanging over the wall from

the adjacent stall. "I know this beautiful lad. I helped breed him out on the downs. We called him Blackseed, although of course he has a new name now. Has he been good for you?" She ran her hands over the gelding's smooth coat and down his legs, teasing at his llirah, trying to gauge his current mood.

Chanti nodded solemnly. "He be a well-behaved animal."

Adehl smiled. "I'm very glad to hear it."

"He like apples with the cores cut out."

"I didn't know that." She reached up to shake the boy's hand. "He's lucky to have you looking after him so well, Master Chanti."

He grinned and reached over the wall with grubby fingers. His hand was warm and work-roughened. But something… Adehl's grip tightened. Something about his llirah felt off.

She unfurled her own energy and reached for his, needing to make sure. Chanti's llirah was bold, vibrant, striking out a melody of sunshine on glass. The boy's whole being seemed to vibrate with it.

"Ow, that hurt, mistress!"

Adehl's gaze sharpened on the boy's face, searching for signs of Fiugreh heritage. His features bore a mix of many races, none of them dominant. But his llirah was bursting out of him. It ought to have been undetectable to casual touch. She probed further to gauge the extent of his raw affinity.

"Please, mistress!"

She became aware of him tugging at his hand, his mouth twisting in distress. His llirah had become so wild she was now afraid to let him go. But she relaxed her grip, and he pulled away, retreating behind the wall, his little head disappearing from her view.

"Chanti!" She rounded the partition into the next stall to

find him sitting in a bed of clean straw, rubbing at his hand. She knelt beside him, and he pulled his hand out of reach.

"You have a fair grip, mistress!"

The boy was shaking. She laid her hand flat, but firmly, on the bare skin of his leg. "Just stay still, please. I'm sorry I hurt you." His llirah gyrated like a firestorm. Adehl doused it as best she could, calming his emotions as she was accustomed to doing for horses. The boy wriggled under her hands. "Chanti, please be still!"

When she'd subdued the wildfire to more of a hearth blaze, Adehl sat back. Sweat trickled from her temples and down her spine. Chanti stared at her, his face pale. He'd stopped protesting after a while, perhaps realising she wasn't trying to harm him. She wondered whether he understood how close he'd come to losing control.

"How do you feel?" Adehl's words came out rough, as though she hadn't spoken for days.

He shrugged.

"Has that happened before?" When he looked wary, she added, "Could you feel the energy inside you? Making you shake?"

Chanti picked at the straw beside him. "Twice before. It happen when I get upset."

"What did you do the other times?"

"Sapling," he whispered. He bounded to his feet and darted past Adehl out of the stall. Fortunately, he didn't go far and pulled open the door of another stall. The bay mare inside nuzzled Chanti's arm as he buried his face in her neck.

"This is Sapling?" Adehl stepped to the other side of the mare's head, stroked her silky black mane. Ellir thrummed through the horse and boy, weaving them together in a meld that anchored Chanti. "She's a beautiful lady."

Chanti didn't respond, other than to press himself closer to the horse. Adehl quietly left the stall but propped herself against the wall outside. She wanted to make sure he was calm before she left. He was at the age when affinity typically manifested in Fiugreh children. Adehl herself had been twelve. A Fiugreh child with affinity would be taken on by the Vuusah as an acoleh, but a pidakah child would have their llirah quelled to a safe level. As would have Adehl, had she not lied her way into the Vuusah. With a pang, Adehl thought of Sorah, the girl back at Fortune Spring. She wondered if the Zehla Guild saw to such things in Dohni. Sapling could not anchor Chanti's rhythm for much longer.

A short time later, she heard Chanti murmuring words to Sapling, then the rustle of straw. He emerged from the stall, tear-stained and dishevelled.

"All right?" Adehl asked softly.

He nodded.

"May I take your hand again? I'll be gentle." She smiled encouragingly, and he allowed her to clasp his hand between both of her own. His llirah had subsided to better levels, but its amplitude was still higher than she'd like. She threaded her own rhythm with his and soothed it further. "Can you feel what I just did?"

He bit his lip. "You made it smaller?"

"Yes. If it starts shifting and burning too much, you come straight to me, and I'll calm it again. As many times as you need me to."

His youthful face softened with relief. "Thank you, mistress," he breathed.

Adehl released his hand. At least he seemed calmer. "Before I leave you to finish your chores, can you tell me how long you've felt the shifting and burning?"

"It be getting worse for a few weeks."

"Can you remember when you first became aware of it?"

He shook his head.

"How long have you had your special bond with Sapling?"

He beamed, looking once again like a twelve-year-old. "Last spring. Sapling understand me."

About six months, then. Thank sweet ellir for the horse. "All right, little colt. Remember what I told you."

He chortled with laughter. "I not be a horse!"

"I was just making sure," she said with a smile.

Outside, the Wild Colt's stable mistress was sweeping the yard.

"Bright day, mistress," Adehl said, then made sure she could still hear Chanti's shovel before continuing. "May I ask you about Chanti?"

Maesenna straightened, broom between her feet. "Is there a problem?"

"No! Well… not exactly. I merely wondered what you know of his family?"

"Sod all," the stable mistress said, with a hint of fondness. "He was a street brat when I found him in the market one time, trying to get acquainted with my horses. He said he had no parents, so I took him in. He's a good boy. The horses will do things for him they won't do for anyone else."

"You're his guardian, then?"

Her gaze narrowed. "Why are you asking? Has he done something?"

Adehl flushed. "No. I apologise. I was just talking to him while admiring your horses. I… He seems to be very fond of Sapling."

"Besotted, poor lad. He'll miss that mare when she's sold."

"She's going to be sold?"

"We have a couple of buyers interested. Sapling's a smart, affectionate horse who'll do best with one rider. She doesn't like being a hire mount."

Adehl would usually appreciate this sentiment. Now, she couldn't think what to say. She didn't know how Maesenna would react if Adehl told her Chanti had anchored to Sapling — or if the woman would even believe her.

She needed to come up with a solution, and she sensed there wasn't much time.

ADEHL MADE three wrong turns on her way to the Zehla Guild, but she finally found Donellon Plaza in the heart of the Old Merali Quarter, surrounded by a maze of narrow streets. When she emerged into the open space, hemmed in on all sides by tall buildings with elaborate entrances, Adehl wiped her brow and headed for a vendor selling something called apple ale in the shadow of the immense Davrayn Trade Hall.

Donellon Plaza hummed with what looked like business activity. The neatly dressed crowd moved purposefully in and out of the trade halls, guilds and lending banks facing the square; many of the more affluent people were trailed by lackeys carrying satchels. The Davrayn Trade Hall was the largest building Adehl had ever seen. Its wide stone steps teemed with merchants and equerries of various nationalities; twin fountains burbled on either side of the steps, and the building's ornate facade was carved with intricate floral patterns.

Fortified by two mugs of apple ale, Adehl ventured through the crowded plaza. Near a bronze statue of Lord Donellon Haas — who, according to an engraved metal plaque, had drawn up the first set of trade regulations for Dohni several centuries ago — she found the Zehla Guild. A modest flight of steps led to wide double doors.

Inside, she found a large entrance foyer flagged in heartrock. For a stunned half minute, Adehl stood motionless as ellir swept up through her feet, skittering like music through her blood. Then someone brushed past her, and she realised she was blocking the door.

Along one of the side walls, two clerks staffed a large desk, before which at least a dozen people queued. Other citizens moved through doors off the foyer or traversed the wide staircase leading up to a mezzanine. Adehl identified several zehla by their braids, mahgans and samahs, but they were easily outnumbered by people bearing the diverse colouring of the Dohni population.

She joined the line before the service desk. No one paid her any attention, but she overheard enough to surmise most of the petitioners sought to engage zehla for a particular task, negotiate long-term contracts or make complaints. The sums of coin bandied about were surprisingly high.

When Adehl reached the front of the line, she met with a sour-faced woman with mid-brown hair wearing a grey gobeila trimmed in sky-blue. Hoping the woman's expression was due to the obnoxious man she'd been serving, Adehl smiled and wished Roh were here to exude charm.

"Soul bright," Adehl said. "I'd like to register as a kalkah zehli, please."

The clerk looked Adehl up and down. "You're a zehli?"

"Yes." Perhaps she ought to have worn her mahgan and samah, after all. She fingered the velinkah beads in her hair.

The woman thrust out her hand. "Documents." When Adehl failed to comply quickly enough, the clerk snapped out, "The line behind you is only getting longer."

Adehl produced her official arrival papers.

The clerk glanced down and frowned. "Where's the rest of it?"

"What else do you need?"

"Zehla papers, letter of recommendation, fixed abode..." Then she named a sum of coin too big to contemplate.

Adehl stared. "I need all that?"

The woman's upper lip curled. "We have standards to maintain."

"But —" Adehl bit off her protest and twisted her features into another smile.

"Come back when you have your documentation in order." The woman made a note in a ledger, then returned Adehl's papers and looked to the next person in line.

"Wait." Adehl moved to block a robust Sevikk man from nudging her aside.

"If you cannot pay, we have reasonable indenture terms," the clerk said.

"What if I can't —"

"All practising zehla *must* be members of the guild and abide by our code of conduct. Rules of the city."

"Code of conduct?"

The clerk gestured at a sign on the wall. "Any zehli breaching the code will be dealt with. Anything else?"

Numb, Adehl shook her head.

The woman tapped the ledger near her hand. "I've logged your kalkah registration inquiry. Be sure to bring all the required documentation soon."

"But —"

"If that is all, please have a bright day."

ON ADEHL'S RETURN TO the Wild Colt, she found Roh sitting alone at a corner table in the downstairs taproom, a mug of ale before him. He looked up when she entered and waited for her to slide onto the bench seat opposite. "You don't look happy," he said.

She nudged his boot with her own by way of greeting. "It's been a strange day."

Roh pushed his mug towards her. "You too?"

She sipped the dark, bitter ale and pulled a face. "You can keep that." At her signal, the server arrived, and she ordered her own drink.

"What's apple ale?" Roh asked.

"A Merali brew I discovered this afternoon."

Roh grunted. He looked… weighed down by something. Perhaps not surprising, given the past couple of days. He hadn't looked this grim since they'd departed her father's house.

"What happened today?" she asked. "Where did you go?"

"I followed some exhorters around for a while."

"And?" Judging by his mood, he'd learnt nothing good.

He toyed with the handle on his mug. "Then I climbed up that great mountain of heartrock. Goldayn Rise. It's the university up there, you know. I met a zehli who claims to be researching ellir."

Adehl blinked at the abrupt change of subject. "How does someone research ellir?"

"I wish I knew." He then launched into a story about discovering a resonator called the Circle of Wind and meeting the First Scholar of a group called the Ellirisi. The words tumbled out rapidly into a heap for Adehl to sort through. Even she felt some shock at the notion of zehla being scholars of ellir, but she found herself intrigued.

"He wouldn't tell you about their research?" she asked.

"Only that they use the resonator." Roh rubbed the back of his neck. "He eventually allowed me to use it. It's… something else. I found you easily."

"When I was in Donellon Plaza?"

"Maybe. I don't know."

Adehl examined his face. "Who else did you find?"

Roh shifted in his seat. "I tried to find exhorters. They're marching around in groups of six…That stands out." A grimace. "I identified at least eleven circahs."

"Eleven."

"At least."

Adehl took a long draught of her apple ale, which had arrived during Roh's recitation. "Could you tell how many would recognise you?"

"Three circahs, I think."

"That's not so bad." She hesitated. "You can avoid them… right?"

Roh nodded, but Adehl sensed what avoiding his brethren would cost him. He picked up his empty mug and frowned, so Adehl offered him hers.

"Why wouldn't the scholar tell you anything?" she asked.

"I rather thought it was because he didn't want me running back to the Vuusah." He sniffed the apple ale and sipped cautiously. "Hey, this is good."

"Does he know who you are?"

A brief nod. "I couldn't avoid the greeting."

"He must have been curious as a cut-eared cat."

"Without doubt." Roh's thumb traced the worn edge of the table. "I didn't know what to tell him."

Adehl blew out her cheeks. She couldn't blame Roh for his low spirits and hated the fact he was in this situation solely because of her. He was Little Atali and deserved to proclaim his identity from the highest peak. This being their third day in Dohni, he'd had time to reflect. Perhaps he was trying to find some way of broaching a difficult subject.

She reached across the table to take his hand, steeled herself for the words that needed saying. "You don't have to do this."

"Do what?"

"Any of it." In the face of Roh's blank incomprehension,

she cradled his hand between her own. "I'm the one who can't go home. I don't even know what comes next."

"You think I'm going to abandon you here?"

"I wouldn't blame you if you did. You know I went to the Zehla Guild today. They won't let me register without my zehla papers. I'll probably have to muck out stables for a living."

"Adehl…"

"If you're going to be Atalah, how can you stay here with me?"

He looked, of all things, hurt. "Stop talking. Just stop."

"I can probably never return to Tarsah or the Humming Downs. I've probably been… expelled." Just saying the word made her want to weep. "If you stay here, too…"

"Enough." He pushed his bench out from the table and held out a hand. "Come here. Please."

Slowly, she rose and circled the table to stand beside him. He pulled her onto his lap. Their llirah threaded together, and he offered candour, showing her the truth of his soul.

"I'm not going to leave you. I know that means…" His mouth worked, as if trying to form words. In the end, he shook his head. "I admit it's… hard. But I'm not going anywhere without you." His fingers toyed with the beads woven into the srih wound loosely around her wrist.

"What happens when they threaten to expel you, too?"

"We'll deal with it. They can't force me to be Atalah, you know."

"You'd give that up?"

He rested his forehead against her temple, his breath warm on her cheek. "Jaleh, I already have."

She believed him. With their llirah melded, she would sense anything untrue. Even so, it hardly seemed possible.

Leaning into him, her heart thudding at all the things he seemed to be saying, at the surety in every ripple of his llirah,

Adehl knew it was time to give him something in return. She needed to accept and believe he knew his own mind, to stop assuming that his impulsive decision to board the *Seabird* would ruin his life.

She needed to trust him.

She lifted her arm. When she had woven her srih as a twelve-year-old, she'd imagined the moment when she'd bestow one of them — where she'd be, how she'd feel, the faceless man. Her brother had teased her shamelessly about the likelihood her srih would be rejected. None of those imagined scenarios came close to the reality of being exiled in a strange city with a man she'd known only a few weeks. Slowly, she began to unwind one of the srih from her wrist.

His hand stilled hers. "Not here," he whispered hoarsely. His llirah had gone wild and irregular, and Adehl sensed him trying to control it. The srih scratched at her suddenly sensitive skin. He nudged her off his lap and took her hand, their drinks abandoned on the table.

Strangely breathless, Adehl followed Roh up the stairs to their room. He fumbled with the lock, releasing her with a curse to use both hands, then shouldered the door open. Adehl closed and bolted the door behind her, leant against its timber surface as Roh paced to the far window and opened it. Then he turned to look at her, and their gazes locked. Adehl's heart pounded fast. She didn't think she could move.

But she had to. The next move was hers.

Once again, her fingers crept to the srih around her left wrist and began unwinding it. She trembled and bit her lip with vexation as the beads and tiny metallic loops caught as they slid past each other. Roh didn't move, his face soft and intent. It seemed to take an eternity, but finally the single long loop of the srih slid off her wrist and dangled from her fingertips.

Holding Roh's gaze, Adehl crossed the room towards

him. He was braced against the windowsill, his knuckles white. She stopped, waited until Roh raised a hand and traced her cheek. Gently, she reached up and caught it. For a long moment, she held his hand between hers, smoothed her fingers along the tanned skin as she studied it. Unable to help herself, she glanced up again, and the heat in his eyes made her mouth dry.

She arranged their left hands to lie palm to palm. His fingers threaded between hers, his grip as strong as the ellir that cascaded through them. With her free hand, she wound the srih around their joined wrists. He stood still as she performed the ceremonial binding. When she was done, she raised her gaze to his once more, reached for her voice.

"Roh, with this srih I bind my heart to yours. Will you consider yourself bound?" The words came out scratchy and soft.

He took a moment to reply. The look he gave her seared her soul, and Adehl could hardly breathe. Finally, his mouth moved, but it was several heartbeats before the words came out. "Adehl, I have been bound by you since first we met. Thank you for this honour in wearing your srih." He drew their bound hands to his breast. "I will guard and protect your heart for all eternity."

"Those aren't the proper words," Adehl said.

"Best I can do under the circumstances," he said shakily, before pulling her to him. They stood together, hands clasped between them, her head against his shoulder. His other hand stroked her back. After a while, he said, sounding more in control of himself, "I thought this day would never come."

"I needed to be sure." When he drew back, she shook her head, kissed him softly. "Not that. I was sure of my *heart*. But..." She stared at their bound hands. "You're giving up everything to stay here with me." She unwound the srih so she could extract her hand.

"Adehl…"

Ignoring him, she fumbled with the srih as it came away. He caught it in his fingers as she pulled it through. "Hold your hand still," she said.

"It's beautiful," he said as she wrapped the srih around his forearm. When she was done, he took her hand and held their identically wreathed wrists at chest level.

"Looks good on you," she said around the lump in her throat.

Gently, he tipped her face up to his, the beads around his wrist tinkling. "Thank you for trusting me."

His face held only sincerity.

In this moment he was hers, always. She looped her arms around his neck and hoped it would be enough.

22. Hunting dogs

ADEHL FITTED the halter and eased Nightdancer out of the stall. He came willingly, nosing at her hair as though expecting to find food there, and stayed relaxed as he walked around the yard. He seemed to enjoy the sun warming his pewter flanks after the cool shadows of the stable.

Maesenna looked up from the saddle she was mending and examined the gelding's walking gait. "That leg's healing nicely." Over the past few days, Maesenna had ceased expressing surprise at Adehl's attentions to the horse. Adehl had visited Nightdancer twice daily and performed a healing ritual with Roh's assistance. Being an empathiser, she usually left healings to others; but she understood the basics, and the strength gained from her meld with Roh had boosted her efforts. The injury had responded well to the gentle enhancement of the body's natural healing processes. "You won't see any coin from old Wonnai, though," the stable mistress added.

Adehl huffed a laugh. "I'm aware."

Payment would have been nice — especially given her dwindling purse — but Adehl would never have withheld her aid. Still, her work with the horse gave her hope. Perhaps she could earn a living tending horses without a kalkah licence. It would be easy enough to hide her empathiser ability if she worked inside a stable or out in a field. Such a role would be similar to that she'd always intended to take on for her father. Uncomplicated. Useful. Rewarding.

She certainly needed to find *some* means of earning coin. After tomorrow, they would owe another week's lodging.

Three days had passed since her first, abortive visit to the Zehla Guild. A return visit to speak with a different clerk had yielded the same advice, along with the information that zehla without papers could instead verify their legitimacy under candour. Additionally, the average indenture period for zehla who couldn't pay the joining fee was three years, while further loans could be secured at high rates of interest. The guild wouldn't budge on the mandatory reference from another Zehla Guild member.

Meanwhile, Roh had taken to long, solitary rambles through the city. Exploring, he said. Acclimatising. Each morning, he'd been gone by the time Adehl had awoken, but she now knew to look for one of his message stones. He'd brought back descriptions of the ancient fortifications along the waterfront, Kinglord Park and its Merali temple, the goods available in the artisan district, Four Nations Plaza across the harbour. More than once, he'd dodged exhorters patrolling the streets, laying eyes on seven different circahs so far, including three from Gentah's company. Each day, Adehl waited for him to tell her he'd been recognised, or that word had arrived, and the hunt had begun.

If she and Roh remained in Dohni, discovery felt inevitable. Especially with Roh tempting fate out in the city.

Adehl didn't call him on it, though. Roh couldn't stay cooped up at the Wild Colt every day. She couldn't even press him to find employment; the notion was laughable.

All Adehl could do was brace herself for the Vuusah to catch up with them. Roh kept saying he wouldn't let them quell her, but what could he do against dozens of Vuusah? She wanted to run far, far away. But, without funds, they were trapped.

And then there was Chanti.

Nightdancer snorted, as though bored with walking in a circle. Satisfied with his progress, Adehl led him into the shade and secured his rein to an iron ring set in the wall. She began working a brush through the horse's soft coat.

From her seat nearby, Maesenna hollered for Chanti, who came bounding out of the stable. "I be here, mistress!"

"Good lad. Draw some water for Nightdancer, please. Then prepare his carrot."

Adehl watched Chanti as he sprang to do Maesenna's bidding — pumping water into buckets and lugging them across the courtyard to fill the trough. Beneath the shock of dark hair, his dirt-smeared face was pale and pinched. When the trough was full, he replaced the bucket on its hook and scampered into the stable. Adehl heard the telltale squeak of the hinge on Sapling's stall.

"Don't forget the carrot!" Maesenna called.

Chanti didn't respond.

Adehl released a breath. Aside from tending Nightdancer, she'd spent hours helping Chanti with his chores as an excuse to keep an eye on the boy. She made sure to calm his llirah each morning and night. He squirmed under her hand — and continued to make frequent visits to Sapling's stall throughout the day. Adehl couldn't tell if this were habit or a sign his llirah was becoming more volatile. Either way, she knew her empathiser skills would soon not be enough.

The thought of Chanti's llirah going wild made her ache. But the more time she spent with the boy, the more she shied away from the obvious solution. Who was she to demand an innocent child be quelled?

Helping Chanti withstand the tug of the heartstorm had become her daily mission. Even had they coin enough to escape Dohni, Adehl knew she could never abandon him.

After a time, Chanti re-emerged with a carrot cut into pieces. He palmed them between Nightdancer's lips, crooning to the horse under his breath.

"There you go, bright lad," Adehl said with a final stroke of the brush. Nightdancer nosed Chanti's ear, and the boy's grin split his face. Smiling, Adehl beckoned for Chanti to follow as she led Nightdancer into the stable. He slipped ahead, opened the door to a loosebox with fresh straw. It wasn't the horse's usual stall, and Adehl raised her brows.

Chanti's face flamed. "I not be finished yet."

Adehl removed Nightdancer's halter and got him settled, then extended her hand. "Let me see."

He put his hands behind his back. "I be fine."

"Is the shifting and burning getting worse?"

"No."

"Has it made you shake again?"

He set his mouth.

"Chanti, remember what I said…"

"I be busy," he said, shoving past her. "Stalls need be cleaned."

Adehl sank against the door, her head thunking on the timber. Behind, the horse snorted, then came the wet pour and stench of urine. Returning with a long-handled fork, Chanti grumbled something about animals abusing fresh straw, then applied himself to cleaning out Nightdancer's usual box. The boy worked in silence, his iron tools scraping stone. Adehl waited. She couldn't leave yet, not until Chanti started whistling.

After a time, he came and fidgeted before her, his eyes pools of dark brown. "I be sorry, mistress."

Adehl suppressed the emotion clogging her throat and took his proffered hand. "It's all right, little colt." His rhythm burned like bright sunshine on glass. She wove her llirah through Chanti's, doused his energy to something resembling dawn light on water. It took longer this time.

Chanti didn't release her hand. "I be scared, mistress."

"I know." She pulled him into a tight hug, his thin, wiry body shaking. He buried his face in her shoulder. "I promise I'll help you, little colt."

Even if she didn't yet know how.

MIDAFTERNOON, Roh arrived in the stable doorway. "And here, again, I find you."

He braced bare arms either side of the jamb, Adehl's srih tight around his left biceps. His grey-and-blue sleeveless tunic flowed over loose grey trousers, a woven holdall slung across his chest. His single braid held strands woven with velinkah beads.

Adehl felt warm at the sight of him. She laid down the bridle she'd been mending while Chanti undertook tasks for Maesenna.

"Come out for a walk with me," he said. "There's music in the gardens."

She hesitated. Chanti had finished the horse stalls without further incident, whistling even. It would be good to get out and see some of the city.

"Please, jaleh. It's not like Maesenna is paying you to

stitch leather…" He let the words fade. "You've been closeted out here for days."

"I like being around horses."

He moved into the building. "I'll start to think you like the horses more than me," he said, his tone only half teasing.

Adehl rose from the hay bale she'd been sitting on. She didn't know why she hadn't mentioned her concerns about Chanti to Roh. But the longer she kept quiet, the harder it became to do so. She put her arms around his neck. "Today, there's no contest."

"You'll come?" Roh said, enfolding her in his warmth.

He smelled of sweat and dust and… incense. "Mmm. What temple have you been visiting?"

"The Temple of Sarkk," he said with a grin. "You should see it. There are a hundred Sevikk priests doing whatever it is they do. They allow visitors into the temple proper for just one hour at midday. But you can still hear the chanting."

"No new Vuusah atrocities, then?"

"Nothing to speak of."

"All right. Let's hear this music."

About half a mile from the Wild Colt, past the Kestali Prayer Hall, the Pioneer Gardens sprawled along the boundary between the Old Merali and Kestali Quarters. Paths wound through shady lawns, the air scented with cut grass. A grove of crepe myrtle trees bloomed in resplendent pinks, crimson and white. From another part of the gardens came the sweet tune of pipe and harp, then the roar of applause.

Roh went over to investigate the performance, but Adehl paused near a massive fig tree, where roots as thick as her torso grappled with the ground. The manicured lawns were nothing like the wild grass of the Humming Downs, but she stooped to unlace her boots, succumbing to the urge to feel grass between her toes. She closed her eyes as ellir bounded out of the ground beneath her bare feet.

After nearly a week in Dohni, she'd seen barely any of the city — just the triangle between the Wild Colt, Donellon Plaza and the wharf. She'd crossed these gardens several times but never stopped to enjoy them. No wonder Roh had dragged her out. He must think her demented to be working for free in the stables instead of exploring the oldest city on the continent of Baljehni.

Keeping her eyes closed, she turned her face towards the warmth of the sun, ellir sweeping through her. She reached out for the hill where the university stood, shivered at its massive energy.

A hand landed on her back. For a heartbeat, she thought it was Roh, but energy clawed at her, intrusive, and she twisted out of the grasp. "Get away from me!"

A pair of white teeth flashed in a dark, broad-cheeked Fiugreh face. The woman wore her bundle of long, narrow braids tied with a piece of cord, and her srih wound around her upper arms. To her zehla brethren moving alongside her, she said, "We were right." One of them kicked Adehl's discarded boots to the side.

"What do you want?" Adehl asked, although she knew. She cursed herself for letting her guard down. Roh had been wandering the city for days without coming face to face with Vuusah zehla, yet Adehl had not lasted half an hour. To think she'd earlier mentally accused Roh of tempting fate. This could be the end of everything, right now. Her heart thudded painfully.

The circah's leader examined her. The sides of his head were shaved beneath a riot of braids, and he wore a gold ring through his left ear. "You a zehli?"

Adehl pulled her rhythm close and gave a tight nod.

"Let me see your kalkah licence."

"Why?"

"It's just routine."

"Routine what?"

"Routine *check*. By decree of the Atalah." He held out his hand impatiently. "Your licence. Otherwise, I'll start to get suspicious."

This was bad — even without the possibility that word of her misdemeanours had already arrived from Tarsah. All kalkah zehla, including those back home, had to apply for licences; there was little excuse for not having one. And if she denied being kalkah, they'd demand to know why she wasn't lodging with the Vuusah.

Roh had told her what they did to zehla who possessed kalkah licences. What would they do to someone who didn't?

Adehl crossed her arms. "You have no right to demand anything of me."

The exhorters laughed mirthlessly and spread out around her like hunting dogs circling prey. Adehl knew what was coming and bolstered her llirah — for all the good it would do.

"Do you wish to reconsider?" their leader asked calmly as they pressed in around her.

"Can't say that I do," she said. "I don't answer to you."

"Don't say I didn't warn you." Two sets of hands grabbed her, twisting and burning her skin. Another invasive probe of ellir as the zehla wove their llirah into a resonant mesh, the ellir in the city's bedrock making it effortlessly strong.

"You insufferable stoneheads," she hissed, trying to fend off their attack. "Take your hands off me!"

"It's just a routine check," the zehli with the earring said, sounding bored. He nodded to the other exhorters.

The resonant mesh engulfed Adehl's llirah, swamping her rhythm. She took a sharp breath. Her sense of self was flattened, overwhelmed by the artificial rhythm enforced by the circle of zehla. It was like drowning without knowing which way was up. The zehli held out his hand. "Let's try that again. Your kalkah licence, please."

Mind swimming, Adehl hardly knew what was happening as her hand dived into her holdall to produce the papers she'd been issued on arrival to the city.

He scanned the documents. "Nice to meet you, Adehl." He looked up. "But I asked for your kalkah licence."

"I don't have one," she heard herself say.

"Why not?"

"I don't have the required documentation."

"What are you missing?"

"All of it."

"Hoi!" The distant cry washed over Adehl as she waited dreamily for the next question. "Chah! Ninah! Leave her alone, you bloodheads!"

"By all the stones," one of them said.

The suffocating press of rhythm abruptly shredded, and Adehl found herself gasping for breath. Around her, the zehla attacking her all stared at Roh bolting across the grass towards them. She wrenched herself out of their slackened grips.

"Keep away from her!" Roh shouldered through the exhorters to get between them and Adehl. "What in the blighted sun are you *doing*?"

AFTER DAYS of dodging and ducking his Vuusah brethren all over Dohni, Roh relished the opportunity to declare his presence and shout at somebody. He'd been forcing his ire into a too-small space since arriving, but the sight of Adehl, face pale and jaw slack, at the mercy of these zehla had made him explode.

The fact they were all zehla he knew from home meant he

could really unleash. "What the fury is going on in this city? It needs to stop!"

Chah had the galling cheek to approach him with a blazing grin. "By all the stones, Roh. What are you doing here?"

Roh only just stopped himself from slapping away the hand Chah raised in greeting. "Answer me! Why are zehla roaming the streets tormenting each other?"

Chah's grin faded into inscrutability. "Routine kalkah check."

"Routine? You were impelling her!" Roh pressed fingers to his breastbone, as though that could keep him from flying apart. "You're Vuusah. You can't just —"

"We can, actually," Chah said. "That's what we're here for, remember?"

"You're supposed to be *regulating* zehla, not violating their person. She wasn't doing anything wrong. They're *never* doing anything wrong. I've lost count of how many times I've witnessed unsanctioned forced candour over the past few days…" He broke off when Chah's eyebrows shot up, and the other zehla shifted uneasily. Over at the open-air theatre, the musicians played a merry tune on pipes and strings.

"Actually, the Atalah did sanction —"

"I don't believe it. I *refuse* to believe it." Roh's words resounded in the charged silence. The six exhorters faced him. Right now, they didn't feel like brethren. Adehl edged up beside Roh, her llirah swirling like a hurricane.

Chah rubbed the side of his shaved head and flicked a glance at Adehl. "You know why we're here, Roh. Why are *you* here?"

Roh struggled to get himself under control. He'd thought he knew all the reasons why exhorters had been sent beyond the borders of the Humming Downs, but now he wondered how much Gentah had concealed from him — and why. Acid climbed up his throat.

But shouting at Chah would not get him answers. He needed to remain calm. At least they'd barely acknowledged Adehl's presence since Roh had arrived. In a more moderate tone, he said, "Why are you holding kalkah zehla inside the lodge?"

"What are you talking about?"

"Don't lie to me. I'm not in the mood. There was a woman, three days ago."

Applause for the musicians playing on the other side of the gardens.

"You were at the lodge?"

"I was on the street," Roh said.

Beside him, Adehl made a stifled sound. He hadn't told her about visiting the Vuusah lodge. *Watching* the lodge, he amended. The first time, he'd forgotten to mention it after learning of the Ellirisi scholars — then she'd bestowed her srih, and his mind had stopped working. He'd returned to the Vuusah lodge the following day. For a time, he'd lurked in the alley across the street, remembering the woman weeping in the dust, until he accidentally caught the eye of Menkah, one of the zehla he knew. Berating himself, he'd fled. After that, he'd been ashamed… of his brethren, of himself.

"Why didn't you come inside?" Chah asked.

"Why did the Vuusah incarcerate and torture a zehli?" Roh held Chah's gaze in a contest of wills. They'd been friends once, but ten months in Dohni had whittled away Chah's openness. Roh's friend wouldn't have clamped his jaw and waited for Roh to throw himself off his horse. Once, Chah would have told Roh anything he wanted to know.

The rest of the circah fidgeted.

Adehl pressed closer to Roh, their arms touching. "Sounds

like torturing kalkah zehla has become a habit," she said. "How long before the Zehla Guild steps in?"

As one, the exhorters swung amber glares her way. Maybe they truly had forgotten her presence, because they obviously hadn't expected to see Adehl pressed up against him. Long-faced Dorteh muttered something under his breath, and Chah's brow furrowed. It was Ninah who wiped sweat off her face and said, "You know this kalkah, Roh?"

"She's not —" He broke off. Adehl would eventually find a way through the guild's obstacle course and secure a kalkah licence. "You could say that."

"Hoi!" Ninah strode forward, her gaze fixed on the srih around Roh's arm. She flicked a finger through some of the beads. "When did *this* happen? Come to that, what are these clothes you're wearing?"

Roh's fingers twitched, but he stopped himself from adjusting the flowing folds of his tunic. The heavy braid tugged at his scalp. The zehla all stared as though he were a stranger.

After a long silence, Chah said, "Is she why you're not staying at the lodge?"

"It's none of your concern."

"She trick you? You need us to take care of it?"

"Of course not!"

Adehl lifted her chin. "Stop talking about me as though I'm not here. I'm the one you stoneheads recently violated, remember?"

Chah exchanged glances with the rest of his circah, and Roh released a slow breath. He'd never had this much trouble with his brethren before. He was the cursed Atalah-in-waiting — at least as far as this lot knew. Drawing himself upright, he wished, not for the first time, for a handspan more height. "Tell me about this so-called Zehla Guild."

A pause, then Chah said, "They're a bunch of fire-cursed

upstarts. There's been little Vuusah intervention in Dohni for centuries, and the Zehla Guild has amassed considerable control. Not only are they charging exorbitant fees, but they've adapted our precepts into their own code of conduct — if you can believe their impudence. But we'll sort them out."

"That's why you're here in such numbers? To reassert authority?"

"Exactly. Believe me, we're greatly outnumbered."

"I heard *all* zehla living in Dohni must join the guild." Roh could still hardly believe it.

Chah scowled. "For the present."

Adehl cleared her throat. "I assume that means you're working under the guild's aegis?" she said.

"I assume you're jesting."

"Not at all. They must have records of all the zehla in the city. It would save you from wearing out your boots chasing after phantom rule breakers."

"I don't recall asking your opinion."

Roh brushed the back of his hand against Adehl's. "How has the guild responded to Vuusah presence?" he asked.

Chah shrugged. "They can't do anything. The Four Nations Council authorised our intervention."

"But why this approach? The street patrols, forcing candour... Surely, it will only aggravate the situation."

"Doyi Palvemah says it's necessary."

"Is it working?" Adehl asked sweetly. "Because it seems to me —"

"Who *are* you anyway?" Chah asked, his brow furrowed.

"Oh, can you not read? I thought, since you've still got my papers..."

Chah looked down at the documents he held in evident surprise. He made a show of reading through them. "Adehl... no named company..."

Adehl snatched them out of his hands, and Roh said, "She's with me."

Ninah sniggered. "We can see that, Little Atali. I'd love to hear that tale over a drink."

Roh flinched at the nickname. Once, he *would* have taken this conversation to a sildai and shared stories over a pitcher of Haiffin wine. But Adehl bristled beside him, almost as though reading his thoughts, and he reflected she had more reason to poison the jug than share it. "Perhaps later," he said.

"You know where to find us," Chah said. He flicked a doubtful glance at Adehl. "One of our circahs reported an encounter with two new Vuusah zehla about a week ago. Was that you?"

"I can't talk about why we're here. Leave it alone."

"Right." Straightening, Chah gathered his circah with a glance.

Roh said, "I still want to know —"

"We need to keep moving," Chah said. "If you have more questions, how about you visit the lodge and speak to Doyi Palvemah yourself?"

"Fine."

Chah glanced at Adehl as his circah moved into formation behind him. "I apologise if we overstepped, zehli." To Roh he added, "We'll see you at the lodge?"

"Join us for ale!" Ninah said.

Roh managed a tight nod.

He couldn't look away as the circah crossed the park, trampling dandelions and sending tibbies into the air. As they passed the towering statue of a figure with outstretched arms, a few of them glanced back over their shoulders. Roh jerkily lifted a hand in acknowledgement.

Adehl crossed the grass to retrieve her boots and sat to pull them on. "Are you going to have an ale with them?"

"No."

"Why not?"

He heard the unspoken accusation in her tone. "I never intended to speak to any of them at the lodge," he said, lowering himself to the grass opposite her. He caught her hand and gently pressed their threaded fingers into the cool blades of grass between them.

"What then?"

"Jaleh, I was only watching, I promise." With his other hand, he drew her forehead to his, resting his fingers against the back of her neck. They sat thus for long minutes, their blended llirah resonating with the heartstorm of ellir. An ant crawled up Roh's arm.

Sitting back, Adehl said, "I'm sorry I let them sneak up on me." She resumed lacing up her boots, tugging so hard one of the laces almost snapped. "So stupid."

"Those bloodheads —"

"Can go die in the deadlands," Adehl said viciously.

"Are you all right?"

She glowered at the patch of grass where they'd caught her. "It was horrible. But I'm fine."

"Sun's blood, when I saw them…"

"I'm just thankful they knew nothing of my other sins."

"Me too." Roh pressed his hands harder into the grass, seeking comfort in the energy. In many ways, he felt better for the confrontation. He'd got some of his questions out, even if he didn't have the answers. But he couldn't change the fact that the Vuusah now knew he was in Dohni, and they knew Adehl by sight and name.

They would be curious, possibly suspicious. Would they search for him immediately? With the resident doyen apparently caring little for Vuusah protocols, he and Adehl would need to be extra careful — especially once the local Vuusah learnt the truth of Adehl's lineage.

"Roh." Adehl plucked a dandelion from the grass, twirled

it between her fingers. "You could go have that ale. Find out what's going on."

He scrubbed hands over his face, then hauled Adehl to her feet.

"You don't want to?" she asked as they started towards their lodging. The lengthening shadows sliced the grass into segments, insects humming and zipping through the air.

In truth, it was tempting. But he suspected his imagined evening of camaraderie and shared stories would unfold somewhat differently. "I think it's too late for that," he said.

23. A FEW INQUIRIES

THE FOLLOWING MORNING, Roh selected a smooth, green stone from his drawstring bag. Cupping the stone between his palms, he infused it with impressions and, upon consideration, left it on top of the door jamb.

"What if I can't reach it there?" Adehl murmured.

"No peeking." He'd thought she was asleep. Instead, she smiled up at him from the nest of blankets, her hair all mussed, features bed-smooshed. He clambered across the bed and kissed her. "Sure you won't come with me? I'll wait."

He was returning to Heights University. Yesterday's encounter with Chah's circah had weighed upon Roh all night. Now the Vuusah knew he was in Dohni, he felt exposed. Worse, it endangered Adehl.

Roh needed to know more about Vuusah activities and why Chah had so blatantly evaded Roh's questions. Confronting the doyen directly felt… unwise. The First Scholar of the Ellirisi had struck Roh as someone who wasn't cowed by the Vuusah. Someone who might be persuaded to provide answers.

Adehl fingered the beads he'd painstakingly threaded through his hair. "Not today." She sounded regretful. "There are things I need to do here."

Roh straightened. "What do you need to do? Mend more tack? Muck out the horse stalls? Are you trying to get employment here?"

"If I can't get a kalkah licence, I'd consider it." Her eyes flashed, but she forbore from asking Roh what *his* plans were for earning coin.

Roh wished he knew what kept her here, day after day. But at least she wasn't out on the streets where the Vuusah could find her. After yesterday, he hated leaving her. "Do you think you could tear yourself away from the stables this evening? I heard there's a Merali festival in Kinglord Park tonight. Apparently, there'll be music and feasting all along the waterfront. They call it Night of the Archer."

Her expression softened. "That sounds lovely."

Holding in a sigh, Roh knelt beside her, kissed her again. "Good. It'll be fun."

This time, Roh found the garden surrounding the Circle of Wind empty — aside from a couple of tibbies loitering at the feet of the stones. Black wings carried the startled birds to the top of the wall, where they perched like tiny guardians, watching him.

Batting away foliage, he went to the central focus stone, trailed his fingers across its warm roughness. The heartstorm hummed sweetly through rock and flesh and bone, opening Roh up to the world. He easily isolated Gordoh's influence — the scholar clearly used the resonator often. Roh couldn't blame him.

He left the resonator and followed the man's trail through a series of courtyards to a building with vines climbing over a covered portico. Inside, framed maps adorned the walls of an airy entrance hall, where a corridor led into the building and a staircase ascended to a second floor. Gordoh's influence imbued everything. Roh peered at objects arrayed neatly on shelves inside a cabinet. They were rocks of different shapes and sizes, some bearing veins of purple crystals, others various shades of purple-grey. He was trying to decide if anyone would mind if he opened the cabinet, when he heard footsteps descending the stairs. A woman of mature years approached, her faded-blond hair cropped short and a scholar's sash across her stout middle. She halted when she saw Roh, arched her brows above blue eyes.

"Greetings, friend. I'm looking for the First Scholar… Gordoh," Roh said.

After a moment of shrewd evaluation, the scholar continued her descent. On reaching Roh, she offered her palm. "Soul bright and balanced. I am Sarenna Braath."

Roh held his arms rigid at his sides. "Is Gordoh here?"

The woman's lips curved. "I'll escort you to him." She gestured for Roh to follow her up the stairs, her hip hitching as she climbed. "We hoped you would return."

"Excuse me?"

She paused and looked back at him. "You are the zehli they call Roh, are you not? Little Atali?" When he still didn't move, she clicked her tongue. "Answers lie up the stairs, young man."

Roh shook himself and followed.

The top of the stairs opened into another foyer and corridor. Sarenna glanced back once and led him to a closed door; after a perfunctory knock, she pushed it open without awaiting a response. Inside, the room was cluttered with shelves of books, and cabinets filled with more strange rocks and other objects carved from stone. A dusty window let in light. In the centre of the room, Gordoh sat at a large desk — the only cleared space — poring over an unfurled scroll, his beaded braids swinging in front of his face. Looking up, he frowned at the interruption, then abruptly stood, the chair scraping across the floorboards.

"I found him downstairs," Sarenna said serenely. She gripped Roh's elbow and dragged him into the room.

Gordoh scrutinised Roh through pale-amber eyes. "It took longer than I predicted."

Sarenna turned to Roh. "Forgive my colleague. Welcome to the Department of Ellirisi."

Roh pulled away from the woman, disturbed by the rhythm he detected from her. He sensed clumsy attempts to read him. But that was impossible.

Gordoh rolled up his scroll and stuffed it into a spare slot on one of the shelves. "Thank you for bringing him to me, Sarenna." His tone was a dismissal.

"Can you doubt any of us would?" Sarenna smiled at Roh, fingers adjusting the sash at her thick waist. She clearly had no intention of leaving.

"You're one of the Ellirisi, too?" Roh asked her with rising misgiving.

"Certainly I am." She hesitated for a few heartbeats, then held his gaze and offered her palm for the second time.

Roh stared at the blatant invitation. Ignoring Gordoh's strangled grunt, he met Sarenna's palm with his own.

Sun's blood. The woman was actually offering him a zehla greeting. He would have laughed if he weren't so horrified.

"It really is providential you returned," Sarenna said into the silence. "Everyone wants to meet you. You could really help with our studies."

"Sarenna, please!" Gordoh said. "Have done."

"I'm simply welcoming Roh to our department."

Mouth dry, Roh pulled away. "What is going on here?" he asked.

"Sarenna, perhaps you could leave us —"

"It's really quite simple," Sarenna said, adjusting her sash again. "Some of us are trying to learn about how zehla interact with ellir — what makes a zehli, so to speak. Who better to answer our questions than you who are in line to be Atalah?"

Roh backed farther away until he hit a shelf, dislodging a fat book. "The Vuusah would never allow it."

Sarenna puffed out her ample chest. "I'm not sure why you think the Vuusah have any say in what we do."

Roh stared at the book splayed on the poorly swept floor, tried to curb his whirling mind into order. He lifted his head to meet Gordoh's clear gaze. "I want to speak to you alone, zehli."

Gordoh's lips tightened. "Please, Sarenna."

"But…" She scrunched up her nose and huffed. "Oh, very well."

Roh let out a breath when she finally left the room. Gordoh strode to the door to ensure it was latched, then rested his back against it. "I don't know what she was thinking to reveal her affinity."

"Bah, it's barely affinity! But that's not the point, and you know it. You have trained her!"

"That's rather overstating it."

"She tried to read me."

That appeared to startle Gordoh, and he released a snort of frustrated laughter. "Most ill-advised."

"Are there more like her?"

Gordoh straightened. "We are scholars, Roh. We study ellir — where it originates, how it works, what makes one person have affinity where another does not." His eyes were alight now. "Some of us are geologists. Some historians. Others are zehla. Most of the Ellirisi are incapable of melding with ellir — but for those who have a trace of affinity, can you honestly think we would deny them the opportunity?"

"Gordoh, you can't teach zehla ways to gravohl

outsiders!" Roh could barely get his head around it. Sarenna's affinity was so negligible as to be non-existent; otherwise, she would have been quelled as a child or gone wild. He would not have deemed it possible for Sarenna to harness ellir in any capacity. "Does the Zehla Guild sanction this?"

"Not exactly."

"Does Sarenna know that?"

"Be sure I'll talk to her," Gordoh said grimly. "She's well aware I don't want certain aspects of our studies known."

His tone held a question, but Roh couldn't answer. He didn't know what he was going to do with this new information. He pushed fingers into knots in the back of his neck. "When you mentioned scholars of ellir, I assumed they would all be zehla. How many are not?"

"Eight."

Blighted sun. If the Vuusah knew Gordoh led eight gravohl scholars of ellir, they would have the man's blood.

"Roh, Sarenna wasn't wrong. Your perspective would be of great interest to all of us."

"What makes you think I'll have anything to do with this?"

The scholar picked up the book Roh had knocked down and replaced it on the shelf. "You did say you were not here on Vuusah business."

"That doesn't mean —"

"Let's say we're aware you're avoiding the Vuusah."

"And how would you know that?"

"We made a few inquiries."

Something unnervingly like laughter threatened to erupt from deep inside Roh's chest. Each day he spent in Dohni tilted him further until he was upside down. He subsided onto the chair Gordoh thrust at him. Maybe he ought to walk out the door, but that wouldn't bring answers… and he had so many questions. "Do you make a habit of spying on zehla?" It was galling after he'd taken so much trouble to avoid being detected by his Vuusah brethren.

"Only those who present a puzzle." Gordoh moved to a cluttered sideboard. From a copper pot sitting on a slab of dark stone, he poured liquid into two cups and handed one to Roh. The beverage was warm, and the aroma of ginger reached Roh's nose, coated his tongue. "Why did you come here today?" the scholar asked.

"I have questions."

"About?"

Roh laughed dryly. "I wanted to learn more about what these exhorters have been doing. I don't like what I've seen so far."

Gordoh nodded and leant against his desk. "We have questions, too." At Roh's lifted eyebrow, he chuckled. "Shall we agree to an exchange?"

Roh's neck still ached no matter how hard he pressed. "What do you want to know that your confounded spying couldn't turn up?"

"Mainly, we want to know where you and your friend stand."

"What friend?"

"The woman with whom you're lodging. And, I think, whose srih you wear."

The ginger tea caught in Roh's throat. "You had spies at our lodging?"

The scholar's mouth twitched. "We made a few inquiries." Then, sobering, he placed his cup on the desk beside him and offered his palm. Roh accepted the offer of candour, and their llirah blended, making deceit impossible. "For obvious reasons, my colleagues and I wish to avoid the attention of the Vuusah. While they don't have much power in Dohni — at least, not yet — they could still make things difficult for us. I promise we mean neither you nor your companion harm."

Truth. "But you want something from us."

A pause as Gordoh considered his answer. Never a good sign under candour. "The Vuusah and the Zehla Guild have been sparring for almost a year. New hooters keep arriving, but it's all more of the same. I know your reputation, Roh. I merely wanted to know if your arrival was going to tip the balance."

Also truth. "And?"

"No one seems to know you're here."

Roh huffed a laugh and pulled away. "They do now. Had a run in with one of the circahs yesterday."

Gordoh crossed his arms. "Your companion registered a kalkah inquiry at the Zehla Guild four days ago. You are not staying at the Vuusah lodge and are clearly avoiding them. You cannot wonder at our curiosity, *Little Alali*."

Even said with irony, Ninah's stupid nickname grated. Again, Roh felt the urge to leave, simply to escape Gordoh's scrutiny. Either that or succumb to the man's compelling personality and unburden his soul. It was almost as if… but, no. Roh detected no signs of Gordoh impelling him.

Sun curse the man, Roh had come here to *ask* questions, not answer them. He collected his wits. "I need to know what the Vuusah are doing. What their objective is," he said.

"I wish I knew," Gordoh said.

"You haven't *made inquiries*?"

"As to that, we're fairly certain the Vuusah wish to assume control of the Zehla Guild. Doyi Palvemah has been meeting regularly with the guild wardens."

"That makes sense…" Roh could imagine how much the Vuusah detested the guild having more control than they. "But you think there's more to it?"

Gordoh picked up his cup. "I can't help wondering why *now*. The Zehla Guild has run things in Dohni for centuries. Why are the Vuusah moving now to wrest back control?"

Roh tried not to betray his ignorance. He supposed the Vuusah had long known about the Zehla Guild. Had they simply not cared about it, until now? "If they're seeking to control the guild," he said, "why are they taking a combative approach? Forcing candour on guild members seems guaranteed to antagonise every zehla in the city."

"I didn't say they were being smart about it," Gordoh said. "If they continue on this path, they will fail." He speared Roh with a look. "How does the Atalah-in-waiting know nothing of this?"

Roh stared into his empty cup. Evidently the scholar saw right through him. "I wish I knew."

Gordoh waited several heartbeats, then plucked the cup from Roh's fingers. He poured more tea for them both and resumed his seat behind the desk.

Sensing the man was about to ask more questions, Roh said the next thing that came into his head. "Tell me about the Ellirisi."

Gordoh's gaze seemed to measure Roh. "As I have said, we Ellirisi seek to understand ellir. We have many avenues of research — collecting stories of old, exploring the distribution of heartrock across the continent and investigating why heartrock holds such high quantities of ellir…"

"But you're not all zehla."

"No." Gordoh folded his hands on the desk. "What I'm about to say, I think you already know. Even if you cannot admit it. The Fiugreh clans have particularly strong affinity, but we are not the only race who melds with ellir."

Roh fumbled for his tea. "Zehla are the appointed custodians of ellir, committed to keeping the heartstorm bright and balanced."

"So says the Vuusah doctrine." Gordoh looked almost amused, but he continued gently. "This world is a large place — bigger than Baljehni, bigger than you or I can know. Is it really so surprising many cultures have their own relationship with what we call ellir?"

Roh took another gulp of tea, wished it were something stronger. In that moment, all he could think was how he wished Adehl were hearing this. "If that's your... your hypothesis, then small wonder you wish to avoid the attention of the Vuusah."

"They could certainly make things unpleasant." Gordoh's voice took on an edge. "They've already appropriated the Stormbowl, and I won't have them near the Circle of Wind."

"Why did you let me use it?"

"I wanted to see how strong you are."

Roh absorbed this. He was coming to realise that underestimating the scholars would be a mistake. He appreciated the forthright answers to his questions, but it also made him wary. "What else did you want to know?"

"Nothing more than I've told you." At Roh's expression, he gave a wry smile. "Very well, I admit I'd rather like to know if it's also your plan to remain in Dohni and register as kalkah. We — that is, the Ellirisi — could smooth the path for both of you."

Roh couldn't misinterpret the man's knowing expression. Gordoh knew exactly what Adehl needed to register her application. Maybe he also knew the weight of their coin purse. "Just a few inquiries, huh?"

"She's not the life companion anyone would have predicted for you."

Roh's whole body clenched with the effort of staying calm. "She's worth more than —"

"You misunderstand me." Gordoh raised a hand to forestall Roh's rant. "I don't mean to disparage Adehl: the opposite, I assure you. We would like to meet her."

Of course the scholar had discovered her name. Roh supposed it wouldn't have been difficult. These Ellirisi seemed to know an awful lot for a bunch of fusty university scholars. Still, Gordoh had pledged no harm to him or Adehl under candour. Although the man assuredly had some agenda, Roh sensed no malice.

"Are you planning to attend the festival tonight?" Gordoh asked after a moment of silence.

"I hope so." Roh knew little of the Night of the Archer, but it sounded like a big deal.

"We would be honoured if you and Adehl would be the guests of the Ellirisi. We will have a private viewing platform; you won't find a better vantage."

"Viewing platform?"

The scholar grinned. "Join us and see."

24. Night of the Archer

ADEHL SPENT over an hour getting ready for Roh's return. She made use of the Wild Colt's tiny bathing chamber and washed her hair, then plaited it into multiple fine braids woven with velinkah beads. She brushed and polished her boots and replaced her grubby mahgan with a clean gobeila in shades of dusky pink. It was one she hadn't worn yet; the soft agave silk whispered against her scrubbed skin.

Throughout the day, each time Adehl had glimpsed the university towering above the roof line, guilt had stabbed at her. She wasn't being fair to Roh, abandoning him to his own devices for days on end. What had he said yesterday? *I'll start to think you like the horses more than me.*

Roh was here, isolated from his brethren, because of her. He'd given up everything. The least she could do was tell him the truth — that Chanti needed her. That the stable lad's affinity soared, and she couldn't bear for anyone to quell him. That she didn't know what to do, other than stay close. At least Chanti had seemed better, today. Less volatile.

Adehl found Roh in the taproom, chatting to some of the

other guests. His smile on seeing her made her insides squirm and her cheeks heat. "Good day?" she asked awkwardly.

He leapt to his feet, twirled her round. "You look… like a pink heath flower."

She put her arms around his neck and pressed herself against the folds of his grey-and-blue tunic. It was the same one he'd been wearing for a few days, and it smelt distinctly of him. "Did you know the Night of the Archer is one of the major festivals of the year?"

"So I hear," he said unsteadily. "Something to do with the Merali god's defender."

"But it doesn't start until nightfall…"

"I heard it doesn't really get going until midnight," Roh said.

Adehl grinned, took his hand and led him up to their room.

By the time they left the Wild Colt, hand in hand, night had long since fallen, and the streets were alive with light and laughter. A full moon shone overhead, and everyone carried lanterns.

After yesterday's encounter with the exhorters, Adehl found herself scouring the shadowy crowd bearing them through the city. Now the Vuusah knew Roh had come to Dohni, they would be looking for him. They would be looking for her. But surely the Vuusah couldn't touch her and Roh among this horde.

The throng led them through the Old Merali Quarter to Kinglord Park, where bobbing lights disappeared into a wall of trees. Despite the moon, the tree canopies remained dark, the only lamps carried by revellers. There were no paths Adehl could see, just grass filling the spaces between trees and scattered shrubs.

They followed the lights deeper into the vast park, which had once been the grazing lands of the early Merali trading houses. After a few minutes, the trees thinned into a massive open space around an ancient temple gleaming pale under moonlight. Torches burned at the tops of five towers, and a great number of people congregated on the temple's flat roof. Thousands more people and lanterns gathered in the surrounding meadow, which extended in a broad arc to the harbour.

"Gordoh said the Ellirisi would be at the western edge, near the water," Roh said.

He'd told Adehl about his visit with Gordoh while they made themselves presentable again. As his story unfolded, her mind had whirled; despite the Ellirisi scholars' intrusive prying, Adehl definitely wanted to meet them. Especially Sarenna Braath, who had tried to give Roh a zehla greeting. Stars and sun, she wished she could have seen his expression. As for the proffered assistance with obtaining a kalkah licence… it was too good an opportunity to ignore.

She hadn't found the opportunity to tell Roh about Chanti.

They squirmed through the crowd. Impeding progress were groups gathered beneath lanterns suspended on poles — there were dozens arrayed throughout the meadow. Each pole marked the location of portable trestles laden with food. Some looked to be vendors selling wares; others hosted private parties. Adehl clung to Roh's hand as they navigated the crush — they'd never find each other again if separated. The crowd was thickest near the temple, where aromatic oils mingled with the stench of sweat. Flaming torches and lanterns added to the warmth of the evening. Adehl received a few elbows in her ribs, probably gave a few, too.

She was relieved when the crowd diminished past the temple. "How are we to find your new friends?" she asked.

"Gordoh showed me their tolkai."

"Their what?"

"Tolkai. They're like signs. Every pattern means something unique." He gestured at the nearest pole, which bore a plaque decorated with coloured tiles arranged in a combination of zigzags and dots in black, crimson and sage green. "Theirs is — *There*. I see them."

Roh almost yanked Adehl off balance as he changed direction. His destination looked to be a group of people gathered on a timber platform positioned with others along the waterfront. Moonlight gleamed on several blond heads and numerous red sashes. Some people sat on cushioned bench seats around the edge of the five-sided platform, faces turned to the moon. Others stood in groups, talking and laughing. Steps ascended to the platform, which stood about two paces above the grass, and lanterns hung at each corner of the structure. As they neared, Adehl made out the tolkai design — swirls of violet and aqua tiles around a jagged charcoal shape reminiscent of Goldayn Rise.

A Fiugreh man wearing a scholar's sash met them at the top of the steps. He wore his hair in a flurry of shoulder-length braids, but his festival clothes were cut in the Merali style — knee-length, split tunic in various shades of ochre over loose-fitting trousers. "Shield favour you this night," he said, thumping his right fist on his heart. His keen gaze met Adehl's, and he smiled. "I'm pleased you both came."

"How could we miss one of the biggest events of the year?" Roh said.

The man laughed. Adehl assumed this was Gordoh. He was younger than she'd expected, especially since most of the other assembled scholars looked to have at least five decades. "You will enjoy this festival, I think," he said. "Come and meet the rest of us."

There followed rounds of introductions, the Ellirisi scholars all bursting to meet *Little Atali*. Grinning at Roh's obvious discomfort, Adehl was happy to stand back and observe. The platform provided a lovely view of the moonlit harbour curving around the Old Merali Quarter. Lights twinkled north-west across the water where, presumably, the Fiugreh Settlement District lay. About the same distance south glowed a lighthouse beacon. Overhead, the moon outshone the canopy of stars, but she spotted the rising constellation of the Archer climbing above the university.

Someone thrust a pewter cup into her hands; based on the cup's small size, she took a cautious sip. The fiery liquid was smoother than the tohba they distilled on the downs and tasted of plums. It went down very nicely. She was on her second cup of the spirit — davinna, they called it — by the time she was introduced to Sarenna Braath. A spark of mischief prompted her to offer the Merali scholar a zehla greeting. Roh uttered Adehl's name in strangled horror, but a grin split Sarenna's face as they touched palms. The woman truly had negligible affinity; but that sliver of training meant Sarenna could touch ellir, even if she could only discern the barest hint. It would give the Vuusah doyens an apoplexy if they learnt of it.

"Soul bright," Adehl said, breaking the contact.

The scholar's cheeks darkened. "You honour me; but on this night, we say 'shield favour you'." She thumped her fist over her heart.

Adehl and Roh repeated the words and gesture. "I confess I've been wondering what this festival was all about," Adehl said.

"The Night of the Archer?" Sarenna turned to the constellation. In fact, most people seemed to be staring in that direction. A burst of several stars sprayed across the sky, and a murmur rose from the crowd. "There — you see?"

"The star falls?" Out on the Humming Downs, star falls were common. "You'd see them better on nights with no moon."

Everyone within earshot laughed. One of the scholars, a zehli whose name she couldn't remember, his greying hair and beard like granite, said, "The moon is the shield!"

"The moon must be full to defend against the arrows." This came from a woman who looked Sevikk, although she spoke with a local accent.

"You tell the story, Sarenna." Gordoh took up a pitcher and circled the group, refilling cups.

"It's a Merali legend." Sarenna said, smiling around a sip of davinna. "It's told that the true god, Venaa, was bathing in a forest pool, when arrows came out of the woods. On the banks, his defender — and, some say, lover — took up a shining shield and waded into the water. Holding the shield before Venaa, the defender blocked the arrows and saved his god — who appointed him eternal defender and transformed him into the moon."

"Which is why," said the bearded zehli, "we celebrate the Night of the Archer when the moon is full."

"Even though the arrows come for around two weeks." The maybe-Sevikk scholar's smile revealed a row of crooked teeth.

"Sounds like it should be called the night of the defender." Adehl had meant it as a jest, but the scholars looked blank, then affronted. She took refuge in her cup of davinna — only to find it empty. Was that her third cup gone already?

Fortunately, another bright spray of falling stars attracted the scholars' attention back to the sky. Gordoh came over with the pitcher, and Adehl held out her cup without thinking.

"Enjoying that, are you?" Roh murmured in her ear.

Adehl grinned at him to disguise the fact her head was swimming. But maybe it only confirmed her predicament, because Roh laughed and put his arm around her.

Gordoh's mouth curved. "Davinna is popular at festivals

here. They make it in Serekka. We always had it in my company, and I forget to warn people of its potency. My apologies." He sounded more amused than sorry.

"Where are you from?" Adehl asked. She leant her head on Roh's shoulder.

"One of the Selgreh clans south of the Talsiah River."

"Ah, near the overland trade route," Roh said. "How did you end up here?"

"I got curious about the Gahmniu deadland." At the zehla scholar's words, a tiny tremor rippled through Roh, and his arm tightened around Adehl. Gordoh watched them as he continued, two braids falling across his cheek, blue beads clinking. "Some of our camps were down near Gahmniu. The deadland always horrified me — but it fascinated me, too. I tried to ride around it once, but the mountains got in the way."

"That sounds like an adventure," Roh said.

Not how Adehl would have put it. Her former company had occasionally roamed the Gahmniu borderlands, but they'd always kept well clear of the marker stones.

The scholar hitched a shoulder. "In the end, I went south and rode around Dagahmniu instead."

"All the way around?" Roh sounded impressed. "Have you ever entered one of the deadlands?"

"Yes."

Adehl shivered at the admission, but Roh's rhythm danced with curiosity. "What was it like?" he asked.

Gordoh drained his cup. "I don't recommend it."

"I've thought about it, but..." Roh chuckled wryly. "I've never been quite brave enough."

Adehl twisted her neck to read his expression but couldn't make it out in the darkness. She couldn't fathom wanting to be brave — or curious — enough to cross the threshold of a deadland.

"For the average person, it's little more than a barren landscape, but for anyone with affinity…" Gordoh grimaced. "As I said, I don't recommend it."

After a moment, Roh said, "Why come here, though? To the university, I mean."

"Knowledge." The scholar's mouth quirked at whatever he saw on Roh's face. "There's little worth knowing about the deadlands that can't be found at Heights University. Scholars come from all over Baljehni — not to mention more distant lands."

"But the deadlands have always been there. What could books possibly have to say about them?"

Gordoh laughed. "There are dozens of accounts of people studying the deadlands over centuries. Besides…" He regarded them intently. "You must have heard what happened to Rungakk. It was only four decades ago."

They were silent for several heartbeats. All Vuusah zehla had heard of Rungakk. It had been a mining and ironworks city in Sevikkland until a deadland had inexplicably formed around it. The city and surrounding lands had been abandoned. Thousands had died.

"You haven't… that is, you wouldn't *visit* Rungakk," Roh said.

"The Sevikks won't allow anyone to go there," Gordoh said. "But the city's destruction instigated a whole new avenue of research." He paused, and Adehl had the impression he held himself in check. "The study of ellir can lead a curious person down all sorts of interesting paths."

"How long have you been here?" Adehl asked.

"Nearly ten years. I never intended to stay forever, but…" He lifted his cup of davinna and smiled at someone behind Adehl and Roh. "My life is here now."

There came a light laugh as the crowd rearranged itself. "It seems we're just in time," said an airy female voice. "I'm sure I warned you against boring our guests, Gordoh. You'll drive them away before I even meet them!"

Adehl lifted her head from Roh's comfortable shoulder and peered blearily at two newcomers. One was a young woman, perhaps a handful of years older than Adehl, wearing a red scholar's sash over an ornate gown gleaming silver in the moonlight. Her colouring and accent proclaimed her Merali descent: she had fair hair intricately styled around her head and a face that was too broad and square for conventional beauty. Her companion bore the armbands of a claithwielder. Adehl had never seen one of these elite Bladekor warriors before. Where the woman was fair, he was dark: hair clipped short and eyes like jet. Clad in black, the leather-bound hilt of a claithsword jutting above his shoulder, he looked powerful and menacing and was clearly there as the woman's protector — which meant she was someone important.

"I believe I've restrained myself admirably," Gordoh said. "You are somewhat late, Kenna. The lights will go out any minute."

"Couldn't be helped." Coming forward to join them, she smiled at Adehl and Roh as they shifted to make space. "I'm so happy to finally meet you. I've been longing to for days."

The claithwielder, all black edges and controlled strength, wedged into a position beside Gordoh and murmured something in his ear. Heat flashed in the scholar's eyes, but he handed a cup of davinna to the woman, then turned to Adehl and Roh. "This is Lady Kenna Auwyn, scholar of the Ellirisi. She is also the niece of Four Nations Councillor Lord Nirran Auwyn and a member of the Dohni People's Body."

"Such a mouthful," Lady Kenna said with an exaggerated eye roll. She indicated the claithwielder. "This is Jaikud. I'm not sure how you tolerate him, Jai. He never introduces you."

"You didn't give me a chance." Gordoh briefly pressed his shoulder against the claithwielder's.

"It's not about me, Kenn." Jaikud's voice was soft, deep and affectionate.

The lady flashed her teeth. "So, my new friends, how do you like our fair city? Let me formally bid you welcome."

A gong sounded as she spoke, loud and resonant in the night. Musicians Adehl had barely registered stopped playing, and thousands of voices swelled into a wave of sound. The night darkened — people covered the lanterns so that lights winked out across the meadow and on top of the temple. It happened so quickly. Soon, every visible light was doused — including those across the harbour — until the only remaining light in the world was that of the stars and moon.

"We did cut it fine," Kenna said softly, as the crowd hushed into an eerie, weighted silence.

Another strike of the gong. Roh put both arms around Adehl from behind, his body warm against hers. From the moon's position overhead, she judged it about midnight. The Archer ascended the eastern sky, stars falling every five or so heartbeats. No one spoke. There came a clatter of something dropped, muffled curses. Otherwise, the night was silent, except for the rustle of clothing and wails of darkbirds in the park.

Thousands of people waited for… something.

Then the gong rang for the third time, and the drums began.

FOR HALF AN HOUR, the air resounded with a hundred drums in powerful syncopation. With every star fall came a gong, and the gathered crowd cheered. Adehl felt the vibrations deep in her chest. Someone kept refilling her cup. The night took on the semblance of a dream.

When the ceremony ended, lanterns were relit. Adehl had lost count of the cups of davinna she'd consumed. Roh's arms encircled her firmly, and she suspected he held her up. With effort, she straightened and disentangled herself. The platform rolled under her feet, but she braced herself on the side rail.

Lady Kenna giggled. "Come talk to me, Adehl. I want to talk to you."

"Then talk to me." She focused on enunciating her words. "What about?"

Another giggle as Kenna came to stand beside her at the rail. Adehl found herself giggling, too. "I want to know some things, please," Kenna said. "Like, why are you hiding from the hooters? It doesn't make sense. And you want a kalkah licence. When you're with the Little Atali. It doesn't make *sense.*"

"I know!" Adehl tried to whisper. "The Vuusah hate me now. Except for Roh. They want to quell me if they can catch me."

Kenna clutched her arm. "*Why?*"

"Because…" A shiver skittered down Adehl's spine. Her impulse was always to deflect, conceal the truth. But her secret was out now and, in that moment, Lady Kenna felt like a friend. She wet her mouth. "They found out I faked my lineage papers." When Kenna's brow furrowed, Adehl leant forward and spoke into her ear. "I'm pidakah!"

"Don't say that!" Kenna slapped a hand on Adehl's mouth, hard.

"Ow!" Adehl rubbed her stinging lips.

"I'm so sorry! But don't say that word."

"Pi —?"

"Don't!" Then Kenna seemed to register Adehl's meaning

and clutched Adehl's arm again. "By the lord's shining locks. They will slay you!"

"It's why I'm hiding."

"But..." Kenna gaped at her for several heartbeats. Then she lapsed into more giggles. Adehl laughed helplessly with the scholar until her chest ached. When they calmed again, both leaning outwards to face the harbour, moon and falling stars above, Kenna broke the silence. "Can I tell you something?" She sounded serious.

"Of course."

"I'm gierfeh. I mean, I *was*..." The scholar bit her lip, then brought up her palm in an unmistakable gesture. Adehl swiped her own suddenly damp palm on her gobeila, then brought it to Kenna's. The energy coming from Kenna was... somehow familiar. It beat out a frustrated rhythm as it tried to take flight within her. Like a bird with its wings clipped.

Adehl searched her swimming mind, then her hand spasmed. Her father. Her father's llirah felt like this — so much potential restrained and suppressed. "You've been *quelled*."

"Yes."

"But..." Adehl shook her head, trying to arrange her thoughts. The davinna was making her stupid. Why would Kenna have needed to be quelled? Even Chanti had a strong dose of Fiugreh blood to account for his high affinity — or so she'd assumed. "You have no Fiugreh blood in you at all?"

Kenna shook her head. "I can trace my Merali lineage for ten generations. It's why I'm here. Doing research."

"What are you researching?"

The woman's chin lifted. "The influence of lineage and environment on affinity for ellir."

Adehl stared. Then burst into another fit of giggles.

"It's not funny! My research is very important." Hand on

hips, she said, "It's fine for *you*. You got to be trained. *You're* not quelled."

"Stars, I'm sorry!" Adehl could barely get the words out. Clapping a hand over her mouth, she tried to get control of herself. It was just too... too *much*. All this time, she'd resented the Vuusah discrimination against pidakah Fiugreh because she'd considered herself Fiugreh in every way that mattered. Now she wondered if she'd been fighting the wrong battle all along.

"Gierfeh don't need *any* Fiugreh blood, if you must know," Kenna said, jaw jutting. "Just look at the Sevikks."

Adehl clutched her aching head. "Stop," she moaned. "No more tonight. Can we talk when I've not consumed an entire pitcher of that death spirit? I have so many questions, and I want to understand the answers."

She speared Adehl with a glittering glance. "I'm just saying things could be different."

Adehl caught her breath. She couldn't mistake the challenge. Ideas effervesced in her mind, bold and brimming with possibility. Nonsensical, perhaps; definitely foolhardy. Fury, these perilous thoughts were doubtless due to the vast quantities of davinna flowing through her veins. She would never touch the substance again.

For years, she had railed privately against the Vuusah stranglehold on ellir. She'd told Sorah that one day things would be different. She'd burned to find some means of helping Chanti. Yet she'd never once considered what she could do. How *she* could make things change.

As the ideas connected and bubbled through her soul, Adehl felt so light she might lift off the ground.

25. RUMBLE OF WHEELS

FRAHTO SPENT most of the voyage to Dohni either curled up in his bunk or retching over the side of the ship. Worse, he hadn't thought to bring a heartstone, which some zehla used to deal with sea voyages. He hadn't stopped to consider what it would be like without ellir present in the world beneath his feet. Some common objects onboard held whispers of ellir, but not enough to soothe his soul or calm his gut.

Gentah couldn't have chosen a better punishment.

Sorah sat with Frahto some of the time, telling stories to pass the hours. He was pathetically grateful for the child's good cheer. She had, of course, been raised on her mother's ship and could scamper around the rigging as well as any deckhand. Or so he'd heard from Ketahl, who was the other person to bring him meals he didn't want, along with ribald anecdotes from the sacks game on deck. When he asked Sorah if she'd ever seen the Shrouded Sea worse than this, she'd burst out laughing and said this was about as calm as it got with a good wind. In the two years he'd known Sorah, he'd never seen her so energetic and confident. Back home, she'd been quiet and reserved. Perhaps even unhappy. He was starting to understand Lenatoh's decision to bring Sorah on this journey.

They'd set sail four days after Roh had absconded with Adehl, two after Gentah and Lenatoh arrived in Tarsah with a handful of others. The old man had stridden into the gatherhall of the Tarsah compound, thin white braids unravelling, already spitting fire and blood. "Where is he?"

Frahto's mug of ale thudded onto the table. It was late, and the gatherhall was largely deserted at that time of night, but Dinah and Ketahl were sitting alongside him, commiserating. "Uh… you mean Roh?"

"Of course I mean Roh, the misbegotten son of a dungbat. Is that woman here?"

"Neither of them is here." Frahto wished he'd known his doyen was going to show up tonight; he wouldn't have drunk so many mugs of ale. Or perhaps he would have drunk more.

The old man fixed him with a glare that would have made his knees wobble had he been unwise enough to stand. "Where are they?"

"Sit." Frahto also beckoned to Lenatoh, who had followed Gentah through the doorway. "You might want ale." He clutched his mug to his chest, spilling some onto his fingers. "You can't have mine."

"What's happened?"

"*Sit.*" Frahto wrestled with his scrambled thoughts. To whoever might be listening, he said, "More ale!"

Dinah patted his arm; then she and Ketahl rose to their feet. "We'll see to it. Good luck."

Lenatoh calmly sat on the bench opposite Frahto, but Gentah followed the zehla to the kitchen, hollering for food. Upon his return, the doyen leant on a nearby, vacant table. "Well, then?"

Frahto opened his mouth, and words tumbled out. He hardly knew what he was saying, but it seemed important Gentah know everything all at once.

"Stop." Gentah was on his feet again. "Speak plainly, Frahto."

Frahto took a deep breath and gripped his mug in two hands. The old man had sent him to learn more of Adehl, so that's where he would start. He forced himself to say the words. "Adehl is pidakah."

Silence, except for low voices in the kitchen. Dinah brought in a tray with a pitcher of ale and two clean mugs. Keeping her eyes lowered, she retreated hastily. Muttering something beneath his breath, Lenatoh filled the mugs and pushed one across the table towards Gentah.

"That's impossible," the doyen said at last, ignoring the ale.

"She admitted it to Doyi Barenah under candour. Faked her lineage papers."

Lenatoh, expression unreadable, leant forward. "You'd better explain."

Frahto nodded. "I looked into her background. Her mother was a zehli, ran away with a pidakah horse breeder. A doyen's son. Wouldn't give him up..." Belatedly he remembered Lenatoh had a pidakah daughter.

Lenatoh drummed his fingers on the table. "Who faked the papers?"

"Don't know. Possibly Dalanah, the grandmother. She's a doyen down south. Sponsored Adehl's application to the Vuusah."

"Does Roh know all this?" Gentah asked sharply.

"Yes." Frahto slumped in his chair. "Lied about it. Said Paluh was her foster-father. I thought she must have lied to Roh too, but..."

"Mercy," Gentah said. He exchanged a heavy, speaking

glance with Lenatoh, then grabbed the full mug of ale and downed a good portion of it. He wiped the back of his mouth. "All right. Where are they?"

"Gone."

"Tell me the whole."

Frahto told them everything he could remember. From the records to Adehl's mishap with the resonator and all the things she'd lied about. All the things she'd confessed under candour. How Roh had lied for her multiple times, helped her escape. "Corrupted his honour," he muttered.

But he didn't admit how Roh had impelled him. Perhaps it was pride that held him back. Or misplaced loyalty to his friend. Were they still friends?

He came to a stuttering halt at the point when Roh had somehow, impossibly, managed to board the ship. "I don't know how it happened," Frahto said feebly. "I don't think he planned it…" But his gear had been attached to the back of his saddle. He'd planned to go somewhere.

Gentah swore long and loud as he paced the room.

"He's always been impetuous," Lenatoh said.

"This is beyond impetuous! Mercy." Gentah kicked over one of the long bench seats, its heavy timbers thundering onto the stone floor. "As if Adehl being *pidakah* weren't bad enough. For Roh to go rogue too…"

"Don't give up on him yet," Lenatoh said.

"I have no intention of giving up on him. We've had the making of him for twelve years. That woman cannot have turned him so quickly."

"It will be difficult to separate them."

"But not impossible."

Lenatoh's fingers drummed, stopped. "It will be difficult without alienating Roh. We may need to… take drastic action."

"We'll do whatever it takes," Gentah said grimly. He

brooded in silence for a minute. Frahto, aware of undercurrents he didn't understand, wondered uneasily what *drastic action* brought that particular glint to the doyen's eye. Eventually Gentah stopped pacing. "I want the two of you on the next ship to Dohni. Take the new circah. Bring him back."

"Me, Doyi?" Frahto was startled into saying.

"Who else?" Gentah's mouth hardened. "I don't delude myself that he would listen to me above the two of you."

Frahto frowned. If Roh had listened to him, they wouldn't be in this situation.

"Deal with the woman in Dohni and leave her there," Gentah added. "I don't want her here in any capacity."

"Understood, Doyi," Lenatoh murmured.

"One more thing." Gentah pinned Frahto with a sharp glance, then Lenatoh. "We need to keep Roh's involvement quiet. When the time comes, I don't want anyone questioning his fitness to be Atalah. I will set it about that he has gone there on an errand for me."

"There were some who saw him leave with her," Frahto said.

"Dinah's circah is accompanying you. Anyone else, I'll deal with."

Frahto didn't want to know what Gentah meant by that. "I'll organise our passage first thing tomorrow."

WHEN SORAH THUMPED on the cabin door and yelled that Dohni was in sight, Frahto groaned his gratitude into the pillow. It had been a long voyage. To secure passage for their entire group at short notice, he'd been forced to book a Kestali merchant vessel that spent a day at each of Port Monys and the Davrayn seaport. Ten days of pure torture.

He dragged himself out of bed and packed his things,

dumped his bag on the floor and moaned back to the bunk. Sometime later, the rocking subsided. Willing his stomach to behave, Frahto staggered up to the deck. His companions waited before a backdrop of mountains under a sunny, blue sky. Sighting him, they whooped and stamped their feet. Frahto was too worn out to react.

It took an interminable time for the horses to be unloaded and the official paperwork examined, but finally — *finally* — Frahto stepped off the wharf onto the street. He shivered at the flood of ellir that reached him, his llirah welcoming the heartstorm. He wished he had better healing skills to appease his ravaged body.

Lenatoh ushered Frahto and Sorah into a carriage drawn by hired horses. Most of the exhorters clambered into a second vehicle, but Dinah and Ketahl mounted the two horses they'd shipped from Tarsah at great inconvenience and expense: Roh's blood bay, Sprig, and Adehl's splendid moonskin. Frahto had noted Adehl's bond with her horse, seen her devastation at giving him up. The wharf official hadn't taken much persuading to sell. Frahto couldn't be sure how much of a lure Sprig would present, but he didn't doubt Adehl would move mountains to regain possession of her moonskin.

Frahto leant his head against the padded upholstery of the carriage, relieved not to have to walk or ride anywhere. He allowed the rumble of the wheels and Sorah's excited chatter about seeing her mother's ship in port to send him into a doze.

He opened his eyes when the motion stopped and Sorah scrambled past him to shove open the door. Outside, Dinah was already at the top of a short flight of steps, greeting a familiar zehli stationed outside the door of a building squeezed into a row of almost identical residences.

"Sun's blood, Nedoyi!" Ninah said, when Lenatoh

followed his daughter onto the street. "Hoi, Frahto! Is the whole company on its way, then?"

"Soul bright, Nin," Lenatoh said. "You remember my daughter, Sorah?"

"Of course." Ninah nodded to Sorah, but paid her scant attention, looking instead to Dinah's circah. "We weren't expecting this lot for another week. What's going on?"

"If you don't mind, Nin," said Lenatoh, "we'll come inside and speak to Doyi Palvemah. And poor Frahto could do with something to settle his stomach."

"I'm fine," Frahto muttered, feeling the heat bloom on his face. He supposed red was better than green.

"Bad crossing?"

"Not in the least," Lenatoh said, hiding his amusement poorly.

After directing Ketahl to take the horses around the back, Ninah admitted them into a small gatherhall, where a group of zehla played a spinning peg game at one of the tables. Among them were Chah and a few others originally from Gentah's company. Frahto ignored the greetings and sank onto a bench seat near the open window. Outside, the hired vehicles pulled away, and Frahto relished the stillness.

"Here you go, brother." Someone plonked a mug of hot herbal tea on the table before Frahto. He identified ginger and liquorice root among the complex flavours and sipped at it gratefully.

When Doyi Palvemah limped into the room, conversation faded. She leant heavily on a crutch, but she wasn't old — perhaps in her fifth decade. The iron-grey braids framing her craggy face were threaded with velinkah beads in different shades of green. She lowered herself onto a chair, then tapped the table beside her. Lenatoh, who had risen when she entered, moved to the bench indicated while she scanned the room. "Is Roh with you?"

Frahto's stomach, which had mostly stopped churning, thanks to the tea, started up again.

Lenatoh's neutral expression didn't change. "No."

Palvemah's eyes narrowed. "Green Falcon, please show our new circah around and get them settled in. Chah, stay for a moment."

"Green Falcon?" Lenatoh asked.

"It helps me keep track." To Dinah's group, the doyen said, "Make sure you choose a good name for your circah. We'll speak later."

"Sorah, go with them." Lenatoh twisted his neck to where his daughter lurked behind him.

"Can't I stay here? Please?"

His face softened, and he brushed her cheek with a bent finger. "We'll go tomorrow, I promise."

Frahto remained by the window as the room cleared. One of the zehla returned almost immediately with a pitcher of wine and a plate of aromatic pastries that, another day, Frahto might have found tantalising. Today, he wished the spices less pungent and clutched his mug of herbal goodness instead.

When the room was quiet again, Lenatoh set his wine aside. "I infer you've seen Roh?"

"Chah spoke to him and his companion two days ago. What's going on? Why didn't he come to the lodge?"

"I would first hear what Chah has to say."

Standing near the door, Chah straightened. "We came across them in the Pioneer Gardens, although we didn't see Roh at first. We asked the woman for her papers according to the standard procedure." He scratched the side of his head. "She, uh, refused."

"What happened?"

"Well... she wouldn't cooperate. So, we forced her to cooperate — if you catch my meaning?"

It took a few heartbeats, but Frahto indeed caught Chah's meaning. It did not help his stomach. Too well did he remember being at Roh's mercy in the pre-dawn shadows back home. "What did Roh do?" he asked.

"He didn't like it," Chah said mildly.

"But what did he do?"

Chah cast a sidelong glance at the doyen. "He shredded our mesh in a matter of moments. From at least ten paces away."

Silence. Frahto flung a glance at Lenatoh, who grimaced. Then Doyi Palvemah said with remarkable calm, "You did not tell me that, zehli."

Chah's fingernail once more dug into his scalp. "Sorry."

The doyen reached for the pitcher and carefully refilled her wine. Frahto was starting to think he needed to abandon the herbal brew and join her. Palvemah said, "Will you please explain, Nedoyi Lenatoh?" Every word enunciated. "I have everything under control. There was no need to send —"

"That's not... Chah, is that what he told you?" Lenatoh asked.

"He said he couldn't tell us why he was here."

"I think you owe me an explanation," Palvemah said. "He failed to identify himself to one of my circahs the day he arrived, and now this. I don't know why he didn't come here to the lodge, unless it's to spy on us and report back to Gentah. And who is the cursed woman?"

"It's not what you think."

"Enlighten me."

"We need to keep this confidential."

Eyes narrowed, the doyen dismissed Chah. Now, only Lenatoh, Frahto and Palvemah remained in the room. "Well?"

Lenatoh's sigh seemed to come from the depths of his soul. "The woman's name is Adehl. She's a zehli recently expelled from the Vuusah, after we discovered she concealed her pidakah lineage. That in itself would be bad enough, but she has ensnared Roh. He helped her flee before we could quell her. We assume they seek refuge here."

Midway through this recital, Palvemah's jaw dropped. She reached clumsily for her wine, knocking her stick to the floor. "How did this happen?"

"The woman brought horses for our company a few weeks ago. We never could have predicted..." Lenatoh rubbed his forehead. "We tried to head it off — even before we knew of her deception. But we underestimated... pretty much everything."

The doyen shook her head. "I can't believe Roh would do this. He knows she's pidakah? Chah says he's wearing her srih."

"It's worse than that," Lenatoh said. "They are injaleh."

The doyen stilled. Elsewhere in the house, several pairs of feet thumped up and down the stairs. "This is going to pose a problem," Palvemah said. "Is Roh aware of what's —"

"No, he's not." Lenatoh cast a sideways glance at Frahto. "That is, there are things we haven't told him yet."

Frahto pretended to be studying the contents of his mug. Thanks to the tea, his brain was working again. He ought not be surprised there were plots afoot involving Roh. Everything *always* revolved around Roh.

He also ought to have realised Adehl was Roh's injaleh. But spontaneous melds like that didn't happen often. He thought if anyone could resist such a thing it would be Roh.

"If they are injaleh..." The doyen rubbed at a spot on the table. "We need to separate them."

Frahto caught the warning look Lenatoh cast Palvemah, and a shiver crawled across his shoulders. "I think it's more than just the meld," Frahto said. "I can't speak for Adehl, obviously, but I know Roh. He was completely smitten by her from the start."

"I agree," Lenatoh said. "And I told him as much. I suspect that was a false step on my part."

"You think she made a deliberate play for him?" Palvemah said.

Lenatoh shook his head. "She couldn't have known they would meld… And she left our camp without him."

"She certainly never intended for her falsified records to be uncovered," Frahto said. "I really thought that would sway him." He wondered what *would* sway Roh. There must be something. It couldn't be possible for someone groomed for over a decade to be Atalah to simply abandon that life without regret.

Palvemah gave the table two thumps with her fist. "All right. The first thing we need to do is find them. I'll send zehla out to comb the streets. They've already found him twice."

"I think he'll come to us, once he learns we are here," Lenatoh said.

"You think it will be that easy?" Frahto asked.

"I do not think it will be easy at all."

"But you think he will come," Palvemah said.

"I've known Roh a long time. Deep down, he believes in the Vuusah and what we stand for. I just hope he listens to his head and seeks my counsel. And Frahto is his closest friend."

Frahto thought back to those last moments in Tarsah two weeks ago. Roh had apologised for impelling him, but Frahto had been too angry to acknowledge it. "We didn't part on good terms," he admitted.

"That may be so," Lenatoh said with a soft smile. "But he is still your friend."

"Maybe she's turned out to be a shrew," Frahto said. "He'll be relieved to see us."

Lenatoh huffed. "We can only hope."

Palvemah fumbled beneath the table for her stick, then

pushed slowly to her feet. Her green beads clinked together as she found her balance. "I will give instructions."

"What happens when we find him?" Frahto asked. "I doubt he will give up Adehl just because we ask him to." Roh had broken multiple Vuusah precepts for her. He wasn't going to apologise and forget he ever knew her.

Palvemah limped towards the door, then turned with a glint in her amber eyes. "If you can get him here, I will make sure he stays," she said with a flash of white teeth. "Once we have control of Roh, we can decide what to do with the woman."

26. No Retreating

Roh ducked behind a horse tethered outside a shop, as yet another Vuusah circah prowled down Moi Boulevard. The exhorters were out in numbers this morning — it was the third group he'd dodged between the Wild Colt and the artisan district.

The circah pulled up nearby, and something brushed Roh's llirah. Cursing silently, he hauled in his rhythm to the barest whisper. He didn't personally know these zehla, but he'd seen them in action: they called themselves the Dancing Owls, and their leader, a tall woman with bony elbows, was quick to draw her sword. The woman now stood rigidly in the centre of a tight circle, her gaze raking the passersby, who were either stopping to watch whatever was about to happen or hurrying past with their heads down.

In the middle of the street, the zehla chanted softly.

Ellir danced at the edge of Roh's awareness. Once again, something brushed — probed — his tightly coiled energy. He didn't move, wished he'd backtracked down the side street. People streamed past, paying him no attention, yet the exhorters would surely notice him lurking behind a horse not fifteen paces distant.

After a few minutes, the leader halted the chant, and the exhorters resumed their progress downhill. Roh released a long breath and patted the horse's neck in thanks.

The exhorters were hunting someone.

It could be unrelated to him and Adehl. The Vuusah could be looking for anyone. Or, after the incident with Chah and Ninah, they might simply be looking for Roh.

But, somehow, he knew word had finally arrived from Tarsah.

With excruciating care, Roh reached out with ellir, then ventured cautiously onto the street. About a hundred paces downslope on Moi Boulevard, the exhorters continued their patrol. They weren't hurrying, but gone was the entitled saunter of the past week, and they looked five times more alert.

He wondered what he would have done had that been Chah's circah; they not only knew him on sight, but knew his rhythm, too. Maybe, instead of hiding, he would have invited them for an ale at the Drunken Mule tavern across the street.

Perhaps he ought to consider meeting his brethren head-on, instead of all this ducking and weaving. He didn't fear them on his own account. They wouldn't hurt him and couldn't impel him.

Still. If they were looking for Adehl, avoidance was best.

Two nights ago, on the Night of the Archer, Gordoh had asked him again why he was in Dohni. He had answered honestly, straight from the heart, helped on by several cups of davinna. "I'm here because Adehl is here."

"And why is Adehl here?"

"She's... on the run from the Vuusah."

"Truly?" Gordoh had contemplated Adehl, giggling with Kenna nearby.

"She's..." Roh caught himself, but Gordoh seemed to draw truth out of Roh like a poultice drew infection. Besides, judging by the earnest conversation those two were having, Adehl was already telling the Merali scholar everything. He blew out a breath. "Adehl is pidakah."

"Storm's oath!"

"The Vuusah found out." Roh lifted an eyebrow at the other man's expression. "I'm surprised your spies didn't uncover this fact."

After a long pause, Gordoh said, "No wonder she's lying low. What are you going to do?"

Braced against the rail, Roh had stared up at the sky, where stars fell like tears. "I wish I knew," he said wryly. "I have responsibilities back home, but I can't leave her."

"She's your injaleh."

Sun's blood, it had felt so good to have someone recognise what Adehl was to him. Even if it were simply a kalkah zehli he'd only just met. He didn't question how Gordoh knew; he felt it must be obvious to everyone.

Roh clung to that fact. He wore Adehl's srih, and they were injaleh. There was no retreating from that, even had he wished to.

But, two nights ago, and again today as he watched the departing backs of his former brethren, he had no answer for Gordoh's question. *What are you going to do?*

IN THE MIDDLE of the stable courtyard, Chanti huddled against Sapling, face buried in the horse's neck. His slight body quivered, and Adehl could have wept with him. A dark-haired girl of about eight sat rigidly on the mare's back, clutching the pommel with two hands, Orkoh holding the reins.

Nearby, a bulky man in a dark-blue Sevikk military tunic cast a critical eye over Sapling's form.

"Chanti, come away now; there's a good lad," Maesenna said. "It's time to bid Sapling farewell. She has a new home now."

As soon as she'd received word the stable mistress needed help with the boy, Adehl had hastened outside. Visions of Chanti comatose in the straw had dissolved on seeing him… But the actual situation wasn't much better. She had hoped Sapling wouldn't be sold yet. After that davinna-soaked conversation with Lady Kenna Auwyn two nights ago, Adehl knew what she needed to do — if she dared. Yesterday's aching head and churning stomach had delayed her taking action, and now it might be too late.

The boy mumbled something into the mare's fur, his fingers clutching, kneading. Sapling whuffed and nudged him with her nose.

"Come now, Chanti," Maesenna said, an edge creeping into her tone.

Chanti tried to bury himself even deeper into the horse. The outpour of emotion made Sapling restless; the girl in the saddle squealed and kicked her legs, spurring Sapling into greater agitation. With a roar, the Sevikk man hauled the girl off the horse. Orkoh grabbed Sapling's bridle, while Maesenna tugged at the boy hanging from the mare's neck. Chanti squirmed and struggled but wouldn't let go.

Moving forward, Adehl threaded ellir through the mare's rhythm to counteract Chanti's turmoil. When the horse settled, Adehl laid one hand on Chanti's head, smoothed back his coarse hair as she calmed him too. With a sob, he turned his face into Adehl's mahgan, his arms tight around her waist.

"Perhaps this horse is not suitable for my daughter, after all," said the perturbed father.

For Chanti's sake, Adehl hoped he would back out of the sale — but it would only delay the inevitable.

"I can assure you, General, this horse is the gentlest of creatures," Maesenna said. "It's just that my stable lad has grown very close to her. She is an excellent choice for your daughter."

The general's shrewd, blue gaze assessed Sapling for long minutes; then he nodded. "Come, girl." He drew his daughter towards the horse. "Will you introduce yourself to this lovely lady?"

She sniffed and took a few cautious paces. The arms around Adehl's waist tightened, and she realised Chanti had tilted his head to watch. His body tensed as the Sevikk girl edged to Sapling's side and, encouraged by her father, fed the mare a piece of carrot. "I'm going to call her Bluebell," she said.

When the general confirmed he would honour the sale, Maesenna couldn't conceal her relief. The girl remounted her new horse, and Adehl kept Chanti tight against her, terrified of what might happen if she released her grip on his llirah. Any tiny emotion could send his rhythm spinning out of control.

"Let me go," Chanti said when the courtyard was empty, his voice flat and broken.

Adehl braced her arms as Chanti tried to pull away. He writhed, hands beating at her with surprising strength.

"Hush. Stop it, little colt." Adehl inhaled to stave off the sudden threat of tears. "You need to be calm."

"I don't care if I die."

"But I would care." Adehl channelled her affection — and, yes, love — into Chanti, this boy who had somehow captured her heart. She swallowed against the lump in her throat. "Mistress Maesenna would care, too. You're her best stable lad, remember?"

He stilled; when he next spoke, he sounded miserable. "I can't stop the shifting and burning without Sapling."

"I'll help you."

"How?"

Adehl looked down into his tear-streaked face. His affinity was so strong. Ellir bounded within him, unfettered as the wind.

She didn't care that further aggravating the Vuusah would be madness. Or that she didn't know the first thing about training anyone.

She was going to do this. A thrill skittered from her shoulderblades down her spine. "I'm going to teach you."

"Hoi!"

Roh checked his step, almost stumbling over a street tabby streaking across his path. The call had come from behind him, and he almost strained something with the effort of not turning around.

"Hoi, Dancing Owl!" Closer — perhaps twenty paces. A woman's voice, familiar.

Ahead, the circah of exhorters he'd been following along Shining Way halted, forcing a mounted courier to veer sharply. Feigning nonchalance, heartbeat rising, Roh ambled to the side of the road, searched for a shop entrance or a loaded cart to provide cover — even another horse would do. He'd been so focused on the circah in front of him, he'd failed to consider another coming up behind.

He spotted a street performer outside a bootmaker's shop and joined the crowd of enthusiastic onlookers. The boy, about sixteen with ragged fair hair and grimy brown clothes, juggled five small sacks with impressive alacrity while maintaining an amusing commentary. The crowd laughed and swelled, dropped coins into the boy's hat. Roh tried to hear the words exchanged by the exhorters behind him on the busy street.

"Ah, Silver Wolf. You're supposed to meet us in Donellon Plaza." Those clipped tones belonged to the Dancing Owl leader.

"It's just up ahead, isn't it?" Fury, it was Dinah. He'd recognise those arrogant tones anywhere.

"Where's Green Falcon?"

"Who knows?" Dinah said. "We don't need minders."

The crowd noise swelled as the juggler added some twirls to his routine, and Roh missed the next part of the exchange.

"You forget, Grendah, we know what they look like," Dinah was saying when the audience quieted. "We've known Roh for years."

"But you don't know the city. Doyi Palvemah wants —"

"Yeah, yeah. We'll let your Dancing Owls show us around the Old Merali Quarter. Wouldn't want to get lost."

Roh risked a glance. The Dancing Owl leader and Dinah faced off, each with crossed arms, the other zehla ranged around them. They were disrupting the traffic flow. Shining Way, as the primary route between Donellon Plaza and the Great Market, was one of the busiest streets in the city. Dinah faced away from Roh, her distinctive twin braids reaching down her back. Her exhorters raked the scene around them with alert gazes. Roh returned to the juggler and strained his ears, his shoulderblades tight and llirah bound into a knot.

He heard little more of their conversation and almost missed their departure. A ripple of motion, bodies and animals shifting en masse, drew his attention in time to view both circahs moving towards Donellon Plaza. Dinah strode at the head of her so-called *Silver Wolf* circah as though she owned the city. It was hard to tell from behind, but Roh sensed she'd edged ahead of the Dancing Owls.

Roh slipped in behind them, keeping a greater distance than before. He'd been trailing the Dancing Owls since Moi Boulevard. They had scoured the undulating streets of the Old Kestali Quarter, trudging down the maze of smaller lanes the exhorters usually ignored, stopping to form a tracking circle every few minutes. Roh had prepared himself to intervene when they drew near the Wild Colt — but they had moved on without hue and cry. With every minute that passed, Roh had felt less inclined to reveal himself.

And now this. More brethren from Gentah's company. He'd known word would come, but he hadn't considered Gentah would send zehla who knew Adehl by sight. He ought to have considered it.

The zehla entered Donellon Plaza through the Shining Gate, a huge arch intricately carved from cream marble. It stood at the eastern corner, between the Artisans and Merchants Guilds. From outside the plaza, the four-storey buildings presented stone walls arrayed with glass-paned windows. Inside, stately entrances and colonnades bounded the immense open space, where prosperous townspeople bustled.

The two circahs plunged into the throng, and Roh edged into the shadows of a colonnade to follow their progress. Grendah flung her hand around, giving Dinah's circah the tour as they veered around the circular pool surrounding the marble statue of Lady Galessa Davrayn.

Farther along stood the statue of Lord Donellon Haas opposite the Zehla Guild, where Lenatoh strode down the guild building's steps.

Roh's heart stumbled. Not what he'd expected. Not *who* he'd expected.

Of course the old man would send Lenatoh.

His friend and mentor wore the same dark-red mahgan he always wore in towns, and his shoulders were hunched — as though against the weight of the buildings pressing in. Lenatoh hated cities. He could barely drag himself to Tarsah. He looked pale and grim and exhausted.

Lenatoh looked up. Through narrow gaps in the swirling mass of people, across a distance of at least a hundred paces, their gazes seemed to meet. The nedoyen checked his step, and the crowd shifted, obscuring him.

For several heartbeats, Roh couldn't move. His llirah lurched like a drunken horse; then he hauled it in and pulled himself behind a column. Breathing was strangely difficult.

He needed to leave. Run. Hide.

He needed to speak to Lenatoh.

The nedoyen had always been able to talk things through rationally and present a side Roh hadn't considered. If he owed anyone an explanation, it was Lenatoh.

27. Spring rain and nectar

Frahto glared out the front window of the Vuusah lodge. The empty street taunted him. Lenatoh had been gone hours on his errand to the so-called Zehla Guild, leaving Frahto to kick his heels in case Roh showed up. Considering they'd only arrived in Dohni yesterday, he judged that unlikely. Yet, while everyone else was out scouring the streets, Frahto was stuck here waiting for something to happen.

A floorboard creaked in the hall; then footsteps padded its length. The front door latch clicked, followed by low voices as someone talked to the zehla stationed on the portico.

They never had guards at the compound in Tarsah.

Frahto had no interest in whoever was leaving, until Sorah stepped onto the street. He swore under his breath. By the time he made it outside, the girl was at least twenty paces away, completely alone and moving quickly.

"Sorah!"

The girl spun, her scarred cheeks reddening. She wore a blue-and-red marbled mahgan and leggings of soft grey wool. Her hair was braided and beaded simply, as befitted a

Fiugreh girl her age, but she lacked srih around her wrists. As though she saw him noticing, Sorah put her hands behind her back, cheeks reddening further. A leather cord around her neck suggested some sort of pendant concealed beneath her clothing.

"Where are you going?" Frahto asked.

"To see my mother." The girl's chin jutted. "The *Samarus* is here. I saw her at the wharf when we docked."

"Your father said he'd take you."

"When? He's not even here! Besides, I'm sure he'll find some excuse not to go."

"You can't go on your own." The wharf was miles away on the other side of the harbour.

"Why not? I know the way."

Frahto shook his head; Lenatoh would slay him if he let Sorah wander the city alone. "Come back inside. I'm sure your father will take you later."

"No." Sorah turned and resumed walking, leaving Frahto following at her heels. He tried reasoning with her as she led him onto a bustling street, but Sorah had become inordinately resolute all of a sudden. Where was the shy, awkward girl he'd known for the past two years? She grinned up at him. "I suppose you can come, too."

Frahto smothered a smile. In truth, it was good to escape the lodge, get his bearings. He'd been too miserable to pay attention when they'd arrived, and now the city bombarded his senses. He kept a close eye on Sorah. She might well feel at home in Dohni, but she'd reached an age when her untamed affinity for ellir made this city dangerous. She would have no means of resisting the heartstorm if it tugged too hard.

Roh, on the other hand, must be revelling in it.

Sorah led the way confidently. She was tall for her age, the top of her head reaching the middle of his chest, her legs long to match, and they soon found a pace to suit them both. The silence between them was not companionable, but it wasn't awkward, either. They crossed the bridge over the harbour, passed into the maze of streets, plazas and gardens of the Old Merali Quarter. Frahto was glad Sorah knew the way, because he would have been hopelessly lost in minutes. He measured their progress by the prominent hill in the east of the city. It grew larger as they drew nearer and eventually entered its immense, midmorning shadow.

At the base of the city wall near the Great Market, Sorah climbed a set of steps. Frahto gained the top, a few paces behind, and stopped to take in the expanse of Dohni's deep-water port. To their left, Commemoration Wharf occupied the eastern shore of an almost fully enclosed cove, dozens of ships clustered like washed-up prickle-shells. Opposite the wharf stood a stumpy lighthouse to guide ships through the narrow entrance. The many seagulls spiralling overhead seemed to enjoy the stiff, salty breeze grabbing at Frahto's clothes. A single ship, sails unfurled, nosed across the gently rolling waters towards the harbour and sea beyond.

Sorah pointed out her mother's ship. The *Samarus*, with its green hull and orange flags, was berthed at the pier closest to their current position on the northern rim of the cove.

When the girl showed no sign of moving towards it, he said, "I assume we haven't come simply to look at your mother's ship?"

Sorah folded her arms as though she were cold. "What if she doesn't recognise me?"

"Of course she'll recognise you."

"But what if she doesn't?"

Frahto stared at the ship and tried to think of the right thing to say. "Then it will be because you've grown up."

"You think?" She turned her wide brown eyes on him, guileless and full of hope.

"Of course. But I'm sure she'll know you. It's only been two years. You'll see."

"All right." She unfolded her arms and wiped her hands on her mahgan, but still she hesitated. "What if she doesn't want to see me? She could be mad at me for leaving…"

"Sorah, it will be fine." Burn it, how did he find himself here? With effort, he gentled his tone. "Of course she'll want to see you. She's your mother. Now, how about you stop worrying, and we go and find her?" He held out his hand and was surprised when she took it, her bottom lip caught between her teeth.

"All right," she said again.

As Sorah led him along the top of the wall, Frahto regretted offering his hand, but couldn't bring himself to break the girl's tight grip. Her unfettered llirah throbbed and surged with a riot of emotion — fear, excitement, guilt — just the sort of thing that could tip her out of control. He attempted to calm her rhythm, wishing his empathiser skills were more accomplished.

"Why did you leave your mother?" Frahto asked.

She tensed and pulled away from him. "I wanted to know my father."

"You would have been safer at sea. With your…" He gestured vaguely, reluctant to say the words.

Her mouth compressed. "Sailors aren't at sea all the time. My mother told me my father could help me."

"Then why hasn't he?"

Lenatoh could have quelled the girl any time these past two years. He was risking his daughter's life.

"He has, but…" Breaking off, she stomped along the wall, oddly reminding Frahto of Rahda, the woman who'd been forced to raise her for the past two years. Then she stopped again. "It's so unfair! The Vuusah don't want me because I'm only half Fiugreh. My mother's people don't want me either, because I'm ti-rei." She gestured at the ugly scars on her cheeks. "I don't fit in anywhere. Where am I supposed to go, Frahto? No one wants me."

The girl looked on the verge of tears. Frahto cast about for something to say. He didn't know what *ti-rei* meant, but he'd wondered about those scars. Did it mean *half-blood* to the Kestali? He'd never heard of that being an issue before. Feeling helpless, he took her hand again and focused on soothing her rhythm. "Your father loves you. He will never cast you out."

"Rahda hates me."

Unfortunately, he couldn't refute that. "I'm sure your mother —"

"I'm an embarrassment to her, too. She was glad to give me over to Da."

Frahto didn't know what to say. He kept hold of her hand, even when she tried to pull it free, too afraid her tumultuous emotions would be her undoing.

"I wish I could be like Adehl," Sorah said in a thick voice.

"You don't mean that."

"I do. She said one day it would be different. That it wouldn't be so bad to be pidakah."

Frahto's heart stuttered. "She *said* that to you?"

"Yes."

The nerve of the woman. He recalled the conversation they'd had about Sorah that very first day. Adehl had chastised him for treating Sorah as less than human, claiming the girl should have srih. He schooled his voice to calm. "She told you she was pidakah?"

Sorah bit her lip. "She hinted at it."

"And you didn't say anything?"

"Why would I?"

Burning bright sun. "Sorah, listen to me." He wasn't sure

if he sounded as calm as he intended. "You do *not* want to be like Adehl. She lied and cheated and —"

"She only did it to be trained as a zehli. It's not like she hurt anyone."

"She's pidakah. And so are you. Your father will have to quell you soon, or else —"

"I don't want to be quelled." Her fingers toyed with something concealed near her throat.

"You have no choice," Frahto said. The girl tilted her chin mulishly, and Frahto tugged on her hand. "Why hasn't he quelled you yet? You should have gone wild by now, with your affinity."

Her brown gaze met his steadily. "Perhaps he doesn't want to."

"He must. For your safety if nothing else." Since he still held Sorah's hand, he probed deeper. Now that he was looking for it, he detected the restraint, the thing that anchored her rhythm. His fingers flew to the leather thong around her neck and drew out the medallion from beneath her mahgan. A deceptively simple metal disk, dull and silver with no obvious decoration. Warm from her skin. Its ellir pulsed with Sorah's rhythm, spring rain and nectar, steady and strong.

Snatching it away from him, she stepped back. "That's mine. I'm not allowed to take it off."

"Is that *claith*?"

"Yes."

"When did he give it to you?"

Her right fist closed around it, knuckles against her throat. "Last winter."

"It helps?" His voice came out rough. When she nodded, Frahto rubbed his temple. He remembered the unprecedented trip Lenatoh had made to Tarsah with his daughter six months ago. Obtaining, *aligning,* a claith medallion would have been no small endeavour — or expense. What the fury was Lenatoh doing? "It's not a permanent solution, Sorah. You must know that." A tiny thing like that couldn't hope to hold her vibrant llirah in check forever. It was merely staving off the inevitable. It was cruel to raise her hopes like that.

The girl gave him a stony glare and turned away. "I'm going to see my mother."

Frahto's gut clenched as he followed her along the top of the wall, the sea breeze whipping at her clothes and hair. For the first time, he felt sorrow that Sorah's mother had conferred Kestali blood on Lenatoh's daughter. Frahto had never allowed himself to consider it before, but it struck him that Sorah would have made a formidable zehli.

28. We call them gierfeh

The message was waiting for Adehl when she bounced in from the stables.

She'd spent a few hours with Chanti, holed up in a horse stall, teaching him the first thing every acoleh learnt: how to touch and isolate his own llirah. How to make his rhythm small and hold it close. Chanti had applied himself solemnly in the wake of losing Sapling, but he'd smiled when he succeeded at constraining his energy.

Adehl's blood hummed, and a weight lifted. For the first time since she'd learnt of the boy's affinity, she could breathe. Chanti would need to remain vigilant and practise, but that was all it had taken for him to gain basic control.

Inside the Wild Colt, Fenaika, the young woman posted at the welcome desk, waved a piece of folded parchment. "This arrived for you, mistress."

Adehl took the missive, which was elegantly sealed with a glob of blue wax. The device was a strange, long-necked bird, wings folded, inside a circle.

"That's House Auwyn's emblem," Fenaika said, her ear ornaments swaying.

"Thank you," Adehl said, ignoring Fenaika's obvious curiosity. She slid her thumb under the fold and scanned the note from Lady Kenna Auwyn inviting Adehl to visit her at the university that afternoon.

Anticipation fizzed through Adehl's blood, and she hurried up the stairs to change clothes. On the Night of the Archer, tongues loosened by davinna, she and Lady Kenna had shared deep confidences. Adehl had thought she'd found an ally. Possibly a friend.

Could she tell Kenna about Chanti? What she'd done?

It was early afternoon when Adehl navigated the twisted streets surrounding the Wild Colt to reach the bustling thoroughfare known as Moi Boulevard. Heading uphill towards the pinnacle of Goldayn Rise, she skirted one group of prowling exhorters who didn't look at her twice, then found the stairway Roh had described.

As she climbed the steps and gained height, she began to appreciate the size of the city. The oldest parts were crammed on the east side of the harbour inside a massive wall, but Dohni had clearly broken free of this restraint long ago. Rooftops cluttered the space outside the walls, bordered to the north by a river and hills rising into mountains. The river merged with two more rivers pouring out of steep valleys, the wide area between cleared for farming.

The western shores of the main harbour bore additional city districts that looked newer, more open, and which dissolved into fields and farmlands farther west. A small, wooded mountain — or perhaps a large hill — with a rocky crown stood proud of the taller range at its back.

At the top of the stairway, almost the first thing Adehl saw was another circah of exhorters. Chah and his minions stood in a tight circle, a stationary group amid a bevy of scholars and students crossing a paved terrace. The zehla looked to be chanting, and Adehl's gut lurched sickeningly. She hauled her llirah in close and eyed a nearby colonnaded building beneath a green dome. Could she make it inside before the exhorters saw her?

Then Chah looked over, and it was too late. He went rigid as his gaze latched onto her. In heartbeats, the entire circah was surging in her direction, shoving aside anyone who got in their way.

Adehl had the distinct impression she ought to run.

"Stand your ground, Adehl," said a breezy voice nearby. Lady Kenna Auwyn rose from a stone bench, the black-garbed claithwielder at her side. In the daylight, her braided hair was a pale, silvery blond, her eyes blue as the summer sky. She wore a gobeila of dark blue, the red scholar's sash draped elegantly. "This looks like it could be fun."

Adehl doubted it, but before she could respond, Chah arrived before her, his eyes glinting. "You're the zehli we saw with Roh. Where is he?"

She paused. "You're after Roh?"

"Our doyen wants to speak to him." Chah glowered at her, the cocky surety of their previous meeting absent. Even if they didn't know about her yet, something had changed. "More pleasant for you if you tell us where you're lodging."

For the first time since breakfast, Adehl wondered where Roh was. He'd gone to visit a leatherworker and ought to have returned long before midday. She'd been too preoccupied with Chanti, and then Kenna's invitation, to notice. "Roh will see the doyen if he chooses to," she said, trying to suppress her misgivings. "I'll pass along your request."

"It's not a *request*." But Chah halted abruptly when Lady Kenna stepped forward, forcing him to acknowledge her presence.

"Think carefully, zehli," the scholar said. "Adehl is my guest this afternoon. I would hate to see her importuned."

"My lady," Chah ground out. "This is Vuusah business."

"Indeed?" Lady Kenna inclined her head. "I understood Adehl was no longer a member of your illustrious order."

Adehl flinched at the words, stated so baldly, even though they were true. Even though she'd intended as much weeks ago. Even though she'd been actively seeking a kalkah licence here in Dohni.

"But..." Chah glowered at Adehl some more. "You were with Roh."

Adehl pressed her lips together. A clump of animated students, seeming oblivious to the confrontation, veered around the exhorters taking up space in the thoroughfare.

"*Roh* is Vuusah," Chah said. When Adehl still made no reply, the exhorter spluttered. "You cannot tell me he's not. I will never believe it."

Adehl wished she could be certain. If Roh never sought a kalkah licence, would he remain Vuusah? They hadn't discussed it.

"Please take your hooters and leave," Lady Kenna said imperiously. "I will ensure your message reaches its intended recipient."

"Thank you, my lady," Chah said roughly. "But —"

"That will be all. Jai, please..."

"Not necessary, I assure you." Chah glared at Adehl. "I'm sure we'll meet again." With a final scowl, he spun on his heel and led his circah towards the stairway.

Adehl's heart thudded almost painfully as Ninah and one other zehli cast dark, curious looks over their shoulders. When the last hooter — Adehl decided she liked the term — had finally passed from sight, she sank onto the bench Kenna had vacated. "That was... that was..."

"I told you it would be fun," Lady Kenna said.

"It was, a little bit." Adehl hugged her upper body as her heart rate gradually settled. "Thank you for your assistance, my lady."

"Just Kenna, please. And you may believe I welcome any chance to mess with hooters." Kenna's fingers stroked the edge of her scholar's sash, and Adehl tried to read her intention — and perhaps the scholar was trying to figure out her, too. But Kenna simply said, "Thank you for accepting my invitation."

"I was pleased to receive it."

"How was your head yesterday?"

Adehl quirked her lips. "How was yours?"

Kenna chuckled. "Come on, then. We can't talk properly here."

The scholar led Adehl to a well-tended path along the cliff edge, the claithwielder bringing up the rear. Since only an old iron railing separated the path from a steep drop, Adehl kept close to the stone walls on her left. They walked in a large curve around the top of the escarpment, with views over the port, the Merchants Quarter, and a long, partially wooded hill on the eastern outskirts of the city. Kenna named the hill Gorannen Rise and said her estate was there. Below, outside the city wall, buildings packed the valley.

Kenna pointed out the high, stone wall dividing them from the Circle of Wind as they passed but did not offer to take Adehl there. Eventually, they left the cliff path and crossed a quadrangle to enter a building covered in climbing greenery.

Lady Kenna's large, third-floor room seemed more like a parlour than an office. Occupying the corner of the building, it commanded a view of mountains and sky through large windows. Afternoon sunlight speared across a sofa and two armchairs arranged around a low table in the centre of the room. The furniture was upholstered in a soft, blue fabric and festooned with cushions in russet and yellow. Shelves of books and a chunky sideboard lined the internal walls, and a large, cluttered desk stood near one of the windows. A breeze drifted in, riffling through parchments weighted down by a rock.

Kenna guided Adehl into an armchair and turned to the claithwielder. "All right, you may go find Gordoh," she said. "But not too quickly."

Jaikud's eyes narrowed. "He's just down the hall."

"I'm sure you'll think of something to do for half an hour."

He hesitated, a tinge of colour in his cheeks. "I will go and *talk* to Gordoh for a while, if you will promise not to leave this room."

"We are going to sit down and drink tea." He held her gaze until Kenna huffed and said, "Very well, I promise not to leave this room." With a nod, the man withdrew, closing the door behind him. Kenna busied herself at the sideboard, where a small kettle sat on a flat stone. She soon set down two mugs. "You must be wondering why I invited you here."

"I rather hoped it was to continue our conversation from the other night." Adehl picked up a mug and sipped what turned out to be hot, ginger tea.

The lady's manicured eyebrow twitched. "Which part?"

"To be honest, it's somewhat hazy," Adehl said with a quick smile. "But I seem to recall you starting to tell me about your research."

"Ah." Kenna sat with her knees and boots pressed together, her gobeila flowing over her lower legs, which were angled to one side. It seemed oddly formal to Adehl, who was still getting accustomed to sitting in chairs and no longer knew what to do with her limbs. Kenna said, "I seem to recall you laughed."

Adehl bit her lip. "There was so much davinna. I'd never

had it before." She smoothed the amber-coloured folds of her own gobeila over her lap. "I laughed because I realised… I realised you were *right*."

"About what?"

"All of it."

Lady Kenna tilted her head. "Right in thinking the Vuusah don't own the world's energy? That the Fiugreh are not the only race who meld with ellir?"

"Yes."

"Because it *makes no sense* that one group of people living in a tiny corner of the continent are the sole custodians of ellir."

Sun's fury. Adehl caught each of Lady Kenna's words, flung like tiny stones, and found a place for them. She felt the truth in her bones — and wondered how she'd ever believed otherwise. It put her personal conflict with the Vuusah into a whole new context. "You used a word. Not pidakah, but…?"

"Gierfeh." Kenna's expression softened. "Anyone who has affinity, no matter their bloodline, we call them gierfeh."

Adehl recognised the old Fiugreh tongue. The word meant spark in the soul… or soulspark. "Gierfeh," Adehl said, liking the feel of the word on her tongue. She thought of Chanti and wondered how many other gierfeh children like him needed to hear it, needed to know they were not alone. Perhaps Kenna, as a child, had needed to hear the word, too. "You must have been quelled when you were quite young."

"I was eleven. Lord Auwyn had several zehla in his retinue. I had no idea what was happening at the time."

Adehl's foot tapped the floor. "But you knew…?"

A sharp nod. "I grew up around zehla. I always knew." In her lap, Kenna's clasped hands were white. "Being a child, I had secretly hoped… but they took it away from me without warning or explanation."

For a moment, Adehl was twelve again. But for circumstance and opportunity, her fate would have been the same. She stilled her foot. "How many gierfeh are born among the Merali?"

"Not so many. Affinity for ellir doesn't run strongly in Merali bloodlines." Kenna paused to take a sip of tea, eyeing Adehl over the rim of the mug. "I suspect my niece might be gierfeh, though."

Adehl tried to conceal her surprise. "How old is she?"

"Eleven." Kenna looked sad, then said, "It's another matter here, though. There's plenty of Fiugreh and Sevikk blood flowing through the citizens of Dohni."

Adehl absorbed that. "Affinity runs in Sevikk bloodlines?" She thought of her father.

"It does indeed. What do you know of the Sevikk goddess, Hyoggi?"

"Only a little. She is the goddess of below and mother of the world…" Her words faded. It seemed suddenly obvious.

Lady Kenna's mouth curved. "Hyoggi's followers believe the divine cadence is her spirit."

"And the divine cadence is ellir."

Kenna nodded. "Around one in fifty Sevikk children are claimed by Hyoggi at the age of maturing. They are either adopted by the Order of Hyoggi, or the goddess takes their soul."

"One in fifty?"

"Thereabouts," Kenna said. "It is similar for Fiugreh, I believe."

These stones were more like rocks, heavier and harder to catch, but Adehl grabbed them with both hands and sought to regain her balance. The Fiugreh didn't worship deities as others did, but there had always been ellir; zehla had been spiritual leaders and guides among her people since time began. If it were true that one in fifty Sevikk children manifested affinity for ellir… Adehl could well imagine how the

Sevikks came to believe in a goddess living in the heart of the world. "So, the followers of Hyoggi…" She couldn't get the words out; it was all too… incredible. "What exactly are you saying?"

Kenna took another sip from her mug. "I think you know what I'm saying."

Adehl drew in a deep breath. "They're like zehla; they meld with ellir."

"They call it communing with the divine cadence." She chuckled. "They're nothing like zehla, though."

Adehl said nothing for at least a minute while this new information settled in her mind. The fact Sevikk bloodlines bore as strong an affinity as the Fiugreh… She thought again of her father, and her blood boiled. "How do you *know* all this?"

"My research." Kenna rubbed at a blue smear on her middle finger. "I've wanted answers for as long as I can remember."

"So you became a scholar?" It seemed a strange occupation for a Merali wellborn.

"I suppose it's rather a foreign concept to the Fiugreh. But most Merali wellborns — and many farborns — are forced to study as children." Kenna gave a conspiratorial grin. "It did require dramatic tactics to persuade my family to let me come here. I don't think they've forgiven me yet, and it's been eight years."

"Hence the claithwielder?"

"Indeed. They wouldn't let me come alone. Now Jaikud's gone and fallen in love with Gordoh, and I'll probably need to buy out his commission and find another to replace him." She smirked. "If you repeat this, I'll deny it, but it has proven useful to have a claithwielder on hand — especially with those abominable Vuusah exhorters."

Adehl took up her mug and drained the lukewarm tea.

She believed Kenna about the Sevikks. It made so much sense. But she didn't know what to do with any of it. Something so fundamental ought to be common knowledge. Not that the Vuusah would ever admit to anyone other than the Fiugreh clans having affinity. Perhaps the Order of Hyoggi was the same. "Why *did* you invite me here today?" Adehl asked.

Lady Kenna's brow twitched again. "I wanted you to know the truth."

"Why?"

"Because even though you *laughed* when I mentioned my research the other night, you told me your truth and listened to mine."

"I didn't mean to laugh."

"I know. The davinna."

"Who else knows about your research?"

"Only the Ellirisi. For now."

Needing time to think, Adehl rose and went to the sideboard. Out the window, a small hawk hovered against the blue sky. She picked up the teakettle. "This is still hot." It had been sitting on a round, flat stone of deep green. Adehl held her palm over the surface, felt warmth radiating from it. "Stars and sun. What's this?"

"It comes from far across the sea. A place called Kasso. Best not touch it."

Adehl retracted her hand and faced Kenna. "But what is it?"

"It's called a bhes." Kenna met Adehl's look with a crooked smile. "Yonnah, one of our zehla, is researching how other peoples engage with ellir. She spent time with the people of Kasso and found these heating stones rather useful, so she brought a few back with her."

"From Kasso, across the sea." It felt like worms squirmed through Adehl's entire body. She pulled herself together and took the kettle across to refill both mugs. "One of these days, I want to know everything. But, right now, I need to talk to you about something."

Lady Kenna smoothed out her gobeila, knees and boots still pressed together, and waited as Adehl replaced the kettle and resumed her seat.

"I've been worried about a… gierfeh boy at our lodging." It was a relief to speak the words at last. "A stable lad. He's about to go wild."

Kenna's eyes flashed. "Poor little thing." She studied Adehl's face. "Do you need me to pay for a noumenor?"

"I didn't mean…"

"Isn't that what you want? The boy will be safe."

"I want him to be safe." The air between them seemed to spark with things unsaid. Adehl had thought, after everything Kenna had already told her, this would be easier. She thought of Chanti's face that morning — initially, after Sapling had been taken away; later, after his first secret lesson in the horse stall. "Is that how things are in Dohni? Is quelling gierfeh children still the only course of action?"

Kenna's finger tapped against the side of her mug. "Most gierfeh children are not found until it's too late to do anything. Those who *are* identified are lucky if their parents can afford a noumenor."

"Back home, gierfeh children — that is, children who are not accepted by the Vuusah for training — are quelled free of charge, regardless of their lineage."

"Dohni is founded on commerce and trade. Nothing here is free."

"But the kalkah zehla… They're all trained by the Vuusah, aren't they? They must be. Surely most of them come originally from the Humming Downs?"

"And they chose to come here." Kenna arched an eyebrow. "The Zehla Guild is mainly interested in charging exorbitant fees and maintaining their exclusivity. I pay for every gierfeh child I can find… For now, it's all I can do."

Adehl's stomach soured as she contemplated this picture of kalkah zehla. She remembered Roh's reaction that first night at Fortune Spring. Is this what he'd believed about kalkah zehla from the start? Back then, she'd thought Roh arrogant, unyielding and prejudiced. But… perhaps that had been her.

Then she became aware of Kenna watching her, and the scholar's other words filtered past Adehl's churning thoughts. *For now, it's all I can do.*

For now.

Adehl pressed her damp palms against her lap. Hoping she understood the scholar's look, she said, "The other night you said things could be different."

"I did." Kenna steadily held her gaze. "I would spend all the coin I have…"

After several heartbeats, Adehl said, "You don't really wish to pay for a noumenor, do you?"

"No." Kenna's form quivered with something like excitement.

Adehl felt a smile take over her face.

29. THE WHISTLING-KITE CALL

By the time Roh returned to the Wild Colt, the afternoon was
well advanced. He hadn't meant to stay away so long. Sun's
blood, he'd been gone all day. Having fled Donellon Plaza,
unsure whether Lenatoh had seen him, he'd found himself
deep in the Merchants Quarter, then circled through the outer
city all the way to the River Gate.

Still, based on the past week, he hadn't expected Adehl to
be gone.

He headed out to the rear courtyard, where the stable lad
whistled merrily as he shovelled a pile of horse dung into a
wooden bucket. This was the boy Adehl had befriended. She
seemed to have spent an inordinate number of hours helping
him with his chores, and Roh wanted to know why.

On sight of Roh, the lad levered himself upright, the
shovel clanging onto the stones. "Oops. I not see you there!"

"Sorry to disturb your work. I'm looking for Adehl," Roh
said.

"She not be here." The words sounded strained, and the
boy squeezed his eyes shut as though focusing intensely on

something. With a low cry, he braced hands on thighs and sucked in long gasps of air.

Roh hurried closer and laid a gentle hand on the boy's back. Wildly fluctuating energy erupted like stampeding loophorns. "Steady," Roh said.

Wide, terrified eyes found Roh. "I can't — I need Sapling!"

Roh's empathiser skills were not as honed as Adehl's, but he wove ellir and attempted to head off the boy's panic. "Deep breaths, now. In… out…" The lad's whole body trembled, but gradually he calmed and his llirah settled. Roh guided him to a bench in the shade. "There you go."

"Thank you, zehli." The lad covered his face with his hands.

Roh hunkered down before him. "You're Chanti, I think?"

He nodded, peeping through his fingers.

"Bright day. I'm Roh." He focused on the boy's rhythm until he was satisfied with its amplitude. "Adehl has been helping with your chores." And stopping him from going wild, apparently.

"Yes."

"I'm sorry I startled you."

Chanti sniffed and uncovered his face to present tear-streaked cheeks. "I be all right now."

Roh straightened, strangely reluctant to leave the boy alone. With a careful thread of ellir, he again searched for Adehl inside the Wild Colt building. "Did Adehl go somewhere?" he asked with misgiving.

"I not know."

"All right." Roh gave Chanti his best smile. "How about you show me these horses I've heard so much about?"

An hour later, Roh had heard all about Chanti's favourite mare, Sapling, getting sold that morning and was teaching the lad how to thread beads in his hair when he felt the familiar presence. He scruffed the boy's head and emerged from the stable to find Adehl barging out the back door of the lodging house. She checked her step. "Is Chanti all right?"

"He's fine."

"Why are you out here?"

"Looking for you." Roh lounged against the outer wall of the stable building. "I've been making the lad's acquaintance."

Adehl stilled; it was almost imperceptible, but they were injaleh, so Roh felt rigidity ripple from her shoulders to her feet.

"Why didn't you tell me?" Roh watched Adehl closely, had no explanation for her heightened colour or the guilt surging across the space between them. "He *is* the reason you've been hiding out here, I assume?"

She jerked a nod, and they faced each other across the width of the courtyard. "If I don't, he'll go wild."

"He almost did just now."

Another wave of guilt flowed from Adehl. "I left him too long. He was anchored to a horse that was sold this morning."

Roh thought about Adehl spending day after day out here, doing half Chanti's work so she could stop his llirah from surging out of control. Even had Sapling remained as the boy's anchor, it was a battle Adehl had no hope of winning. The poor boy would only grow more unstable, and she couldn't be with him all the time, indefinitely. Roh loved her more for trying. "Jaleh, I could have helped you," he said.

She eyed him as she chewed her lip. "I know."

"We need to find him a noumenor."

"No."

"Do you want me to find one?"

"*No.* Besides, they're too expensive."

"I think… That is, I know noumenors among the Vuusah. I could ask…"

Adehl's eyes widened. "You can't bring any of them *here*."

"I know. Sorry." He pushed fingers into the back of his neck. Sun's blood. He was forgetting his own adventures of the day. And she'd been out on the streets, alone. "Jaleh, where have you been? The streets are swarming with exhorters looking for you."

"Actually… they're looking for you," Adehl said. "Where have *you* been? I was worried."

Roh was across the courtyard in three steps. "I'm sorry. I didn't think." He wrapped arms around her. "I followed a circah acting strangely, and…" Her words sank in, and he pulled back to see her face. "What makes you think they're hunting *me*? What happened?"

Adehl drew him over to the same wooden bench he'd guided Chanti to earlier. This late in the afternoon, the bench sat in deep shade, but the stone wall of the lodging house behind it still radiated warmth from the sun. Adehl seemed… excited about something — eyes shining, colour heightened, llirah dancing. Now that her initial alarm had dissipated, Roh saw it had been there all along.

"Lady Kenna invited me to meet with her," she said. "That's where I've been. Your friends from the other day were at the university."

"They saw you?"

She grimaced. "I could hardly avoid them. They wanted to know where to find *you*."

"Did they —"

"No." She smiled, and another burst of excitement flowed into Roh. "Lady Kenna and her claithwielder were there."

He hadn't seen her like this before: simmering with unbridled hope and… exhilaration. Something had happened. Something to do with Lady Kenna. Not a surprise, exactly.

On the Night of the Archer, they'd giggled like co-conspirators. Seeing the buoyancy in her soul made him realise how weighed down she'd been in the scant weeks he'd known her.

"Do you think Lady Kenna will help you?" Roh asked.

"Help me with what?" A shield of wariness instantly shuttered her elation.

"Keeping you safe from the Vuusah. She has influence in this city, and now word has come…" He saw her confusion and realised he'd neglected to mention the most important news. "Adehl, I saw Dinah and her circah on the streets today. The ones who were in Tarsah with us. They're out hunting with all the others." He sucked in a breath. "And Lenatoh is here, too."

The weight came down upon her again, and she sighed. "We always knew they would come after you."

"You mean us."

"Chah didn't seem to know about me."

"Maybe not yet."

"Lenatoh is your nedoyen, right? Did he see you?"

"I don't know." Sun's blood, was it too much to hope Lenatoh hadn't recognised him? Roh slid closer to Adehl across the bench seat and took her hands. "We need a backup plan. Somewhere safe for you to go. Because it's only a matter of time before they come after you. Do you think Lady Kenna will help?" She likely never went anywhere without that claithwielder.

Adehl rested her brow on Roh's shoulder. He thought he heard her mutter a string of choice curses into the side of his neck. Then, cheeks flushed, she lifted her head. "As it happens, Kenna *will* help us. She's already offered. She knows… That is, I've told her everything that's happened. And she's told me… so much." The light was back in her eyes. "I think — if we stay here — the Ellirisi will very much be our friends."

Roh tried to read her expression, wished she hadn't bound her llirah so close. Adehl squeezed his hand. For several heartbeats, they didn't speak, and Roh felt bare beneath Adehl's scrutiny although he wasn't sure why.

"Jaleh," Adehl said gently, and it was the first time she'd called him that. "What are you going to do?"

That question again. He didn't feel any closer to an answer. "I don't know," he said. Although… maybe that wasn't entirely true.

On seeing Lenatoh, Roh had run. But he couldn't deny that the nedoyen's proximity, a short walk across the harbour, niggled at Roh like a grass seed in his sock. It would be so easy to walk up to the lodge and demand explanations.

He told himself he wanted explanations. In truth — a truth he barely acknowledged — Roh wanted Lenatoh to pat him on the shoulder and tell him everything would be all right.

The following morning, Roh slipped out of their room and made his way to the Fiugreh Settlement District. He didn't stop to think about what he was doing or what he'd do when he saw Lenatoh. He only knew he needed to see the nedoyen like a silverbark nut needed fire.

Outside the Vuusah lodge, three exhorters stood watch, mouths set in straight, determined lines. Two he recognised from his travels around the city; the third was Ketahl from Dinah's Silver Wolf circah. Roh eased back into the lane, knocked his head softly against the wall.

He nudged a stone out of the way with his boot. An enormous tabby cat, sprawled along the top of the opposite sun-drenched wall, opened his eyes. After watching Roh for several minutes, the animal jumped down to sidle against his legs. Roh crouched to trail fingers through soft fur and felt the cat's llirah pulsing with curiosity.

Blighted sun. He couldn't stay here all day patting a cat. The impressive tabby rubbed his face against Roh's hand and held his head for scratches.

On the street, out of sight, a door closed, and Roh heard voices. New voices.

Familiar voices.

One almost as familiar as his own. He jerked to his feet, and the tabby bolted down the alley.

He didn't need to look but couldn't stop himself. Carefully, Roh peered around the corner of the lane. Frahto, garbed in his dark-green town mahgan, stood chatting with the three zehla on watch. On the street, clearly waiting, was Lenatoh's daughter, Sorah. The girl edged along the street until she was almost level with Roh's hiding spot — as though sensing his presence, she glanced in Roh's direction. Cursing silently, he retreated farther down the lane, seeking better cover. He was almost certain Sorah had seen him, but he heard no outburst to indicate she'd told anyone. His chest weirdly tight, he ducked behind a parked wagon, where he waited and watched.

A few minutes later, Frahto and Sorah passed the mouth of the lane, Sorah chattering away as though nothing were out of the ordinary. Perhaps she hadn't seen him, after all. Roh braced his forehead against the rough timber of the wagon, breathed until the ache subsided, then clambered to his feet.

He picked up Frahto's trail on Founders Road, the district's main commercial thoroughfare, and ended up in a market field. Alongside pickets holding dozens of horses were tents selling tack, feed and other horse supplies.

Produce and artisan markets occupied the opposite side of the field.

In the horse market, Roh cupped his hands around his mouth and let out the whistling-kite call they'd used as boys. Frahto stiffened, silenced Sorah with a gesture. His gaze swept the market, skimmed past the saddle stand Roh lurked behind, swung back to meet Roh's. It held for one beat, two, Frahto's expression unreadable. Roh didn't wait any longer. Knowing his friend would follow, he circled behind the market tents towards an unoccupied corner of the field and a small copse of trees. Waiting on a dappled patch of meadow grass, Roh shifted his weight from one foot to the other. Adjusted his braid where it pulled at his scalp. Flicked a stray cobweb off his tunic.

When Frahto at last broke free of the tents, his gaze locked again onto Roh's. Without hesitation, Frahto approached with long strides across the grass. He pulled up about five paces away.

They stared at each other. Roh scrutinised his friend — the shadows below his hooded eyes, the hard line of his mouth, the haphazardly beaded braids. Frahto hadn't shaved in a few days, which gave him a roguish appearance.

Examining Roh in turn, Frahto's eyes narrowed. "Lenatoh was right," he said, after an agonising silence. "He predicted you'd come to us."

Roh had a feeling this was a mistake. "I didn't expect to see you here."

"Why should you have all the adventures?" They could have been facing off about who got to claim the loophorn kill. Then Frahto closed the gap between them, pulled Roh into a rough hug. "You idiot," Frahto said.

Roh allowed a brief embrace then shrugged Frahto off. Those hunting expeditions on the downs seemed very long ago.

Frahto's expression grew bitter. "So that's it? Some woman comes along, and we're not friends anymore?"

"We can be friends."

"Are you sure?" Frahto crossed his arms and glared. Roh wondered if he were thinking about that last morning in Tarsah. "What are you doing, Roh? Where's your pidakah sidekick?"

"I don't expect you to understand."

"Understand? I'm miles away from understanding!" Clouds drifted across the sun, casting a shadow over the world. "Don't throw your life away over her!"

Roh shook his head. "I'm not —"

"You've broken multiple precepts. Gone rogue with a woman who lied and cheated her way into the Vuusah. How can you…" He broke off, mouth turning down.

The accusations were not unfounded. He couldn't even blame Frahto for making them. Roh had done things he wasn't proud of. "I'm not throwing anything away." Roh held Frahto's gaze, tried to make him understand one thing at least. "She's my injaleh."

"She's also pidakah!"

"I don't care."

Frahto's brow furrowed so deep the ridges looked permanent. Over in the horse market, an auctioneer's voice rang loudly across the grass. After a long pause, Frahto said, "You truly have changed."

He had. Roh hardly recognised the man he'd been a month ago. And it was all due to Adehl — although not for the reason Frahto thought. She'd made him question, made him think. Once he'd tugged on that thread it seemed never to end. "I've come to understand that some Vuusah beliefs are… limited. Misguided." He noted Frahto's shocked expression. "If you stay in Dohni, you'll see."

"I will *not*."

"The Vuusah are despised here, Frahto. They have no true power, yet they patrol the streets like militia and harass every zehli they come across. I've seen them force candour without cause in the middle of the street. You talk about breaking precepts…"

Frahto shifted a few steps, revealing grass and a stray leaf flattened beneath his large boots. He didn't meet Roh's gaze. "Doyi Palvemah says it's necessary."

"Is it *necessary* to hold and punish zehla inside the lodge?"

"That's not happening."

"Are you certain? Because I saw the aftermath." Roh couldn't think of that day without feeling nauseated. "I never thought I'd be ashamed to be Vuusah."

Frahto sucked in a breath. "You don't mean that." Then, voice rough, he said, "We're your family. You're supposed to be Atalah one day."

Roh wished he were anywhere else. He wished he didn't have to do this. "I'm sorry. Not anymore."

The words might as well have been a punch. Frahto reeled, colour blooming then draining from his face as a gust of wind rattled the leaves in the canopy overhead. After a silence as loud as a wail, Frahto said, "Ever since you met that woman, I don't know who you are."

"Her name is Adehl," Roh said. His heart pounded out a dirge of sorrow and guilt and pain. He and Frahto had been friends for a long time. This felt like the end.

Another long silence, punctuated by the distant call of the auctioneer. The sun had never returned, Roh realised, banished by rainclouds accumulating overhead.

Frahto straightened. "You need to come with me." His voice had gone cold, hard.

"No."

"Lenatoh wants to speak to you."

Roh's cracking heart couldn't take much more. He'd made

his choice, and now he needed to get away. There was no longer any point running to Lenatoh for guidance. And if Roh thought to explain himself — what could he possibly say that the man didn't already know? "Tell him to go home."

"Roh, don't you dare…"

Roh gathered his strength and dragged himself away from the man who had once been closer to him than his brother. "Don't try to follow me," he said.

FRAHTO WALKED WOODENLY towards the picket where he'd left Sorah fawning over a jet-black mare. He stopped once to brace himself against a hay cart, bowing his head until the nausea subsided. The air rang with voices, everyone speaking loudly to make themselves heard over the horse auction.

Sorah wasn't where she was supposed to be.

Wretched girl. He supposed she'd moved on to another horse, or the mahgan stall she'd been pestering him about. He had better things to do than search for the child. He ought to be following Roh.

She's pidakah!

I don't care.

"Burning bright sun," Frahto muttered. He hadn't been prepared. That was why it had gone so badly. Roh had looked almost unrecognisable with his hair bound in a single braid, wearing strange blue town garb and boots with designs stitched into the leather. Not to mention the srih flamboyantly spiralling from wrist to elbow. When the whistling-kite call had sounded in the middle of the market, Frahto's llirah had fizzed, his thoughts gone wild. Every sense focused on Roh — on the fact Roh had sought *him* out. Roh would talk; Frahto would hear his confession and bring him back into the fold. Frahto's own lapse in judgement would be forgiven, and Adehl would be dealt with.

I never thought I'd be ashamed to be Vuusah.

We're your family. You're supposed to be Atalah one day.

Not anymore.

Frahto had always assumed Roh wanted the same things he did — standing and respect within the Vuusah. But Roh had that already, didn't he? And the impetuous, arrogant bloodhead had thrown it away.

Someone shoved past Frahto. He stumbled, blinked, found himself scowling at the pretty black mare, who sidled nervously. With effort, Frahto calmed his expression and his llirah. All around, people scrambled to escape a sudden downpour of rain.

They had eight circahs scouring the city for the man, and Frahto had let him walk away.

Despite this fire-cursed rain, it was time to find Sorah and see if he could pick up Roh's trail.

Don't try to follow me.

Yeah, right.

30. Outmanoeuvred

Roh trudged with his head bowed against the rain. The squall had gusted in with a cold wind before he'd left the Fiugreh Settlement District. Growing weary of slogging through the downpour as he neared Four Nations Plaza, he ducked into a narrow lane between buildings, where overhanging eaves provided cover. Squatting, his back to a wall, Roh laid his hand to the clammy stones at his feet.

He found Frahto's rhythm quickly; his friend was still in the market field, consternation emanating from him. Roh wondered whether the rain always blew in so suddenly in Dohni.

A trickle of water found its way down his neck, and he jolted. Ugh. Standing, he shook out his legs, then noticed someone — a girl — peeking around the corner of the building. Their gazes met, and the girl ducked out of sight. But Roh recognised her, and it took but a moment to confirm Sorah's presence via a thread of ellir. He thunked his head gently against the building and waited. A burly man holding a sack above his head crossed the lane entrance; a door squeaked. When Sorah's face next appeared, Roh crooked his finger.

She reached him, glowing and breathless. Saturated, too: braids dripping, mud smearing her mahgan, as though she'd been hiding in dark corners. Her wide smile almost obscured the scars on her rosy, wet cheeks.

Roh crossed his arms against the chill of his own sodden clothes. "I have a feeling Frahto is scouring the market field for you."

Her face fell. "I couldn't tell him where I was going."

"And where are you going?"

"I want to see Adehl."

Surprise swept through him, but he couldn't miss the earnest pleading in her voice. It didn't seem like an idle request. "Why?"

"She was kind to me. She said…" Sorah fingered a metal medallion at her throat. "I thought she might help me."

"Sun's blood," Roh muttered. He could only imagine what Adehl might have said to this pidakah girl with rampaging affinity. Adehl had obviously spent more time with Sorah at Fortune Spring than he'd realised. "She can't help you, Sorah. Your father is the best person for that."

"My father doesn't want me around."

"Isn't that an anchor around your neck?" It looked to be made from claith, an expensive alloy with ideal properties for use as an anchor. When she shrugged, he said, "I think your father cares for you greatly. He'll tear apart the city if he thinks you're lost in it."

She shook her head. "He'll think I've gone to visit my mother."

Roh regarded her doubtfully. Given her wildly fluctuating llirah, he thought it more likely Lenatoh would think her soul-lost in some alley.

"Please, Roh? I promise I won't tell anyone."

It occurred to Roh that, dripping alley aside, they stood right next to the main thoroughfare between the Vuusah lodge and the bridge over the harbour. Hopefully his former brethren would hole up in a tavern somewhere instead of patrolling in the rain. He reached out with ellir to erase any careless traces of his own influence, then, sighing internally, began erasing the trail Sorah had laid in following him. Frahto wasn't a great tracker, but if he picked up Sorah's influence, he could probably follow it.

"You need to return to Frahto," he said. "Your father will blame him for losing you."

"I want to come with you."

"Sorah…"

"I'll follow you."

"You cheeky little…" He glared at the girl, but she lifted her chin in a manner that reminded him of Adehl. Fury, Adehl would probably slay him if he sent Sorah away. She'd probably delight in torturing herself over two children about to go wild, instead of one.

This was ridiculous. Beyond impelling the girl, he couldn't stop her. He'd evaded exhorters for over a week, only to be outmanoeuvred by a thirteen-year-old.

Other than personally restoring her to her father — which is what he *ought* to do — he couldn't see any alternative. He massaged the back of his neck. This was a terrible idea.

CHANTI'S BROW wrinkled as the little tortoiseshell cat dug her claws into his bare leg. He sat cross-legged in the straw, knee to knee with Adehl, holding his llirah steady as a shield against the heartstorm. Carefully, he allowed the amplitude of his llirah to grow, pulse to the extremities of his being.

Then he pulled it close again, holding it tight in his chest. He repeated the cycle.

"Ow," Chanti murmured as the little cat rearranged herself on his lap.

"Keep going," Adehl said. The small distraction was good practice. Chanti had grasped the gaerah cycle quickly, but the exercise needed to become like breathing. Adehl remembered spending her first weeks as an acoleh practising this one thing, over and over, until basic control of her llirah became second nature.

The little cat purred, loud enough to penetrate the sound of rain outside, her sweet chin resting on Chanti's thigh. With a smile, he stroked her fur. "She tickle." Then he said, "I feel her."

Adehl straightened and gently took Chanti's other hand. "Keep steady. Don't get distracted."

Too late. Chanti's llirah was already losing form. The cat's slinky sunshine rhythm weaved around the boy like a temptress. Adehl waited a few heartbeats to see if Chanti could pull himself together, then intervened.

When he was safe, she squeezed his hand. "Can you tell me what happened?"

"Lulu not be like Sapling." Chanti squirmed to dislodge the cat, who jumped into the straw, tail swishing. He rubbed at his skin where her claws had dug in.

"Do you know what you should have done?"

"Held energy close."

Adehl nodded. "We'll practise some more."

They continued, Lulu curled up in the straw nearby, untroubled by the rustling of mice in other parts of the stable. Outside, the rain grew heavier, pelting the tiled roof like stones.

Adehl monitored Chanti's efforts, ready to intercede again if anything went wrong. For the first time in weeks, she knew in her bones she was doing the right thing — even if she wasn't entirely sure she was doing it correctly. But if Chanti could master how to hold his rhythm, how to withstand the pull of the heartstorm, he wouldn't need to be quelled. It was such a simple thing. And it was *working*. Yesterday, when Sapling was sold, Chanti had almost gone wild, and Adehl had stepped in out of desperation; today, he had already managed ten gaerah cycles, despite cheeky cats who wanted his attention.

The outer door slammed open, and footsteps squelched towards the empty horse stall they occupied. Chanti jerked, his llirah flaring.

"Easy," Adehl murmured, her thumbs soothing his white-knuckled fingers. "See if you can get it back." But this distraction proved too much, as Chanti stared wild-eyed at the new arrival. Adehl knew without looking that Roh stood there; she could only imagine his expression.

"Sorry, mistress," Chanti said, pale-faced, as she helped him regain control.

"Do you have it now?" When he nodded, she released his hands. "That's enough for today, little colt. You'd better get on with the rest of your chores."

Chanti scrambled to his feet. The sudden movement roused the cat, who leapt up onto the wall between stalls and dropped out of sight. "Thank you, mistress," the boy said. With Roh braced in the doorway, Chanti looked tempted to follow Lulu, but he ducked under one of Roh's arms and fled.

Adehl brushed straw off her old mahgan as she stood. Roh's saturated hair and clothes were smeared against his body, his amber eyes a little fierce. His gaze followed Chanti's exit, then swung back to Adehl.

"I think you scared him," she said.

"What were you doing?" he asked in brittle tones.

She made herself hold his gaze. "I'm making sure Chanti's llirah doesn't go wild."

"You said Lady Kenna would pay for a noumenor."

"She *offered*. As a last resort. This way, Chanti won't need to be quelled." From somewhere came a small gasp, and Adehl stiffened. "Who's there?"

Roh grimaced and said, "Adehl, you can't…"

A small face peeked past Roh, eyes shining above damp cheeks. Adehl blinked. "Stars and sun, Sorah." Adehl opened her arms, and Sorah bolted past Roh, thudded against Adehl, knocking her a step backwards. Laughing, crying, Adehl hugged the sodden and shaking girl. "What are you doing here?"

Sorah launched into a garbled, disjointed account of her life since Adehl had bade farewell to Fortune Spring. How she'd thought about Adehl's words every day. How she'd begged her father to go with him to Dohni on the mission to get Roh back. How she'd sneaked away from Frahto and coerced Roh into bringing her here.

"And I thought — I thought you might help me — You're helping that boy, aren't you? You hinted you were like me — I didn't tell *anyone* — I don't want to be quelled."

Adehl's heart squeezed so hard she thought it might rupture. She hugged Sorah tighter and darted a glance at Roh, leaning against the wall with his arms crossed and his mouth set in a straight line. He'd been gone from the Wild Colt when Adehl had awoken, but she'd known where he was going, who he'd wanted to see. "Frahto came to Dohni, too?"

A curt nod. Roh held himself tightly bound.

Adehl returned her attention to Sorah. The girl shivered with cold and reaction, her rhythm flaring bright. *One day, things will be different.* When Adehl had said those words weeks ago, she'd never dreamed anything would come of them. "Of course I'll help you," she said.

"No." Roh pushed off the wall, leaving a damp smear on the wood. "Adehl, you need to stop this."

"You know I can't." She lifted her chin, willing Roh to understand. "It's what I need to do."

"Do you want to make everything worse? Sorah is Lenatoh's *daughter*."

"Then perhaps he'll thank me! If he wanted to quell her, he'd have done it already. It's just the gaerah cycle — so they don't lose control."

"But —"

"It's not harming anyone! Just think of all the pidakah — that is, *gierfeh* — children back home who wouldn't need to be quelled if they learnt this one thing." Her father. Her brother. "Is it really so bad?"

Roh came closer, as though intending to grab Adehl's shoulders, but he didn't touch her. She couldn't decipher all the expressions that rippled across his face and wondered if she'd pushed him too far. It took a long time for him to reply. "It's always one more thing with you," he said.

Adehl shivered at the flatness in his tone. But she had no answer and no defence. Nor did she wish to defend her actions. Perhaps Roh would never understand; she could almost see the Vuusah shackles weighing him down. "What did Frahto have to say?" she asked awkwardly.

"Nothing surprising."

"They want you back."

Roh glared, and Adehl's stomach turned over. "I'm not leaving you here," he said. But, for the first time, he looked like he wished he could.

31. Find them

The rain had stopped by the time Frahto reached the Lokk Janikk Bridge. Covered carts rumbled towards him across the slick stones, splashing through puddles without care for the sodden pedestrians. Behind him, in Four Nations Plaza, street performers struck up a tune. The music seemed muted, distant, except for the deep, booming drum. Frahto shivered and uselessly tried to peel his wet mahgan away from his skin.

Still no sign of Sorah. Or Roh, for that matter.

Back in the market field, he'd looped three times past each stall, then forced himself to slow down, take each circuit progressively slower to ensure Sorah wasn't lurking somewhere out of sight. In the end, he'd entered every tent, but none of the sellers recalled seeing a girl of her description. Not even the mahgan maker, whose garments Sorah had coveted.

He'd found no trace of Sorah at all, until he returned to where he'd last seen her and detected a hint of her rhythm in the soil and grass rapidly churning into mud. His own frustration gave way to misgiving. He'd painstakingly followed the remnant to the street, then along the street to the busy intersection the locals called *Cahto's Horse* — at which point her trail of determination and excitement had petered into nothing, as though washed away by the teeming rain.

It might have been his own inability to isolate Sorah's influence among the chaos. His roiling gut told him otherwise. He knew of only one person who could have so emphatically wiped away all signs of the girl's presence, along with his own.

With some vague hope Frahto would come across either Roh or Sorah — perhaps both — he had trudged through the downpour towards Four Nations Plaza. It was miserable going in his sodden clothes, even after the rain stopped.

Another cart rumbled off the bridge, and the drumbeats echoed around the plaza. Frahto found himself pulled onto the span by some invisible hook in his gut. In the middle of the bridge, he stopped, gripped the side balustrade to physically anchor himself to the stones. Silver gulls squawked and launched into the air, then settled again along the balustrade's length.

He reached out through ellir, knowing it was futile. The worked stone of the bridge carried uncountable rhythms inflicted by daily traffic. He doubted even Roh could untangle them. Beyond, past where the bridge abutted the banks of the harbour, he couldn't detect anything but the muted cadence of the heartstorm. The span of the bridge was not a large enough conduit to carry nuances from the city.

He withdrew, hands clenching the balustrade as if it would help him extract more ellir. The bridge held him suspended in the centre of the city, cradled by the sweeping harbour, at least a dozen boats on the rolling waters below.

To the north, mountains. At the head of a wide valley rose Kindoh, the so-called *storm mountain*; at its pinnacle was the powerful resonator known as the Stormbowl. Frahto had not been up the large hill yet, but the other zehla had been telling him about the perfect bowl carved out of heartrock by the early Fiugreh clans. The kalkah zehla of Dohni had apparently been using the Stormbowl for centuries. The notion was infuriating.

Frahto glowered at Kindoh under the darkened sky. He considered making his way up there; perhaps the Stormbowl could help him locate Roh.

He huffed a defeated laugh. Who was he kidding? Not even a resonator could help with this. First, he'd lost Roh, now Sorah. Lenatoh was going to slay him.

Frahto dragged himself back to the lodge. Ketahl and two others, still stationed outside, watched him approach as though he were the most interesting sight of the morning. They looked almost as bedraggled as Frahto felt.

"Where's the girl?" Ketahl asked, idly swinging her samah to dry in the breeze. Without the waist sash, her mahgan hung from her lean frame like a sack. "Thought you'd been appointed nursemaid."

Frahto shook his head and ascended the steps, hoping — mostly — Lenatoh hadn't departed the premises. Sure enough, the nedoyen remained closeted with Doyi Palvemah in the room the doyen used for private conferences. The pair had been arguing over how to deal with Roh since Lenatoh had sighted him yesterday in Donellon Plaza.

Raised voices emanated from behind the closed door, and Frahto made out Lenatoh exclaiming, "Only as a last resort!" A muffled response from the doyen followed, then Lenatoh again said, "He is *my* responsibility." A floorboard creaked under Frahto's foot. He tensed and began to retreat, but the door flew open. Lenatoh looked like he could set fire with his eyes. "Did Sorah get what she wanted?"

It took a moment for Frahto to remember he'd originally escorted Sorah to the mahgan stall. "You sound busy. I'll come back."

But Lenatoh stayed him with a gesture, eyes narrowing. The deep red of his town mahgan lent weight to his anger, dark against his skin. "What is it?"

Frahto chewed his cheek. Lenatoh had, after all, known him a long time. He decided to start with the almost-good news but pitched his voice low. "I saw Roh."

The nedoyen's gaze sharpened, then he slipped into the corridor, leaving the door ajar behind him. "Where?"

"In the horse market."

"You spoke to him?"

"Briefly."

A hand bell sounded from within the room. "What's happened?" demanded the doyen. She gave the instrument another, exasperated shake. "Don't stand there gibbering in the hall. Come in here."

Lenatoh pressed his lips together and gestured for Frahto to enter the room. The chamber held little more than a long table lined with empty chairs, a large curtained window overlooking the street, and a sideboard piled high with papers. On the table, amid the remains of a meal, a lamp burned against the gloomy day. Doyi Palvemah sat at the head of the table, her crutch propped against the wall behind her. Near her elbow stood a brass bell with a rearing horse for a handle. In the few days Frahto had known her, she'd left this chamber rarely, preferring to ring for zehla when she felt like issuing orders.

Frahto took the chair Lenatoh pulled out for him, wished he'd changed out of his damp clothes first. He eyed a plate of flaky pastries and realised the hour had gone past noon.

The doyen crossed her muscled arms, drawing attention to the green-and-white beaded srih adorning each biceps. "Well?"

"A development," Lenatoh said, pouring ale. He jerked a nod for Frahto to proceed.

Heeding the warning in Lenatoh's tight expression, Frahto gave the short version: that Roh had summoned him with the whistling-kite call, that they'd spoken briefly, that Roh had refused to come to the lodge. As he ground out the words, hating how inadequate they made him feel, Palvemah's intense scrutiny reminded him of a raptor waiting to strike.

The doyen leant forward, head tilted like a bird's. "If he refused to come here, what was he doing in the horse market?"

Frahto reached for a pewter mug etched with a scene that might have been an artist's impression of Fortune Spring. "I think he came to speak to Lenatoh."

"And?" Her gaze pinned Frahto in his seat. "Why did he not, after all, speak to Lenatoh?"

"I don't know… he saw me first." And changed his mind. Fury, Frahto really had messed this up. "He's furious and confused."

"Furious?"

"Roh, uh, doesn't like being kept in the dark," Frahto said, casting a sidelong glance at Lenatoh. "He seemed to think he ought to have known about the situation here." He couldn't bring himself to mention Roh's scathing remarks on the subject.

The doyen sat back in her chair. "At least that's consistent with everything I've heard of the young miscreant. Well, I don't care if he's piqued. He needs to do his duty."

Lenatoh had been toying broodily with the handle of his mug, which he now set aside. "What happened next?"

"He left."

"What's that supposed to mean?" asked the doyen. "Where did he go?"

This was the part Frahto had been dreading. Or, at least, dreading the most. He stole a mouthful of ale. "I don't know for certain. I presume he returned to wherever he's lodging." Then, he said inanely, "It started raining."

The doyen scowled. "You let him leave?"

"I needed to return to Sorah."

"She wasn't with you?" Lenatoh asked sharply.

"I wanted to speak to Roh alone." He met Lenatoh's gaze with effort. "I left her looking at some horses."

His friend and mentor simply nodded, and Frahto would have blurted out the rest of it, but the doyen interrupted. "You were gone hours, Frahto. Could you track him?"

"I tried, but I'm not very good at it; and Roh is... not easy to track if he doesn't want to be found."

The doyen muttered something unintelligible, then grabbed the bell and rang it vigorously. Instead of waiting for her summons to be answered, she reached for her stick. "I'm sending a circah to the market. They can stay out all night as far as I'm concerned." She stood awkwardly, limped to the door and pulled it open. "Tallah!"

With the doyen issuing orders to her favoured circah, Lenatoh closed the door behind her. "Tell me the whole. Quickly."

Frahto steeled himself. "First, I need to tell you that I couldn't find Sorah."

Lenatoh looked startled, then went still. "She didn't return with you?"

"She left the market while I was talking to Roh. I tracked her as far as I could..."

Out in the corridor, footsteps thumped down the stairs, doors opened and closed. Lenatoh pressed two fingers to his temple. "It's not safe for Sorah alone in the city."

"She knows her way around —"

"That's not what I mean!"

Frahto rose and placed a hand on Lenatoh's shoulder. "I think she'll be all right. I'm pretty sure she followed Roh."

Lenatoh stared.

"And I think she found him." He described how he'd managed to track Sorah's influence and how it had ended at Cahto's Horse. "Roh's the only one who could have erased her passage like that."

"Sun's blood," Lenatoh said faintly, leaning against the door.

"Roh won't let any harm come to her."

"There's no guarantee —"

"You gave Sorah a claith anchor."

Lenatoh's head dropped. "I know." The words came out as a groan. "She has so much affinity, Frahto. It breaks my heart. But even if she is with Roh, he's not a noumenor. I've been —"

The door opened, and the nedoyen broke off. Braced on her crutch in the doorway, Doyi Palvemah said, "Frahto, I want you to take the Blue Fox to where you spoke to Roh."

"Of course, Doyi."

"Stay with them when they pick up his trail. Your knowledge of him will be useful."

Frahto wondered if he ought to mention Sorah's involvement; it would give them another tracking option. Perhaps with the strength of a circah behind her, Tallah could pick up something Frahto had missed. He opened his mouth, but Lenatoh gave a head shake so tiny Frahto might have imagined it.

"They are waiting for you, zehli," the doyen said, gesturing to the door.

With a regretful glance at the pastries, Frahto rose. Then he plucked his mug from the table and drained it. When he reached the corridor, Tallah's circah was already out the door.

FRAHTO SPENT the next several hours trawling the streets — from the Fiugreh market field to the bridge and into the Old Merali Quarter. The Blue Fox circah paused every few minutes to construct a tracking mesh — and when that inevitably failed to detect any trace of Roh, the exhorters aggressively questioned passersby for a man matching the description Frahto had provided. In some cases, they forced candour. *The Vuusah are despised here, Frahto.*

Returning to the lodge late afternoon, Frahto was about ready to eat his own leg or else kick something with it. He headed straight to the gatherhall — where he found Sorah gleefully tucking into a meal.

Looking up, her braids messy, the wretched girl grinned. "Da says you almost drowned looking for me."

Frahto took a seat opposite. A serving platter held slices of bread and cold roast beef, fresh leafy greens and segments of a tangy red fruit the locals called tomatai. With a sidelong glance at Sorah, he selected a slice of bread and piled it high with toppings.

"You needn't have worried, you know," Sorah said, hands loosely clasped around her mug. "I was perfectly fine."

Frahto allowed the silence to stretch until he'd finished his first slab of bread. The roast beef was seasoned with a zesty spice he didn't recognise. "Where did you go?"

"To see my mother. I told you I wanted to."

"You said you wanted a new mahgan."

"I do." She chewed her lip. "I didn't think you'd want to go to the docks again."

He assembled another slice of bread. "Did you see Roh?"

Colour swept across her cheeks. "From a distance."

"Did you see Adehl?"

She shook her head and glared. "I told you I went to the docks."

She was lying. Even without the telltale hitch in her llirah, Frahto knew. He crossed his arms and would have pressed, but Sorah sprang to her feet and ran from the room.

Frahto made short work of the food, though it now tasted like dust. He was certain Sorah had intercepted Roh and seen Adehl. The girl had made all the zehla searching for Roh — Frahto included — look like fools. It would be for her father to extract the truth. Sun help the wretched girl if the doyen got wind of her escapade first.

He found Lenatoh brooding on a stone bench in the rear garden courtyard. Swathes of weeping grass carpeted the walled area, interspersed with clumps of long feathergrass, strappy flax-lilies and shrubs with delicate pink flowers. A flowering crepe myrtle tree, forked limbs smooth and pinky-brown, bestowed white petals among the greenery like spots of snow. The garden smelt of damp soil and lush grass and home.

"You need to talk to Sorah," Frahto said.

Lenatoh brushed a few tiny petals off his knees. "I've already tried."

"What did she say?"

"The same story she gave you, I assume. That she visited her mother."

Frahto ran his fingers through a sheaf of feathergrass seeds, then plucked it with a twist of his fingers. "Why is she lying?" He thought of his conversation with Sorah the other day. *I wish I could be like Adehl.* "She thinks…" He shied away from the thought. "Can't you force her to tell you where she went? Palvemah will."

Lenatoh gripped the bench seat below him, knuckles white. "The doyen *cannot* know."

A second bench stood nearby, and Frahto lowered himself onto it. "What haven't you told me?" He kept his voice low. He faced the rear facade of the lodge, and plenty of windows overlooked the garden. The single back door stood to the right and, at the other end of the building, a flight of steps led down to what Frahto assumed was a basement.

"First, tell me what happened with Roh earlier," Lenatoh said. "Don't leave anything out."

"You might wish I had."

"Frahto, please. Before anyone comes."

This time, the whole story did come tumbling out. The moment Frahto had embraced Roh and thought everything was going to be all right. The realisation that Adehl meant more to Roh after a few weeks than his brethren of more than a decade. He didn't soften any of the blows. *She's pidakah! I don't care… I never thought I'd be ashamed to be Vuusah.*

"He was angry about the exhorters forcing candour." Frahto chewed his cheek. "He said we're not his brethren anymore."

Lenatoh winced. He looked older than his years and sadder than Frahto had ever seen him. "Best not let the doyen hear that."

"Why? What will she do?"

For a time, the nedoyen stared at nothing. He hardly seemed to breathe. "Doyi Palvemah has spoken of a realignment."

Every one of Frahto's bones turned to ice. A realignment was something reserved for criminals… "You mean for Adehl?"

Lenatoh transferred his gaze to his hands. "No."

"You can't mean… She can't intend to realign *Roh*?" To realign someone's llirah was to change the fabric of their being. Roh would retain his affinity, but he wouldn't be himself anymore. It could even remove his memories. *"Why?"*

"Because we need him."

"Need him for what?"

Lenatoh pressed his lips together and shook his head.

After a long, numbing silence, Frahto said, "You can't let that happen, Lenatoh. If you care for him at all…"

"I love that boy as though he were my own son."

"Then we need to make him see reason!"

"How? You've already tried and failed."

"If he knew what the doyen intended, he might relent."

"Be serious, Frahto. When has Roh ever…" Lenatoh rubbed his temple. "Besides, we need him onside, not coerced…"

"Realignment isn't coercion?"

Lenatoh grimaced. "He wouldn't know about it."

Frahto couldn't believe what he was hearing. What could be so important that Lenatoh would consider carrying out such a ritual? For the task would fall to Lenatoh as the senior noumenor. "You would truly do that? Realign Roh?"

"Sometimes… sometimes, sacrifices must be made." Lenatoh seemed to force out the words.

Frahto swallowed. His mind whirred, sorting through and discarding ideas. A gust of wind blew more snow-like petals onto the grass. "Maybe the injaleh bond will diminish if she's quelled," Frahto said. "Maybe *then* he'll see reason."

The music of a distant wind chime filled the silence. "I hadn't considered that," Lenatoh said slowly.

"If we can find Adehl… I'll bring her back here, and that'll be one problem solved." If anyone were to be sacrificed, it ought to be her.

"It might work."

Relief flooded Frahto. They had a plan — one that didn't

involve realigning Roh. Frahto was more than happy to make Adehl his target. "Sorah needs to tell us what she knows."

Lenatoh shot him a glance. "Keep your voice down." When he next spoke, Frahto could barely make out his words. "You need to find them first, Frahto."

"I will."

"But you can't warn Roh about… any of it. We can't risk them fleeing the city."

Frahto wished he understood what the blight was going on. "I'll find them, I promise."

"We need to keep Roh away from the doyen until there's no other choice."

Frahto nodded, stroked the plucked feathergrass head lying on the bench beside him. "I think it will be harder than the doyen thinks to control Roh."

"The fire-cursed woman thinks of everything." Grimacing as though he'd bitten into an unripe apple, Lenatoh produced a key from the front pocket of his mahgan. "Go take a look in the basement."

Frahto took the key reluctantly and eyed the basement steps.

"Go on," Lenatoh said grimly.

Damp grass slithered against his boots as Frahto crossed the garden. The steps descended to a new-looking door fitted with a shiny lock. Roh's words came back to him. *Is it necessary to hold and punish zehla inside the lodge?*

The door opened onto a short, dark corridor with stone walls and a door on each side. One room was an unlocked storeroom filled with sacks, barrels and crates, lit by a high window running the width of the chamber. The door to the room opposite was bolted and featured a grille at approximately eye-level. Through narrow bars, the dim and windowless chamber looked plain and unremarkable, little more than a cell constructed of pale stone. Yet Frahto's fingers trembled as he drew back the bolt and pulled open the door.

Some dread whisper warned him not to step inside. With a single finger, he touched the stone cladding on the internal wall of the room. Recoiled, as from a savage bite.

It was worse than anything he could have imagined. The chamber was a travesty. Its plain and unadorned appearance concealed a monster.

Frahto slammed the bolt closed and staggered up the stairs into the light.

32. Haiffin wine

For the third day in succession, Roh slouched in a corner and ordered a pitcher of ale. The serving boy scampered away to the bar and returned at a slower pace, careful not to spill a drop. He seemed familiar, and Roh glanced around the taproom to make sure it was a different establishment from yesterday. Wide windows looked onto a busy plaza on the outskirts of the Great Market. Inside, the long tables bore carved designs that accumulated crumbs and spilt ale. Definitely nowhere he'd been before.

Grinning, the server asked if Roh wanted food. The boy looked about Chanti's age and had similar colouring — and that was probably why he seemed familiar. Roh grunted refusal and took a long draught of ale. He didn't want to be reminded of Chanti.

The serving lad brought Roh a second pitcher. A third. Roh was drinking faster today, and he really ought to stop.

He was staring blankly at the wall when someone nudged his elbow. "This isn't like you, Little Atali." Frahto loomed over him in a rumpled dark-blue mahgan Roh hadn't seen before. He looked haggard and still hadn't shaved.

In the back of his ale-soaked mind, Roh suspected he ought to be alarmed. "How did you find me?"

"You're drunk, and I was looking." Frahto lowered his large frame onto the bench opposite and signalled for more ale. The lad bounded away to fill the order.

Roh frowned and belatedly reined in his turbulent llirah. A first season acoleh could probably have located him. "What do you want?"

"To have a drink with my friend."

"There's no point talking —"

"We won't talk, then." Frahto leant against the wall and closed his eyes.

Roh sipped his drink, then pushed the mug away. He debated leaving the taproom, but Frahto would follow him this time, and Roh couldn't lead him anywhere near the Wild Colt. It would be bad enough for Frahto to learn where they were lodging, but if he discovered Adehl's latest transgression of Vuusah precepts... Thank the sun Roh had taken the precaution of obliterating any trace of Sorah's visits. He ought to have stopped her from visiting all together, but he couldn't seem to deny Adehl anything.

Adehl had been challenging Vuusah ideology for weeks, and now Roh found himself clinging to his last beliefs like a man dangling on the end of a rope. Part of his current consternation, he was fairly sure, lay in his suspicion it was time to let go.

They didn't speak for long minutes; then Frahto made some unimportant observation about the occupants of the next table, and soon they were discussing the merits of Dohni's Great Market. The conversation was safe, familiar, uncomplicated — on the surface. Roh could almost convince himself nothing had changed between them.

Of course, the camaraderie couldn't last. Everything had changed.

Frahto flicked an invisible crumb from the table. "Roh, we need to talk about —"

"Don't." Roh wanted to keep pretending, extend this fragile peace another hour. "Not today."

"It has to be today. There's no time. You need to listen."

Roh groaned. "I meant what I said the other day."

"They will *not allow it.*" Frahto pressed both hands on the table and leant forward. "Do you understand me?"

Blighted sun, Roh was tired. "I wish you would understand that I'm done. I'll register as kalkah if I must."

"You don't mean that."

Roh was surprised to find that he did. "The Vuusah don't own me, Frahto. I won't let them dictate my life anymore."

A strange expression travelled across Frahto's flushed face. He sat back and drained his mug, replaced it on the table with a loud thunk. "You're an arrogant, ungrateful bloodhead, tossing away something most of us could only dream about. If I'd been the one besotted, do you think Gentah would have sent you to retrieve me?"

"I'm sorry he did send you. You could have refused." Roh knew this was unfair, but he was past caring. "I suppose, as usual, you're trying to win his favour. It's not as great as it looks."

"*Don't* make this about me." Frahto's fingers flexed as though he wanted to throttle Roh. "This has nothing to do with me. This is about your betrayal of your brethren. You owe the Vuusah more than a quick change of loyalties because you can't keep it in your breeches."

"Hoi!" Roh straightened so quickly he almost tipped the bench over. "Watch your mouth."

Frahto's jaw jutted. "If not for your infatuation —"

"Do you really think this is only about Adehl? Don't be

naive! You must have seen by now something's going on at the lodge. Whatever it is, I want no part of it."

"Where would you be without our brethren? The Vuusah *made* you."

"You're right!" The laugh clawed its way out of Roh's throat. "Gentah made me into something I don't want to be."

"He's always let you do anything you wanted!"

"Until the day I decided to think for myself. Until the day I caught him trying to *impel* me."

"Just like you impelled me?"

Roh winced. They were attracting attention in the taproom, and he lowered his voice with effort. "I'm sorry it came to that." He doubted Frahto would care for his excuse. "But you know Gentah's been manipulating me for years. I can't trust him anymore. I can't trust any of them."

For several heartbeats, Frahto wouldn't meet Roh's gaze. Then, voice like gravel, he said, "Do you even understand how much forbearance they've shown over this thing with Adehl? She's been officially expelled, you know. She's a cursed criminal."

Roh waited, chest aching, to hear he too had been expelled.

"Despite all that, they want you back. You won't like what they have in store for you, but I'm starting to think you deserve it."

His words could have rattled the windows. Roh forced himself to consider how difficult it must have been for Frahto all these years. His closest friend, unwaveringly loyal, always riding alongside while Roh had basked in Gentah's approbation and taken everyone's adulation as his due. Always second, frequently overlooked, despite being a talented noumenor in his own right.

Hands unsteady, Roh refilled his mug, then Frahto's. He tried to think of something to say.

After a time, Frahto broke the silence, sounding calmer. "I know you're lodging near here."

The ale soured on Roh's tongue.

"I know you've seen Sorah and that she's almost as obsessed with Adehl as you are," Frahto said.

Roh inwardly reviewed Sorah's visits over the past few days. They'd known it was a risk Sorah coming to them, but Adehl had insisted — and Sorah had been confident no one cared where she went. Roh had put her ability to roam the city freely down to her father's preoccupation. Still, he'd made sure no one could track her movements to the Wild Colt. "Does Sorah know you've been following her?"

"I assume so, or she wouldn't have evaded me so easily."

Sun's blood. The wretched girl had said nothing — at least, not to Roh. The thought of Frahto discovering Adehl while Roh was off somewhere sulking gave him chills. "You could have forced her to tell you."

Frahto glared. "We wouldn't do that."

"I bet that sun-cursed doyen would."

"She doesn't know about Sorah's… movements." Frahto chewed his cheek. "We're trying to find you before Palvemah's people do."

"Why?"

Frahto pressed his lips together, then said, "I'm on your side, Roh, whatever else you may think."

"Then leave Adehl alone. Leave us both alone."

Frahto's frown was answer enough. Did they honestly believe Roh could return to the fold, resume his former life as Atalah-in-waiting?

"You can't hide forever," Frahto said.

No, they couldn't. Roh had been hiding in taverns. Hiding from everything. He needed to stop.

"It'll be easier on everyone if you just tell me where you're lodging," Frahto said.

"I'm not *that* drunk." In fact, Roh's buzz had completely gone.

Frahto crossed his arms. "I'm in no rush."

THE SHADOWS outside were lengthening when Frahto judged it time to leave the alehouse. He propped Roh against the wall, almost exactly as he'd found him hours ago, and paid the hefty bill with Vuusah funds. It had taken a few bottles of expensive Haiffin wine to render Roh into the ideal state for Frahto's purposes — pliable without being comatose. Frahto wasn't proud of resorting to such a tactic, but the case was getting desperate.

It had been sheer luck he'd found Roh this morning. For three days, Sorah had sneaked out of the Vuusah lodge and somehow managed to evade all Frahto's attempts to follow her. The first morning, he'd trailed her at a distance across the bridge and into the Old Merali Quarter, only to lose her in the hustle and bustle of Janikk Way. The next, he'd missed her departure all together. This morning, he'd approached Sorah as she passed through Bridge Gate, hoping to appeal to her common sense. She'd taken one look at him and bolted. He'd eventually lost her in the Great Market's dense crowds and twisty passages.

Frahto had wanted to scream. Instead, he'd circumnavigated the market, staring down each of the main roads radiating out from it, casting out to see if he could determine which road she'd taken. Then he'd wandered up and down each street, searching.

He'd discovered no sign of Sorah... but he'd caught a trace of Roh.

"Come on, Little Atali," Frahto said, getting an arm under Roh to help him off the bench seat. "Let's get you home."

"Can walk on m'own."

"I know." Frahto supported at least half Roh's weight as they navigated past tables onto the street. "What's the name of your lodging house?"

"Wild Colt." Roh almost tripped over his own feet. "Ugh. Ground's moving."

Frahto could have kissed him. "It's all right. I've got you."

They staggered along Sairsanall Street towards the Pioneer Gardens, Frahto debating his best course of action. It would be easy enough to obtain directions to the Wild Colt lodging house.

First, he needed to get Roh out of the way.

Then he could make his move on Adehl.

33. Hands bound

ADEHL HELD Sorah's hand as they sat cross-legged on the bed facing each other. The girl's other hand was clenched around the claith medallion at her throat. It would make no difference to its efficacy as an anchor: the metal only needed to touch Sorah's skin. But Adehl understood the reflexive need to squeeze.

Softly, Adehl said, "Feel your rhythm extend through your body until your flesh and bones are singing. Keep it in tune with the medallion… *Good*. Now, pull it in. Make it the tiniest whisper."

In the three days Sorah had been coming to the Wild Colt, she had almost mastered the gaerah cycle. It gave Adehl a thrill to see the girl's confidence bloom as her control improved. Adehl's instructions, issued in a low, steady tone, were as much to aid Sorah's concentration as remind her what to do. It made Adehl's blood boil that Lenatoh had been strengthening his daughter's alignment to the anchor each morning and night, instead of teaching this basic exercise. She wondered if he'd noticed Sorah's improved control.

Sorah completed the tenth cycle and grinned. "I can do it. I can really do it!"

Adehl smiled so hard it hurt her cheeks. "I knew you could."

The girl glanced up through her lashes. "Could we try something else?"

"Not yet."

"Please?" Sorah flung herself off the bed and prowled around the room.

Outside, the covenant bells chimed for at least the tenth time that afternoon, interrupting some ravens having a loud conversation. The sharp light indicated the day was further advanced than Adehl had realised. She'd expected Roh hours ago. The past two days, he'd returned midafternoon, the scent of ale on his breath the only hint of how he'd passed the time. Adehl understood the internal battle he waged and knew he needed time and space to work through whatever he was feeling.

At least he hadn't tried to stop her from teaching the gaerah cycle to Sorah and Chanti.

Sorah trailed fingers along the wall. "I want to feel ellir in the stone like you do. I want..." She paused at the dresser, snatched an item sitting on the timber surface. Returning to Adehl, she thrust out her cupped palm. "How about this?"

She held one of Roh's message stones, swirly blue agate, polished smooth, about the size of a quail's egg. Adehl took it up and closed her fist around it, tuned in to its tiny tangle of rhythms. Roh's enforced impression had long since dissipated, leaving the agate wild, untamed.

Adehl considered the stone and its correspondingly small energy. Not enough to disrupt a novice, surely. And her bedchamber, being upstairs, would provide isolation from the heartstorm.

Could it hurt?

Sorah, evidently reading Adehl's expression, clapped her hands. "Thank you, thank you!"

Misgiving tugged at Adehl, but she gestured for Sorah to sit and took her hand. Impatience and anticipation radiated from the girl, her llirah unconstrained, as though it would burst out of her.

"First, calm down," Adehl said, assisting with a soothing thread of ellir. "Control it, Sorah."

Sorah took several long, slow breaths. "I'm calm."

"Hmmm." Adehl waited another few minutes, then placed the polished blue stone in Sorah's hand. "All right. Now, *carefully* relax your grip on your rhythm the tiniest amount — and keep it small…" Monitoring Sorah's llirah, Adehl waited, her heart racing with apprehension. Still, Sorah was doing well. Adehl kept her voice steady. "Now, feel the tiny rhythm of the stone in your hand. It's like a butterfly's wings against your skin. Just notice it's there."

Sorah's mouth stretched wide in a smile. "It is like a butterfly!"

Outside, in the cobbled square, cantering horses clattered to a halt. Then the jingle of tack and raised voices. Sorah's shoulders hunched, and Adehl cursed inwardly. "I think that's enough," Adehl said.

The bright wonder faded from Sorah's face, and her breath came in short gusts, her teeth gripping her bottom lip.

"Keep your rhythm small," Adehl said. "Haul it in, Sorah."

"I'm trying." Sorah's breathing became ragged. "The stone's pulling me."

The ruckus below grew louder; it sounded like about eight horses immediately below the window, but Adehl tried to block them out. Someone thumped on a door downstairs, and a voice she half recognised made loud demands.

Sorah's eyes shot open, and her llirah surged into a roiling catastrophe.

Adehl sucked in a breath. "Ignore the stone! Your medallion. Focus on its rhythm…" Sorah squeezed her eyes shut and shuddered.

Heavy feet stomped up the stairs, and the door rattled. "Adehl? Open the door." Frahto's deep voice easily penetrated the timber. "I have a circah of armed exhorters downstairs. Sorah — are you in there?"

"Noooo!" Sorah wailed. "I can't get it back!"

With fear clamping her chest, Adehl tried to grasp hold of Sorah's wildly fluctuating llirah. She dimly registered Frahto pounding on the door and shouting, but she had no attention to spare.

The door splintered open, and Frahto strode into the chamber. "What are you doing?"

"Unless you're here to help, get out!"

He paused, then swore and hauled Adehl off the bed. She scrabbled back to Sorah, but Frahto fended her off. "Get out of my way!" he snarled. "Or by the burning bright sun, I will break your arm."

"You're a noumenor, right? Help her!"

Frahto grunted and took Sorah's hand. Adehl crept around the bed to the girl's other side. She cursed herself for succumbing to Sorah's plea, but Sorah reminded her so much of herself…

"I'm sorry." Tears streaked Sorah's pale, scarred cheeks. "I couldn't hold it!"

"It'll be all right," Frahto said soothingly, though he speared Adehl with a venomous glance.

"You're not going to…?" Sorah gazed at him imploringly.

His mouth set. "Your father ought to have quelled you long ago."

"He's been aligning her twice a day," Adehl said.

"I'm aware."

"Please don't," said Sorah, gripping his arm.

"I'm going to strengthen your bond with the medallion. Like your father has been doing."

Adehl knelt beside Sorah, not trusting Frahto to keep his word. But Sorah lay obediently still as he performed the alignment. Quiet fell over the darkening room, ushering in the mutter of sounds from the street.

Now that Sorah was safe, the severity of her own situation crashed upon Adehl. Frahto had brought hooters to the Wild Colt, and Roh had still not returned. She scrambled off the bed to the window. Seven horses milled in the plaza below, most with zehla at their heads. Chanti held the reins of a large moonskin. Adehl stared, reached out with a thread of ellir through the walls of the building. A bolt of joy made her skin tingle, and her hands became fists. Sensing her presence, Cloud tossed his head and whinnied. "Stars and sun," she breathed.

"He's a beautiful animal," Frahto said. Rising, he smirked. "Up to my weight."

She was going to cut him into tiny pieces. To Sorah, she said, "How do you feel?"

"All right." Sorah clambered towards Adehl and uncertainly eyed Frahto across the crumpled bedcovers.

"I won't let him hurt you," Adehl said.

Frahto scowled. "You achieved that on your own."

"It's *your* fault she lost control. She was doing well until you lumbered up the stairs like an overgrown shaggybeast."

"She was about to go wild because *you* weakened the bond to the anchor with your meddling." He swelled in anger, seeming to take up most of the room. "First, you put ideas in her head, and now I find you —"

Someone cleared their throat, and Adehl became aware of a woman lurking in the doorway, impassively watching proceedings. She looked like one of the hooters Adehl had encountered in Tarsah. "This is fun," the zehli said. "Perhaps we should take it to the lodge?"

"Dinah." Frahto straightened. "Has Roh shown up?"

The zehli shook her head.

"He must have been more drunk than I thought." Frahto's voice held an odd mix of satisfaction and regret.

Cold crept through Adehl. Why hadn't she taken more notice of Roh's prolonged absence? "What did you do?" She reached out with her limited farsensing ability, tried searching the streets around the Wild Colt. "Where's Roh?"

Frahto smiled unpleasantly. "Didn't I mention our reunion in a tavern this afternoon? Roh never did have a head for Haiffin wine."

"You conniving cutsnake," Adehl said, her biting fear morphing into fury. "If he's murdered in an alley, I will use your bones as clapping sticks." After that, if it turned out he'd got drunk with Frahto and revealed their location, she'd use Roh's.

Dinah chuckled darkly. "If that comes to pass, you won't be the only one."

Frahto strode across the room and gripped Adehl's arm so tightly she bit back a yelp of pain. "Let's go. Sorah, you're coming too."

Frahto almost wrenched Adehl's arm out of its socket as he dragged her down the stairs. Two hooters waited in the entrance hall, swords bared, while Fenaika stood rigidly against the wall, staring at the floor. Adehl managed to gasp out this was all a misunderstanding, before the zehla shoved her out the front door.

In the plaza outside the Wild Colt, Adehl released her llirah and linked with Cloud. He whinnied at full volume, hooves clattering on the stones. The gathered horses rumbled into turbulence, their handlers swearing.

"Chanti, let go of the reins!" Adehl squirmed in Frahto's grip; if she could free herself, she could be away. Cloud snorted and plunged through the other horses.

Frahto cursed. "Come and hold her!" Other hands grabbed Adehl, more fingers pressing into her flesh, leaving bruises. Frahto bound her hands in front, a lead rope attached, while Dinah grabbed Cloud's reins and tied them to a hitching post. Her horse didn't take kindly to this and whinnied again. Adehl shouted at her captors to let her go. Futile, of course, but she had no intention of going quietly.

Maesenna and Orkoh arrived at a run. Whether or not they understood the situation, they responded as might be expected of the Wild Colt's stable employees. Within half a minute, they'd taken command of the horses, freeing the remaining zehla to draw their weapons.

Chanti, white-faced, wide-eyed, clung to the reins of a blood bay. Adehl wanted to tell him that he would be all right now, that he knew what to do to stay in control, but she didn't dare.

Frahto grabbed her upper arm again. Adehl sensed the restrained violence in that grip, also the triumph. The six hooters confronted her, short swords gleaming. For several heartbeats, she wondered if they intended to cut her down and say it was an accident.

"Hoi! Swords *down*."

The cry came from the opposite side of the plaza. Adehl yelped as Frahto's hand tightened, and his energy flared with consternation. Some of the zehla turned their heads; some even lowered their blades.

Roh arrived at a run, startling two horses. From the crumpled state of his tunic, he might well have been sleeping in an alley. "Do *not* point them at her!"

"Roh," Frahto said dangerously. "Don't interfere."

Roh's eyes flashed. "This has gone on long enough. Release Adehl, and I'll come."

THE SIGHT of Frahto with his hands on Adehl, *hurting* Adehl, made something inside Roh snap. It had been bad enough the time he'd interrupted Chah's circah forcing candour on his injaleh. That violation had been worse in many ways, but Chah hadn't known who she was. They had simply been doing their misguided duty.

This attack, this betrayal, was personal.

Curse Frahto for knowing Roh's weakness for Haiffin red. He'd been almost sober by the time it had arrived, but Frahto had lured him into complacency by recounting his woes during his voyage from Tarsah. Then his friend had comically described Gentah's fury upon discovering Roh's truancy. Roh had guffawed, poured more wine and ended up with his head on the table.

After that, he'd been too drunk to remember everything he'd said. Everything he must have revealed. Moreover, he'd ended up comatose on one of the ledges of the vacant, open-air theatre. If not for the young sweeper, who had apparently struggled to wake him, Roh might have been there still.

Blighted sun, Roh was a fool. After their bitter argument and everything that had gone before, Roh had wanted to recapture his old camaraderie with Frahto so badly. Only to have the bloodhead drowse him.

In front of the Wild Colt, Adehl stood at sword point with her hands bound before her, Frahto still gripping her arm in his massive hand. Her gaze sparked when it met Roh's. He clenched his fists in an effort to keep himself under control. "Get your hands *off* her." The words held so much gravel they scratched his throat.

"We're taking Adehl for judgement," Frahto said. Fortunately for him, he transferred his hold to the rope attached to her hands. "I suggest you don't make further trouble."

"She's not a cursed criminal. Put away the swords."

"That's a matter of opinion. Do you know —?" He broke off and looked about him, then tugged Adehl to face him. "Where's Sorah?"

"Is she not here?" Adehl asked. "That girl has a mind of her own."

Roh couldn't tell how much Frahto knew. He'd already spotted Chanti amid a group of horses and sensed Sorah's presence inside the lodging house.

Frahto cursed and thrust Adehl's rope at the two nearest exhorters, then disappeared inside the building. Roh realised he knew these zehla hastily sheathing their swords. They were Minuh and Ketahl from Dinah's Silver Wolf circah, the newest arrivals. He wanted to throttle them all for pointing swords at Adehl.

Dinah eyed Roh speculatively. "It's nice of you to show up," she said.

"I wish I could return the sentiment." Inspired by Frahto's earlier actions, Roh began forming a plan. "Put your swords away. Someone might get hurt."

"That is rather the point," Dinah said, but she gestured at her zehla, and steel slammed into leather. The exhorters surrounded Adehl, eying Roh uncertainly.

"Roh, you should leave," Adehl said, an edge to her voice.

"You jest, jaleh." He steeled himself. He had drunk ale with these zehla around the fire at Fortune Spring a month ago. It made what he was about to do both easier and more difficult. He took a step forward.

"Stay back," Dinah said, her hand returning to her sword hilt.

Roh held his hands wide. "I'm not armed." He took another step towards Minuh, who held the rope attached to Adehl's bound wrists, Ketahl beside him. With a quick glance, Roh tried to warn Adehl to be ready.

Dinah drew her sword. "I said stay *back*."

"Calm down." Honing his llirah, Roh brought his hands up, laying one on Minuh's shoulder, the other on Ketahl's. "I'm just greeting old friends." Then, he ruthlessly tweaked the rhythms of the two zehla. Between one heartbeat and the next, they slumped in a heap on the cobblestones. Roh winced, but there was no time to worry about bruises.

Adehl twitched, her rope trailing on the ground. He gave her a look and she ran.

Dinah stared at her two fallen exhorters. "What did you do?"

"Nothing," Roh lied. He grabbed hold of Eranah, about to pursue Adehl, then Ahro. They too succumbed to sleep. A moonskin horse tethered to a rail whinnied and kicked its hind legs, knocking Dinah off her feet. Sun's blood. Was that Adehl's horse, Cloud?

"Roh!" Frahto's yell echoed around the darkening plaza. From the front door of the Wild Colt, he gaped at the four unconscious zehla, at Dinah groaning on the stones, clutching her hip. Bortoh, the remaining exhorter on his feet, backed away from Roh. Frahto said, "Have you lost your mind?"

The question warranted no answer. Sorah loitered near Frahto, one hand around her medallion. At a nod from Roh, she slipped past in the direction Adehl had fled.

"Sorah!" Frahto lumbered forward, but Roh blocked his attempt to follow. Frahto's hands came down heavily on Roh's shoulders. From the man's bared teeth, Roh suspected he was lucky those hands weren't clamped around his throat. The next moment, Roh found himself thrust aside. He grabbed at an outdoor table to avoid smashing his knees on the cobbles. Frahto hunkered beside the collapsed zehla.

"They're merely drowsed," Roh said icily.

"Stay back!" Frahto swivelled to glare at Roh, then roused the zehla one by one.

Roh would have offered a hand to Dinah, gingerly testing her limbs after Cloud's kick, but the woman's scowl deterred him. While she was consulting with Frahto in a low voice, Roh scanned the other horses: sure enough, Sprig jostled among them. How devious of his former brethren.

He took a step in his horse's direction, but Dinah and Ketahl raised their swords. Without averting her attention from Roh, Dinah sent four zehla on foot in pursuit of Adehl and Sorah.

"The steel isn't necessary," Roh said. Neither of the exhorters lowered her weapon. "Are you really going to keep me from my horse?"

Frahto's hands formed fists at his sides. "You have no idea what you've done."

Reluctantly, Roh turned away from Sprig. "I didn't —"

"Burning bright sun, Roh! Can't you see it's only going to get worse? The doyen wants to —" Frahto cut himself off, his mouth twisting.

Dinah and Ketahl stepped closer, their swords still bared. "Let's go before he tries anything else," Dinah said.

Inexplicably, Roh thought of a day early in the summer when he and Dinah had teamed up to track and kill a feral wildcat threatening their camp. They'd been friends, once. "You have my word I'm coming with you willingly. It's time I spoke to Lenatoh."

A soft groan escaped Frahto. His mouth worked as though he wanted to say something, then he jerked a nod. "So be it. Walk with me," he said.

34. Touch of cold steel

ADEHL RAN. Hands bound, she felt as ungainly as a three-legged horse, but she ran.

In the plaza behind, Cloud's whinny preceded shouting; then light, rapid feet gave pursuit. Sun's fury, she'd hoped for a greater head start after Roh's little demonstration.

The footfalls drew nearer, and Adehl tried to run faster but her balance was compromised. When the pursuer reached her, she spun awkwardly.

"It's just me." Sorah steadied Adehl with an arm.

Adehl dragged in a couple of breaths. "Are you all right?"

"Yes. Come on."

Sorah took the lead as they zigzagged through the streets of the Old Kestali Quarter. Expediency had driven Adehl downhill initially, and they crossed Dailis Way into a maze of the oldest streets and alleys. Adehl judged their pursuers would be several minutes behind. Roh couldn't have drowsed all of them, but he'd done enough. She and Sorah had no chance of outrunning mounted exhorters, but if they could get far enough ahead, the zehla would need to track them on foot.

With a glance over her shoulder, Sorah squeezed into a gap too narrow for horses to pass through. Adehl hesitated at the mouth of the murky passage, which seemed to have swallowed Sorah whole. She stumbled in the girl's wake, her shoulders scraping the grimy walls; the air smelt of dead animals. The alley led farther into the maze of dim, narrow streets, stone buildings pressing close, until they arrived at the plaza behind the Prayer Hall for He-Beyond, where a birthing exchange ritual was underway.

"Stop for a minute," Adehl said, pausing in the tiny space between two buildings. Her heart pounded hard enough to break a rib.

Light bloomed from the many windows of the prayer hall, and clumps of people crossed the darkened plaza towards the wide-open rear doors. They spoke in hushed tones out of respect for the rei-tarn, but there was an undercurrent of excitement, too. The covenant bells had been ringing all afternoon, so the bestowal must be close. Adehl grimaced at the thought.

Nearby, Sorah leant against a wall, breathing heavily. Adehl wanted to ask if she were all right. After hearing the bells for almost two weeks, Adehl had learnt more about the Kestali exchange ritual and why Sorah had those barbaric scars on her cheeks. It couldn't be easy for Sorah to confront the ritual head-on. But before Adehl got the words out, the bestowal bells sounded from the tower overhead. From here, they were deafening.

With a groan, Sorah slumped to the stones, bracing her head on her knees. Adehl hunkered awkwardly before her. With hands bound, she could only lightly grip Sorah's arm. Belatedly, she realised it wasn't the exchange ritual bothering the girl, but her wayward llirah. "Steady," Adehl murmured, melding with Sorah's llirah to help stabilise her rhythm. "You know what to do."

Sorah shuddered but wrestled her rhythm down. "I don't know why this is happening!"

"Shhh. Focus on the rhythm of the medallion. You are in control." Adehl wished she didn't have Frahto's words ringing in her ears, louder than the bells overhead. *She was about to go wild because* you *weakened the bond to the anchor…* Adehl needed to get Sorah off the stones, away from the tug of the heartstorm. "Can you stand?"

"I think so."

Adehl was about to help Sorah up, when two people outside the prayer hall caught her attention. "Wait," she said. Two exhorters held conference, stationary amid the swirl of people hurrying to enter the temple. Crouched in the shadows, Adehl and Sorah kept still. The hooters joined palms, and Adehl drew her llirah close, hoping Sorah managed the same. She felt the tiniest brush of rhythm, but perhaps the bells had deadened the hooters' wits, because they didn't use their eyes.

Sooner than Adehl expected, the zehla broke the meld and departed abruptly towards the front of the prayer hall. Then she felt another, familiar rhythm entwine with her own and understood.

Roh stood on the main street with a handful of others. His llirah conveyed apology, reassurance, resignation. Adehl had known he would go with Frahto to the Vuusah lodge.

She hadn't let herself think about Roh revelling with Frahto all afternoon. She didn't know how it had come about or why Roh had allowed Frahto to reach the Wild Colt first — but Roh would never intentionally jeopardise her freedom. Her heart clattered at the thought of Frahto, his oldest friend, trying to cajole him back into the fold.

Roh had asked her many times to trust him. *I'm not leaving you here.* So… she would.

At least the Vuusah wouldn't harm Roh. He would find her when he could. Adehl needed to focus on reaching the safety of Lady Kenna's estate.

Ignoring Sorah's protests, Adehl led them back towards the Wild Colt, taking minor streets and trusting in the gathering darkness to conceal their passage. When they neared the rear gate of the lodging house, the bestowal bells were still ringing, and the streets had cleared. Adehl reached out with a careful thread of ellir, directing her senses towards where she had last seen Cloud outside the front of the Wild Colt. Her heart gave a lurch of joy at his familiar, beloved rhythm. Sensing her, he whinnied, the sound faint behind the chiming bells. Beside Adehl, Sorah breathed in harsh gasps, but the girl had clamped her llirah into a tight ball. Adehl would have hugged her if she could. "Hold on, little sparrow."

Chanti met them excitedly at the stable gate. "Mistress, careful!" he said, pulling them into the stable, where the lantern glowed on its usual hook. He procured a knife and carefully sliced through the ropes around her wrists. "There be hooters out front!"

"How many?"

"Two."

"And my horse? The big moonskin. Is he still tethered?" She helped Sorah onto a nearby hay bale, hoping it would provide sufficient isolation for a few minutes.

"Oooh, yes. He be a wild one. He not let anyone near. Even me!"

Adehl scruffed his hair. "Tell me what happened."

In a hurried, barely intelligible stream of words, Chanti recounted events since Adehl and Sorah had fled. Adehl couldn't help smiling as he described all seven horses and their behaviour in great detail — especially the part about Cloud kicking the circah leader and not allowing Frahto to get near him. She reminded Chanti she needed to know about the hooters, to which he replied four had pursued her on foot, but two had since returned to guard Cloud. The remaining two hooters had departed with Frahto and Roh.

"Right now out front, there be five horses," Chanti said, hopping up and down. "There be a nightmoon, two autumnals, a starskin and the wild moonskin. The moonskin truly be yours?"

"He is." Cloud was bait, of course. Why else transport him all the way from Tarsah? "Can you find out if the other hooters have returned?"

"Ai! Wait here, mistress!"

While the lad was gone, Adehl threaded calming strands of ellir towards Cloud. This rescue operation would have been easy had he not been hitched to the rail. She could ask Chanti to slip him free, but that would draw attention to the boy. She ignored the several other obvious solutions munching on hay in the stalls nearby.

Sorah sat with knees drawn up, wayward strands of hair partially obscuring the twin scars on her pale cheeks. "I'm proud of you," Adehl said, putting an arm around her. "In a few minutes, I'm going to get my horse. You'll need to be ready at the gate."

"I understand."

"Tell me honestly… Do you need your father? Or Frahto? They're noumenors, and —"

"No."

"Are you sure? Because we could ride after Frahto. Otherwise, I believe Lady Kenna would pay for one to see you, but —"

"*No.*" Sorah lowered her legs and straightened her

mahgan over her lap. "They'd quell me, eventually. I want to stay with you."

Stars and sun. Was this what she had been like at Sorah's age? Adehl pulled the girl into a quick hug. "All right, little sparrow. Hold on."

ADEHL EDGED along the side of the Wild Colt building, making the most of deep shadows and the cover of the four horses tethered along the wall. Her thudding heart threatened to drown out the incessant chimes of the bestowal bells. She'd grown impatient waiting for Chanti to return. She wanted her horse and she wanted away.

Light spilling from the lodging house bathed the small plaza out front. There were still only two hooters, swords dangling at their hips. One gripped Chanti's narrow, squirming shoulders, the other Cloud's rein.

"Where is she?" The male zehli shook Chanti roughly. He looked young, barely eighteen, his chiselled jaw smooth. "Did she ask you to steal her horse?"

"I be not *stealing*!"

"It's not your horse, is it?"

"I be making sure the horses have water," Chanti said with youthful dignity.

The female zehli holding Cloud's rein glanced at the brimming water trough several paces away. "They've all had plenty of water," she said, her voice light and mellifluous. "I watched you fill that trough earlier."

"The pidakah scumbeat must be here somewhere," the young hooter said, not releasing Chanti. His braids flew around his head as he scanned the area. "Adehl! Show yourself! We've instructions to kill the moonskin if you don't turn yourself over to us!"

Adehl's fists clenched. She didn't believe them, not for a moment. A zehli would never murder a horse. Not even the hooters she'd encountered so far in the city. She'd seen these two in Tarsah, which meant they'd been out on the downs a month ago. They would *not* slaughter a horse simply to capture her. They were not monsters.

Chanti screamed, writhing against the hands restraining him. "No! You not touch him! I not let you!"

"Enough!" The hooter shook Chanti again; then the boy twisted his neck and sunk his teeth into one of the hands gripping his upper arms. "You little..." The man shoved Chanti onto the ground.

The boy yelped and sprawled on the cobbles, panting as though he'd sprinted for an hour. Adehl winced and waited for him to scramble to his feet. Instead, Chanti moaned.

"Easy, Ahro. He's only a child." Still holding Cloud's reins, the female hooter edged closer to Chanti. "What did you do to him?"

"Nothing! *He* gnawed on my hand!"

The woman thrust Cloud's reins at her companion and knelt beside Chanti, who moaned again and pressed small hands over his eyes. "His llirah is all over the place," the zehli said.

Adehl was already moving. She ducked under the neck of the nearest horse and rushed into the pool of thin light, thudded to her knees beside Chanti. "Focus, Chanti," she said. "You know what to do. You are in control."

"I can't..."

"You can."

Adehl was vaguely aware of the woman pushing to her feet, of drawn swords, of the touch of cold steel at her neck. She ignored them. All her attention was on Chanti, her rhythm anchoring his while he battled for control. The boy gripped her fingers until they hurt. His llirah was starting to fray, torn apart by the heartstorm, and Adehl had no idea how to reconstruct it.

After a time, the murmur of voices, new arrivals, penetrated the fog of panic spiralling to the haunting tune of the bestowal bells. "What's going on?" a woman demanded loudly.

"The pidakah woman is here," Ahro said loudly from overhead. His blade pricked Adehl's skin. Chanti's clasp slackened, his rhythm like a tattered flag in the wind.

"What's she doing?" Frahto asked.

Mindful of the swords at her throat, Adehl's gaze wrenched towards him. She didn't care why Frahto was here so soon after departing with Roh. Frahto was a noumenor. "Please," she said. "I need your help."

Frahto's expression tightened. He strode forward and dropped on Chanti's other side.

"Please help him." Adehl's words were thick with tears.

He took in the thin form of the stable lad and shot Adehl a dark, disbelieving glance. "*Another* one?" But he gently touched the skin at Chanti's collarbone. The boy's eyes were closed above his messy dark hair, and he barely seemed to breathe. Adehl held his small, grubby fingers.

It took longer than before, when Frahto had aligned Sorah. Adehl stayed melded until Frahto told her to get out of his way. She reluctantly withdrew her energy, bitterly aware of her failure. Ahro and the woman had drawn back to join their circah, all six present now, encircling Adehl with drawn swords ready to cut her down the moment she moved.

At last, Chanti gasped in a breath and wailed. "I can't. I can't."

Adehl squeezed his hand, smoothed his hair. "I'm here." Meeting Frahto's flat gaze, she swallowed. "Thank you."

"I'm not finished." With his hand still near Chanti's throat, he regarded the boy's pinched face with grim intent.

Adehl's heart faltered, and she couldn't breathe. "Don't. Please." No no no no. But she was helpless to stop Frahto. Chanti's llirah flared with a last beautiful flourish, before Frahto ruthlessly subdued it, locked it into place. It happened so quickly. One moment, dancing sunlight, then doused. Not completely snuffed, but all the energy and amplitude removed.

Frahto retracted his hand. "Does Roh know what you've been doing?"

Adehl screamed something wordless at him, then pulled Chanti into her arms, tried to rouse his llirah, but she had no idea where to start.

"Don't be a fool." Frahto rose to his feet. "Where's Sorah?"

Chanti's eyes fluttered open.

"It's all right," Adehl said. Only, it wasn't. "You're safe now."

He dragged in air and coughed. Spotted Frahto and the ring of armed hooters, looked quickly up at Adehl. "I be sorry, mistress. I… I…"

"Oh, Chanti." Adehl hugged him, blinking back tears.

He frowned and pushed away. A sharp breath. "It be… it be all calm inside." He chewed his lip.

"Look at me." Adehl helped Chanti to stand and knelt before him. "You're *safe* now, all right? You don't need Sapling, or me, or anyone."

"But you said… You said…"

"I know." Adehl wanted to tear up the stones with her fingers and hurl them in Frahto's face. "I thought I could help you…"

"Adehl!" Frahto's voice cracked the silence. Adehl hadn't noticed when the bestowal bells had stopped. The barest hint of light lingered in the western sky beyond the dark rooftops. "Where's Sorah, you misbegotten bloodhead?"

"Leave Sorah alone," Adehl said. She clambered to her

feet amid the circle of swords and put an arm around Chanti's trembling shoulders.

"She needs to come with us, too."

"You've done enough!"

"It's *you* who's —"

"I'm here," Sorah said.

Adehl couldn't pinpoint the girl at first, but Chanti jolted, and Frahto's jaw tightened as he stared towards Cloud. The hooters had released Cloud's rein in their haste to point swords at Adehl, but her horse hadn't drifted far from where she'd last seen him. Sorah now sat astride his back, clutching his mane with shaking hands, the rein trailing on the ground.

"Sorah, do you know how to ride?" Frahto asked in a strange tone.

"No."

Warmth swelled inside Adehl, and she fought against a smile. Clever, brave girl. Sorah met Adehl's gaze, flexed her grip on Cloud's mane.

Bending her head to Chanti's ear, Adehl said, "I'll find you later, little colt. Don't despair, all right?"

"I try, mistress."

"Good lad. Now, don't get in the way of any swords." She straightened and addressed the leader of the circah, a zehli with twin braids she remembered from Tarsah. "You're pointing weapons at a traumatised child. Let him through."

After a long, hard look at Adehl, the woman lowered her blade and indicated permission with a head jerk that rattled her beads. Chanti hesitated, looked up at Adehl, but she squeezed his shoulder and pressed him forward. He slipped out of the circle and disappeared into the shadows.

Adehl released a breath. She hated abandoning Chanti so soon after Frahto had quelled him, but at least he was safe.

Frahto, meanwhile, was edging towards Cloud's head.

Pinned by the hooters' blades, Adehl couldn't go to her

horse. But she didn't need to. Cloud whuffed a happy welcome when her llirah threaded with his. She rapidly sent him images of what she wanted him to do and yelled at Sorah to hold on.

As Frahto reached for Cloud's halter, the horse retreated several paces into the gloom. Sorah gasped at the sudden movement, but she adjusted her weight and kept her seat when the horse suddenly reared. Frahto yelled and fell back. More importantly, the hooters gawked. Without pausing to consider the wisdom of brushing past bared blades, Adehl seized her opportunity.

She ducked to the stones and rolled past the distracted hooters closest to Cloud. They shouted as she passed, struck out with their swords. Bright pain flared in her thigh, but she was on her feet in heartbeats. Frahto, who had been focused on Sorah, spun and tried to grab Adehl, but Cloud shoved the large man to the ground. Sorah squealed and began to topple.

Adehl leapt forward to catch Sorah, agony tearing through her wounded leg. She bit back a curse and steadied the girl, pushed her back into the saddle. "Hold on."

Frahto picked himself up, his glare like twin daggers as Cloud muscled forward. Behind Frahto, loose horses plunged into the mix, forcing the hooters to sheath their blades or risk injuring their mounts. From the edge of the Wild Colt building, beside a row of dangling, empty halters, Chanti gave her a quick grin.

"Sorah, you need to come down." Frahto grabbed Cloud's dangling rein, taking control of the horse. Behind him, three exhorters lunged after the loose horses. The other three stalked towards Adehl. "You're coming with us to the lodge," Frahto said. "Both of you."

"Sorah is free to do as she chooses," Adehl said, hobbling to keep Cloud between herself and Frahto. She swiftly unbuckled the halter and fumbled it off the horse's head. "For my part, I decline your generous invitation."

"Wait…" Frahto stared at the empty halter in his hand.

Adehl swung onto Cloud's back behind Sorah, almost screamed as pain flashed through her leg. Frahto lunged for Cloud's mane, but her horse plunged out of reach.

"Don't make this worse than it already is, Adehl! Don't make things worse for *Roh*."

That gave Adehl pause, but only briefly. The Vuusah would never hurt Roh.

She put her arms around Sorah and strengthened her meld with Cloud. After weeks of separation, it was like stepping into a warm bath. Cloud lunged past the hooters, launched into a canter, and they were away.

35. More guard than escort

Night had fallen by the time Roh reached the Fiugreh Settlement District accompanied by the Blue Fox circah. They strode around the faintly gleaming statue of the stone horse, two exhorters walking ahead of him, two behind, one on either side. No one spoke — except for Tallah, who maintained a steady flow of general conversation, as though trying to distract Roh from the fact her circah was more guard than escort.

Frahto had tried to warn Roh of… something. The Blue Fox circah had intercepted them earlier as they cut through the Pioneer Gardens, fruit bats swooping above the trees. The moment the other circah came into view, Frahto had cursed and slowed their pace.

"Roh, there's something… You need to be careful." Frahto spoke so softly Roh barely heard him over the chime of the bestowal bells.

He recognised Tallah's loping stride from the day he and Adehl had arrived in Dohni. "Of course. But I'll be fine. I just want to talk to Lenatoh."

"It's not…" After several more steps, Frahto said, "Lenatoh is not the one in charge."

Roh grunted. He'd seen enough of the exhorters under the doyen's command to be wary. And he hadn't forgotten the distraught kalkah zehli stumbling to her knees outside the lodge. But the Vuusah wanted Roh to abandon Adehl and return to his role as Atalah-in-waiting. He was in no danger. They wouldn't harm him and couldn't control him. He would get this over with and leave.

Frahto eyed the approaching circah. "Listen to what I'm saying! You think they can't hold you, but —" He broke off as Tallah motioned her zehla to a halt before them.

Tallah quirked an eyebrow. "Roh, I presume?"

"Soul bright, Tallah of the Blue Fox." Roh summoned his cockiest grin.

"Hmmm." She glanced at Roh's companions, Frahto walking alongside, Dinah and Ketahl riding behind — the former on Sprig, confound her. "Where are the others?" Tallah asked.

"Rounding up Adehl," Dinah said.

Despite the situation, Roh felt grim satisfaction: outside the prayer hall, Minuh and Bortoh had failed spectacularly to discover Adehl and Sorah hiding nearby. Roh had allowed himself the briefest of melds with Adehl, before doing what he could to confuse the trackers. He hoped they stumbled around in the tiny lanes of the Old Kestali Quarter for hours.

Frahto started to give directions for retrieving Adehl and Sorah, but Tallah shook her head. "We're here to make sure Roh comes along."

"I believe I am coming along," Roh said.

Tallah showed her teeth. To Dinah and Ketahl, she said, "You should return to finish the job."

"I'll head back with Roh," Frahto said.

Tallah scratched a spot on her neck. "As to that, I believe Nedoyi Lenatoh requested you retrieve his daughter."

Under different circumstances, Roh might have laughed at Frahto's expression. He would prefer to have Frahto's company than that of the Blue Fox exhorters, who seemed cannily named.

"Don't worry, we'll take good care of him," Tallah said as her exhorters arranged themselves around Roh. Ellir swirled beneath his feet as the zehla melded — not a resonant mesh, not yet. More the launching point for one. Tallah grinned.

Frahto held Roh's gaze for several heartbeats. Another warning. It was certainly worrying that these exhorters sought to threaten Roh with a mesh. They would learn their mistake if they tried anything.

"We'll catch up," Frahto said.

"Don't get too close to him," Dinah said with a pointed glance at Roh.

Tallah laughed. "Oh, we've heard the stories."

"I'll wager you haven't heard all of them." Dinah reined Sprig around and left, with Frahto jogging alongside.

Tallah raised a quizzical eyebrow. "How intriguing."

The Blue Fox circah marched Roh across the Lokk Janikk Bridge, then towards the Fiugreh Settlement District. Loping alongside Roh, Tallah seemed unconcerned about Dinah's words, and Roh wished she would cease her endless diatribe about how the Vuusah planned to spend Wintersmorn — a mere ten days hence. He mulled over Frahto's warning. *You think they can't hold you, but…* As warnings went, it was vague as all blood.

Roh ought to be planning what he would say when they reached the lodge. He wasn't looking forward to explaining himself to Lenatoh, who was closer to him than the father he no longer knew. This conversation had been coming since that night at Sage Well.

When they reached the Vuusah lodge, light blazing at its windows, Tallah strode up the steps and thrust open the door. The zehla stationed outside straightened, but Roh didn't recognise them. His senses confirmed Lenatoh was inside, but Roh mounted the steps slowly and held his llirah ready.

Tallah ushered Roh into a ground-floor room with unadorned white walls, and thick blue curtains framing a window. Oil lamps burned on a long sideboard, and a dozen chairs lined a table strewn with parchments. Lenatoh stood at the window, facing the street with rigid shoulders. Seated at the table, an older woman looked expectantly at the door as Roh entered.

"This is Roh, Doyi," Tallah said from behind him. "The Silver Wolf circah is tracking down Adehl and the girl."

The doyen furled the scroll before her but did not rise. When the latch had clicked closed behind Roh, she drawled, "Little Atali. What have you to say for yourself?"

Roh pressed his lips together. He wanted to talk to Lenatoh alone, but the man had not turned from the window.

"Answer me, zehli."

"I have come to clear the air. Voluntarily, I might add."

"And?"

"I would prefer to speak to Lenatoh."

"You will speak to me."

Roh didn't answer. Surely it must be obvious what he wanted — needed — to say to his friend and mentor, but he had no intention of baring his heart in front of this woman he didn't know.

"Let me put it another way," said the doyen. "Unless you have come here to pledge your unconditional loyalty to the Vuusah and disavow the pidakah woman known as Adehl, you can have nothing further to say."

Roh stayed silent. At the window, Lenatoh twitched but still did not turn around.

The doyen's face grew hard. "Choose carefully, zehli."

"Do you think I have done any of this lightly?" Roh said. "She's my injaleh." He hovered in front of the closed door. He wanted to leave, but Tallah and her cronies were stationed on the other side. He wondered if they would actually use their swords against him. His stomach felt queasy. "If Adehl cannot be Vuusah, then nor can I."

A sharp silence filled the room. At last, Lenatoh turned, and Roh almost flinched at the nedoyen's haggard features. His feathered braids looked days old, and he still wore the same town mahgan, crumpled and askew, one of the front fasteners undone near the throat.

"You need to rethink this, Roh," Lenatoh said. "Please."

"I suspect you always knew I would choose Adehl."

"You must not." Lenatoh fidgeted with the beads on Rahda's srih, gathered loosely around his forearm. "When you understand why —"

"No," said the doyen.

Lenatoh scowled. "Let him make an informed decision!"

"No," Doyi Palvemah said again. "I won't bargain with a rogue zehli, no matter who he is. We need unconditional loyalty, Nedoyi. He has made his choice."

Lenatoh pressed his lips together, and Roh held his breath. *Lenatoh is not the one in charge*, Frahto had said. Roh could almost taste his mentor's fury and sorrow and desperation roiling through the room. Uneasily, Roh wondered what *informed decision* Lenatoh had been alluding to... but, ultimately, it didn't matter. Roh would still choose Adehl.

The doyen watched Lenatoh closely as he stepped forward and roughly pulled Roh into a tight embrace. "I'm so very sorry, Roh." It felt like a farewell.

Relief suffused Roh. They were going to let him go. Putting his own arms around Lenatoh, he said, "I wish I could explain..."

"No need." Lenatoh's rhythm now held an added thread of grief. "Where is Sorah?"

"She's with Adehl." Roh squeezed the nedoyen's shoulder. "She'll be all right."

With a grimace, Lenatoh pulled away. "And when we have retrieved my daughter and Adehl, what will you do? If you give her up now, you could save her."

The doyen uttered a strangled oath, and Roh smiled wryly. "Adehl will never be safe from the Vuusah, no matter what I decide."

"Then can't you see this will be for nothing!"

"Nedoyi!" The doyen's tone was implacable. "It's too late. We've lost him."

Lenatoh looked as though a spear had caught him in the chest.

Roh chewed his lip. "I'm sorry things have ended like this." He opened the door.

"We cannot let you go, Roh," the doyen said grimly.

Roh gathered his llirah. "How are you going to stop me?"

"Like this," said Tallah of the Blue Fox, then brought down her sword hilt on his head.

36. Enough waiting

Lady Kenna's high-walled estate stood on Gorannen Rise, a ridge of hills in the outer-eastern reaches of the city. Reining in Cloud at the gates, Adehl beat back waves of pain and dizziness. Though she'd hastily bound her thigh using half her gobeila, blood soaked her remaining garments and smeared the horse's pale flanks.

By torchlight, Lady Kenna's guards did not miss the blood. A grizzled veteran stalked to Adehl's side and caught her before she toppled. "Send word," he said over his shoulder and lifted Adehl in his arms. "Easy, lass."

Another guard helped Sorah down and went to Cloud's head. The gates opened and admitted them into sprawling, shadowed grounds. Farther up the hill, a grand villa blazed with light.

"Are you all right?" Sorah hovered near Adehl, still being carried by the guard.

I'll be fine… Adehl wasn't sure whether she got the words out and closed her eyes.

She came around to find herself lying on a settee in an

opulent parlour lit with lamps and mirrors. Someone had tended and bandaged her thigh, replaced her ruined gobeila with a soft house robe the pale green of brizah grass. Adehl tried to rise, gritted her teeth against flashing pain.

"Rest, Adehl. You've lost a great deal of blood," said Lady Kenna from a settee opposite. She was similarly attired, though her robe shimmered blue-green like the ocean.

"Where's Sorah?"

"I'm here." Sorah huddled in an armchair, knees drawn up. Her hair was damp and loose, and she wore another of Kenna's robes — or so Adehl assumed. It was too long for Sorah and bunched around her feet. She looked young and scared.

Adehl extended a hand, and Sorah crossed to kneel at her side. The girl held her llirah tightly bound with effort. "When Roh gets here, he can try to strengthen your bond with the medallion," Adehl said. Though Roh wasn't a noumenor, he could probably manage an alignment better than she. He would come. It was what they'd agreed: to accept Lady Kenna's offer of refuge. "Until then, don't go outside… Are we upstairs?" She arched an inquiring brow at Kenna.

The Merali scholar nodded, her eyes glistening. "You're safe here, Sorah. I promise."

Relieved, Adehl subsided against the soft cushions of Kenna's furniture. Days ago, when Adehl had told Kenna about Sorah, her second gierfeh pupil, her friend had wanted them to relocate here immediately. Kenna would give every gierfeh a chance, even though she herself had been denied.

Fury, Adehl was tired. She hoped Roh got here soon.

By midnight, when Roh still hadn't turned up, Adehl was

about ready to get Cloud and rampage through the streets in search of him.

She braced her hands on the windowsill, her injured leg bleating. The dark city sprawled below, three lighthouses blazing around the harbour entrance, and an additional light tower at the university atop Goldayn Rise. Somewhere on the far side of the harbour, miles away, lay the Vuusah lodge. Was Roh still there — or had he gone somewhere else?

"I need to go." Head swimming, Adehl limped three steps across the blue rug and collapsed onto her settee. More spikes of agony jagged through her leg.

Kenna looked up from the book she'd been squinting at by lamplight. Sorah had long since retired to a bedchamber. "You can barely walk."

"I can't just sit here." Adehl breathed through the pain, wished her head would clear. Earlier, she had performed a rudimentary healing on herself to help the wound knit faster. Kenna's healer had stitched up the gash, which was fortunately only a flesh wound, but it continued to throb relentlessly.

"I'm sure Roh is simply swapping stories with his friends. He'll probably sleep at the lodge and send word in the morning."

It was what Adehl had been telling herself, but she couldn't suppress the nagging feeling that something was wrong. Frahto had seemed almost panicked. *Don't make this worse than it already is, Adehl! Don't make things worse for Roh.*

Kenna laid her book aside. "I've met the doyen, and I don't believe she would harm a Vuusah zehli of Roh's standing. She's shrewder than that."

"He's important to them. They want him to renounce me and go back to being the Atalah-in-waiting."

"Exactly. They won't hurt him." Kenna rose, saying

gently, "Go to bed, Adehl. We can do nothing tonight. I'll get you another draught for the pain."

"No."

"If he's not here in the morning, you can take my carriage."

Reluctantly, Adehl allowed a couple of servants to help her walk. She checked on Sorah, who was sleeping peacefully; then Kenna guided her into an ornate bedchamber.

Sleep eluded Adehl, at first — despite her exhaustion and the most comfortable bed she'd ever lain on. Her leg throbbed. Chanti was quelled. Roh had not come. Adehl wanted to pound on the door of the lodge. She wanted to pummel Frahto's face.

At some point, she must have slept, because she woke to find the room awash with silver moonlight.

She groped her way to the window, gritting teeth at her leg's protest, to find the waning gibbous moon high over the city. From this vantage, she easily made out the curve of the harbour and, farther south, the sweep of Haventown Bay. Moonshine glimmered on thousands of rooftops and limned the swaying foliage covering the eastern slopes of Goldayn Rise. Below, the city was waking, and she judged it about an hour before dawn.

Enough resting. Enough waiting. She searched for her clothes.

Unfortunately, Adehl didn't have any clothes. Those she'd been wearing were both blood-ruined and ripped into pieces, and the rest were in her room at the Wild Colt. She would have paced her chamber waiting for the household to rise, but her leg hurt too much. Instead, she went back to bed and stared at the ceiling.

Fortunately, it turned out Lady Kenna had a wardrobe large enough for ten people. After the healer changed bandages and checked stitches, Adehl donned the plainest garments laid before her by Kenna's chief attendant — a midnight-blue-and-indigo gobeila woven from the finest agave silk, paired with a grey waist sash and leggings, finished with slightly too large, short boots of soft, black leather.

At the breakfast table, Adehl forced down a slice of bread that tasted like sawdust, then guided Sorah through ten gaerah cycles. The girl's llirah had calmed down since yesterday, but Frahto's scathing denouncement still weighed heavily. "Do you need your father?" Adehl asked. "I didn't mean to weaken —"

"No," Sorah said. "What you did… what you showed me was amazing. I've never felt anything like that before. I *felt* the rock's rhythm. I want to feel that again."

"Are you sure? If Frahto hadn't shown up…"

"Please don't make me go back."

"I won't make you do anything you don't wish to do." Adehl chewed her lip. "Just… try to stay upstairs."

Sorah rolled her eyes. "I know." Then she stuck her tongue out, acting her age for almost the first time since Adehl had known her.

"Noted." Adehl smiled and drained her lukewarm mug of ginger tea. Then she staggered to her feet.

She was braced on the back of a chair, waiting for the jabbing pain and dizziness to subside, when Lady Kenna entered the room with her claithwielder. "I don't suppose I can talk you out of this?" Kenna looked every inch the Merali wellborn, coiffed and draped in a long, sea-green agave silk tunic over matching wide-legged trousers.

"I need to find Roh."

"What exactly are you intending to do?"

"I'll start at the Vuusah lodge. If I can get close enough, I'll be able to sense if he's there."

"And if he is?"

Adehl swallowed. "Then I'll know he's all right."

Kenna tapped her thigh a few times. "My carriage is waiting for you out the front. Jai, please go with her."

Jaikud speared the scholar with a look. "I trust this means you intend to remain here?"

"I'll do my best to entertain Sorah," Kenna said, snappishly. "You make sure my friend does not get nabbed by hooters. Try not to kill anyone."

The corner of Jaikud's mouth lifted. "Understood."

ADEHL DIDN'T RECOGNISE the zehla stationed outside the building she assumed was the Vuusah lodge. They looked alert, casually glancing at Lady Kenna's elegant vehicle sweeping past. Similar slate-roofed buildings lined the wide street; pedestrians and horses comprised most of the traffic.

The carriage pulled up outside a building several doors down, a large tabby cat sunning himself on the steps. Adehl lifted the door latch of the vehicle, but Jaikud stopped her with an arm. "I need to get out," Adehl said.

"I'll go first."

She eyed his distinctive black uniform and sword hilt jutting above his shoulder. "You'll attract too much attention. I'm not going far. I'll stand at the door." All she needed was proximity to the ground.

"You can barely walk." With one arm, he held her in place and leapt neatly out to hold the door open for her.

To spite him, Adehl considered disembarking via the opposite door, but that would put her in the direct eye line of the hooters. She allowed Jaikud to assist her out of the carriage, conceding that his supporting arm was preferable to falling flat on her face.

Propped between the carriage and the claithwielder,

Adehl reached for ellir. It flowed through the ground, not as chaotic as on the eastern shores of the harbour but every bit as strong. She embraced her llirah and melded herself with the energy. When Roh was nearby, she could always find him.

She directed her attention to the Vuusah lodge, feathering past the two zehla on guard, careful not to betray her presence. Inside the building, the ground floor held at least two dozen zehla; upstairs, it was more difficult to identify individuals, but if Roh were there, she'd find him.

Roh wasn't there. He wasn't anywhere.

Frahto was inside, his llirah becoming familiar. But not Roh. "Burn them all black," Adehl muttered.

Jaikud's grip tightened on her arm. "Trouble?"

Adehl swept through the lodge one more time. All she found were too many hooters and a strange, distorted rhythm coming out of the basement. She widened her search, wished she were better at farsensing. "I can't find him."

"We should go."

As she'd predicted, local passersby were starting to clog the street around Jaikud. Claithwielders weren't too common, especially on this side of the harbour; the whole district would probably be here soon. But Adehl didn't want to leave. She'd been so sure Roh would be at the lodge. Could he have returned to the Wild Colt? Or perhaps the university? She didn't know where else he'd go.

She accepted Jaikud's assistance into the carriage and stared out the window as they retraced their path. The lands on this side of the harbour, where the Fiugreh clans had first settled, were more open, less built up than the eastern shores, and the northern band of mountains rose out of flatter terrain. She eyed the rocky pinnacle of the large hill she'd first noticed from the university. In the morning sunlight, the grey crown shimmered faintly purple, indicating more heartrock.

Ignoring Jaikud's protests, Adehl directed the carriage

driver to the rear courtyard of the Wild Colt. When the carriage rumbled through the gate, Orkoh arrived at a run, his brow furrowing at the fancy equipage. He went to the horses' heads, and Adehl leant out the carriage window. "Bright day, Orkoh. Apologies for the disturbance. I'm here for our belongings."

Chanti came to the carriage window, his drawn face splitting into a grin when he saw Adehl. "Mistress, careful! There be hooters out front."

"Have you seen Roh since yesterday?"

A wild shake of his head, shaggy dark hair flying.

"All right." She forced her worry down. Chanti looked like he'd had a rough night. "How are you feeling?"

His lip trembled. "I be missing Sapling. It be all quiet inside."

"I know…" Adehl could hardly get the words out. "I'm sure she's missing you, too." Adehl nudged open the door, extended a hand. "Will you help me down?" Muted strands of sunlight twinkled in his rhythm, still essentially Chanti, but subdued. Adehl wanted to cry with him; she gave him a quick hug instead. "Stay safe, little colt. Do what the hooters say, all right?"

The boy nodded solemnly.

Jaikud helped Adehl hobble upstairs to the bedchamber she and Roh had occupied for the past two weeks. She half expected the room to have been cleared out already, or at least searched, but their gear lay strewn about, just as they had left it. While Jaikud stood watchfully at the door, Adehl stuffed meagre belongings into their one bag. It was mostly clothes and grooming items, but she carefully gathered Roh's polished stones from the dresser. An idea struck her, and she melded with each one to see if Roh had left a clue as to where he might have gone. She received nothing more than muddled impressions.

Running her gaze around the room to make sure she'd packed everything, Adehl felt strangely reluctant to leave. It had been a good room, a sanctuary after their flight from Tarsah. On arrival, she and Roh had barely known each other; it was in this room she'd bestowed her srih.

Downstairs, the proprietor bustled up to awkwardly request payment for a third week's lodging. The woman fiddled with one of her dangling ear ornaments, said the hooters had been here and she didn't want any trouble. Fenaika lurked behind, her eyes wide.

"Thank you for your hospitality, mistress." Adehl smiled at both of them and hefted her bag. "We have vacated the room. You may tell anyone who asks we are to be the guests of Lady Kenna Auwyn for a time."

The woman shifted, eyed the claithwielder and swallowed. "Very well."

Adehl pulled open the back door, only to have Jaikud reach over her shoulder and push it closed. "Me first, remember?" He gently manoeuvred in front of her and stepped out — then immediately drew his claithsword. "Stay there!"

The stable yard was full of hooters with drawn blades. Chah's circah this time. He and three others waited to confront whoever came out the door. The carriage had been turned so the horses faced the gate, but Ninah had a sword in the driver's face and offered Adehl a wicked grin. Beyond the horses, Orkoh and Chanti huddled against the stable building, guarded by a sixth zehli. Orkoh's strong arms were wrapped around Chanti, trying to prevent the squirming boy from impaling himself.

The door behind Adehl nudged her over the threshold and slammed closed. The sudden movement jarred her leg, and pain bloomed white hot. She collapsed back against the timber and heard the bolt ram home. Meanwhile, Jaikud stood between her and the hooters, his stance relaxed. He held his sword angled towards the ground.

Chah looked past the claithwielder. "You can't keep running, Adehl." Morning sunlight glinted on the gold in his ear.

"Where's Roh?"

"Safe from you." Chah pointed his sword at her. "I heard what he did to the Silver Wolf circah yesterday."

"You mean put them to sleep? What a villain."

"He's out of control because of you. The doyen is furious."

Adehl laughed without humour. "Right. He's out of *their* control."

"As to that…" Chah scratched the shaved side of his head.

Adehl narrowed her gaze. The Vuusah must have detained Roh — but considering what he was capable of, she couldn't think how. "Roh isn't at the Vuusah lodge. Where is he?"

Chah looked uncomfortable.

"What have they done to him?"

"Are you ready to come with us quietly?"

They wouldn't harm Roh. They *couldn't*. They wanted him back. Propped against the door, not wanting to reveal the extent of her injury, Adehl crossed her arms.

Jaikud looked at Adehl. "Have you heard enough?"

Not really. Roh was in trouble, and she didn't know how to save him. But these hooters weren't going to tell her anything. She said, "More than enough. *I* don't mind if you kill someone."

Jaikud laughed as he launched into action.

From the back doorstep, Adehl could only gape as the claithwielder danced with the hooters. His blade flashed hints of indigo as it arced through the air in time with his movements. He dodged and weaved and disarmed the zehla in less than a minute. One by one, four short swords clanged to the cobbles, kicked away expertly as he moved. Ninah and the remaining hooter leapt towards their brethren, only to confront the threatening edge of the claithsword. Wide-eyed, all six zehla retreated to huddle in a corner of the courtyard.

"Get in the carriage," Jaikud said, over his shoulder.

"Don't let them form a mesh." Adehl gritted her teeth and limped across the empty space, her bulging bag slung across her back.

Jaikud made a sound of acknowledgment.

Adehl wished she could enjoy the sight of Jaikud shouldering through the group to disrupt their meld, but her leg screamed at her, and she somehow needed to climb into the carriage.

Chanti arrived at her elbow. "I help you, Mistress Adehl."

She wanted to take Chanti with her. Instead, she leant on his shoulder and hauled herself up two steps, her thigh almost exploding with agony. At last, she sprawled, panting, on the padded bench seat inside Lady Kenna's comfortable vehicle. "Thank you, little colt." She gripped his grubby fingers. "If you need to find me, go to Lady Kenna Auwyn at the university. Got that?"

Eyes wide, the lad nodded and closed the door.

It opened again almost immediately, and Adehl jolted upright, inciting another jag of pain; but it was Jaikud who sprang inside, grinning. His sword was once more sheathed across his back, and he adjusted its position as the carriage rolled forward.

"What did you do with the hooters?" Adehl asked.

"Locked them in the stable building. It'll delay them long enough for us to leave."

"Any of them get injured? Perhaps fatally?" She was not entirely jesting.

Jaikud snorted. "No need." He frowned at the damp dark-red patch on Adehl's borrowed leggings, and she hastily covered it with the folds of the tunic. "Home, I think," he said.

"Not yet. There's one more thing I need to do."

He squinted at her. "What's that?"

"We're going to the university." At this point she was willing to try anything. "I want to use the Circle of Wind."

THE WROUGHT-IRON GATE CREAKED OPEN, and Adehl limped after Gordoh into a walled garden of rampant greenery. Although Roh had described the Circle of Wind, it took her several heartbeats to spot the pillars lurking in the foliage. She felt them, though. The circle's power thrummed through her body before she'd even stepped within its bounds, dwarfing the strength of the resonator in Tarsah.

At the sudden, painful memory of her father, bound to a pillar, bruised and bloody at the hands of zehla, Adehl checked her step, injured leg twinging. She hoped he had forgiven her.

Having entered the garden behind Adehl, members of the Ellirisi fanned out, batting away foliage and taking places beside the pillars. Among the Ellirisi who Gordoh had dragged out of their offices were Merroh, the bearded zehli from the Night of the Archer, and a woman called Lanikka, whose Sevikk features suggested she was not a zehli at all.

Adehl's leg throbbed. Jaikud assisted her to the central pillar, where Gordoh stood. Being a limnor already attuned to the Circle of Wind, he would lead the farsensing ritual.

"If he's out there, we'll find him," Gordoh said, his hand resting on the focus stone.

"Are you sure?"

"As long as he's... able to be reached." The First Scholar

looked momentarily grim. "Your presence as his injaleh will help."

Adehl breathed, nodded. Refused to wonder what that grim set of his mouth had meant. "I'm ready."

Gordoh offered a brisk nod in return, then lifted his voice in a goreyah chant. It was the same chant the Vuusah had used three weeks ago, but Gordoh set a slower tempo. His voice soared in a pleasant tenor, the words in the ancient Fiugreh tongue. Then, one by one, going around the circle, each zehli joined the chant, some choosing a harmony more comfortable for their vocal range. The chorus resounded through the garden as the chanters tuned in to the Circle of Wind and each other.

Adehl clung to the focal pillar. Her arms went around its girth, her whole body pressed against its radiating warmth. Ellir hummed within the stone, bounding out of the thick core of heartrock embedded in the hill.

Gordoh had earlier explained how the Ellirisi had tuned the Circle of Wind, and by extension the whole hill, into a particular, recurring rhythm that never completely dissipated. She felt the underlying pattern strengthen as the goreyah chant continued. Strand by strand, rhythms juxtaposed, blended, conformed into a single cadence.

It was like a raucous crowd deciding on a melody, then blending into one voice, clear as a bell.

The chords of the chant filled the air, and the mesh of ellir strummed her soul. That single honeyed tune shivered through Adehl's flesh and bones and blood, welcoming her into the meld. There were no unruly vibrations, only a sweet, harmonious hum. Her body felt weightless, incorporeal, a bundle of light.

She sensed each of the individual scholars participating in the ritual, their llirah blended into the mesh, including Gordoh, preparing to wield it. The city below and all around became a mass of chaotic energy beyond the mesh. So many people, so many llirah, so many echoes. She couldn't fathom how anyone could make sense of this mess.

As Gordoh had requested, Adehl focused on Roh — on his llirah, almost the match of her own. He might be able to remove his echoes, but he couldn't hide himself, no matter how tightly he bound his energy. Not from her. She breathed deeply and allowed Gordoh to bear her away.

Time passed. Strands of rhythm resolved into individual llirah. Hundreds of people. Thousands. Animals, too. A whole city's worth on both sides of the harbour. Gordoh sorted through them too fast for her to follow, searching for the one that would sing to Adehl's soul. But every single rhythm jarred against Adehl's own.

More time passed… then, much later, a hand came down on her shoulder. "Adehl." The voice was deep, rough. "Come away."

No. She hugged the pillar more tightly. They couldn't be finished. Gordoh must have missed something. Roh could not have simply vanished.

"We're not going to find him this way," Gordoh said. The garden was silent now, except for the chirps of noisy mynas and the wind in the leaves. She hadn't noticed the mesh dissipating.

Adehl shook her head, wincing as her jaw scraped rock. Her heart thudded painfully.

The hand on her shoulder squeezed. "I'm not saying I think he's dead."

"Good, because he's not." She would know if he were dead. She would have felt… something.

"Come inside. I think I know where he is."

She turned. "Where?"

Gordoh extended a hand to help her up. Aside from

Jaikud, the garden was empty of people. High overhead, the sun burned hot on Adehl's skin.

"I think he's locked in the Vuusah lodge," Gordoh said wearily.

"But he's not there, I checked."

"We've heard reports of a chamber in the basement. The doyen had it constructed from stone salvaged from the lost city of Rungakk."

Adehl's heart almost stopped. Rungakk was in a deadland. "You mean… dead stone?"

A grim nod. "The chamber is isolated from the heartstorm."

"Isolated?" Adehl's words were a hoarse whisper.

"The doyen likes to… neutralise zehli who don't do her bidding."

Bile rose up Adehl's throat. Surely they wouldn't put Roh in such a place. He was *Little Atali*. They wanted him back. They wouldn't… *torture* him like that.

But it would explain how he seemed to have disappeared.

Roh shivered.

Cold.

Cold pressed into his back, and he came to realise he lay sprawled on something hard. A stone floor. But why so cold? His mind felt numb with it, as though his flesh would never be warm again.

Instinctively, he reached for his llirah, felt an odd relief when he touched it. Muted, though. Like a single candle trying to light up a vast cavern. It didn't banish the cold.

He reached out farther and found a void.

Roh bolted upright, opened his eyes to dimness. Panic

and a splitting headache rocked him into a shudder. He pressed hands into the floor, sought ellir.

It was as if all the air had gone out of the world. The stone was lifeless, dead. He couldn't breathe, his limbs felt heavy and weak, and his ears rang with dense silence.

Sun's blood. Something was very, very wrong.

Tallah had clobbered him on the head. And now he couldn't reach ellir — and this cursed silence was too — and the freakish cold — and why wouldn't his lungs work?

He forced himself to take slow breaths until his pulse settled to something approaching normal, and the throbbing behind his eyes eased. All was still, except for his llirah, deep in his core. Clinging to his llirah desperately, Roh felt like a flame about to be smothered.

He was in some kind of dimly lit cellar. No windows. Faint light came through a grille on the closed door. The walls and floor were made of dressed stone blocks, carefully fitted together. Roh dragged himself to his feet and tried the door. Locked. It was made of stout timber, oddly pale and very hard. He pressed his fingers into the surface, reached for its energy. Not a flicker.

Not wood, then. Couldn't be wood. Because a tree wouldn't grow without ellir.

All the stones were dead, too. The whole floor, the walls. None carried any hint of ellir.

Not good. Not good. Not good.

Hunched on the floor of the empty cell, Roh cradled his aching head in his arms and breathed.

A tiny rhythm whispered against his cheek. He brought his arm down and found the ornaments on Adehl's srih. Tiny pebble-beads and links of gold, slivers of ellir within each one. He pressed them against the skin below his collarbone, wrapped his other hand over the top. On the floor, curled in a ball, he rocked and tried to get himself under control.

He wasn't quelled. He clung to that thought. He could still reach his llirah and meld with the pebbles and gold links on the srih. It wasn't much, but it was something.

The chamber was constructed entirely of materials containing no trace of ellir. The cell — and anyone inside it — was isolated from the heartstorm. He was unable to reach out. Unable to be reached. Roh would have thought it impossible for such a chamber to exist. The strength of ellir in rocks varied, but there was always something.

Then he thought of the deadlands. The cold, vast regions of nothing no one could explain.

Roh thought of the kalkah zehli who had stumbled out of the lodge and wept on the stones of the road. He thought of the strange pattern of ellir flowing from the basement of the Vuusah lodge.

He thumped on the door, yelled for both Lenatoh and Frahto until he was hoarse. The silence was unnerving. All his senses were dampened — every scuff of his boots on the floor, every rasp of his breath swallowed up by the thick air.

No one came.

There was only the cold, hard, lifeless stone.

37. In the basement

The only thing worse than listening to Roh's increasingly hoarse bellows was the silence after he stopped.

Seated against the outside wall above the isolation cell, Frahto bowed his head over raised knees and adjusted his weight on the grass. His buttocks were going numb, but he bore it. Numb buttocks were nothing compared to what Roh was going through inside that cursed basement. The distorted flow of ellir around it was awful, but Frahto bore that, too.

He didn't know how long he'd maintained this futile vigil. Long enough for the daylight to fade. Long enough to consume three pitchers of ale. Long enough for Roh to stop shouting.

Roh had been locked in that horrible cell since the previous evening. Frahto had returned to the lodge after his second failed attempt to capture Adehl and retrieve Sorah, and Tallah had gleefully related the full story — including how she'd poured a sleeping draught down Roh's throat to keep him quiet. The doyen wasn't willing to rely upon drowsing, Tallah said. Not against Little Atali.

Through the grille in the bolted door, Roh had looked dead. If not for two exhorters stationed outside the cell, Frahto would have dragged him out of there immediately. Lenatoh had been no help, closeted with Palvemah, their low-voiced conversation muffled by the closed door. How could Lenatoh permit Roh to be treated like this?

The night had seemed endless.

At daybreak, Roh still lay comatose, and Frahto had a headache from trying to reach Roh via ellir. He retreated to pace around the garden courtyard; it didn't help his headache and, by midday, he'd given himself a blister.

Sometime after that, the shouting began.

Frahto had rushed to the basement — but the zehla stationed there wouldn't let him talk to his friend. Doyen's orders, they said. He'd then rushed to find Lenatoh, but the nedoyen had once more vanished into Palvemah's conference chamber. Shouting came from there, too.

Fuming, despairing, not knowing what else to do, Frahto had retreated again to the garden. He needed to be outside among the grass and wind, where the heartstorm could reach him. Where he could be near his friend, even if Roh never knew about it.

Chah and Ninah joined him for a time, telling him of their latest encounter with Adehl — who had been accompanied by a claithwielder no less. The idea of Adehl showing up to collect her belongings, so she could take refuge with an influential Merali wellborn while Roh languished in that torture chamber, made Frahto so angry he started shaking. Did she even care she could secure Roh's release by handing herself in? Adehl didn't deserve Roh's love and loyalty.

The thought they would no longer be injaleh if Roh were realigned was cold comfort.

The day faded into another mild night with abundant

stars, the moon not yet risen. Crickets chirped in the garden, and from inside the lodge came the familiar murmur of Frahto's brethren at their evening meal. The noise surged as someone came out the back door and scuffed down the steps to the basement. Frahto tipped his head back against the wall and closed his eyes. It sounded like meals had arrived for the zehla guards.

A short time later, the door opened again, expelling several sets of feet that rustled the grass on approach. "You look like loophorn muck," said Dinah, from close by.

Frahto opened his eyes to find the woman with a few zehla from her circah. One carried a lantern, the others pitchers and mugs. They arranged themselves cross-legged in a rough circle and sloppily poured. Frahto shook ale off his hand. "Thanks. I ran out some time ago." He took a long draught. "Did they send some in for Roh?"

"He received water and gruel, I believe." With a grimace, Dinah lowered her voice. "That cell is brutal."

Frahto grunted. "I'd call it barbaric."

"Ninah said the doyen paid a fortune for the stones," Ahro said. "How would anyone get them? I thought Rungakk was lost."

"They know where it is, idiot," said Ketahl. "It's just no one is supposed to go there." She shuddered. "Who would want to?"

Cold crept over Frahto's skin at the thought. Decades ago, Rungakk had been a thriving steelmaking city, far to the north, in Sevikkland. No one knew how or why the land had died around it. No one knew how any of the deadlands formed. Most of the wastes were older than time. "Do you know how long they intend to keep Roh inside there?" Frahto asked.

"As long as it takes," said Dinah.

Ahro leant forward. "Tallah said they've held zehla inside for as long as ten days."

The ale curdled in Frahto's gut. "As long as it takes for what?"

"For Roh to break," Dinah said.

"To renounce Adehl?"

"I…" Dinah adjusted the srih on her left arm. "I get the impression it's more than that."

Frahto sagged against the wall at his back, tried to ignore his brethren speculating softly about what *breaking* Roh might entail.

He hated how easily they accepted this. A month ago, Roh had been revered as the Atalah-in-waiting by these zehla. They would all have done anything he asked.

MUCH LATER, as the half-moon lifted over the rooftops, the rear door opened, and Lenatoh strode into the garden. Hands cradling the back of his head, he paused beneath the crepe myrtle tree, his rigid form clearly delineated by moonlight.

Frahto hadn't moved from his position against the wall, though the Silver Wolf circah had long since bidden him goodnight. The crickets, too, had gone to sleep, and Frahto clearly heard grass rustling and twigs cracking when the nedoyen began pacing the same route Frahto had worn down earlier.

Frahto shifted, about to rise and cross to Lenatoh, but the door opened again, and the doyen clomped down the steps.

"I need your oath, Nedoyi," Palvemah said.

"There must be another way."

"This is the best way."

Lenatoh completed another loop of the garden. "I want to speak to him."

"We've already been over this." The doyen sounded annoyed.

"Five days in that cell is too long! You said they go mad."

Frahto hardly dared breathe.

"I'm weary of repeating myself, Nedoyi," the doyen said, propped awkwardly on her crutch. "Now, give me your oath."

Lenatoh halted, moonlight revealing his tortured features. "You don't know what you're asking."

"I'm not asking. You swore an oath to the Atalah."

"Not to do *this*!"

"You swore to do whatever was necessary to ensure Roh was ready."

"Not this." Lenatoh sounded like he might be ill.

"Then you should have ensured the boy didn't abscond with that woman!"

In the ensuing silence, Frahto felt sure they would hear his heart pounding. Cramp built in his leg, and he cursed silently. His position remained in shadow, but if he stretched, they would surely see him.

"The Vuusah order needs you to do this, Lenatoh," Palvemah said implacably. "Roh is vital to our plans. If we lose him, it will set us back years."

"And if I don't?"

"You would break your oath to the Atalah?"

Lenatoh turned away.

The doyen lowered herself onto a stone bench. "Sometimes we must make sacrifices to achieve a greater goal. No one — not even Roh — is more important than what we're trying to achieve."

Frahto strained to hear Lenatoh's next words. "I wish I could believe that."

"Your opinions don't matter." Palvemah's voice hardened again. "We do the Atalah's bidding in this."

Lenatoh muttered something under his breath. Frahto thought it sounded like *For how much longer…*

"I expect you to honour your oath, Nedoyi. You won't like the consequences if you don't."

"You wouldn't…"

"Have you not been listening? There is nothing I wouldn't do. We must be ready for the next phase. We are all expendable. All replaceable."

"Except Roh."

"Except Roh."

A voice jerked Frahto awake. It took him several disoriented and rapid heartbeats to recognise he had fallen asleep outside, his head pillowed on grass. Warbling tibbies proclaimed the dawn, though the sun had not yet breached the horizon. He shivered in the cool air.

Lenatoh hunkered beside him and said again, "Get up."

Frahto groaned, every muscle protesting after a night on the ground. The past weeks had made him soft.

"Pull yourself together." The man's voice rang with tension. "Are you drunk?"

"No."

"Good. The doyen intends to have Roh realigned today."

"Today?"

Frahto sat up and scrubbed at his face. He'd sat outside for hours after overhearing Lenatoh eventually submit to the doyen's demands and not-so-veiled threats. In halting, bitter tones, the nedoyen had given his oath to realign Roh if Palvemah asked it of him. But it had sounded like the doyen intended Roh to languish in the isolation cell for a few more days before taking further action. "What's going on?" Frahto asked.

"I warned you this might happen." Lenatoh's words carved slices out of the dawn air.

"I thought she was softening him up first." Frahto's mind had turned into mud. "Why now? What's the rush?"

Lenatoh looked grim. "The Merali woman from House Auwyn is making noise."

"What Merali woman?"

"The one who has my daughter and is sheltering Adehl." Some barkwrens pecking at the grass took flight at Lenatoh's raised voice. "The doyen wishes to make sure of Roh before Lady Kenna Auwyn can interfere."

"Lenatoh…" Frahto's gut churned. "Would you truly do it? No matter what oaths you've sworn… This is *Roh*."

The nedoyen stilled. "How long have you been out here?"

"Since, uh, yesterday."

"How much did you overhear?"

Frahto chewed his cheek. "You don't want to do this."

"It doesn't matter what I want."

"You can still refuse."

"I swore an oath to the Atalah," Lenatoh said, his voice cracking. "Get up!"

Frahto scrambled to his feet and followed Lenatoh to the top of the basement steps. They arrived as Doyi Palvemah emerged from the lodge, her crutch knocking against stone. Her expression hardened at the sight of Frahto, but she did not prevent him from following her halting descent.

In the basement, Palvemah spoke softly to Tallah and the other zehla on watch. Lenatoh glanced through the grille into the isolation chamber and stiffened. Then he drew the bolt and pulled open the door. Frahto stared over Lenatoh's shoulder. Roh huddled in the corner, shaking, his back to them. His braid had come unravelled, and his clothes were dusty and dishevelled. He curved his whole body around something clutched tightly to his chest.

"Roh?" Lenatoh's voice came out strangled.

Roh stilled. For several heartbeats, he didn't move; then he dragged himself around to sit with his back against the wall. One hand remained fisted against the front of his tunic.

From the doorway, Lenatoh asked, "How do you feel?"

"Do you care?" Roh sounded exhausted.

"I…" Lenatoh swallowed. "How is your head?"

Roh laughed, the sound shocking and wild. "You want to know whether my head hurts?"

Lenatoh clenched the doorframe, then recoiled. Frahto pushed past him and went inside. The enveloping, unnatural stillness was suffocating. "Sweet ellir."

Another hollow laugh from Roh. "Funny. Ha ha. That's just what you won't find in here."

"We've got to get you out of here," Frahto said.

"Come away, Frahto." The doyen had joined Lenatoh in the doorway.

"*Please*, Roh," Frahto said. The ceiling seemed to press down on him and expand into nothing, all at once. "They won't let you out until you renounce her."

Roh stared at Palvemah, met Frahto's gaze fleetingly; then his eyes shuttered and his body hunched over his raised knees. "It seems I might as well get comfortable here."

"Roh, I'm begging you." Lenatoh sounded distraught. "You've forced our hand."

Roh's attention snapped to the nedoyen. After several heartbeats, he swallowed and said slowly, "You will not quell me." He'd never sounded so uncertain.

"You deserve to be quelled for your behaviour over the past few weeks," Palvemah said. "But as it happens, we have something else in mind." She stepped back to provide space for Tallah and two of the Blue Fox circah to enter the chamber with their swords drawn.

Roh's eyes widened. "What's going on?"

Tallah produced a vial of liquid. "Drink this, please."

From the floor, Roh eyed her incredulously over the steel; then his gaze flicked to the vial. "What is it?"

"Merely another sleeping draught," said the doyen.

"What are you going to do?"

Frahto hated this. Hated all of it. No one was saying anything, but Roh deserved to know. He wet his mouth and forced the words out. "Realignment." In case Roh hadn't heard, he forced himself to say it louder. "You're going to be realigned."

Roh paled. He adjusted his grip on something in his hand. "You're lying."

Frahto shook his head, denying any involvement, but guilt stormed through him regardless. "I wish I was."

"Lenatoh?" Roh said, his tone disbelieving.

White-faced, the nedoyen pressed his lips together and withdrew from the doorway.

"Will you drink this or must I tip it down your gullet?" Tallah said, proffering the vial.

"You can *try*," Roh said.

Palvemah gestured at Frahto. Shaking his head, Frahto stumbled back until he crashed into the cold, dead wall.

"We've got this, Doyi," Tallah said.

"Get your hands off me!" Weakened from spending a day and a half in this cursed chamber, Roh struggled against the grip of the two exhorters, the object falling out of his hand. They held him down while Tallah poured the contents of the vial down his throat. "Go away, all of you!" Roh said.

Roh sagged against the wall, his hand groping at the stone floor. A braided strip threaded with tiny stone beads and gold loops lay in the dust, out of his reach. Adehl's srih. Roh leant, reaching for the srih as though his life depended on its retrieval. But it was too far, and he toppled, smashing his face against the stone. He groaned, fingers clawing at nothing, then was still.

Frahto stared down at the unconscious body of his friend as Palvemah and her minions left the chamber. Roh's hair flowed over the grimy stone. Frahto wanted to gather him in his arms, carry him to safety and warmth. He glanced at the door, but two more of Tallah's circah looked on.

"We can't leave him like this," Frahto said. He stooped to retrieve the srih. After a pause, gut churning, he wound it securely around Roh's arm.

"Come away, Frahto," Lenatoh said from the doorway.

"I can't just leave him here!"

"They're about to take him to the Stormbowl."

Frahto registered the distant sound of Palvemah barking instructions.

"Come away," Lenatoh said again in a low voice.

Outside, the day had brightened, and everything was wrong. The stable courtyard was already abustle as zehla prepared a horse-drawn vehicle and opened the back gates. A gust of wind swirled around the courtyard, whipping at Frahto's hair. The thought of Roh being realigned made him see stars. He needed to stop this.

"I'm getting Adehl," Frahto said. He would *not* let Roh be realigned because of Adehl. It was time to see whether she would make a similar sacrifice for him.

"She's under protection —"

"I want to look her in the eye and tell her what's about to happen. Perhaps she'll surprise us." And if she didn't, Frahto would drag her to that hill by the hair. "Who's the Merali woman?"

"Lady Kenna Auwyn," Lenatoh said, his shoulders straightening, and Frahto remembered these women also had Lenatoh's daughter. "Her estate is in the hills beyond the city. You don't have much time."

"I'll get Sorah, too."

Lenatoh gave a stiff nod. "Take the sunskin. He'll bear you."

"Stall them." Already moving, Frahto tossed the words over his shoulder.

"Go quickly," came the soft reply.

38. ONLY ONE THING TO DO

WHEN THE PALE glow of dawn finally lifted the dark edge of night, Adehl threw off the bedcovers and dressed as quickly as her wounded leg allowed.

She had spent the night staring at the ceiling. Weeping and shaking at the thought of what Roh must be going through. Planning. She wished she could believe the Vuusah wouldn't put Roh inside a chamber such as Gordoh had described. He was *Little Atali*. They wanted him back and onside. Didn't they?

Kenna had promised to get him out of there, but it would take too much time. Adehl needed to rescue him herself.

There was really only one thing to do.

She opened the door of Sorah's room, lamplight filtering in. The girl barely made an impression in the massive bed. "Sorah, can you wake up for me?"

Sorah moaned softly and pulled the covers around her shoulders. "It's still dark."

"I need you to go through the gaerah cycle."

"What, now?" She was quiet a moment. "I'm fine."

Adehl reined in her impatience. None of this was Sorah's fault. "I need to make sure."

Sorah rubbed her eyes and pushed up on her elbows. Her unbraided hair flowed, messy and loose, over the sleeping shift Lady Kenna had found for her. "Why are you wearing riding breeches?" the girl asked.

"Gaerah cycle, little sparrow."

"But your leg!"

"It's better." Not quite a lie. She'd attempted another healing, and the pain was less. Or so she told herself. Adehl lowered herself to the edge of Sorah's bed. "Come on. This is important." Huffing dramatically, Sorah subsided and closed her eyes. After the girl executed ten perfect gaerah cycles, Adehl couldn't help a smile. "Excellent. Now you can go back to sleep."

"Where are you going?"

Adehl hesitated.

"If you're going to the Vuusah lodge I want to come with you."

"Why?"

"I want to see Da." She shucked off the blankets and swung her legs out of bed. "Please?"

It was a terrible idea. Adehl couldn't imagine the nedoyen letting Sorah out of his sight if given the opportunity. But Sorah was only thirteen years old; she had every right to see her father. Or return to him, if that was what she wanted. "Are you sure?"

"I want to say goodbye." Sorah began tugging on clothes.

"There's a risk —"

"I'll be careful."

Adehl chewed her lip. She couldn't bring herself to verbalise the true risk. But if the Vuusah got their hands on Adehl, Sorah would be better off with her father, anyway.

The household was quiet as they stole downstairs. Adehl

braced her weight on the banister to spare her leg, gritted her teeth against the pain. They easily evaded the kitchens, where someone clinked dishes, and made their way to the stables in the soft dawn light.

Cloud whickered a greeting and dropped his nose over the door of his stall. Kenna's staff had cleaned off the blood, and Adehl took a moment to hug his neck.

In the courtyard, she led Cloud over to a block and was thankful no one but Sorah witnessed her ungainly mounting endeavours. Her beautiful boy pranced excitedly, so Adehl calmed him with a thread of ellir, then pulled Sorah up behind her. The girl's arms snaked around her waist.

The light grew steadily as they crossed the city. They descended from Lady Kenna's estate on Gorannen Rise to the Merchants Quarter, already lively with carts of goods travelling in all directions and sailors stumbling after nights of indulgence. Sorah quietly pointed out her mother's ship at Commemoration Wharf; then they were through Traders Gate and crossing the Old Merali Quarter.

They came to the Lokk Janikk Bridge as the sun breached the hills and drenched the bridge's stones in sunlight. Traffic teemed across the span, and fishing boats swarmed the waters beneath it. Four Nations Plaza was sparsely populated at this hour, mainly a few licensed vendors setting up stalls.

Due to her injured leg, Adehl had kept Cloud to a walk as they crossed the city. Now, the unmistakable sound of a galloping horse made everyone turn their heads.

The rider entered Four Nations Plaza from the landward side opposite the bridge. He rode his sunskin mount with the consummate skill characteristic of the Vuusah, effortlessly weaving past anyone who got in his way.

Sorah pressed her face against Adehl's back. "It's Frahto."

"I can see that," Adehl said.

Frahto pulled up with a clatter, his cheeks unshaven and

braids unravelled. He appeared to be alone and looked both surprised and relieved to find them. "Are you here to stop this?" His words reverberated in the stone plaza.

"What's happening?"

"You need to come with me." He reached across and grabbed the cheekpiece of Cloud's halter.

Adehl clawed at his hand. "Let go, you stonehead!"

Frahto ignored her and yanked Cloud in a circle until his own horse faced the direction he'd come. Adehl almost fell out of the saddle and bit back a yelp of pain at the extra stress on her leg. Seated behind, Sorah gasped and clung tighter to Adehl's waist. The horses lurched into a trot, the gait agony for Adehl, when she couldn't brace herself properly against the movement.

"What's happening?" Adehl asked again, shoving at Frahto's arm, trying to disconnect him from Cloud. With her hand on his skin, she felt his llirah roiling like a savage sea. "Where's Roh?"

Frahto shook her off, releasing his hold on Cloud's halter. "No time to explain."

"Tell me!"

His nostrils flared. "Realignment!" he snarled. "Unless we get there first, they're going to realign Roh. We need to hurry." With that, he kicked his horse into a gallop.

Adehl was vaguely aware of urging Cloud after Frahto, her mind locked in shackles of ice. The pain in her leg became an anchor to reality, like Sorah's arms squeezing her waist, the clatter of hooves on stone.

Realignment.

Not Roh. They wouldn't.

Sharp morning light cut extra edges into the trees and grand buildings lining the boulevard. Handfuls of pedestrians scattered, and a flock of rosy parrots took to the air. Without slowing his pace, Frahto took a hard right turn. They flew past more buildings for a few minutes — then the road broke abruptly out of the city to forge through fields of recently harvested crops. The rising sun speared the corner of Adehl's right eye.

She spurred Cloud alongside Frahto. "Where are we going?"

"Kindoh." Frahto nodded towards the isolated hill at the head of the range Adehl had noticed before. In the old tongue, *Kindoh* meant *storm mountain*. Grassy pastures clustered at the base of steep, wooded slopes crowned by an outcrop of heartrock glistening purple in the sunlight. She could just make out tiny figures moving at the pinnacle.

"What's up there?"

"The Stormbowl," Frahto said and urged his horse faster along the dirt road.

Adehl's heart thudded as Cloud matched the sunskin for pace. "What's the Stormbowl?"

"The biggest fire-cursed resonator in the world."

For about a mile, the road undulated through farmland, heading north. Kindoh climbed towards the sky, almost above them, its crown now obscured by trees. To their right, cradled by foothills, sprawled the fertile flatland between the Siadon and Davrayn Rivers.

When they arrived at the Siadon River, Frahto took a route upstream, eventually entering the narrow Siadon valley, behind Kindoh. Dense, scrubby forest pressed around them, rising steeply both sides of the river, and the road roughened to little more than a track. They slowed their pace and followed the track up the flank of a wooded spur. The Stormbowl lay somewhere high to their left, beyond the canopy of trees. Voices — and laughter — reverberated through the surrounding hills, and Adehl's gut tightened.

They burst out of the trees onto a grassy saddle between Kindoh and another, higher, rocky hill. At least a dozen horses grazed over the slopes, where a cart had been abandoned. From this vantage, the stunted summit of Kindoh looked as though it had been chopped off. People clambered in and out of view. Adehl strained her eyes looking for Roh, but it was too hard to distinguish individuals from this distance. No one appeared to pay any attention to their arrival.

Frahto helped Sorah down. "Are you all right?" he asked.

Adehl didn't hear the girl's answer. Dismounting, she winced as her leg jarred against the ground, then tied up Cloud's reins. Adehl wished Sorah weren't here. She didn't know how to protect her from whatever was about to happen.

Adehl calmed her mind and reached for Roh's llirah. His energy engulfed her, carried by the heartrock in the hill. She released a breath, a fragment of tension dissolving. But when she entwined their rhythms, it was like hugging a log of wood. "He's unconscious," she said.

"He's drugged." Frahto released his own mount.

Sun's fury. "Hurry!"

Her heart thundered with fear and exertion and pain as they headed along a ridge towards the Stormbowl. Frahto led the way at a pace Adehl couldn't match. Sorah got under one of her arms and helped her along the uneven path. There were at least a dozen Vuusah up there, their words indecipherable, muffled. Roh's llirah remained strong but unresponsive to Adehl's touch. She didn't know what a realignment ritual involved, but she didn't think it had started yet.

Ahead, Frahto reached the base of a narrow staircase carved into the crag. The steps climbed some thirty feet, cutting across the face of the rock, then doubling back. Adehl eyed them with misgiving. The steps seemed to ascend into clear air, and her head was already swimming. Assuming she made it to the top, what then? She hoped her presence would be enough.

Frahto scowled at Adehl. "What's wrong with you?"

Adehl pressed her lips together.

Sorah said, "The hooters stabbed her in the leg."

"At least they managed that much." Frahto bent forward and hoisted her over his shoulder.

"Put me down!" Adehl kept her voice low and pinched the skin on his arm through his clothes.

"Enough." Frahto adjusted her weight and began climbing the precarious steps. "Don't squirm or it will go badly for all of us."

Adehl sucked in a breath. The trees below looked upside down and very far away.

Two humiliating minutes later, Adehl found herself deposited on a five-foot ledge ringing a large, shallow bowl carved out of heartrock. The bowl was about thirty feet in diameter and perfectly round. Its smooth contours dipped gracefully towards the centre, perhaps five feet lower than the rim where Adehl stood. A cool wind whipped at her clothes and her hair. The terrain fell away seaward: sprawling agricultural lands, then the city clustered around the harbour. Northwards, hills ascended in waves towards the mountains.

There were Vuusah zehla everywhere, at least two circahs. Most were positioned around the rim of the bowl, only air at their backs, but a small group clustered at its base where Roh lay trussed on a plinth, close enough for Adehl to make out the steady rise and fall of his chest.

Adehl lurched towards him, just as Frahto gave a shove. Her injured leg buckled underneath her. As she toppled, she tried to tuck into a roll but smacked her head against the hard surface.

Pain flared, and the world went dark.

39. Down and down
and down

Frahto winced as Adehl tumbled headfirst into the Stormbowl. He hadn't meant for that to happen; he'd forgotten she was injured. But at the sight of Doyi Palvemah hunched over Roh's unconscious form, neatly laid out on the plinth for sacrifice… He'd needed to make sure the doyen knew he'd found Adehl.

Palvemah's head jerked up. All conversations died, everyone stilled, and there was only the sound of wind. Most of the zehla were perched around the rim of the bowl, having taken up positions for the ritual. They were all from the Blue Fox and Dancing Owl circahs. None of them knew Roh beyond his reputation.

The doyen glanced dispassionately down at Adehl sprawled unmoving on the concave surface. "This is the pidakah woman, I assume?"

"We have her now, Doyi," Frahto said. "If we quell her, Roh won't want her anymore. You don't need to —"

"We will certainly quell her." Palvemah gestured at some of the zehla. "Restrain her, please."

Sorah reached the top of the stairs, gasping for breath. She looked about the bowl wildly, and Frahto grabbed her before she fell off the rim. "What happened?" she wailed, as two zehla rolled over Adehl's inert form and tied her hands. "What are they doing?"

At this, Lenatoh spun around from where he'd been checking on Roh. He mouthed Sorah's name silently. Perhaps he would have come towards her, but Adehl suddenly moved. She writhed and twisted like a mad thing, rolling into the doyen's withered leg. Palvemah toppled, cursing, in a pile of bones and braids. There followed a flurry of kicks and blows and bellows. A zehli flung himself across Adehl's legs, inciting a scream, which cut off when another grabbed her in a chokehold.

The doyen shakily regained her feet with Tallah's assistance. "We'll do her first," Palvemah said.

"No," Sorah said.

"It's for the best," Frahto said, holding her steady.

Sorah squirmed out of his grasp. "Stop it!" she shrieked. "Let her go!"

Only Lenatoh paid her any attention. He stepped around the zehla restraining Adehl and approached to within a few paces of his daughter. Balanced on the curve a couple of feet below the rim, he reached out a hand. "Sorah. Come here."

"Stay where you are, Sorah!" Adehl sounded winded, but her voice carried.

"Come with me now, and all will be well," Lenatoh said.

"I don't believe you!" Sorah's voice grew thick. "Why are you doing this? She's done nothing wrong. What are you going to do to Roh?"

"It is not for you to question what this woman's done —"

"Why not? She's like me!"

Lenatoh flinched. Then he took another awkward step, reached up and grabbed his daughter's arm. He pulled her into a rough embrace. "Fool girl," he muttered. "I'm sorry it has to be like this."

"Don't take her away from me." Sorah sobbed into his shoulder.

"She's no good for you, Sorsha."

Sorah pushed him away. "Are you going to quell me, too? Perhaps you should bind me as well." She presented him with her wrists held together. Lenatoh simply stared.

Frahto's heart ached. It had been cruel of Lenatoh not to quell her a year ago. That claith anchor around her neck had given her false hope, and Lenatoh's naked expression suggested he realised it. Of course, Adehl's interference hadn't helped matters. Frahto said, "Not today, Nedoyi. Not Sorah. Not like this."

"Yes, today! With Adehl." She pulled away and ran to Adehl, just as the zehla heaved the woman's trussed form onto the plinth. Roh had been lifted off and discarded a few feet away, where the bowl's sides curved upwards.

Lenatoh drew a sharp breath as Sorah clung to Adehl. "No, Sorah," Adehl said. "You don't need to be here."

Sorah shook her head. "It's not fair!"

"I know, little sparrow."

The zehla looked to Palvemah, then Lenatoh. Lenatoh looked beseechingly at Frahto. Burning bright sun. *He* wasn't her father. But Frahto climbed down into the bowl in time to hear Sorah say softly, "I remember."

Frahto laid a gentle hand on Sorah's shoulder. "Come away…" He stopped. Sorah held her rhythm, a melody of spring rain and nectar, tightly contained. He'd known what Adehl was doing, yet somehow he'd forgotten. He cast a quick look at Lenatoh.

"What is it?" Lenatoh asked, approaching cautiously.

"She's taught Sorah the gaerah," Frahto said under his breath.

Lenatoh stared at Adehl and laid his hand to the back of his daughter's neck. Sorah beamed up at him.

"You don't need to quell your daughter, Nedoyi," Adehl said. "If you would just *think* about it, you don't need to quell anyone."

Lenatoh retracted his hand and pressed fingers to his temple, eyes closed. Then he turned to address the doyen. Palvemah had settled on the rim, bringing the number of zehla positioned around the circumference of the bowl to thirteen. Most of them sat cross-legged, a position they would need to hold for up to an hour. "I believe we are ready to begin, Doyi," Lenatoh said.

"Wait," Frahto said. "Don't subject your daughter to this spectacle, Nedoyi. Sorah, come away."

But Sorah shook her head and clambered onto the plinth beside Adehl, ignoring her protests.

"I'm sorry, Sorsha," Lenatoh said sadly. "I should have done this long ago."

Adehl's eyes flashed. "You've avoided it for a reason, Nedoyi."

Lenatoh's mouth firmed into a line.

Frahto chewed his cheek. Sorah was pidakah. Of course she needed to be quelled. He'd almost lost sight of the real reason he had come. "Let me take Roh away from here."

"Yes." Lenatoh wiped his brow. "We don't need —"

"No," Doyi Palvemah said. "Roh stays."

Lenatoh said, "Surely if the woman is quelled, Doyi…"

"He stays." The doyen's voiced cracked through the bowl. "Things have gone too far."

Frahto went cold. No! He'd brought Adehl so Roh would be safe. "Lenatoh, you *can't*."

"Doyi, I beg you. Let me quell the woman and talk to Roh," Lenatoh said.

"No." She leant forward, a hawk about to strike. "Remember your oath, Nedoyi."

Lenatoh braced both arms on the plinth and bowed his head. "Sit with him, Frahto," he said woodenly. "Make sure he doesn't wake up."

"You're making a mistake!" Adehl writhed in her bonds. "He'll never forgive you!"

"Silence her," the doyen said.

"Are you sure you want to make an enemy of your precious Atalah-in-waiting?" Adehl yelled, as Tallah clambered down into the bowl. When the zehli pulled out a knife, Frahto held his breath. But Tallah sawed off strips from Adehl's mahgan and fastened a rough gag to muffle her outrage.

Sorah, eyes red and puffy, took Adehl's head in her lap with a defiant glare at her father. Adehl's ragged braids fell over the girl's knees.

Lenatoh's lips pressed together and he said, "Begin."

Around the rim of the bowl, thirteen zehla began to chant.

Frahto went to Roh, who still hadn't moved, his crumpled body unnaturally still. Guilt and despair smacked him in the gut. Frahto had never seen his friend so... inert — but his llirah pulsed strongly, thank the sun.

Holding Roh's hand between two of his own, Frahto knelt back on his heels, threaded their llirah together. It took him a few heartbeats to realise Roh's llirah was already entwined with someone else's. He felt a prickle on the back of his neck and found Adehl watching him, eyes hollow above the gag.

For a long moment, she held Frahto's gaze. He didn't know what she read in his expression, but after a moment she gave a small nod and withdrew. Frahto ought not be surprised she worried about Roh despite her own predicament. Roh never inspired anything less than complete devotion from anyone.

He settled himself more comfortably. The moment of collusion made his skin crawl, but at least the problem of Adehl would soon be over. It would all soon be over.

The goreyah chant continued, thirteen voices in unison, lifting and reverberating through the surrounding hills. Ellir swirled through heartrock into coherent form, a resonant pattern forged by the circle of zehla, amplified by the Stormbowl. Sustained by so many zehla, the mesh of ellir would be strong. It already pulsed through Frahto until he thought his bones might shatter. The doyen was taking no chances.

Beside the plinth, Lenatoh stood with one hand on the stone, his face turned to the cloudless blue sky, attuning himself to the mesh. Soon, it would be coherent enough, robust enough, for him to impose his will on Adehl's llirah. She would fight him, but not even Roh was capable of withstanding this.

Frahto drew Roh's hand to his chest, and Adehl's eyes burned. At her head, Sorah sat with a straight back, chin tilted, watching her father with sad eyes.

After perhaps ten minutes, the doyen made an impatient gesture for Lenatoh to start. With a nod, he laid a gentle hand on his daughter's arm and took a less gentle grasp of Adehl's. The resonant pattern of ellir thrummed as the noumenor claimed its power.

A spasm shuddered through Adehl's restrained body; then the battle began.

Sorah hunched beside Adehl, undoubtedly terrified as the goreyah chant resounded in the air. Across the distance between them, Frahto reached out with some thought of soothing her. He found Sorah's rhythm, a distinctive flicker beneath the torrent of ellir spiralling around the bowl. She turned her head to look at him, as though sensing his presence. Her breaths came deep and even, no sign of panic.

Someone was already calming her, channelling away her fear and absorbing her pain. Someone else, an empathiser far more skilled than he.

Frahto's mind reeled. He stared at Adehl.

Her head was thrown back, her whole body arched with the agony of having her llirah slowly and inexorably suppressed. He'd been wrong to think she'd only try to save herself. Half her attention was on Sorah. While opposing Lenatoh's relentless attack on her core energy, she was protecting the man's daughter.

Something snapped in Frahto's chest. Without stopping to think things through, he got to his feet and stumbled into the centre of the circle.

ADEHL WAS ABOUT to pass out. She willed herself to hold it together, even as her bones threatened to fly apart and her core got hammered into a pulp. She needed to keep beating back the black veil of agony, over and over. Passing out was simply not an option.

She gripped her llirah. With every heartbeat, its amplitude diminished like slivers of rock chipped off a pillar. Who would she be when this was over? Despair threatened to overtake her, borne into the air by the chanting voices.

Sorah trembled against her, thin arms tight around Adehl's ribs. Holding her together. Adehl wished she could put her arms around the girl in mutual comfort, but all she could offer was the thread of calming energy. It was pointless. Staving off Sorah's fear and devastation would not prevent Lenatoh from quelling his daughter once he'd finished with Adehl. But she couldn't abandon Sorah now.

Roh's llirah brushed the fading edges of her own. Frahto knelt beside him, restricting her view of Roh's face; but at least, for the moment, she could feel his energy. The touch was without purpose, the connection subconscious; but Adehl clung to it, inhaled deeply, as though she could breathe him in across the six or seven paces that separated them.

Adehl closed her eyes, aware of pathetic sounds deep in the back of her throat. She sounded like a tortured animal, but maybe no one could hear past the gag. At least it stopped her from screaming.

Beat by beat, her llirah yielded to the noumenor's will. She felt crushed by an avalanche. Flattened and torn. She clung to the remnants of her llirah, but her control was slipping.

For the moment, though, she could still help Sorah.

She could feel Roh dragging himself into the now.

She didn't know for how much longer she could feel anything.

The arms around her tightened. Adehl's eyes opened in time to see Frahto reach for Sorah, his face set in a mask of determination. He grabbed the girl around the waist and attempted to drag her away from Adehl.

Pulled by Sorah's grasp, Adehl toppled off the plinth. Although Frahto scrambled, cursing, to brace her fall, Adehl's face slammed into the hard surface of the bowl for the second time that morning.

Sorah yelped. "Adehl!"

The chanting faltered, and the force chipping away at Adehl's llirah stopped. She found herself sprawled at the base of the plinth, gasping for breath through the gag. One of her braids, caught somewhere beneath her body, pulled painfully at her scalp, and her injured leg cramped.

Do not pass out. Do not pass out.

She tried to shift into a more comfortable position, her cheek scraping the rock painfully as she flailed and flipped over.

"Frahto?" Lenatoh's voice held shock.

Sorah's sobs punctuated the silence. Adehl harnessed the remnants of her llirah, but without physical contact she could no longer reach the girl, let alone soothe her. She stared into the blue sky, wished it would take her up.

"Focus on *her*," Frahto said.

Adehl floated in a sea of pain and sluggish energy. She hadn't realised how much comfort she'd been taking from Sorah's presence. Now she was alone.

The zehla lifted their voices again, and before long they had reestablished the mesh. Each note stabbed at Adehl's bruised soul, and she no longer had enough strength to resist Lenatoh's relentless will. Now there was only the forced suppression of her energy. Her amplitude pushed down and down and down.

The smaller it got, the less it hurt. Numbness consumed her, taking away the rest of the pain.

She wanted to pass out now, wanted it to be over.

Soon, she would be reduced to nothing.

40. Mountains and sky

Ellir hummed through Roh, stroking his soul. He drifted, energy thrumming through flesh and bone. His mind conjured lush spring grass and hot immersive pools. If only he could curl up and sleep forever, his infernal headache would go away…

He couldn't sleep, because there was chanting, loud and all around him. Every note stomped on his throbbing temples. He tried to cover his ears, but his arms wouldn't cooperate.

The surface beneath him was hard, unyielding. It pressed and scraped at his skin. It was warm, though. Warm and humming with a mesh of ellir. He sank into its embrace, allowing it to soothe his head and sweep him away.

The world went blessedly quiet, and he drifted, found his dreams again.

"Roh." Someone shook his shoulder.

Again, voices filled the world like thunder. He wanted to ignore them, to submerge himself in the mesh of ellir until his head stopped hurting, but hands pulled him up. A flask bumped his lips, and ale filled his mouth.

Reflexively swallowing, he struggled to part the cloying fog in his mind. "Wh—?"

"Open your eyes."

Too much effort. At least his arms worked now.

"Roh, I swear if you don't wake up right *now* —"

"*What*?" Roh opened his eyes.

Frahto knelt before him, hands gripping Roh's shoulders. The man looked rough: red-raw eyes, feathered braids, stubble. Above, a ring of chanting zehla. Beyond, mountains and sky.

"Where?" The word came out a moan.

"The Stormbowl. It's a resonator."

Roh felt a flicker of recognition.

He stared up at the zehli seated cross-legged above him, chanting powerfully in unison with her brethren. He had always found goreyah chanting beautiful.

"Get your head together." Frahto gave him more from the flask. The man's crumpled mahgan sat askew, and he smelt like sweat and horse.

Sorah's face swam into view, her golden-brown eyes brimming full. "You need to help Adehl!"

"Hush." Frahto pulled Sorah away. "He needs to help himself."

"Whaat…?" Roh struggled to make sense, find words. The mesh of ellir swirling through the bowl soothed him. He remembered a terrible time when there was none…

Memory flooded back, and he groaned with the pain of it. The isolation chamber. Tallah forcing something bitter down his throat. Frahto and Lenatoh watching on.

"You let them drug me."

"I couldn't stop it."

Blighted sun and stars and moon combined. A resonant mesh of this magnitude was only used for the most difficult rituals. And Roh had been lying here, drugged and defenceless. Frahto had said… *realignment*… and Lenatoh hadn't refuted it. Horror and betrayal curdled Roh's gut. "Why is Lenatoh going along with this?"

His friend grimaced. "The Atalah has some plan."

Sorah clutched Roh's arm and tugged. "Roh, they've got Adehl! You need to help her!"

The girl's earlier words finally penetrated. *Adehl.* "Where is she?"

"There's nothing you can do for her," Frahto said. "It's done."

Roh's blood froze. Pushing himself up on his elbows, he quested frantically. His eyes found Adehl, twisted and unmoving at Lenatoh's feet. But his senses… No no no!

His head swam, gut churned. He couldn't find her. Couldn't find her. Couldn't — *there.* Her beautiful llirah reduced to a whisper.

Desperately, he threaded her energy with his own.

Lenatoh shifted, turned his head to meet Roh's gaze. A shadow passed over his former mentor's face, followed by his hand, wiping sweat away.

Roh's hairline was damp, too. He gritted his teeth and held Lenatoh's gaze, while he channelled everything he had into protecting what was left of Adehl's llirah.

All things being equal, Roh would back himself in a one-on-one tussle with Lenatoh. But things were not equal. Lenatoh wielded the mesh, and Roh's mind was swimming. Roh could hold him off for perhaps a few minutes.

Not enough.

Roh forced down the upsurge of rage. With the drug still coursing through his blood, he felt as unsteady as a baby loophorn, but there was no time to stop and wonder whether this would work.

"Roh…" Frahto's voice held both a question and a warning.

Roh would have to abandon his defence of Adehl, which meant he needed to act quickly. She didn't have much left.

As though she felt his thoughts, her head turned, and the hollowness in her gaze made his throat tighten. Roh had to stop himself from leaping to her side. Or trying to. He sent a thread of energy with all the love and hope and encouragement he could muster.

"Sorah," he said. "Distract your father."

A small gasp, then the girl was on her feet.

Roh reached out to the mesh. It was strong. An intricate weave of rhythm within the heartrock, amplified by it. Moreover, the zehla in the circle were trained to work together — and there were a lot of them.

Taking one out of the circle would barely disrupt it. Which was why he needed to harness the mesh instead. But Lenatoh held the prime position at the focal point of the bowl. The entire weave was constructed around him.

Sorah reached her father. Roh homed in on the energy where it channelled into Lenatoh and tried to wrest control.

For several heartbeats, it worked. When Sorah tapped Lenatoh on the arm, he started and his control wavered, leaving ellir swirling through the heartrock bowl. Roh pulled the focal point towards him. He experienced a rush of energy that made him giddy.

But the other man still had the huge advantage of position. In moments, Lenatoh reasserted his dominance — then turned to Roh in shock, fending off Sorah with one hand.

Roh stabbed at the focal point, tried to sever Lenatoh's connection with the weave, disrupt the pattern — anything. It wasn't working. Lenatoh maintained control.

But at least fighting Roh took his attention from Adehl. She uttered a moan of relief or pain or despair. Roh longed to go to her.

"Are you insane?" Frahto muttered. "Don't do it, Roh. The doyen is looking for any excuse…"

Roh followed Frahto's gaze and spied Doyi Palvemah forming part of the circle. She glared down at Roh and seemed to have stopped chanting. But none of the other zehla were paying attention. They were immersed in the goreyah ritual, seated with eyes closed, faces turned to the sky. No wonder the resonant pattern had not faltered.

Lenatoh continued to fight off all attempts to distract him. Worse, with the drug still in his system, Roh could feel his own strength fading.

His chest hurt, and he realised he'd forgotten to breathe.

Adehl moved. Sun's blood, she was bound hand and foot, gagged. Trussed up like live crabs for market. But she somehow hitched herself up onto her knees. Flung herself at Lenatoh's legs. Took them out from under him.

A startled shout. Arms flailing, Lenatoh collapsed on top of her, his head smashing onto the hard surface of the bowl.

Roh pounced. Before Lenatoh could reassert himself, before the goreyah chanters could react, he seized control of the energy. He needed the mesh.

He wielded the mesh.

FOR SEVERAL, critical heartbeats, Frahto had no idea what was happening.

Sorah screamed when her father fell and didn't get up. She bounded to his head, then recoiled, her hands slick with blood. Doyi Palvemah's mouth moved frantically, her words drowned out by the chant. The zehla all had their eyes closed, focused on the ritual.

Then, between one syllable and the next, the words died on their lips, and each zehli slumped forward. Had they not been seated already, some would surely have fallen headfirst into the bowl.

"— end it! End it now!" The doyen's words sliced through the sudden silence.

Stillness. Then Palvemah moved her head, surveyed the twelve unconscious zehla sprawled around the rim, glanced at Lenatoh's prostrate form, her mouth hardening as her gaze came to Roh. "What have you done?"

Roh's eyes held a dangerous glint. "I formally decline to serve the Vuusah," he said. "Find some other fool to enact your schemes."

"That is *not* acceptable —" The doyen's eyes widened, blinked, then closed as she, too, slumped into unconsciousness.

Frahto's mind was spinning. He'd known from Roh's expression that he was going to try something impossible, but drowsing a dozen zehla in the space of a heartbeat was beyond comprehension. The Stormbowl looked like a battlefield strewn with corpses. There was even the smell of blood.

Roh rolled onto his hands and knees, moving as if he were drunk. He crawled to Adehl and pulled her out from under Lenatoh, fumbled the gag off and hauled her into his arms.

Frahto couldn't tell if she were conscious. Given the way Roh rocked her against him, maybe she was dead. He scrubbed his face with his hands and tried to think.

"Frahto, help me!" The wailing plea came from Sorah, covered in her father's blood.

A stream of blood trickled sluggishly to the lowest point of the bowl, pooling along the corner where the plinth stood.

With his knife, Frahto sliced two thick strips off his own mahgan, made one into a pad and bound it tightly to Lenatoh's head with the other. Although Frahto couldn't wake him, the man's pulse seemed strong. Head wounds always bled a lot.

"He's going to be all right," he murmured to Sorah, hoping he spoke the truth.

"I'm sorry. I didn't mean for that to happen," Roh said, mainly to Sorah, Frahto thought. Roh took the knife and sliced through Adehl's binds. Her eyes were open, and she watched Roh with the intense focus of someone who was barely holding on.

Frahto wanted to ask whether she were all right, but he bit off the words. "What about the others?" He indicated the fallen zehla.

"They should come around in a few hours," Roh said grimly.

"Why did you leave me awake?"

"I want you to do something for me."

Roh's words rang loud in the cool morning air, gathered and tossed around by the mountains. A prickle of premonition crept across Frahto's shoulders. He examined Adehl, fragile and broken in Roh's arms, her llirah suppressed and damaged. She might not be fully quelled, but Frahto sensed she didn't have much left. "I can't do anything about..." He gestured vaguely. "Lenatoh knew what he was doing."

"I know."

Roh's sorrow stuck in Frahto's heart like a knife, gave a twist. That probably wasn't what Frahto was supposed to feel. He'd *wanted* Adehl quelled, had done everything in his power to make it happen. This ought to feel like a victory. "What can you possibly need from me?"

Roh stroked Adehl's hair. "You're a noumenor, Frahto."

"I'm aware."

"She's my injaleh."

"That too is apparent." And it was, too. It had proven a vain hope that quelling Adehl would reduce the strength of the bond.

Understanding snapped into place. Frahto's head swam, and he forced himself to acknowledge the truth: Roh would never give up Adehl. He felt the stirrings of shame.

"I was going to wait until Wintersmorn," Roh said. "But I want *you* to soulmeld us here, now."

"Roh, no…" Adehl stirred, lifted her head. "You can't want —"

"Shh." He kissed her temple. "I do want. Always."

"But I'm —"

"It's going to be all right." He rearranged her to lean against his chest and wrapped his arms around her. "We'll stay right here, and Frahto can do it."

Frahto closed his mouth and scrubbed his face again.

"Please?" Roh had never used that tone with Frahto before. Humble. Imploring. He held Adehl as though she were the most precious thing in the world.

"I don't have a mesh," Frahto said.

"You don't need one. This is the lord of all resonators, and we're almost melded already."

"Are you just going to keep running? Hiding?"

"If necessary." Roh held Adehl even closer. Her eyes were dull with grief and exhaustion. "Look, it's done. I can't change it, but…" His voice had thickened, and he paused to expel a deep breath. "The Vuusah need to let us both go." That pleading tone again.

So typical of Roh to believe that anything he desired would happen through the force of his will.

The sky held no answers. Nor did the mountains, rising silent and solid around them. Frahto dreaded what Palvemah would say when the Vuusah awoke to find their prizes gone.

He told himself they would be gone regardless of whether or not he soulmelded them first.

His heart felt as though it would shatter his rib cage. He needed to get Lenatoh to a healer. He needed his soul to stop aching.

Roh waited quietly, his chin on Adehl's shoulder. Sorah watched from her father's side, her brown eyes holding hope like flecks of gold.

To Adehl's bowed head, Frahto said, "This is what you want, too?"

Roh murmured something into her ear, and she twisted her neck to look at him. "Are you sure?"

Roh touched her cheek. "Please?"

She searched his gaze for several heartbeats, then turned to Frahto. "This is what I want."

"Very well," Frahto said.

The Vuusah could never know about what he was about to do, but Frahto couldn't fight Roh anymore. Not when he was more accustomed to doing anything Roh asked. For Roh, he would do this thing.

It was always for Roh.

ADEHL STARED at a falcon soaring against the sky. It passed directly through her line of sight, its ambivalence towards human activities oddly comforting. The steady thud of Roh's heart against her back was another source of comfort. His tight embrace stopped her from flying apart.

Frahto sat cross-legged on the plinth, opposite Adehl and Roh. Once he'd agreed to Roh's request, he'd spoken quietly to Sorah, who was sitting beside her father, then checked each of the unconscious zehla. Now, he was centring himself to perform the ritual. Adehl didn't know why he had agreed.

Adehl forced herself to stop asking Roh if he were sure. Her llirah, what was left of it, nudged at her senses like ripples at the edge of a lake. Docile. Barely a reminder the heartstorm existed at all.

At least she could still feel it. Roh had somehow managed to stop Lenatoh from completely quelling her. She didn't yet know how much affinity she had left, whether she could influence anything, but she still had this.

"Are you ready?" Frahto asked roughly. She heard the unspoken question he directed at Roh, the same one she'd asked over and over.

"Just do it." Roh's voice caught.

His energy gushed through her, swamping her in yearning, sorrow, love. She felt for his hand, threaded their fingers together across her belly. His mouth was soft and warm at her neck. She didn't know why she wasn't afraid. It wouldn't take much for Frahto to change his mind and finish quelling her instead. But Roh trusted Frahto, and that seemed to be enough.

"Don't worry about the words," Roh said. "They're not important right now."

"I wasn't planning to."

Then Frahto began to chant. His voice was lighter and clearer than Adehl had expected, rising in a different goreyah chant to the one the hooters had used earlier. Working alone, Frahto couldn't create a resonant mesh, but the Stormbowl had its own amplifying power. Adehl longed to be able to feel it.

She leant into Roh. From the beginning, they had been in tune, their rhythms melding together effortlessly; but, over time, their llirah had shifted subtly, become more closely matched. This then would be the final stroke to match them perfectly. Frahto would nudge their rhythms into perfect alignment, perfect synchronicity. A complete melding of souls.

Adehl wondered whether she'd be able to distinguish her ripple from Roh's maelstrom.

Without warning, pain ripped through her, and she cried out. Frahto was quelling her, after all! No, please no. Her body shuddered; her throat constricted. Tears burned in her eyes, and despair closed in.

"Ssh." Roh rocked her. "It's all right. I've got you. You're strong. You can take this."

"Don't let go of me."

"I won't. Not ever." He kissed her neck, her cheek, her mouth when she turned to face him. "It'll be over soon."

Her whole body felt as though it were being mangled. She gritted her teeth against it and closed her eyes, focused on the ellir surging through her and Roh.

And it *was* different from before. Instead of being suppressed, beaten down and down and down, her llirah was being knocked about. Wrenched into something else. She felt as though she were being picked apart and stitched back together differently.

Roh held her through it all, his own body shuddering and shaking almost in time to Frahto's melodious chant. When Adehl screamed, Roh groaned in echo.

She clutched at his arms, which tightened around her with every one of his cries, louder and louder, until she thought he must be getting shredded into tiny pieces. Adehl twisted in his embrace, flung her arms around Roh to hold *him* together, because he was screaming now, like an animal being tortured.

And then it was over. The terrible ripping of her insides stopped as abruptly as it had started — to be replaced with a gentle humming balm.

Roh groaned and panted in her ear, and Adehl gradually regained her wits. Hard, warm rock dug into her hip and her elbow. Roh's breath rasped against her face, and his body shuddered. She was partially underneath him, his weight numbing her arm.

She turned her head to nudge his face. "Are you all right?" She kissed him softly on his jaw and stroked his back with the arm that wasn't pinned. He seemed incapable of moving. "Roh?"

"That was hard on him." Frahto gently lifted his friend off Adehl, laying him beside her on the plinth. "Give him another minute."

Adehl looked warily at Frahto as she retrieved one of Roh's hands. Frahto appeared to have shoved his hostility beneath the surface for the time being.

"How do you feel?" Frahto asked.

"I don't know…" She stroked Roh's hand. "I suppose I should thank you."

"I didn't do it for you."

That was obvious. Tentatively, Adehl reached for the residual energy at her core and found Roh there.

They truly were melded, their rhythms identical. It was almost impossible for Adehl to detect where she ended and he began. His energy was majestic, beyond comprehension. As for hers — she felt like weeping. She might as well have been quelled.

Roh tugged her hand, and she felt his reproach clearly, as though the emotion were her own. "You're still you, jaleh." He kissed her hand. "This is us."

Adehl couldn't speak with her chest so tight. Roh held her gaze, his sunlight eyes full of emotion.

A few deep breaths later, she squeezed his fingers and managed to form words. "I think we need to get out of here."

Frahto grunted his assent and helped them both to their feet.

Roh twitched when Adehl tried to put weight on her leg,

doubtless feeling the jagging pain. "What happened?" He tried to steady her despite his own lack of balance. To avoid toppling, they wound up side by side, braced against the plinth.

"One of them, two days ago." Adehl gestured at the unconscious zehla, who still lay where they had fallen. "Will they be all right?"

"They're just in a deep sleep. I'm not sure what they'll remember."

"Sun's blood," Frahto said with more resignation than heat. He raked hair off his face but didn't look at either of them. "I don't know how I'm going to explain any of this, but if you're leaving, then… please just leave."

"We're leaving," Roh said. But he didn't immediately move, perhaps because Frahto squatted beside Lenatoh, whose head was still in Sorah's lap.

The girl stroked her father's cheek, then threw Adehl a beseeching look. "Can I come with you?"

"No," Frahto said.

Adehl remembered Frahto dragging Sorah from the circle. "You stopped her from being quelled."

Without looking away from Lenatoh, he said, "I wanted to spare her the humiliation of being quelled at the same time as you."

"I want to go with Adehl." Sorah clambered out from underneath her father and laid his bandaged head carefully down.

Frahto grabbed her wrist. "No. Your father needs you. I can't…"

For the longest time, Sorah hesitated. Then she bent to kiss her father's cheek. "I'm going with Adehl and Roh, Dada," she said softly. "You don't have to worry about me anymore." Frahto looked reluctant to release her, but she eventually tugged free of his grip, and they both stood. "I don't want to be quelled, Frahto. I want to learn…"

"Who's going to teach you?" he asked roughly. "Adehl isn't up to it anymore."

Adehl flinched, but it was true. She couldn't help anyone, not even herself. Those days were over.

"I don't know. It doesn't matter," Sorah said. "But I need to be with people who don't mind that I'm pidakah and don't despise me for being ti-rei." She gestured at the scars on her cheeks. "I need to stay here."

Frahto stared at something in the distance. He looked to be searching for words, arguments that might persuade her, but in the end he exhaled deeply. "Your father will miss you."

Sorah flung her arms around Frahto, her head reaching the middle of his chest. "Thank you." Rising up on her toes, she kissed his cheek. "Thank you for everything."

His arms came around her shoulders awkwardly, briefly; then he stepped back and turned to Roh. "Look after her," he said.

"We will," Roh said, his voice hoarse. "I hope we'll see each other again." He held out his free palm, which shook slightly.

Frahto swallowed and touched his palm to Roh's. Their fingers interlocked, and they held each other's gaze over their clasped hands. "I hope so too."

Adehl shivered. It was impossible not to feel the depth of Roh's emotion. It cascaded through her like a summer storm.

After a time, he nodded and released Frahto's hand, but they held each other's gaze for several more heartbeats, Frahto's eyes bleak. Then Roh turned to Adehl. "How do we get down from here?"

The descent was steeper than Adehl remembered, and her legs not nearly as steady as she would have liked. Roh, lurching behind her, was in worse condition, the drug in his system affecting his balance. Sorah silently brought up the rear.

It seemed to take an interminable time to reach the bottom.

Adehl didn't look back until they had reached the horses, where Roh made a happy noise and summoned a blood bay grazing among them. Silhouetted against the sky, Frahto's still figure watched them go.

41. Come to terms

None of the Vuusah knew exactly what had happened that day at the Stormbowl.

Frahto had allowed the doyen, at present overseeing a training drill below Frahto's bedchamber window, to believe Roh had drowsed Frahto along with the rest of them. Frahto hadn't confided the truth to Lenatoh, either.

Three days had passed since the debacle — as the doyen referred to events. Three days of the doyen stomping through the lodge like a thunderstorm. Three days of verbal tongue-lashings and difficult questions. Frahto found Lenatoh particularly difficult to be around. Something inside the nedoyen seemed broken. The once calm and rational man had become short-tempered and brittle. Frahto knew Lenatoh worried about Sorah; but Frahto couldn't forget, would never forget, the nedoyen agreeing to realign Roh.

Homesickness for the Humming Downs ached through Frahto. He wanted to be anywhere but here, staring aimlessly out a window, watching rain clouds gather. Unfortunately, the earliest available ship to Tarsah didn't leave for another two days.

Downstairs, a bell rang, and Frahto turned away from the window. Then someone bolted up the stairs to arrive at his door. He opened it to find Ninah, her broad cheeks flushed, grinning at him.

"Why are you holed up in here?" She leant a shoulder against the doorjamb.

"Was that another courier?"

"Uh huh."

Frahto waited. Over the past few days, several missives had been exchanged between the doyen and Roh via Lady Kenna Auwyn's secretary.

"He's agreed to meet with Lenatoh," Ninah said.

"When?"

"This afternoon at Heights University." Ninah eyed him. "You're invited, too."

"The doyen?"

She shook her head. "Roh's giving Lenatoh the opportunity to see his daughter."

Something flickered in Frahto's gut, a fleeting warmth. "Tell Lenatoh I have Roh's gear."

"You won't go?"

Frahto shrugged. He and Roh had already said their farewells, and he had no desire to pick at that wound. But he couldn't admit to his last conversation with Roh. "I have nothing to say to him."

Ninah's eyes widened and, when Frahto declined to speak further, she departed. Frahto closed the door behind her, momentarily rested his back against it. He didn't care what his brethren thought; it was better they believe him bitter than learn the truth. Better they didn't know the extent to which his own foundations had been shaken.

He lifted Roh's battered bag from the floor and dumped it

on his bed. Back in Tarsah, the idiot had left all his possessions fastened to Sprig, and Frahto hadn't so far found the
opportunity to return them. In all these weeks, he hadn't
bothered untying the fastenings: he knew the contents of
Roh's bag almost as well as his own.

He opened the bag. As expected, it held mostly clothes.
There was also a small pouch of velinkah hair beads, along
with a hairbrush and other personal items. A satchel
containing horse-care equipment. And a leather bag of
smooth pebbles Roh had collected over the years. Nine stones
of various sizes, the largest the size and shape of a fowl's egg.
Frahto remembered Roh's delight in finding the *egg stone* in
the shallows of a stream.

Roh's egg stone wasn't the one Frahto selected, though.
His fingertips sought the smooth, dark-grey disc of heartrock
found during their first year as acoleh. They'd been set the
challenge of navigating in pairs to various landmarks around
their camp using ellir. Frahto had been captivated by Roh's
lively observations about life in Gentah's company, their
zehla tutors and fellow acoleh, barely noticing Roh leading
him across the downs to complete the daylong challenge in a
couple of hours.

It had been the first day Frahto had understood the extent
of Roh's raw talent, his charismatic flair. Roh had retrieved
the round, flat piece of heartrock from the base of a cairn at
one of their checkpoints, pressed it between their joined
palms as they melded and pledged friendship forever.

Now, in a gloomy bedchamber far from the Humming
Downs, Frahto held the stone snugly between his hands.
Hints of his friend's energy fluttered against his skin,
imprinted from Roh's habit of frequently handling his
favourite rocks. Frahto caught smatterings of joy, fury, amusement. The heightened nature of the emotions was so typical
of Roh that Frahto smiled.

He returned most of the stones to the drawstring bag, but not the one in his hand. That stone he held awhile longer, then slipped it securely into the front pocket of his mahgan.

ADEHL FINGERED the red scholar's sash Kenna had dropped onto her lap. The soft folds slipped through her fingers, but she didn't put it on.

"Your new rooms are quite nice," Kenna said, remaining on her feet instead of joining Adehl on the lush quadrangle grass of Mainwick Hall, one of Heights University's oldest residential lodges. "A pity you aren't in them."

They were nice rooms — a suite on the ground floor, with comfortable furniture and large windows looking out onto expansive grounds towards the mountains. Twice the size of their chamber at the Wild Colt.

Kenna eyed Adehl, then the gathering clouds overhead, then the grass. As always, Jaikud hovered nearby. "Why are you out here?"

"I'm waiting," Adehl said. Kenna knew well enough that Roh and Sorah were about to meet with Lenatoh. Adehl's fingers tightened around the sash's red fabric.

"Of course. I completely understand why you're sitting outside, in plain view, unaccompanied. It makes perfect sense."

"Lenatoh came alone. I'm quelled, not stupid." Bile rose as she spoke the man's name. Roh needed to confront Lenatoh; she understood that. And the nedoyen was Sorah's father. No matter what Lenatoh had done to Adehl, she couldn't begrudge Roh and Sorah this final audience.

Kenna's feet shifted, her lavish garments rustling; she wore pale greens and golds beneath her sash, today. Then, with a huff, she lowered herself carefully to the lawn. "I think, if you're going to wander at will through the university, you're going to need your own claithwielder."

It was so absurd, Adehl burst into laughter. Then she couldn't stop. Huge waves of uncontrolled mirth rolled out of her contorted mouth until her cheeks ached and stomach muscles burned, until the maniacal laughter became wails — because it wasn't funny. Not really.

When she got herself under control, Adehl mopped at her eyes with the scholar's sash.

"You can have a good life here, Adehl," Kenna said, eying the damp, crumpled agave silk. "I know it's not the life you wanted, but…"

Adehl nodded. Over the past few days, she'd done her best to come to terms with her new situation. But her entire identity had been centred on her affinity for ellir. She'd had no idea how much she'd relied upon her empathiser skills — with horses and other animals, with people. Even now, she instinctively reached for the heartstorm to be met with… the faintest, silent hum. "I wanted to make a difference," she said, strangling the garment in her hands. "Now I can't even help myself."

"You can still make a difference," Kenna said, leaning forward. "That's what we Ellirisi *do*."

"It's not the same."

"That depends on you."

Adehl didn't need ellir to interpret Kenna's exasperation and endeavoured to shake off her despondency. But, although the Ellirisi seemed quietly excited by the prospect of Roh and Adehl joining their ranks, Adehl had no notion of how to be a scholar. All she knew was horses. She'd briefly entertained the idea she could do more… but the Vuusah had ruined everything. Her llirah flickered with suppressed rage.

"By the lord's shining locks." Kenna poked Adehl in the knee. "What do you *want*, Adehl?"

"You know what I want. Wanted."

A group of students walking down one side of the quadrangle stopped to stare at the sight of Lady Kenna Auwyn seated upon the grass. Jaikud sniggered, and the lady narrowed her eyes. "Humour me."

Adehl had never explicitly stated her dream out loud. She hesitated.

"Go on," Kenna said softly.

"I wanted to help gierfeh children." Chanti, who Frahto had quelled. Sorah and untold others. She swallowed. "I wanted to teach them how to meld with ellir. I wanted any gierfeh child to be able to come to me and know they never need be quelled. I wanted to open some sort of school —" Adehl slapped a hand over her mouth.

Kenna grinned and clapped her hands twice. "A school… that's a brilliant idea!"

"Until the Vuusah find out about it. Or the Zehla Guild, I suppose."

"If it were a normal school on the surface, we could teach the zehla skills in secret."

"But I can't…"

"Adehl." Kenna's voice held a mix of sympathy and calm authority. "It's *your* brilliant idea, and there would be plenty for you to do. Have you discussed it with Roh?"

"No." Adehl had barely acknowledged the outrageous prospect to herself. "When he found out I was teaching Chanti, he spent three days in alehouses."

"Did he try to stop you?"

He hadn't. Instead, Roh had made it possible for Adehl to teach Sorah, too — and that was before the Vuusah had shattered his heart. Since the Stormbowl, Roh had taken Sorah under his wing, spending hours guiding her through the gaerah cycle. Roh was a surprisingly patient teacher — more patient than Adehl had been. "Roh's shown himself able to break precepts for my benefit and now Sorah's," Adehl said. "But I don't know what he'd say to something as audacious as… a school." The final word caught on her tongue.

Was a secret school truly possible? Kenna spoke as though it were merely a case of deciding.

Adehl allowed herself to dream. She imagined a group of students like Chanti, lively and eager to learn. She imagined them sitting in a circle, right here on the quadrangle grass, learning to farsense. She imagined them learning how to read emotions.

Pressing her fingertips into the grass, Adehl reached for the roots and the soil. Reached for the heartstorm below… Gradually, the barest trickle of ellir filtered through her. It left her wanting more.

She would always want more.

"I was going to be the one to teach them," she said. "At least some of it."

"I know," Kenna said.

"Then what…" Adehl stopped.

Ellir thrummed at the edge of her senses. She didn't have much left, but she still had this. It was like standing in the shallows at the beach, the tide rippling across her toes. Her llirah fluttered like a scrap of seaweed caught on a rock.

Wouldn't the seaweed eventually be freed if the tide pulled hard enough?

For the first time since the Stormbowl, Adehl allowed herself to hope. Roh had interrupted Lenatoh. Instead of being completely quelled, unable to touch her own llirah, Adehl could still control the tiny amount of energy she had left. She couldn't do much with it — but it wasn't *nothing*.

Adehl had believed she might as well be quelled. What if she were wrong?

Her brief association with the Ellirisi scholars had shown there was plenty the Vuusah didn't understand about ellir.

The Ellirisi had a library of books and scrolls going back centuries. Moreover, Kenna had revealed the Ellirisi didn't limit their studies to Baljehni. *It comes from far across the sea. A place called Kasso.*

"I'd love to know what you're thinking right now," Kenna said.

Adehl grinned and smoothed out the scholar's sash across her lap. "I suppose I also need an avenue of research if I'm going to join the Ellirisi."

Kenna's smile split her face. "You've thought of something?"

"I have," Adehl said. She slipped the sash over her head and adjusted it to sit neatly. "I'm going to investigate how to reverse a quell."

"THOSE LOOK PRETTY, SUNGIRL," Roh said as Sorah fidgeted with the srih she wore on each forearm. "Are you worried about what your Da will think?"

She dropped her hands, a hint of colour in her cheeks. After visiting an exclusive beadmaker with Kenna and Adehl, Sorah had woven the srih yesterday under Adehl's guidance. The beads were expensive ones: spheres of polished agate, smooth pebbles of purplish heartrock, and broad rings of delicately etched pewter. "A little," Sorah said. "I'm still getting used to wearing them."

Roh fingered the beads around his own arm; when he'd first started wearing the srih, it had ripped out hairs. "I know what you mean. But you'll get accustomed, I promise. And don't worry about what your Da might say. Just remember what we've practised."

"I will."

They were crossing the university towards the

Department of Ellirisi, where they would meet one last time with Lenatoh. The prospect of confronting his former mentor made Roh's gut seethe, but they needed to reach a formal understanding if Roh and Adehl were to have any kind of freedom, and Sorah needed to see her father.

Gordoh met them at the corner of the building, his usual mahgan a bright flare of orange against the wall. "Are you sure about this?" he asked.

Roh nodded. "He's alone?"

Gordoh gestured down the length of the building. "On the terrace as you requested."

Roh had known Frahto wouldn't come but sensed Sorah's disappointment. "Don't worry. You'll see the big oaf again one day, I'm sure of it. Are you ready?"

Sorah chewed her lip, took a deep breath and pulled in her llirah to give the appearance of being quelled. "Is that all right?"

"Perfect," Roh said.

It was essential Lenatoh — and thus the Vuusah — believed both Sorah and Adehl to be quelled. In Adehl's case it was mostly true. Roh hoped Lenatoh would believe the rumours that Kenna had hired a noumenor to quell Sorah and felt confident the man would probe his daughter's llirah rather than ask her outright. If Sorah could hold her energy in that unnatural state, it ought to allay Lenatoh's fears.

Still, things might not go to plan. To Gordoh, Roh said, "You'll wait here?"

"I'm not going anywhere." The zehla scholar leant his back against the wall. "Shout if you need me."

With that, Roh really couldn't put this off any longer.

The terrace where Lenatoh waited stood at the end of the building and overlooked the broad, flat-bottomed valley between two hills. The lower slope of Goldayn Rise, below the university, was filled with trees, their open crowns swaying in a strong, gusty wind; but the valley and lower slopes of Gorannen Rise, opposite, held more of the city.

The nedoyen faced the view over trees, hands clasped at his back, the folds of his mahgan snapping in the wind. His head was bandaged, reminding Roh of the injury Lenatoh had suffered when Adehl toppled him at the Stormbowl. It must have been a minor head wound for Lenatoh to present himself alone, three days later. Roh searched his heart but felt no remorse.

With a squeak, Sorah ran forward. Lenatoh must have heard and turned to catch her, staggering back a couple of paces with the force of her arrival. "Fool girl," Lenatoh said, holding her close. "You could have gone wild."

"But I didn't."

"I promise I'll do better. Once we're home."

Sorah leant back. "I'm staying here, Da."

Emotion rippled over his haggard face. "You can't stay here. You're my daughter."

"I can't go back to the Humming Downs."

"Your mother's ship is no place for you."

"I'm staying *here*," Sorah said with gentle emphasis, pulling away. "In Dohni. As the ward of Lady Kenna Auwyn."

Lenatoh stared. "The Merali woman?" He darted a confused glance at Roh, standing several paces back.

Roh nodded. Adehl had wanted to assume the role of Sorah's guardian, of course; but Lady Kenna had advised them that the Four Nations Council would be more likely to rule in Kenna's favour than Roh and Adehl's, penniless and adrift as they were. With Sorah's permission, the Merali scholar had instigated proceedings already — just as she'd fended off demands from the Vuusah about all three of them.

Adehl and Roh might have found themselves sleeping in back alleys or fleeing into the mountains without Kenna.

"Why does Lady Kenna Auwyn take such interest in my daughter?"

"She's very generous," Roh said.

"The woman's a stranger!"

"Not to me!" Sorah's words rang across the terrace. "And she's not ashamed of me, either."

Lenatoh stilled.

"I'm sorry." Sorah's voice thickened. "I'm thankful for the time I spent with you, Da. But the Vuusah all hate me. They're mean. Adehl and Roh… and Lady Kenna have been very kind. They *want* me to live with them." She sniffed and swiped a hand across her eyes.

Roh winced, but Lenatoh appeared not to notice what Sorah had almost said. "Sorsha." Stepping forward, he caught his daughter's arm, brought it closer to examine the srih. After a time, he swallowed. "These are lovely. They suit you very well."

"Thank you," Sorah said in a small voice. "Adehl helped me."

Lenatoh nodded. As a flock of rosy parrots swooped, chittering, among the treetops downslope, he closed his eyes. Roh recognised the signs of Lenatoh melding and gave Sorah a sharp, warning glance. She gripped her lip between her teeth and concentrated, Roh hoped, on appearing quelled. At the same time, Roh held himself ready and hoped Lenatoh didn't probe too deeply.

Lenatoh opened his eyes and released a long breath. "You're certain, Sorah?"

"Yes." Sorah retreated to stand beside Roh. "I'll be happier here."

Roh felt her struggling to keep her llirah in check. He nudged her gently with his shoulder. It was time for her to go find Gordoh before she betrayed herself.

"I'm sorry I ran away, but I'll be all right now," Sorah said.

"You won't need to worry about me anymore." After a small hesitation, she ran back to Lenatoh and kissed his cheek.

"Sorah…"

"Goodbye, Da." With a quick glance at Roh, she bolted.

It was just Roh and Lenatoh on the terrace, now. Over the past several minutes, the world had darkened as rain clouds swept in. Roh wanted to get this over and done with. "You were going to realign me," he said.

Lenatoh snapped his head towards Roh. He'd been gazing after Sorah, his shoulders slumped, but now he straightened into something resembling a slab of granite. Roh sensed that, beneath the impenetrable, hard surface, Lenatoh's energy roiled. "You're not innocent in this," the nedoyen said.

"I haven't harmed anyone."

The other man's mouth formed a straight line. "I didn't think you capable of such betrayal."

"Nor I you. All I did was get on a ship."

"I can see you believe that." Lenatoh inclined his head. "What of your responsibilities, your *loyalties*, to the Vuusah? What of your decision to free one who violated our most sacred precept?"

It occurred to Roh that he no longer felt any guilt over freeing Adehl back in Tarsah. Not because she was his injaleh — which had been his reasoning then. But because he no longer believed in the first precept. *Only the pure blood of Baljehni can meld with ellir…* It seemed ludicrous.

Lenatoh's voice shook as he continued. "How could you, Roh? We gave you everything." But if Lenatoh felt any contrition, he'd buried it deep. All Roh sensed from his former mentor were anger and grief.

"You wanted to control me! You and Gentah have been doing it for years." When Lenatoh's mouth tightened, Roh knew he'd scored a hit. They'd been grooming Roh for some secret scheme he still didn't understand. All those years, he'd thought they trusted him above all others. "That's why you gave me *everything*. It's why you intended to realign me." He clenched his fists. "And it's the true reason you quelled my injaleh."

"I understand you're upset —"

"Is that what you'd call it?" Roh lowered his voice with effort. "The Vuusah could have made an exception for Adehl being pidakah. I was certain they would — even if only for me." Yes, he'd been that arrogant and stupid. "But Adehl knew you wouldn't. And thank the bright sun I listened to her, because the Vuusah are wrong, Lenatoh. Our so-called most sacred precept is *wrong*. Adehl doesn't deserve to be quelled, simply because of some stupid Vuusah belief that means nothing. Just as your daughter doesn't deserve to be quelled. I'm glad I jumped on that ship. I'm glad I came to Dohni. Because now I understand more about the world than I ever did before. The Vuusah are not the custodians of ellir; they are its oppressors."

Roh stopped to gather his thoughts. He'd said more than he'd intended — yet somehow it didn't seem enough. Lenatoh looked incapable of speech — and like he needed a chair.

"Look," Roh said in a calmer tone. "I don't know what game the Atalah is playing, and I don't suppose you'll tell me, but I need to know the Vuusah will leave me and Adehl alone."

Lenatoh still didn't respond. He seemed to be staring at a tibbi scratching around in a small patch of garden.

"Lenatoh!"

The bird took to the air, and Lenatoh's gaze travelled back to Roh. "You've said enough."

"I need to know Palvemah will leave us alone — that no more harm will come to Adehl. She's quelled. They can have no further interest in her."

A nod. "We do not speak her name."

Roh felt a knot in his gut. He knew she'd been expelled, but… "You've declared her anathema?"

"It will be the Atalah's right to do so."

"And me?"

"That will be for the Atalah to decide." Lenatoh had regained his earlier hard, expressionless facade. The only movement around him seemed to be the rising breeze blowing his garments and long hair. A few spots of rain fell.

"I see." Despite everything, it hurt. But if Adehl were declared anathema, the Vuusah, believing her quelled, would no longer acknowledge her existence. Roh didn't know what it meant for him. "Dohni law requires me to register with the Zehla Guild," he said.

"I'm aware."

Roh hesitated, then said, "Why did you come here, today, Nedoyi?"

Slowly, Lenatoh brushed a splash of water off his mahgan. "I wanted my daughter and…" He looked at his feet. For the first time, Roh noticed a familiar bag dumped on the paving stones. "As for the rest, it hardly matters."

"You brought my gear."

"You can thank Frahto."

Roh nodded and wrestled with a surge of regret — not for anything he'd done, but for the loss of Frahto, his friend. And for the loss of this man who had been like a father. "I can't forgive you for quelling Adehl."

"You've stolen my daughter. Perhaps we're even."

42. WINTERSMORN

IN THE SOFT, dawn light of Wintersmorn, Adehl stood barefoot in the garden surrounding the Circle of Wind.

Roh, also barefoot, stood alongside. His hand felt warm and large around Adehl's, his thumb softly stroking her skin. Her damaged llirah fluttered in response to Roh's torrent, but she no longer feared being flattened by the meld. Instead, she allowed Roh's energy to buoy her up.

They'd come alone to the resonator as first light bloomed. Birdsong filled the garden, echoing off the surrounding buildings, and a biting breeze caught at the foliage. Adehl's bare feet were warm, though, thanks to the storm of energy in the heartrock below. She couldn't sense ellir like before, but she remembered.

"Let's do this, jaleh," Roh said, drawing her hand to his cheek. His long, dark hair, bound only by a dozen fine braids around the crown, flowed over the subtle grass motif woven into his mahgan.

Adehl smiled, didn't ask him if he were sure. They'd been soulmelded for eight days, after all. Together, they stepped into the circle of stones, the lush grass gliding against her feet. At the central pillar, she placed her hand against the rock, felt its warmth, tried to feel it humming.

Their private ceremony didn't require witnesses. Roh shaped ellir into a mesh and guided himself and Adehl into a meld. Ellir rippled through Adehl, amplified by the resonator and her link with Roh. She clutched at the heartrock pillar, drawing the energy into her. Not enough, but more than she could now achieve on her own. Her llirah thrummed.

They exchanged a few heartfelt words under candour: ancient promises of strength and honesty and love. Adehl knew all would be well.

The sky had lightened around them while they stood within the circle, and the tops of neighbouring buildings caught the sun. "One last thing," Roh said, smiling.

He reached inside the front pocket of his mahgan and withdrew two claith medallions suspended on leather cords. The identical discs were about two finger widths in diameter, a design etched into the front of each. The finely wrought claith shimmered silver and violet, so beautiful Adehl could barely breathe. "How… *When?*"

"They're a gift from Kenna. She took me to see a claith-smith a few days ago." Roh placed one of the discs on her palm.

Adehl's shaking fingers closed around it. She felt the tiny flutter against her skin, an extension of her own rhythm. "They're aligned to us?"

"They are." Roh held the other up by the leather cord, knotted through a hole in the disc. The polished metal glinted in the rising light as it dangled between them. "I personally assisted the smith. It took hours, but she said I was a natural."

Adehl huffed a laugh. "Of course she did."

Roh grinned and fastened the medallion behind Adehl's

neck, so it rested against the skin just below her throat. "Perfect." He leant forward and kissed the disc where it lay.

She gently pushed him away. "Be still." With fumbling fingers, she moved aside his braids and lifted the matching medallion to his neck, tied it off. "These must have cost a fortune."

"The Ellirisi seem very keen for us to join them."

"You think…"

"I sense no malice, jaleh. I believe they are good people. But they have an agenda they think we can help them with."

Adehl thought over her dealings with the Ellirisi — especially Kenna, who would spend all the coin she had to help gierfeh children like Sorah. Kenna had proven herself a genuine ally and friend.

As for Gordoh: from what Roh had told her, the First Scholar had seemed keen to recruit Roh from the start. The Ellirisi had already endorsed and paid for Roh's kalkah licence, plus enthusiastically supported Adehl's crazy idea for a school. They seemed remarkably well resourced, even better informed, and not cowed by either the Zehla Guild or the Vuusah. Adehl and Roh could do far worse.

At least, with the departure of Frahto and Lenatoh for Tarsah a few days ago, Roh seemed to have broken free of the last remaining Vuusah shackles.

He'd been sober after his confrontation with Lenatoh. The news that Adehl, and probably Roh, would likely be declared anathema had given them both a jolt. Adehl had expected to be shunned, but it was unexpectedly hard to have it confirmed after everything she'd done — everything her family had risked — to gain acceptance into the Vuusah. It meant she could never return home.

In Roh's case, he said it had cut off any path for reconciliation and made his position clear. But Adehl knew he grieved. How could he not?

Still, the Vuusah had, so far, left Adehl and Roh alone. Adehl wasn't so naive to assume they were safe forever; but, even if Ellirisi aid came with strings attached, the scholars provided a robust shield. She and Roh could certainly do far, far worse.

"Do you mind?" she asked.

Roh shrugged. "I suspect the Ellirisi agenda aligns with… I was going to say yours, but I probably mean *ours*." He took her hand, bringing together their forearms and matching srih. "We're in this together, jaleh. Whatever happens next."

"Even if we found a secret school for gierfeh children?"

He smiled crookedly. "Who better to teach them than me?"

The end

Thank You

Beyond the Humming Downs is my debut novel, the product of blood, sweat and years. Thank you so much for reading!

If you enjoyed the book, please consider telling your friends or leaving a short review in the usual places to help other kindred readers find it. Word of mouth means everything to the independent author.

More information about Beyond the Humming Downs and future works can be found on my website ellenstarsmore.com, where you'll find a glossary and downloadable map.

If you enjoyed discovering the land of Baljehni, there are definitely more adventures to come in this world. I hope you'll join me there.

Acknowledgements

When you've been on a journey as long as mine, there are many, many people who have played critical roles along the way. I extend my heartfelt thanks to the following:

Simon, PhD buddy and earliest critique partner. I'll never forget developing and printing photos in a darkroom as undergrads one afternoon and discovering our shared love of reading and writing fantasy. Without your friendship and support, I might never have attended that first convention and found Australia's fantasy and speculative fiction writing community.

The somewhat ghostly Supernova writers group. We've all moved on from those days of intense short story critiquing, but I treasure everything I learnt over the years and, especially, the enduring friendships I've made. Many of you read early chapters of Beyond the Humming Downs, and some read a complete draft several years ago. I'm 100% confident you all feel it's time for me to declare this baby *ready* and let it fly.

My Page Turners friends, who have watched my writing journey from afar for 25 years. Now, you finally get to read one of my creations! Special thanks to Ania, who read a draft of Beyond the Humming Downs earlier this year to check my horse-related content.

Nat B, who has gone above and beyond in providing

endless design advice and moral support. If not for you, I might still be rocking in the corner.

My Dungeons and Dragons crew — including Lita, Jason and Peter. Who would have thought we'd still be rolling dice more than a decade later? Your friendship, advice, feedback, shared international (and imaginary!) adventures and moral support over the years mean more than I can say.

Kirstyn and Deb, mad witches forever. We were going to make gin together, before covid, then tragedy, struck. I hold those early planning (and tasting!) days dear, because they remind me of Ada. As authors and friends, you've been my primary sounding board for pretty much everything over the past few years. Deb in particular, living just around the corner, has been subjected to numerous drop-ins wherein I downloaded my exploding brain. Thank you both for always being there and generally being awesome humans.

My mum, dad and siblings: Susan, Michelle and James. You've been there every step of the way — since I bought my first desktop computer and installed it in my bedroom, so I didn't have to share. I've been so lucky to have your quiet support all these years, even when it must have seemed like this day would never come. A special thank you to my nieces Hannah and Jessica, who have provided a Gen Z perspective — but particularly Jessica, who read a complete draft of Beyond the Humming Downs earlier this year.

And finally, Tracey. Our meeting in that long-ago short story critique workshop, and my subsequent introduction to the then NOVA (new or very awful) writers group, marked a turning point in my development as a writer. As a critique partner, you've always connected with my work, and your steadfast friendship and support over the years mean everything. Here's to many more weekends away writing, feasting and talking about words. I can't thank you enough for editing this novel.

About the Author

Ellen Starsmore's love of fantasy began with her dad reading The Hobbit around a campfire. She's been an avid fantasy reader since her teens, inspired by quests through wondrous worlds. These days, she writes fantasy with love, hope and adventure, primarily focused on character journeys and discovery. Beyond the Humming Downs is her first novel.

Once a materials engineer, Ellen also writes for companies in the engineering and industry space. Some of these interests sneak into her fantasy world building too. She lives with a feline animal companion and a horde of carnivorous plants in Melbourne, Australia (Boonwurrung Country).

Her website is at ellenstarsmore.com.

www.ingramcontent.com/pod-product-compliance
Lightning Source LLC
Chambersburg PA
CBHW031734180726
48283CB00005B/1508